KING OF FOXES

D0893011

Also by Raymond E. Feist

Magician
Silverthorn
A Darkness at Sethanon

Faerie Tale

Prince of the Blood
The King's Buccaneer

Shadow of a Dark Queen
Rise of a Merchant Prince
Rage of a Demon King
Shards of a Broken Crown

Krondor: The Betrayal
Krondor: The Assassins
Krondor: Tear of the Gods

Talon of the Silver Hawk
King of Foxes
Exile's Return

Flight of the Night Hawks
Into a Dark Realm
Wrath of a Mad God

Rides a Dread Legion
At the Gates of Darkness

With Janny Wurts:
Daughter of the Empire
Servant of the Empire
Mistress of the Empire

With William R. Forstchen:
Honoured Enemy

With Joel Rosenberg:
Murder in LaMut

With Steve Stirling:
Jimmy The Hand

Voyager

RAYMOND E. FEIST

KING OF FOXES

Conclave of Shadows
Book Two

HarperCollins*Publishers*

Voyager
An Imprint of HarperCollins*Publishers*
77–85 Fulham Palace Road,
Hammersmith, London W6 8JB

www.voyager-books.com

Published by Voyager 2005

16

Copyright © Raymond E Feist 2003

The Author asserts the moral right to
be identified as the author of this work

A catalogue record for this book
is available from the British Library

ISBN 0 00 648358 5

Typeset in Janson Text by
Palimpsest Book Production Limited,
Polmont, Stirlingshire

Printed and bound in Great Britain by
Clays Limited, St Ives plc

All rights reserved. No part of this publication may be
reproduced, stored in a retrieval system, or transmitted,
in any form or by any means, electronic, mechanical,
photocopying, recording or otherwise, without the prior
permission of the publishers.

ACKNOWLEDGEMENTS

It has become a tradition that I begin each acknowledgement with a heartfelt 'thank you' to the original creators of Midkemia, and this book is no different. So, again, I acknowledge my never-ending debt to Steve, Jon, Anita, Steve, Bob, Rich, Tim, Ethan, April and Conan. As I explain at every opportunity, yours are the 'other voices' that permeate my work.

To Jonathan Matson of the Harold Matson Company, Abner Stein of the Abner Stein agency, Nicki Kennedy of the Intercontinental Literary Agency, and the folks at Tuttle-Mori Agency for taking care of the franchise around the world.

To Jennifer Brehl and Jane Johnson for being amazing; they know how to make a writer look better.

To so many friends for keeping me upright and sane over the last few years.

To the members of the Feist Fans Mailing List at Cornell University who are not shy about telling me what they like and dislike but who have also become virtual friends, and a few who've become more than virtual. Thanks for keeping things interesting.

To Jennifer, Roseanna, Rebecca, Milisa, and Heather for keeping things lively.

To Jamie Ann for keeping things interesting and lively.

To my mother, for so many reasons, and my children, for even more reasons.

And, lastly, but certainly not least of all, you, the readers, for keeping me working at a craft I love.

Raymond E. Feist
San Diego, CA July, 2003

For Jessica
With all the love it's possible for a father to give.

Contents

PART ONE

Agent

'In the service of Caesar, everything is legitimate'
Pierre Corneille, *La Mort de Pompée*

CHAPTER ONE

Return

A BIRD SOARED OVER THE city.

Its eyes sought out a figure in the throng on the docks, one man amidst the teeming surge of humanity occupying the harbour-side during the busiest part of the day. The Port of Roldem, harbour to the capital city of the island kingdom of the same name, was one of the most crowded in the Sea of Kingdoms. Trade goods and passengers from the Empire of Great Kesh, the Kingdom of the Isles, and half a dozen lesser nations nearby came and went daily.

The man under scrutiny wore the travel clothes of a noble, all sturdy weave and easily cleaned, with fastenings which allowed him to remain comfortable in all weathers. He sported a jacket designed to be worn off the left shoulder, leaving his sword arm unencumbered. Upon his head was a black beret adorned with a silver pin and a single grey feather, and upon his feet he wore sturdy boots. His luggage was being offloaded and would be conveyed to the address he had specified. He travelled without servant, which while unusual for a noble was not unheard of – for not all nobles were wealthy.

He paused for a brief second to drink in the sights. Around him people scurried: porters, sailors, stevedores, and teamsters. Wagons loaded so high their wheels appeared on the verge of buckling rolled slowly by him, cargo heading into the city or out to the ferry barges which would load them onto outbound ships. Roldem was a busy port by any standard; not only were goods delivered here, but also transhipped, for Roldem was the trading capital of the Sea of Kingdoms.

Everywhere the young man looked he saw commerce. Men bargaining over the cost of goods to be sold in distant markets, others negotiating the price of offloading a cargo, or insuring one against pirates or loss at sea. Still others were agents of trading concerns eagerly watching for any sign that might prove an advantage to their sponsors, men who sat in coffee houses as far away as Krondor or as close as the Traders Exchange, just one street away from where the young man now stood. They would dispatch young boys with notes who would run to those men who awaited news on arriving cargo, men trying to sense a shift in a distant market before buying or selling.

The young man resumed his walk, and avoided a gang of urchins dashing past with determined boyish purpose. He forced himself not to pat his purse, for he knew it was still where it was supposed to be, but there was always the possibility the boys were sent by a gang of pickpockets on the look-out for a fat purse to rob. The young man kept his eyes moving, seeking out any potential threat. He saw only bakers and street vendors, travellers and a pair of guardsmen. It was exactly who he would have expected to see in the crowd on Roldem's docks.

Looking down from above, the soaring bird saw in the press of the crowd that another man moved along a parallel course and at the same pace as the young noble.

The bird circled and observed the second man, a tall traveller with dark hair who moved like a predator, easily keeping his eye upon the other man, but using passers-by as cover, dodging effortlessly through the crowd, never falling behind, but never getting close enough to be discovered.

The young noble was fair-skinned, but sun-browned, his blue eyes squinting against the day's glare. It was late summer in Roldem and the dawn mists and fog had fled, burned off by mid-morning to a brilliant sunny sky, made tolerable by a light wind off the sea. Trudging up the hill from the harbour, the noble whistled a nameless tune as he sought out his old quarters, a three-bedroomed flat above a moneylender's home. He knew he was being followed, for he was as adept a hunter as any man living.

Talon of the Silver Hawk, last of the Orosini, servant of the Conclave of Shadows, had returned to Roldem. Here he was Talwin Hawkins – distant cousin to Lord Seljan Hawkins, Baron of the Prince's Court in Krondor. His title was Squire of Morgan River and Bellcastle, Baronet of Silverlake – estates producing almost no income – and he was vassal to the Baron of Ylith; a former Bannerette Knight Lieutenant under the command of the Duke of Yabon, Tal Hawkins was a young man of some rank and little wealth.

For almost two years he had been absent from the scene of

his most significant public triumph, winning the tournament at the Masters' Court, thus earning the title of World's Greatest Swordsman. Cynical despite his youth, he tried to keep the illusion of superiority in perspective – he had been the best of the several hundred entrants who had come to Roldem for the contest, but that hardly convinced him he was the best in the world. He had no doubt there was some soldier on a distant battlement, or mercenary riding guard-duty somewhere who could cut him up for fish-bait given the chance; but fortunately they hadn't entered the contest.

For a brief instant, Tal wondered if fate would allow him to return to Roldem in three years' time to defend that championship. He was but twenty-three years of age, so it would only be circumstance that would prevent him from returning to Roldem. Should he do so, he hoped the contest would be less eventful than the last. Two men had died by his sword during the matches – a very rare and usually regrettable outcome. Nevertheless Tal had felt no regret, since one of the men had been among those responsible for the destruction of his nation, and the other had been an assassin sent to kill him. Memories of assassins turned his mind to the man following him. The other man had also boarded at Salador, yet had managed to avoid direct contact with him aboard the small ship for the duration of the voyage, despite their being nearly two weeks at sea.

The bird wheeled overhead, then pulled up, wings flapping as it hovered, legs extended downward and tail fanned, as if watching prey. With its telltale cry, the predator announced its presence.

Hearing the familiar screech, Tal looked up, then hesitated for a moment, for the bird above the throng was a silver hawk. It was his spirit guide and had given him his naming vision. For an instant Tal imagined he could see the creature's eyes and hear a greeting. Then the bird wheeled and flew away.

'Did you see that?' asked a porter nearby. 'Never seen a bird do that.'

Tal said, 'Just a hawk.'

'Never seen a hawk that colour, leastways not around here,' answered the porter who took one look at where the bird had hovered then returned to lugging his bundle. Tal nodded, then moved back into the throng. The silver hawk was native to his homeland far to the north, across the vast Sea of Kingdoms, and as far as he knew, none inhabited the island kingdom of Roldem. He felt troubled, and now by more than the presence of the man who had followed him from Salador. He had been subsumed so long in the role of Tal Hawkins that he had forgotten his true identity. Perhaps the bird had been a warning.

With a mental shrug he considered that the bird's appearance might have been nothing more than a coincidence. While still an Orosini at heart, in all ways he had been forced to abandon the practices and beliefs of his people. He still owned a core being – Talon of the Silver Hawk – a boy forged in the crucible of a nation's history and culture; but he had been shaped and alloyed by fate and the teachings of outlanders so that at times the Orosini boy was no more than a distant memory.

He wended his way through the press of the city. Shops displayed colourful fashions as he entered a more prosperous part of the city. He lived at just the right level to convince everyone he was a noble of modest means. He was charming enough and successful enough as Champion of the Masters' Court to warrant invitations to the very best Roldemish society had to offer, but had as yet to host his own gala.

Reaching the door to the moneylender's home, he reflected wryly that he might crowd half a dozen close friends into his modest apartment, but he could hardly entertain those to whom he owed a social debt. He knocked lightly upon the door and then entered.

The office of Kostas Zenvanose consisted of little more than a tiny counter and there was barely enough room to stand before it. A clever hinge allowed the counter to be raised at night and put out of the way. Three feet behind the counter a curtain divided the room. Tal knew that behind the curtain lay the Zenvanose family living-room. Beyond that lay the kitchen, bedrooms, and exit to the back courtyard.

A pretty girl appeared and her face brightened with a smile. 'Squire! It's wonderful to see you again.'

Sveta Zenvanose had been a charming girl of seventeen when Tal had last seen her. The passing two years had done nothing but turn a pretty lass into a burgeoning beauty. She had lily-white skin with a hint of rose on her high cheekbones and eyes the colour of cornflowers, all topped off with hair so black it shone with blue and violet highlights when struck by the sun. Her previously slender figure had also ripened, Tal noted as he quickly returned her smile.

'My lady,' he said with a slight bow. She began to flush, as she always had when confronted by the notorious Tal Hawkins. Tal kept the flirtation to a minimum, just enough to amuse the girl, but not enough to pose any serious issues between himself and the girl's father. While the father posed no threat to him directly, he had money, and money could buy a lot of threats. The father appeared a moment later, and as always Tal wondered how he could have sired a girl as pretty as Sveta. Kostas was gaunt to the point of looking unhealthy, which Tal knew was misleading, for he was lively and moved quickly. He also had a keen eye and a canny knack for business.

He moved swiftly between his daughter and his tenant, and smiled. 'Greetings, Squire. Your rooms have been readied, as you requested, and I believe everything is in order.'

'Thank you.' Tal smiled. 'Has my man put in an appearance?'

'I believe he has, otherwise you have an intruder above who has been banging around all day yesterday and this morning. I assume it's Pasko moving the furniture to dust and clean, and not a thief.'

Tal nodded. 'Am I current with our accounts?'

As if by magic, the moneylender produced an account ledger and consulted it, with one bony finger running down the page. With a nod and an 'ah' he said, 'You are most certainly current. Your rent is paid for another three months.'

Tal had left the island nation almost two years previously, and had deposited a sum of gold with the moneylender to keep the apartment against his return. He had judged that if he didn't return within two years, he'd be dead, and Kostas would be free to rent out the rooms to someone else.

'Good,' said Tal. 'Then I will leave you to your business and retire. I expect to be here for a while, so at the end of the three months, remind me and I'll advance more funds against the rent.'

'Very well, Squire.'

Sveta batted her lashes. 'Good to see you home, Squire.'

Tal returned the obvious flirtation with a slight bow and smile, and fought down a sudden urge to laugh. The rooms above were no more his home than was the palace of the King. He had no

home, at least he hadn't since the Duke of Olasko had sent mercenaries to destroy the land of the Orosini. As far as Tal could
judge, he was the sole surviving member of his people.

Tal left the office. One quick glance around the street told
him that the man who had followed him from the ship was out
of sight, so he mounted the stairs next to the door, climbing
quickly to the entrance to his rooms. He tested the door and
found it unlocked. Stepping in he was confronted by a dour-
looking man with a droopy moustache and large brown eyes.

'Master! There you are!' Pasko said. 'Weren't you in on the
morning tide?'

'Indeed,' replied Tal, handing his jacket and travel bag to his
manservant. 'But as such things are wont to be, the order of
landing was dictated by factors of which I am ignorant.'

'In other words, the ship's owner didn't bribe the harbour-
master enough to get you in early.'

'Most likely.' Tal sat down on a divan. 'So expect the luggage
to arrive later today.'

Pasko nodded. 'The rooms are safe, master.' Even in private,
Pasko observed the formalities of their relationship: he the ser-
vant, Tal the master, despite the fact that he had been one of
Tal's instructors over the years.

'Good.' Tal knew that meant Pasko had employed various
wards against scrying magic, just as he would have inspected the
premises against more mundane observation. The chances of
their enemies knowing that Tal was an agent of the Conclave
of Shadows were small, but not out of the question. And they
had sufficient resources to match the Conclave in dealing with
opponents.

Since his victory over Raven and his mercenaries, avenging

his own people's slaughter, Tal had lived on Sorcerer's Isle, recovering from wounds – both mental and physical – learning more of the politics of the Eastern Kingdoms, and simply resting. His teaching had continued in various areas, for Pug and his wife, Miranda, had occasionally instructed him in areas of magic that might concern him. Nakor the Isalani, the self-proclaimed gambler who was far more than that, instructed him in what only could be termed 'dodgy business', how to cheat at cards and spot others cheating, how to pick locks and pockets, as well as other nefarious skills. With his old friend Caleb he would go hunting. It had been the best time he had known since the destruction of his people.

During that period he had been allowed to glimpse some of the dealings of the Conclave on a level far above his station; and had thus gained the sense that the Conclave had agents numbering in the hundreds, perhaps thousands, or at least had links to thousands of well-positioned individuals. He knew the organization's influences reached down into the heart of the Empire of Great Kesh, and across the sea to the lands of Novindus, as well as through the rift to the Tsurani home world, Kelewan. He could tell that enormous wealth was at their disposal, for whatever they needed always appeared somehow. The false patent of nobility that Tal carried in his personal portfolio had cost a small fortune, he was sure, for there were 'originals' in the Royal Archives on Rillanon. Even his 'distant cousin' Lord Seljan Hawkins had been delighted to discover a long-lost relative who had been victorious in the Masters' Court, according to Nakor. Tal didn't feel emboldened enough to ever visit the capital of the Kingdom of the Isles, because while the elderly Baron might believe that some distant cousin had fathered a lad who had some versatility with the sword, the possibility of Tal failing to be convincing when it came to small-talk about this or that family member made such a visit too risky to contemplate.

Still, it was reassuring to know that these resources lay at his disposal should he need them. For he was ready to embark upon the most difficult and dangerous portion of his personal mission to avenge his people: he had to find a way to destroy Duke Kaspar of Olasko, the man ultimately responsible for the obliteration of the Orosini nation. And Duke Kaspar happened to be the most dangerous man in the world, according to many sources.

'What news?' asked Pasko.

'Nothing new, really. Reports from the north say that Olasko is again causing trouble in the Borderlands, and may be once more seeking to isolate the Orodon. They still send patrols through my former homeland to discourage anyone who might think to claim Orosini lands.' Then he asked, 'What is the news in Roldem?'

'The usual court intrigues, master, and quite a few rumours of this lady and that lord and their dalliances. In short, with little of note to comment upon, the nobles, gentry and wealthy commoners turn their attention to gossip.'

'Let's confine ourselves to matters of importance. Any sign of Olasko's agents here in Roldem?'

'Always. But nothing out of the ordinary, or at least nothing we can see that's out of the ordinary. He builds alliances, seeks to do favours in exchange for social debts, loans gold, and insinuates himself in the good graces of others.'

Tal was silent for a long moment. Then he asked, 'To what ends?'

'Pardon?'

Tal leaned forward in his chair, elbows on knees. 'He's the most powerful man in the Eastern Kingdoms. He has blood ties to the throne of Roldem – he's, what? Sixth in line of succession?'

'Seventh,' replied Pasko.

'So why does he need to curry favour with Roldemish nobility?'

'Indeed.'

'He doesn't need to,' said Tal, 'which means he wants to. But why?'

'Lord Olasko is a man with many irons in the fire, master. Perhaps he has interests here in Roldem which might require a vote of the House of Lords?'

'Perhaps. They ratify treaties enacted by the Crown, and verify succession. What else do they do?'

'Not much else, save argue over taxes and land.' Pasko nodded. 'Given that Roldem is an island, master, land is of great importance.' He grinned. 'Until someone discovers how to build dirt.'

Tal grinned back. 'I'm sure we know a few magicians who could increase the size of the island if they felt the need.'

Pasko said, 'So, what are we doing back in Roldem, master?'

Tal sat back and sighed. 'Playing the role of bored noble looking to find a better station in life. In short, I must convince Kaspar of Olasko I'm ready to take service with him by creating a muddle here that only he can get me out of.'

'Such as?'

'Picking a fight with a royal seems a good choice.'

'What? You're going to smack Prince Constantine and provoke a duel? The boy's only fifteen years of age!'

'I was thinking of his cousin, Prince Matthew.'

Pasko nodded. Matthew was the King's cousin. He was considered the 'difficult' member of the royal family; more arrogant, demanding and condescending than any other member of the King's family, he was also a womanizer, a drunk and he cheated at gambling. Rumour had it that the King had bailed him out of very difficult straits on a number of occasions. 'Good choice. Kill him and the King will privately thank you . . . while his executioner is lopping off your head.'

'I wasn't thinking of killing him, just . . . creating enough of a fuss that the King would be unhappy with me remaining in his country.'

'You'd have to kill him,' said Pasko dryly. 'As Champion of the Masters' Court you could probably sleep with the Queen and the King would pass it off as a boyish prank. Why do you need all this bother? Olasko offered you a position when you won the tourney.'

'Because I wish to appear the reluctant petitioner. I would have undergone close scrutiny had I accepted his offer immediately after the tourney two years ago. If I were to appear suddenly requesting that position today, I would undergo an even closer examination. But if I'm merely forced by circumstances to seek out his patronage, then my motives are obvious – at least I hope they are.

'While at Sorcerer's Isle, I was . . . prepared, to withstand a great deal of examination.'

Pasko nodded. He understood what was being said. Tal had been conditioned by Pug and the other magicians to deal with any magic that might uncover his true allegiance.

'But the circumstances of my seeking service with Kaspar must also be credible. Being in his debt for my life seems an obvious motive.'

'Assuming he can keep you off the headsman's block.' Pasko rubbed his throat. 'I've always thought beheading a barbaric choice. Now, the Kingdom hangs its felons. A short drop –' he snapped his fingers '– and the neck is broken, and it's over. No mess, no fuss, no bother.

'In Great Kesh, I've been told, they have many different choices of execution, depending on the location and nature of the crime: decapitation, burning at the stake, being buried up to your neck next to an anthill, drowning, exposure, being pulled apart by camels, being buried alive, defenestration –'

'What?'

'That's throwing someone off a very high place onto the rocks below. My personal favourite is castration, then being fed to the crocodiles in the Overn Deep after having watched them first consume your manhood.'

Tal stood up. 'Have I ever mentioned that you have a seriously morbid streak? Rather than contemplate the means of my demise, I'll spend my energies on staying alive.'

'Then, to a practical concern?'

Tal nodded.

'While I suspect Duke Kaspar would intervene on your behalf in such a circumstance – the humiliation of Prince Matthew, I mean, not the feeding to crocodiles thing . . .'

Tal smiled.

'. . . isn't it going to be difficult for him to do so from across the seas?'

Tal's smile broadened. 'Nakor had intelligence from the north just as I left Salador; Duke Kaspar arrives within the week for a state visit.'

Pasko shrugged. 'In aid of what?'

'A little hand-holding for his distant cousin, I imagine, prior to doing something that might otherwise earn the King's displeasure.'

'Such as?'

'We have no idea, but the north is constantly on a low roil, and Kaspar only has to raise the heat in one place or another for a kettle to boil over somewhere. That's one of the many things I wish to find out.'

Pasko nodded. 'Shall I draw you a bath?'

'I think I'll take a walk to Remarga's and indulge in a long massage and tub there. Bring suitable clothing for an evening in town.'

'Where will you be dining, master?'

'I don't know. Somewhere public.'

'Dawson's?' The former inn was now exclusively a dining establishment for the noble and the rich, and had spawned a dozen imitators. 'Dining out' had become something of a pastime for those in the capital city.

'Perhaps that new establishment, the Metropol. It's considered the place to be seen, I have been told.'

'It's a private club, master.'

'Then get me an invitation while I bathe, Pasko.'

With a wry expression, Pasko said, 'I'll see what I can do.'

'I must be seen in public so word will spread I'm back in the city, but I need to be alone tonight when I finish supper and return to these quarters.'

'Why, master?'

'So I can find out who's been following me since I left Salador, and what's on his mind.'

'A spy?'

With a stretch and a yawn, Tal said, 'Probably an assassin.'

Sighing, Pasko said, 'So it begins.'

Nodding as he headed for the door, Tal said, 'Yes. So it begins.'

Fog shrouded the city. Mist hung so thick it was impossible to see more than three feet ahead. The bright lamps at each corner of the merchants' quarter were reduced to dim yellow spots in the distance, and even the occasional lantern beside a tavern door became just a faint pool of light across the street. There were places on long streets where no light was visible, and the senses were confounded, distances were meaningless and the entirety of the universe was murk.

Even sound was muted. The taverns he passed offered just a murmur of voices rather than the raucous cacophony normally heard. Footfalls were a soft grinding of heel on caked mud rather than a clatter of leather on stone.

Even so, Tal Hawkins knew he was being stalked. He had known that the instant he had departed Lady Gavorkin's home. He had lingered over dinner at the Metropol – it had taken only minutes for Pasko to gain an invitation on behalf of the owner of the establishment for the Champion of the Masters' Court to dine as his guest – and Tal had left with a free membership in the club. He had been impressed with the décor, the ambiance and the service. The food was only just acceptable, and he planned on having words with the chef, but he could see this club business might be a useful enterprise.

Roldem lived on commerce more than any nation in the east, and this new club was in a location where nobles and wealthy commoners could come together in casual surroundings to socialize in a fashion impossible to imagine anywhere else in the city. Tal suspected that over the coming years fortunes would be lost and titles gained, marriages arranged and alliances formed in the quiet interior of the Metropol. Even before he had finished dining, a note from Lady Gavorkin had been handed to him, and Tal judged it as likely he would encounter his stalker on his way to her townhouse as he would back to his own. He had not, however, been accosted by whoever followed, and had spent a pleasant two hours, first being scolded for his long absence, then being ardently forgiven by Lady Gavorkin.

The lady was recently widowed, her husband having perished in a raid against a nest of Ceresian pirates operating out of an isolated bay off Kesh. His service to the Roldemish Crown had garnered Lady Gavorkin a fair amount of sympathy, some guarantees of a modest pension in addition to her ample estates and holdings, and an appetite for a new husband as soon as the proper mourning period had been observed. She was childless, and her estates stood at risk if the Crown decided that another noble would better able manage them. Ideally, from the royal perspective it would be ideal that Lady Gavorkin, Countess of Dravinko, should marry some other noble who was favoured by the Crown, which would tie up two loose ends nicely.

Tal knew he would have to sever all contact with Lady Gavorkin soon because he would never withstand the close scrutiny reserved for those marrying into Roldemish nobility. A minor squire's son from a town outside a distant Kingdom city who was socially acceptable as an escort for galas and festivals was one thing, but someone who wed the widow of a recently departed war hero was another matter entirely. Besides, being tied down to anyone, even someone as attractive as Lady Margaret Gavorkin, held limited appeal for Tal, her substantial wealth, holdings, and energetic lovemaking notwithstanding.

Tal listened as he walked and let his hunter's instincts serve him well. He had learned years earlier that a city was nothing but a different kind of wilderness, and that the skills he had learned as a child in the mountains to the far north, across the sea, could keep him alive in any city. Each place had its own rhythm and pace, its own dynamic feeling, and once he was comfortable within that environment, threats and opportunities for a hunt would be recognized, just as they were in the wild.

Whoever followed him was desperately trying to keep a proper distance and would have gone unnoticed by anyone less keenly aware of his surroundings than Tal. Tal knew this area of the city as well as anyone born here, and he knew he would be able to lose his stalker at whim. But he was curious as to who was following him, and more to the point, why.

Tal paused for half a step, just enough of a break in the rhythm of his walking for his stalker to reveal his whereabouts, then continued. He turned right at the corner, and stepped inside a deep doorway, the entrance to a tailor shop he had frequented. Forgoing his sword, he deftly removed a dagger from his belt and waited. At the moment Tal expected, the man following him turned the corner and stepped in front of him.

Tal reached out and grabbed the man's right shoulder, bearing down and twisting as he pulled. The man reacted, but Tal was quicker; the stalker did exactly as Tal anticipated, hesitating for an instant before reflexively pulling away. Tal yanked upward using the man's own motion to spin him completely around. Suddenly the stalker found himself hard against the door with Tal's dagger at his throat.

'Why are you following me?' Tal asked, his voice a hissed whisper lest he arouse those asleep upstairs above the shop.

The man was quick, for his hands were moving towards his own dagger before the last syllable was uttered. He was also no fool, for he recognized he was in a hopeless situation a scant moment before Talon would be forced to plunge the blade into his throat. He slowly raised his hands to show they were empty. In a whisper, he answered, 'Magnificence! I mean you no harm! My sword and dagger are still at my belt!' He spoke in the language of the Kingdom of the Isles.

'Who are you?'

'I am Petro Amafi.'

'Amafi? That's Quegan. But you speak the language of the Isles.'

'I have resided in Salador many years now and, to tell the truth, my command of the Roldemish tongue is lacking, so I employ the King's Tongue.'

'Tell me, Amafi, why are you following me?' Tal repeated.

'I am an assassin by trade. I have been paid to kill you.'

Tal took a step back, leaving his blade against the man's throat, but gaining a perspective on him.

Petro Amafi was a half-head shorter than Tal's two inches over six feet, with broad shoulders and a barrel chest. His clothing marked him as a foreigner; he wore a curious long tunic, gathered at the waist by a black leather belt, and rather than the long wide-bottomed trousers affected by the style-conscious in Roldem this season, he wore leggings and a courtier's slippers. He sported a moustache and goatee and upon his head he wore a felted wool beret with a clasp and feather on the left side. His face was narrow, with deep eyes that revealed his menace more than his vulpine appearance. 'You mean me no harm, but you're an assassin sent to kill me. Something of a contradiction, don't you agree?' observed Tal.

'I gain nothing by hiding the truth, Magnificence. My life is preserved by your ignorance. Should you kill me this moment, you will wonder who hired me.'

Tal chuckled. 'That is true. So, then, we are at an impasse, for should you tell me, then I must kill you. So it is to your benefit not to tell me. But as I cannot spend the rest of my life waiting for you to divulge who sent you, so I gain nothing by keeping you alive.'

'Wait!' said Amafi, holding out his hand in a conciliatory gesture. 'I did not come to kill you. I was hired to do so, but I have been observing you since nearly a week before you departed Salador and I wish to bargain.'

'For your life?'

'More, Magnificence. Let me serve.'

'You'd take service with me?' said Tal in dubious tones.

'Willingly, Your Magnificence. Any man of your skills would be a worthy master, for I have seen you duel in the Court of Blades in Salador, and I've watched from the corner as you play cards in the ale houses; you win just enough to raise no suspicions, yet you are a master cheat. You are welcome in the homes of the great and near-great. You are admired by men and desired by women. What's more, no one has ever done what you just have, turned me from hunter to hunted. But most telling of all, you are Champion of the Masters' Court, the greatest blade in the world, and a rumour circulates that you are secretly in the service of Duke Kaspar of Olasko, and one who serves such as Kaspar can only prosper greatly. I wish to prosper greatly with you.'

He gently moved the tip of Tal's blade away from his throat with one finger, and Tal permitted it. 'As you can see, Magnificence, I am getting on in years, nearly sixty of them. The assassin's trade requires skills that are fading as I age. I must think of my latter days, and while I have kept some part of the fees paid me over the years, it is not enough. I have fallen on hard times.'

Tal laughed. 'Bad investments?'

Amafi nodded. 'A trading concern out of Salador, most recently. No, I wish to take my bloody skills and use them to a more permanent advantage. Were I your man, then I would rise with you. Do you see?'

Tal put away his dagger. 'How can I trust you?'

'I will swear an oath in whatever temple you require.'

Tal considered. Few men would willingly break oath, even if they weren't as honour-bound as the Orosini. 'Who told you I was in Kaspar's service?'

'A rumour here, there, nothing more. You were reported to have been seen in the region of Latagore where Duke Kaspar has interests, and it is well known he sought you out after you won the competition at the Masters' Court two years ago. Duke Kaspar employs only the most gifted and ambitious young men, so it is assumed you are his.'

'Well, I'm not,' replied Tal, intentionally turning his back on Amafi. He knew he took a risk, for as much as the assassin claimed age was slowing him down, Tal judged him capable of a swift attack from behind if given the opportunity. The attack didn't come.

Instead, Amafi fell into step beside Tal. 'You wish to know who sent me?'

'Yes,' replied Tal.

'Lord Piotre Miskovas, though I am not supposed to know this.'

'He does hold a grudge,' observed Tal. 'I haven't slept with his wife in more than two years.'

'As I understand it, she became intoxicated at a gala given by Lady Amsha Detoris, and threw the facts of your . . . liaison into her husband's face over supper some months after you last left the city. The couple are yet not reconciled and she abides in her suites here in the city, while he resides at their estates in the country. He blames you.'

'He should look to his own philandering,' remarked Tal, 'for had he not been so quick to bed every pretty face he saw, his wife would not have been so eager to receive my attentions.'

'Perhaps, Magnificence, but it takes a man of unusual character to openly confront his own shortcomings. It's so much more convenient to blame others.

'Upon hearing of your planned return, he sought out an assassin – far less discreetly than he should have – and I was hired to remove this –' he pointed at Tal '– blot on his honour. He was at least intelligent enough to have used a . . . broker . . . in Salador, lest blame fall upon him here in Roldem. I have "failed", so I am honour-bound to return his gold, and seek to turn this failure into a triumph. Employ me, Magnificence, and I will serve you. My oath upon it!'

Tal considered his next move. He had been back in Roldem for less than a day and needed reliable eyes and ears. 'Until such time as you can successfully betray me without risk?'

Amafi grinned. 'Possibly, my lord, for I have never been a man of constant heart. But oath-breaking does not come easily even to one such as me, and given your rare talents I suspect such a time would never exist, for it would require an opportunity to become even richer than I hope to become in your service.'

Tal laughed. Amafi had a refreshing candour that made Tal think he could trust the assassin – up to a point, anyway – and as long as he didn't attempt to press him beyond that point, he should prove a reliable servant. 'Very well, let us to the Temple of Lims-Kragma, where you will swear an oath.'

Amafi grimaced. 'I was thinking perhaps Ruthia or Astalon,' he said, naming the Goddess of Luck and the God of Justice.

'I think wagering your chance at being reborn to a higher station a good hedge against betrayal,' said Talon, putting away his weapon. 'Come along. And, we must work on your Roldemish. We may be here a while.'

If Amafi thought even for an instant to draw his weapon and strike, he masked the impulse completely, quickly moving to fall into step beside his new master as they vanished into the fog shrouding the city.

The magician stood in the corner, his features veiled in shadow. Tal knew his face even if he couldn't see it in the gloom. A single candle burned in the apartment, and that was on the table in the next room, casting a faint light through the open door.

'Where's your new man?' he asked.

Tal said, 'I sent him on an errand. What did you find out?'

Stepping out of the shadows, the magician revealed himself to be a tall man of lean features, a striking face with a long straight nose, dramatic cheekbones and startling blue eyes. His hair was so pale, it appeared almost white. He said, 'Informants in Queg have vouched for Amafi. At least they have vouched for his reputation as an assassin.'

'A reputable assassin,' said Tal. 'That's a quaint notion.'

'He's considered something of an "honourable" man in the context of his trade,' declared Magnus, son of Pug of Sorcerer's Isle, and one of Tal's many teachers over the years.

'It's beginning,' said Tal. 'Lady Gavorkin confirmed last night that Duke Kaspar is to arrive by week's end and will be ensconced in the palace with his cousin the King. Pasko? How many invitations arrived today?'

'Seventeen, master,' he answered.

'By month's end, I imagine I will be in a position to make the re-acquaintance of the Duke at one gala or another.'

'Your plan?' asked Magnus.

'I need to establish a link with Kaspar, then find a reason to call out Prince Matthew.'

'Is that necessary?'

'Almost certainly,' said Tal. 'For while I'm vague on the details I think I have anticipated Duke Kaspar's larger goals in his manoeuvrings over the last few years.'

'This is something you didn't mention before leaving the island,' said Magnus.

Tal nodded. 'Because I didn't fully see the pattern until a few hours ago. And I may be wrong, but I believe all his actions in the north to be nothing more than a bloody, murderous ruse, and his anticipated invasion of the Kingdom through Farinda a feint.'

'To what end?'

'To keep the Kingdom busy up north while he works towards his true goal in the south.'

'And that is . . . ?' asked Magnus impatiently.

'I have no idea. But it could involve Roldem or Kesh, and keeping the Kingdom occupied along a long, empty border would work to Kaspar's advantage.

'I'm no military expert, but it seems to me if he sends a force into the Kingdom of the Isles, they will respond in strength. If Kaspar sends in small companies, each can occupy a much larger force if they scatter across the plains. From the foothills at the border to the Blackwood north of Dolth, you've got almost a thousand miles of grasslands. King Ryan of the Isles would be forced to tie up a huge number of men hunting down a relatively small army.

'So, the question is, if Kaspar wants that army up in the grasslands, where does he plan on striking?'

Magnus said, 'I will convey your theory to Father.' He put a broad-brimmed felt hat on his head, and removed a device from within his dark grey robe, an orb that glowed with copper highlights in the candlelight. He depressed the surface with his thumb and suddenly he wasn't there, the only sign of his departure being a small inrush of air.

Pasko said, 'But why?'

'Why?' echoed Tal. 'Why what?'

'Why all the plotting? Kaspar is as powerful in his own way as the King of Roldem. He effectively rules Aranor; the Prince does his bidding. He either controls or intimidates every nation surrounding Olasko, and he has the King of Roldem's ear. Why does he want this war with the Isles?'

Tal sat back. 'I thought it obvious. By destabilizing the region, opportunity arises for Kaspar to gain what he wants most of all.' Tal laced his fingers together and stared at the candle over balled fists. He tapped his chin lightly with his hands as he muttered, 'Men of power seek only one thing: more power.'

• CHAPTER TWO •

Reception

*T*AL SMILED.

This was his first time in the palace since his victory in the Masters' Court Tournament two years earlier. The King had sent an invitation for Talwin Hawkins to attend the welcoming gala to celebrate the arrival of the Duke of Olasko.

Tal had waited patiently in line for his turn to be presented, behind all the nobility of Roldem, most of those from other nations, and just ahead of the wealthiest commoners. A squire from the Kingdom of the Isles stood barely above a ribbon-maker with a great deal of gold in the eyes of the Roldemish court.

Even so, Tal stood resplendent in a pair of new wide-legged trousers – the current fashion – with his boots covered to the buckles, and a broad black leather belt, but he chose to wear a currently out-of-fashion tunic – a yellow doublet sewn with seed pearls. While other nobles were wearing the off-the-shoulder military singlet which was now all the rage, Talon had chosen to wear the jacket which had been given to him as a gift by the King two years ago.

When last he had met the King, Tal had been the centre of attention, the winner of the Tournament of Masters, the recipient of the golden sword, emblematic of his being the world's greatest swordsman.

Now Kaspar of Olasko was the focus of the gala, and Tal but a minor participant. When he at last heard his name called, Tal moved forward briskly and approached the throne. He took in the tableau before him as he reached the point where he was expected to bow before the Crown. King Carol sat on his throne, his wife Queen Gertrude to his right. On his left hand sat Crown Prince Constantine, heir to the throne. Tal remembered the Prince as a quiet boy with curious eyes, one given to slight smiles as he listened closely to the banter of the adults around him. Tal suspected he was an intelligent child. The younger members of the royal family were absent, the other two Princes and the Princess no doubt being made ready for bed by their servants and nannies.

To Constantine's left stood a man dressed in a burgundy-coloured tunic of velvet, fastened with loops and frogs made from diamonds. He wore black leggings rather than this season's wide-bottomed trousers, and his feet were encased in polished, but serviceable boots. He wore the same black hat Tal had seen him wearing two years before, a large velvet thing which hung over his right ear almost to his shoulder, with a gold badge on the left.

It was the Duke of Olasko.

Kaspar of Olasko studied the young squire while still engaging the young prince in conversation, a skill which Tal observed, for while Prince Constantine was being kept occupied by his distant cousin, Olasko was assessing Tal closely. Tal considered it possible that Kaspar was one of those men who could focus on two things at the same time. Even among the magicians Tal knew, that was a rare gift.

Out of the corner of his eye, as he bowed before the King, Tal reacquainted himself with Kaspar. He was a burly man with a broad chest and powerful shoulders, and muscles revealed by the tight leggings suggested he might also be a man with some speed. He glanced at Tal in such a way that the younger man suspected the Duke recognized he was being appraised. His face was round, but his chin jutted a bit, robbing him of any comic cast to his features. He sported a thin-cut black beard, with his upper lip shaved, which gave his chin an even more aggressive appearance. His hair was still mostly black, though a sprinkling of grey hinted he was a man in his early forties. His eyes were those of a predator, black and searching. And his mouth was full, sensuous without being decadent, and set in a near-smirking smile Tal had seen several times before.

Tal straightened from his bow and the King said, 'Squire Hawkins, it is good to have you in our court again.'

'I am pleased as well to return to Roldem, Majesty.'

The Queen beamed as she said, 'And I see you return to us in the garb we presented you upon your victory.'

Tal gave Gertrude his most endearing smile. 'Majesty, I have worn this gift only once before, on the night of my triumph, and have vowed that it will never again be worn, save in the presence of your august selves.'

The King nodded in pleasure and said, 'You are most considerate. Again, welcome.'

Tal knew he was now excused, so he moved over to the gathering on the left side of the King to watch those behind him being presented. He stole a couple of quick glances at Kaspar, but the Duke seemed focused on his quiet conversation with the Prince.

Eventually the last presentation was made and the Master of Ceremonies moved to stand before the throne. 'With Your Majesty's permission?' he said bowing.

The King waved his hand and the Master of Ceremonies turned and declared, 'My lords, ladies, and gentlemen, please retire to the banquet hall and await Their Majesties!'

Tal watched as the royal family departed, with the Duke of Olasko following close after. He knew they'd retire to a nearby apartment in the palace and wait until all the guests were seated before moving to the head table.

Tal waited patiently in line, but it moved quickly as more than two dozen pages and squires had been detailed to the Master of Ceremonies who consulted the master seating plan. Once instructions had been whispered into the page's ear, a guest had only to pause for a moment before being escorted to their place in the hall.

Tal was pleasantly surprised to discover he was being seated at the King's table. He quickly counted chairs and realized that there would be no more than two or three people between him and the Duke of Olasko. He suspected his position at the banquet was more a result of Kaspar wishing him to be near to hand than because of his prestige as reigning Champion of the Masters' Court.

When the royal family arrived, everyone rose and bowed slightly, then remained standing until the King was seated and the Master of Ceremonies struck the floor with his iron-shod staff of office. At which point everyone sat and servants began pouring wine and providing food.

Tal found himself next to a local court baron and his wife, whom Kaspar engaged in conversation for a while. The Baron at last turned to Tal and introductions were exchanged. Then the Baron launched into an enthusiastic retelling of Tal's victories as if Tal hadn't been there. On Tal's left sat a pretty woman of middle years and her husband, rich commoners who seemed content simply to be at the King's table and who demonstrated no need to speak to anyone else. They lowered their heads slightly and spoke in whispers as they glanced around the room, apparently trying to espy people who might know them and be impressed by their place at the head table.

Throughout the dinner the Duke ignored Tal's presence, save for one slight nod and smile as the first course was being served. During the course of the dinner, entertainers provided distraction in several locations around the great hall. Deft jugglers, acrobats, and sleight-of-hand magicians. A particularly gifted poet spun verse to order, flattering the ladies and gently mocking the men. His wit was dry and his rhyming clever. On the other side of the room a jongleur from Bas-Tyra sang love songs and ballads of heroic sacrifice. Tal could hear enough of his song to know he was excellent.

As was the meal and every other aspect of the gala. And why not? Tal thought. Roldem was considered to be the seat of all things cultural and refined in the world, or at least this part of it. Fashion, literature, music, all flowed from the court of Roldem.

Given his travels, Tal reflected that much of that influence was lost as you moved away from the island nation; those in the west of the Kingdom seemed completely indifferent to matters of fashion, while only in Salador and Rillanon was there some of the same concern that one saw here.

But gazing around the room he realized that whatever others might think – that it was vainglorious and pointless – it was also sumptuous and regal. The women were beautiful in their finery and the men cut handsome figures, or at least as handsome as nature permitted.

When the meal ended, the court turned its attention to the centre of the royal table. No one was permitted to leave until the King and his family left the table. Those who had finished their meal early sat sipping wine or ale, watching those around them, or engaging in idle conversation with their neighbours.

Suddenly, Tal heard Kaspar say, 'So, Squire, you're back with us again?'

Tal turned in as relaxed a manner as he could, and trying to show deference to the Baron on his right, spoke past him to the Duke. 'For a time, m'lord.'

Kaspar took a sip from a wine cup and asked, 'Have you completed that "family business" you spoke of when last we met?'

'Indeed, Your Grace. It took longer than I had anticipated, but it is now a matter in the past.'

'So, you are now free to seek your fortune?' The Duke's eyes were narrow and appraising even as he kept his tone light.

Tal feigned a laugh. 'Given my luck at cards lately, I am in need of a fortune, m'lord.'

The King rose, and a half-second later, Kaspar did as well. As he turned to follow his cousin, Kaspar looked over his shoulder and said, 'I am hunting at first light. Join me at the southern gate. I'll have a horse ready. Do you have a bow?'

'Yes, m'lord,' said Tal, to Kaspar's retreating back.

The court baron turned. 'Quite the coup, young Hawkins.'

'Sir?'

'The Dukes of Olasko have been hunters for generations. They say this duke's grandfather once hunted dragons in the west of the Kingdom of the Isles. To be invited to hunt with him is a mark of distinction.'

Tal smiled and nodded, attempting to look suitably flattered. The Baron and his wife departed.

Tal felt it necessary to make one circuit of the hall, then determined to stay close to the exit and wait until someone else departed. He had no wish to mark himself by being the first to leave, but he wished to be out of the palace as soon as possible.

As he made his way through the throng, he was occasionally stopped by this acquaintance or that and several times by strangers who wished simply to introduce themselves to the current Champion of the Masters' Court. As he came near the King's cortege he was struck by how many people were being kept at bay by the servants, who were acting as guardians of the royal privacy as much as providing titbits and drink – though who could eat or drink after such a meal? Tal wondered.

Without intending to, Tal caught the King's eye, who waved him approach. Tal instantly turned and as he moved towards the King, the servants parted enough to let him pass. Tal bowed, 'Majesty.'

King Carol smiled. 'Hawkins, it is good to have you with us again. Would it be possible to arrange a demonstration of your skills here in the palace?'

'I am at Your Majesty's disposal,' replied Tal. 'Whatever time you require.'

'Oh, good, young sir. Prince Constantine is of an age and needs to learn his weapons. His instructors say the boy has promise, but still, I think watching experts in such matters tends to give a lad something to emulate. Don't you?'

Tal couldn't disagree, and besides it would be impolitic to do so. 'Most learning begins with mimicry, Majesty.'

'Quite. What say you, a week from today?'

'At any time you wish, Majesty.'

'Say mid-morning. I find the wits are keener in the morning than the afternoon.' Turning to his wife, he said, 'Assuming my wits are keen at any time of the day, what, my dear?'

The Queen smiled and patted her husband's arm. 'You are a man of very keen wit, m'lord . . . sometimes.'

The King laughed aloud, and Tal couldn't help but smile. King Carol of Roldem was the only monarch Tal had encountered in his travels, but Tal doubted most were as self-deprecating as this one.

'Shall I bring an opponent, Majesty?' Tal knew that any student from the Masters' Court, and most of the instructors, would welcome an opportunity to come to the court. Royal favours had been curried with less than a sword match in the past, Tal knew.

'We have an ample supply of swordsmen here in the palace, Squire,' answered the King. 'Just be here at the appointed hour.'

'Yes, Your Majesty,' said Tal with a bow, taking it to mean he was dismissed.

He noticed that a few guests were departing and decided it was safe for himself to leave as well. But halfway across the floor he heard a familiar voice. 'Squire, a moment of your time.'

Without turning, Tal said, 'Constable, what an unexpected surprise.'

Constable Dennis Drogan came to stand before Tal and with a smile and nod said, 'Glad to see you again, Squire.'

'What brings you here?' asked Tal.

Dennis, a middle-aged, broad-shouldered man, had a head that looked to be perfectly round. He kept his hair cropped close and seemed impervious to the effect that had, for it emphasized his left ear, which had been half bitten off during a scuffle in his youth. His nose looked as if it had been repeatedly broken over the years. Tal recognized him for what he was, a brawler, tough, unrelenting and dangerous. More so, for he was the Crown's law in the city.

Drogan smiled. 'My uncle is still Bursar to the household here in the palace, and I am technically a member of the Royal Court.'

'Ah, of course, but rather, what brings you here?'

Putting his hand on Tal's shoulder, Drogan moved him towards the door. 'You do, Squire.'

'Me?' Tal fell into step beside the shorter man. 'Why?'

'Because people have an annoying habit of turning up dead when you're in the city. I thought it best to have a word with you before we start accumulating corpses again.'

Tal didn't try to feign innocence, but he did look aggrieved. 'Dennis, you and I have never been close friends, but we have been affable acquaintances. You know that in every instance, someone ended up dead because my life was at risk. What am I supposed to do? Stand by and say, "Oh, if I defend myself the Constable is going to be annoyed, so I'd better let them kill me"?'

The grip on Tal's shoulder tightened, just enough to convey

emphasis without causing pain. 'No, by all means, should your life be put at peril, defend yourself; I'm just suggesting you try to avoid finding your life at peril any time soon.'

Caught halfway between amusement and irritation, Tal said, 'I'll do my best.'

'That's all I can ask.'

Tal slipped out from under the Constable's meaty hand and left the palace. Outside, as guests waited for carriages, Tal wended his way through the crowd and exited through one of the pedestrian gates. He was only a few yards from the palace, moving downhill on a thoroughfare lined with the homes of the wealthy, when someone fell into step beside him.

'Evening, Tal,' said a familiar voice.

'Evening, Quincy,' answered Tal without looking. He had spied the merchant from Bas-Tyra in the crowd at the palace.

'Lovely evening, isn't it?'

Tal stopped and started to laugh. 'You didn't ambush me outside the palace to discuss the weather, my friend.'

Quincy halted, also. 'Well, I saw you on your way out when the Constable intercepted you; I know you walked to the gala rather than booking a carriage, so I just left before you and waited.'

'How have you been, Quincy?' Tal asked, looking at his old acquaintance under the lantern light. Quincy de Castle was in his thirties, perhaps early forties, with a rapidly-balding pate. His features were undistinguished save for his eyes, which were as close to an eagle's as any man Tal had known. He wore fashionable, but not extravagant clothing, a jacket of a charcoal hue, double-breasted with a swallow-tail cut, and matching trousers tucked into knee-high boots. It was, as Tal knew, the latest fashion in the Kingdom of the Isles, as it was *last* year's fashion in Roldem.

'I have been well enough.'

'Recently back from the Kingdom, I see.'

They resumed walking. 'Yes, the clothing. I just arrived and had no time to have new garb made. Besides, all this slavery to fashion seems very . . . unproductive. If someone thinks less of me for wearing last year's style, let him. It but works to my advantage should we negotiate.'

Quincy was one of the most astute merchants in the city. He was a native of Bas-Tyra, the second most important city in the Eastern Realm of the Kingdom, and specialized in high-quality luxury goods. As a result, he numbered nobility, even royalty, among his customers and was invited to all the better social functions. Tal also suspected him of being an agent for the King of the Isles. There was something about him that made Tal wary, something very unmerchantlike in his bearing.

'I see,' said Tal. 'You needing an edge in business seems hardly likely, but I'll grant that taking one where you can find it is logical. Now, what is it that you wish of me?'

'What makes you think I want something?' said Quincy with a smile.

'Because it's not your habit to lurk in the shadows and leap out upon me in the night. This is hardly a chance meeting.'

'Hardly. Look, I'll get to the point. The first reason is I wish to invite you to a small gathering at Dawson's on this coming Fifthnight. I am inviting a few likeable chaps for supper, drink, and then perhaps we'll go on to some cards or dice.'

'A note to my man would have sufficed.'

'There's another reason,' Quincy answered as they turned a

corner and started down a steeper hill towards Tal's quarters. 'You are to hunt with Duke Kaspar tomorrow, am I right?'

'Bribing the waiting staff, are we?'

Quincy laughed. 'I've let it be known in the palace that a bit of news here or there that might prove useful would be rewarded. Now, is it true?'

'Yes, tomorrow at sunrise I hunt with the Duke and his party. Why?'

'If you are in the Duke's favour, I wish you to present me to him.'

'Why?' asked Tal, stopping for a moment.

'Because he really is the most difficult man to see. I can get an audience with the King more readily than I can with Duke Kaspar.'

'Only because you're selling gems to the Queen at cost.'

'I lose no money and it earns me a great deal of social access. But not to Kaspar.'

'Why are you so anxious to meet with Kaspar?'

Quincy was quiet for a moment, then he resumed walking, gesturing for Tal to accompany him. As they proceeded he said, 'Trade with Olasko is . . . difficult. It's as if somehow every trading concern in the duchy has . . . decided to do business the same way.

'They send their agents to Rillanon, Roldem, Bas-Tyra, Ran, down to Kesh, but if I send one of my agents to Opardum, it may as well be for a holiday. For no one will entertain an offer to trade. It's always their agents, in our cities, on their terms. Take it or leave it.'

'Are they bad trades?'

'No, otherwise I wouldn't care. Often they're very good business. But the essence of commerce is regular trade routes, with goods being dependably provided. It keeps the market alive.

This hit or miss . . . I can't help but feel that a vast opportunity is going to waste because of these trading concerns.

'I feel if I can get Duke Kaspar's ear, perhaps convince him to speak to some of the wealthier trading concerns, or even to let me visit his court . . . if I come from the Duke's court to the offices of a major trading concern, like Kasana's or Petrik Brothers, then they would have to take my offers seriously.'

Tal listened and nodded, as if agreeing. To himself he thought, and if you can get your agent up into Opardum, especially if he's trading with the Duke's chancellor, then the King of the Isles has a pair of eyes and ears near a troublesome neighbour.

'I'll see what I can do,' said Tal. 'But for the moment, don't count on anything.'

'Why not?'

'Because the Duke is likely to offer me a place in his court and I will almost certainly turn him down.'

'Why in the world would you do that?'

'Because it is not in my nature to wish to serve another,' Tal lied. He knew that before the supper on Fifthday at Dawson's, half of Roldem would hear about Kaspar offering a position to Tal that he refused. 'And, besides, I have some other prospects that may suit me better.'

'Well, don't offend him too deeply,' said Quincy, dryly.

'I'll try not to.'

They reached the street upon which Tal resided and parted company. Tal went quickly to his quarters where Pasko and Amafi waited, passing the time with a game of cards.

'Master,' said Pasko, rising as Tal entered.

'Awake me an hour before dawn,' Tal instructed as he crossed to the door of his bedroom. 'Dress for a hunt.'

'A hunt?'

'Yes, the Duke of Olasko has invited me out to slaughter some helpless animals and I will oblige him.' To Amafi he said, 'Tomorrow I hunt with the Duke. When I return, we'll visit several villas and estates nearby. It is then we introduce you to the world as my retainer and bodyguard.'

'Magnificence,' said Amafi.

Pasko said, 'Unroll that bedding in the corner. You'll sleep here.' He indicated to Amafi a place on the floor near Tal's doorway. 'I sleep in the kitchen.'

Then, Pasko followed Tal into the bedroom and closed the door. Helping Tal unlace the fancy jacket, he whispered, 'All goes well?'

'Well enough,' Tal whispered back. 'Knowing Kaspar's reputation, the animals won't be as helpless as I indicated. Something nasty like lion or giant boar, I expect.'

'He seems that sort of man,' observed Pasko.

'What do you think of our new friend?'

'He's a bad card player.'

'Bad player or bad cheat?'

'Both.'

'What else?' asked Tal as Pasko pulled the linen shirt over his head.

'He's a weapon. Very dangerous, despite his claim to old age. He may be useful if you don't cut yourself.'

'I take your meaning.'

'I will keep an eye on him for a while,' said Pasko.

'He took oath.'

'That is as it may be,' answered the wily old servant, 'but he wouldn't be the first man to forswear in history.'

'I made him swear at the Temple of Lims-Kragma.'

Pasko considered as he pulled off Tal's boots. 'Some men are not even cowed by the Goddess of Death.'

'Does he strike you as such?'

'No, but did Nakor strike you as particularly dangerous upon meeting him for the first time?'

'Your point is made. Keep an eye on him for a while.' Tal pulled off his leggings and small clothing and slipped under the quilted comforter on his bed. 'Now, get out so I can sleep.'

'Yes, master,' said Pasko as he stepped stealthily through the door.

Tal lay quietly for a while. His mind was busy and sleep was a long time in coming. For years his purpose had been only one thing: to avenge the destruction of his people. Of all those involved, only two principals were left: the Special Captain of Kaspar's household guard, Quentin Havrevulen, and the Duke himself. Tal had already killed the others.

He forced himself to calm, using one of the mind-relaxation drills taught him at Sorcerer's Isle, and sleep finally came. But it wasn't a relaxing sleep. Rather, it was filled with dreams and images of other places and times, his village in the mountains and his family, his mother, father, sister, brother and grandfather. The girl he had dreamed of as a child, Eye of the Blue-Winged Teal. In his dream she sat upon a seat, one leg crossed under the other, wearing a simple buckskin summer dress, a faint smile on her lips. He awoke with a painful longing he thought he had eradicated in himself years before. He rolled over and willed himself back to sleep, and again the dreams came. It was a restless night and he felt little benefit from his slumber when Pasko came and awoke him for the dawn's hunt.

• CHAPTER THREE •

Hunt

*T*HE HORSE PAWED THE ground.

Tal brought his gelding's head around slightly, forcing him to pay attention to something besides his own boredom. The morning was crisp at first light, with a breeze coming off the ocean, but Tal knew it would be very hot by midday in the hills to the northeast of the city. Even before Duke Kaspar appeared Tal knew they were after big game, lion or bear, perhaps even one of the more exotic creatures reputed to inhabit the higher mountains, the giant boars – whose tusks reputedly grew to three feet in length – or the valley sloth, twice the size of a horse and despite the name fast when it needed to be, and armed with claws the size of short swords. The array of weapons in the luggage told Tal what he needed to know about the coming hunt: there were boar-spears with cross-pieces fastened above the broad blade to prevent the animal from running up the haft and goring the spearman; there were giant nets with weights at the edges, and heavy crossbows that could punch a hole the size of a man's fist through plate armour.

A dozen servants, another dozen guards, and livery boys to care for the horses also waited patiently upon the appearance of the Duke. Another six men had been leaving as Tal had arrived, trail-breakers and trackers wearing the King's livery, who would mark the most likely game trails. Tal found it intriguing that the hunting grounds lay less than a day's march away, for Roldem was an ancient land, and he would have expected wildlife to have been pushed far into the mountains by the encroachment of civilization. Having hunted for his entire boyhood, and on many occasions since, he knew that rarely was big game within a day's ride of a city.

Tal let one of the servants oversee the disposition of his travel gear, which was modest compared to the rest of the baggage being stowed on the horses. Tal knew they'd be following trails that wagons couldn't negotiate, but it looked as if they could use a pair. Two animals alone were being used to carry what could only be a pavilion. Tal had no problem with sleeping on the ground, but realized the gentry of Roldem might find that objectionable.

Besides Tal, two nobles of Roldem – Baron Eugivney Balakov, and Baron Mikhael Grav – waited patiently. Tal knew them by reputation. They were young, ambitious, and held modest but important positions in the King's court. Balakov was assistant to the Royal Bursar and he could expedite or slow a request for funds. He was broad-shouldered, with a brooding look, his dark hair cut close as was his beard. Grav was also associated with the Bursar's office, but was seconded to the office of the Royal Household Guard, being primarily responsible for seeing that the palace troops were armed, clothed, fed and paid. He was a thin man with blond hair and a slender moustache he obviously worked hard at keeping perfectly trimmed. Both wore extravagant clothing, a long way from the modest leather tunic and trousers Tal had selected to wear.

As the sun lit the sky behind those distant peaks, Duke Kaspar and a young woman emerged from the palace, quickly making their way to a pair of waiting horses. Tal glanced at the young woman, wondering absently if it might be the Lady Rowena of Talsin, who in reality was another of the Conclave's agents, Alysandra.

Tal had been frustrated during the time he had spent on Sorcerer's Isle in determining just what she had been doing in the Duke's company, for either people didn't know or they weren't telling. All he could discover was that it had been Miranda, Pug's wife, who had dispatched the girl to Olasko at about the same time Tal had been training in Salador.

This woman was unlike Rowena, but she had one trait in common: she was equally beautiful. But while Rowena had been fair with eyes the colour of cornflowers, this lady was dark, her skin touched by the sun to a warm tan, her eyes almost as dark as her black hair. The Duke said something and she smiled, and instantly Tal knew who she was, for there was a hint of resemblance to the Duke.

As if sensing Tal's thoughts, Duke Kaspar said, 'Ah, young Hawkins, may I have the pleasure of presenting you to my sister, the Lady Natalia.'

Tal bowed in his saddle. 'My honour, m'lady.'

It was obvious that the other two nobles were already acquainted with the Duke's younger sister, who appeared to be in her late twenties or early thirties. Both fell in behind the Duke and Natalia, leaving Tal either to follow or ride on the flank.

Duke Kaspar said, 'We have a half-day's ride before us to get near our quarry.' He looked again at Tal. 'That's a serviceable-looking bow, Talwin. Do you know how to use it?' His voice was light and playfully mocking.

Sensing the mood, Tal smiled. 'I'm a better archer than I am a swordsman, Your Grace.'

That brought a laugh from everyone, for Tal, as Champion of the Masters' Court, was accounted the greatest swordsman in the world. Lady Natalia looked over her shoulder at him, giving him an excuse to ride forward a little. 'Are you making a jest, sir?' she asked.

Tal smiled. 'In truth, no, m'lady. I have hunted since I was a child, while I only took up the sword after my fourteenth birthday.'

'Then you must be the world's greatest archer, sir,' said Baron Eugivney wryly.

Keeping his smile in place, Tal replied, 'Hardly, sir. Elven archers cannot be matched by any man.'

'Elves!' said Baron Mikhael. 'Legends. My father used to tell me stories about a great war in my grandfather's time, against invaders from another world. Elves and dwarves figured in it quite prominently.'

'We'll talk as we ride,' said the Duke, urging his horse forward.

Tal found himself beside Baron Mikhael, as Baron Eugivney rode forward to flank Lady Natalia. 'Not legends, my good sir,' said Tal. 'My home is near Ylith, and not too far to the west live those elves of legend. And to the north, in the city of LaMut, many descendants from that other world now live.'

Mikhael looked at Tal as if deciding whether or not the young man was jesting with him. 'You're serious?'

'Yes, Baron,' said Tal. 'And those elves boast archers unmatched by any man living.' Tal didn't know this from his childhood, but rather from long conversations with Caleb, one of his teachers on Sorcerer's Isle; Caleb had lived with the elves in Elvandar, their home, for a time. He spoke their language and claimed only one or two men had come close to matching their skill with a bow.

'Well, then, if you say so,' conceded Mikhael as if that put a close to the matter. To the Duke he said, 'Your Grace, what are we hunting today?'

Over his shoulder the Duke said, 'Something special if luck holds. A report has reached the King that a wyvern has flown up from Kesh and is nesting in the mountains. If that's true, we have a rare opportunity before us.'

Baron Eugivney blinked in confusion. 'A wyvern?'

Mikhael's expression also revealed uncertainty. 'I'm not sure . . .'

Tal said, 'Small dragon. Very fast, very mean, and very dangerous . . . but small . . . for a dragon.'

Lady Natalia glanced from face to face, then smiled with Tal at the obvious discomfort exhibited by the other two men. 'You've seen one, Squire?'

'Once,' said Tal. 'In the mountains when I was a boy.' He neglected to mention those mountains were close to Olasko.

The Duke looked over his shoulder as they rode out of the

palace gate and turned up the high street that would lead them northward out of the city. 'How would you go about hunting one, Squire?'

Tal smiled. 'I wouldn't, Your Grace, any more than I would go looking for a forest fire or tidal wave. But if I must, there are two ways.'

'Really? Say on.'

'Stake out a sheep or deer on a high plateau in plain sight. Have archers nearby and when it lands, keep shooting until it's dead.'

'Sounds like little sport,' observed the Lady Natalia.

'None, really,' agreed Tal. 'Most of the time, the objective is to kill a marauding predator, protecting nearby herds, not sport.'

'What's the other way?' asked the Duke.

'Find its lair. Wyverns like shallow caves or deep overhangs in the rocks. According to my grandfather –' Tal halted himself. For the first time in ages he found himself on the verge of slipping out of character. He forced Talon of the Silver Hawk down in his mind and continued, '– who heard this from a Hatadi hillman up in the mountains of Yabon – wyverns don't like to go deep underground the way dragons do.'

Baron Mikhael asked, 'So you find its lair, then what?'

'Flush it out. Lay nets over the mouth of the cave if you can, some heavy ropes, anything to slow it when it comes out. Then toss in some flaming brands and have long spears, ten-, twelve-foot stakes, ready. Impale it as it comes out and then wait for it to die.'

'Has any man taken one with a bow?' asked the Duke.

Tal laughed. 'Only if he has a couple of dozen other bowmen along.'

'No vital spot? No quick kill?' asked Duke Kaspar.

'None that I've ever heard of,' said Tal. Realizing he was beginning to sound like an expert, he quickly added, 'But that doesn't mean one doesn't exist, Your Grace. It's just my grandfather was trying to impress on me how dangerous they were.'

'I think he succeeded admirably,' said Mikhael.

Talk continued on the topic of hunting as they rode through the city. In less than an hour, they were out of the city proper and into rolling foothills dotted with small estates and farms.

'After noon,' announced the Duke, 'we'll reach the edges of the Royal Hunting Preserve. The King has graciously permitted us to hunt there.'

That answered Tal's question as to how large game could be situated this close to the city.

'Your Grace,' asked Baron Eugivney, 'doesn't the preserve extend for several hundred miles?'

'We're not going to hunt all of it,' said Kaspar with a laugh. 'Just the interesting bits.'

Their course followed the highway upward. It was the major trading route to the northern provinces, but when it turned westerly, they took a smaller road to the northeast. At midday they paused to take a meal and rest the horses. Tal was impressed at how quickly the servants erected a small pavilion, complete with clever folding chairs made of canvas and wood, so that the Duke and his guests could relax in comfort. They paused to dine in a large rolling meadow, with a few dairy cows grazing at the other end.

Talk turned to the gossip of the court, for the Duke had been away from Roldem almost as long as Tal, Natalia even longer. Both barons made it clear they saw a potentially beneficial match in the Duke's younger sister, and kept their attentions focused on her. Not only was she clever and beautiful, she was also a stepping stone to power. Olasko might be a small duchy compared to the vast expanses found in the Isles or Kesh, but it was a very influential one, second in the region only to Roldem.

After the meal, Duke Kaspar said, 'Walk with me a bit, young Hawkins.'

Tal nodded and rose from his seat while the Duke waved the two barons to keep theirs. 'Sit, gentlemen. Keep my sister amused, if you will.'

When they were a few yards away from the pavilion, the Duke said, 'So, young Hawkins, have you given any thought to the offer of employment I made to you after the Tournament of Champions?'

'In truth, Your Grace, I have. I am very flattered, honoured even, but the fact of the matter is I prefer to be my own man.'

'Interesting,' said the Duke as they reached a stand of trees. 'Excuse me a moment, while I relieve myself.'

The Duke unceremoniously undid the fastening on his breeches and stood with his back to the Squire. After he finished, he said, 'Now, that is what I admire about you, Squire.'

'What, Your Grace?'

'Your independence.'

'Sir?'

'Look at those two,' he said, pointing over to where the barons were talking with Natalia. 'They hover over my sister as if she were a prize in a festival tournament. They wish to ingratiate themselves with me through my sister. I am surrounded by sycophants and those seeking favour and it is a rare day when I encounter someone who wishes nothing from me. Those are the men I value the most, because I know with certainty that should they serve me, they will do so to their last breath.' Lowering his voice as they walked back towards the pavilion, he added, 'Those and others like them may find better terms from other masters attractive at the most inopportune times.'

Tal laughed. 'So I have heard. I must admit, while I have distant kin in the court in Krondor, my own experience with royal politics is limited. In fact, last night was only my second visit to the palace.'

'You should come to Opardum. While not as grand an edifice as Roldem's palace, my own citadel above the city is rife with enough politics to last a lifetime. Besides, it would do my sister some good to spend time with a young man who wasn't trying to convince her of his undying devotion so as to gain a position in my service.'

Then they walked back to rejoin the others. As they approached the pavilion, the Duke raised his voice. 'Let us again to the chase!'

The servants quickly bound up the pavilion and tied it to the packhorses, while others put the dishes and food in baskets. Within ten minutes they were mounted again and riding northeast, into deeper forests.

Tal signalled. He pointed up the trail. The Duke nodded. It was nearing sundown, with perhaps another hour and a half of usable light, and they were following a game trail.

Tal had been surprised to discover the entire royal game preserve was as its name suggested, preserved wilderness. No logging had been conducted in this area for generations, though there were heroic stands of old-growth trees that would yield timbers for ships and houses should they be harvested. As a hunter, he appreciated that the kings of Roldem had been willing to make shipbuilders forest many miles farther away and haul lumber down the mountains in order to keep this region pristine. He silently acknowledged the practice was most likely begun in ancient times to ensure that the royal family had game to eat in times of famine, but whatever the original motivation, it had left a stunning wilderness within a day's ride from the largest city on the island kingdom.

They had reached their campsite two hours earlier and a large pavilion had been established, with several smaller tents for the guests. The Duke had insisted on starting the hunt at once, rather than waiting for morning. Tal had agreed that game often was plentiful near sunset when both predators and prey sought water. From the lie of the hills Tal judged as many as half a dozen good-sized streams were likely to be in the area. Certainly there were game signs everywhere. He had already seen the tracks from a heart of forest boars, a sow and her young. Half an hour earlier he had spotted cat prints, most likely a leopard or catamount from the size of the prints, rather than the much larger, black-maned cave lions.

Of their intended prey, the wyvern, there was no evidence. As far as Tal was concerned, if they never saw a hint of the creature, so much the better. There were other ways to die he found preferable to being devoured while trying to demonstrate his hunting prowess to a bunch of idle nobles.

Duke Kaspar led the hunt, with Tal on his right flank. Between them was the Lady Natalia, who held a small bow as if she knew exactly how to use it. The two barons were on the left. A full company of guards, servants and trailbreakers were waiting back at camp. A half-dozen mounted crossbowmen were ready to answer any call for help, though Tal's experience told him that with a wild beast, the matter would usually be resolved before help could arrive. He just hoped there would be no trouble. Lingering closer were two servants holding a variety of weapons, including a heavy crossbow and a pair of boar-spears.

Tal was surprised how quiet the Duke was at the point, and how noisy the two barons were. Both were very uncomfortable at being on foot, apparently, though they claimed to be serious hunters. The Duke stopped, and signalled for Tal and the others to join him.

He was looking at the ground as they approached. 'Now, look at that,' he said very softly.

Tal went to one knee and examined the print. He put his finger in the soil and judged the imprint to be no more than a few minutes old.

He stood up and said, 'Bear.'

Baron Mikhael whistled. 'But look at the size of it.'

'That's the grandfather of all bears,' said the Duke.

Tal had heard tales of such bears, but they had been hunted to extinction in his grandfather's grandfather's day. They were the *Ja-haro Milaka*, or Grey-Muzzled Bears, of his people's legends. Perhaps limited hunting here in Roldem had kept them alive. To the Duke he said, 'I know this breed by reputation. They are aggressive at the best of times. It's spring, and it's almost certain one this big is a male, so he will be looking to mate and will not look kindly on *anything* encroaching his territory.' Tal glanced around. 'He's close. There's still moisture in the depression. The air would have dried it out in less than an hour.'

'How big do you judge him?' asked the Duke.

'Twelve feet if he's an inch,' said Tal. He motioned towards the servants. 'Arrows will only irritate him. We need heavier weapons.'

'What do you suggest?'

'Did you bring a catapult?'

The Duke smiled. 'I've hunted bear before.'

Ignoring protocol, Tal said, 'As have I, Your Grace, but the largest brown bear you've seen is nothing compared to the Grey-Muzzled Bear. You can't stop it even with a heavy bolt to the shoulder if it's charging. With other bears you can drop and play dead and perhaps they'll get bored after mauling you a bit and wander off.

'These creatures will shred you. They can bite a man's head off if they are in the mood.'

'Sounds like it's best to retreat at first sight,' said Baron Eugivney.

'You can't outrun it,' said Tal as he started to move towards the servants. 'In a short burst, it can run down a horse from behind and cripple it with a blow to the spine.'

The Duke didn't move, while the others started to follow Tal. 'You're not suggesting I don't hunt this creature, Squire?'

'No, Your Grace, but I am suggesting a better choice of weapons.'

The Duke nodded. 'What, then?'

'I would rather have heavy lances from horseback, or heavy spears, but these boar-spears should suffice,' called Tal over his shoulder.

Duke Olasko took a single step towards the others when from behind him there came a roar to shake the trees. It was a low howl with a strident note, coupled with the grating sound of a piece of wood being torn in half. Tal swore nothing living could make such a noise.

He turned for a second while the others froze and saw a massive brown shape explode from the trees less than ten yards from the Duke. Kaspar spun as if ready to meet a human attacker, in a crouch, his bow held in his left hand, his dagger seeming to fly to his right.

The Lady Natalia remained motionless but cried, 'Do something!'

Tal threw aside his bow and with two quick steps yanked the boar-spear from the hands of an open-mouthed servant who looked to be on the verge of fleeing. To the other servant, Tal called, 'Follow me!'

As he ran uphill past the two barons, he shouted, 'Distract it!'

The Duke didn't move until the animal was almost upon him, and at the last instant threw himself to the left. The bear swatted at him with his left paw, propelling him in the direction he was already heading. Had it gone the other way, Tal knew, the Duke would be dead with a broken spine. And, for all Tal knew, he was already.

Kaspar had taken a punishing blow and he wasn't moving, either unconscious or playing dead. The bear's momentum took it on for a few yards farther, then it wheeled and turned, ready to charge. The two barons and Natalia let fly a volley of arrows and two of the three struck the animal. It turned and howled, giving Tal the time he needed to reach the Duke. Tal came to stand above him.

Seeing an opponent that wouldn't flee the bear slowed its charge and continued forward at a quick walk. Tal raised the boar-spear high above his head with both hands and shouted as loud as he could, an inarticulate approximation of an animal's howl.

The bear pulled up just a few feet away and reared on its hind legs. It roared a challenge, and Tal ducked low, thrusting the boar-spear under the animal's breastbone. The bear howled, stepping back. Once more Tal ducked under and thrust. The broad-headed blade cut deep into the muscle and blood flowed, streaking the beast's brown fur. Howling in pain, the bear retreated once again, but Tal followed, continuing to duck and thrust into the same spot below the breastbone.

Soon blood gushed like a river down the animal's torso, pooling in the ground at its feet. The huge creature waved its paws, and again Tal thrust home with the boar-spear.

Tal lost count, but after close to a dozen cuts, the animal staggered backwards, and fell on his left side. Tal didn't wait, but reached down and grabbed the Duke, gripping his right upper arm and dragging him downhill. Kaspar said, weakly, 'I can get up, Squire.'

Tal helped Kaspar to his feet. The Duke seemed slightly dazed, but otherwise unhurt, though he was moving slowly. 'I'll be feeling that blow to the ribs for a week with each breath I take.'

'Are you all right?' Natalia cried, arriving at a run.

The two barons approached, bows in hand, and Mikhael said, 'I've never seen anything like it.'

Kaspar said, 'How did you do that, Squire?'

'My grandfather,' said Tal. 'He told me once of a boyhood hunt. The great bear rears up to challenge. It is the only way to kill one, he said. If you run, he'll take you down from behind, but if you stand and threaten him, the bear will rise on his hind legs. Then, said my grandfather, you must strike upward, just below the breastbone, hard and fast, for there is a great artery under his heart and if you can nick that with a deep thrust of a spear he will quickly lose consciousness and bleed to death inside.' He looked over to where the now-comatose bear lay bleeding out, and said, 'Apparently, Grandfather was right.'

'Your grandfather must have been an amazing hunter,' observed Baron Mikhael quietly.

For an instant emotions threatened to overwhelm Tal as the image of his grandfather, Laughter In His Eyes, came to him, smiling as he always did. Tal forced that memory aside, using every mental discipline he had been taught at Sorcerer's Isle to keep composed. He said softly, 'He was that.'

'Well, Squire,' said the Duke, wobbly enough to allow Baron Eugivney to help him down the hill, 'I owe you my life. What can I do to repay that?'

Tal suddenly realized that without thought, he had just saved the life of the man he had sworn to kill, but Kaspar read his confusion as modesty. 'Come. Let's go back to camp and rest, and we'll talk about it.'

'Very well, Your Grace,' said Tal. For a moment the irony of the situation came down on him in full force and he was caught halfway between wanting to laugh aloud and wanting to curse.

He took a glance back at the dying bear, then shouldered the spear and followed the Duke.

That evening, the Duke lounged in one of the chairs with his feet propped up on cushions, nursing his injured ribs. Tal was amazed at how much strength the man possessed. In his prime, Kaspar was a powerful man with the shoulders of a wrestler or dock worker, and arms knotted thick with muscle. When the servants had removed his shirt, revealing the huge blackening area from the deep bruise dealt him by the bear, Tal saw there was very little fat on the man. In open-handed combat, he would be extremely dangerous.

He was also tough; every breath had to be a trial, for Tal suspected the Duke had cracked ribs, yet he lay back comfortably, chuckling at one or another remark during the evening meal, one arm draped over the back of the chair for support, the other holding a cup of wine.

He ate little, but he consumed a prodigious amount of wine. Tal's opinion was that the wine would help the Duke sleep soundly. At the end of the evening, he directed a question at Tal: 'So, Squire, have you given any thought to what reward I can offer to set right my debt to you?'

Tal lowered his head a little as if embarrassed and said, 'Truth to tell, Your Grace, I acted without a lot of thought. I was attempting to save my own life as much as yours.' He tried to look modest.

'Come now. That may be, but the effect is the same. You saved my life. What can I do to repay this?'

Tal smiled. 'I am currently in need of little, sir. But I assume at some point in the future things may not be as sanguine for me as they are today. Should I fall upon hard times, then perhaps I might redeem your favour?'

'Fair enough. Though I suspect a man of your resources should make his way through life without too much difficulty.' He stood up slowly. 'Each of you has a tent prepared and a servant to provide for your comfort. Now, I must bid you good night and come morning I'll see how I feel. I would hate to shorten our hunt, but I fear I am in no manner of form able to confront a dragon, even a small one.' The others laughed. 'So, I suspect we shall be back at the palace this time tomorrow. Sleep well.'

He departed and after a moment, Tal excused himself, leaving the two barons alone to contest for the Lady Natalia's attentions. He found the 'tent' put aside for him was another small pavilion, large enough for Tal to stand in and disrobe with the help of a servant. The serving man took Tal's clothing and said, 'These will be cleaned and ready for you in the morning, Squire.'

Tal sat in the middle of a pile of cushions, upon which a pair of thick quilts had been placed. On top of that lay a satin comforter, far more than he needed.

Breathing deep the mountain air, he ignored the hints of conversation that carried from the main pavilion as Eugivney and Mikhael tried to amuse Natalia and turned his mind to the odd events of the day. The bear had come so quickly he had reacted like a hunter, without thought, grabbing the best weapon at hand, and charging straight at the beast. He could have just as easily taken a bow and peppered the animal with useless arrows until it had finished mauling Kaspar to death. Then he would have only one man – Captain Quint Havrevulen – to kill, and his people would have been avenged.

Tal had endured enough mental exercises with the magicians at Sorcerer's Isle to know the futility of agonizing over why things had transpired as they had. What could have happened . . . did, as Nakor used to say. Obviously, there was to be no simple solution to the problem that lay before Tal. But one thing now felt clear; watching Kaspar die would have afforded him no joy. He found he didn't hate the man. He was wary of him, as he would be of any wild and dangerous creature. But he somehow couldn't reconcile the charming host with whom he enjoyed a goblet of wine with the calculating murderer who ordered the death of an entire nation. Something here didn't jibe and Tal wondered what it could be.

Another hand was in the mix, he suspected. The magician Leso Varen was said to have great influence over Kaspar, and Tal wondered if he might not have been the architect of the Orosini's destruction.

When Tal emerged from his reverie, he realized the camp had grown quiet. The Lady Natalia must have bid her suitors good night. He also realized he was still very much awake and that sleep would come hard for him if he didn't relax. He was sitting nude upon the comforter, so he crossed his legs and put his palms down on his knees. He closed his eyes and began a meditation to calm the mind.

Time stilled and he felt his heart rate slow and his breathing deepen. He was nearly asleep when he felt the tent flap open.

Before he could move a shadowy figure took one quick step from the opening and grabbed him by the throat. As he came fully alert he smelled soft perfume and heard a whisper in his ear. 'How sweet. You waited up for me.' Then he felt Natalia's lips press hard on his as she pushed him over on his back, and pressed him down upon the pillows. He blinked and in the gloom saw her beautiful face inches from his as she quickly unfastened her sleeping robe and cast it aside. Playfully slipping one hand down to his stomach, she said, 'My brother may not be able to think of a way to thank you for saving his life. But I have several ideas.'

Then she lowered her head and kissed him again.

• CHAPTER FOUR •

Choice

*T*AL SAT DOWN.

He sank heavily into the cushions of the divan while regarding the figure standing quietly in the corner. 'Pasko has run Amafi down to the market on a pointless errand before the market closes, so we're alone for a few minutes,' he said, raising a cup of wine. 'Join me?'

The tall figure stepped out of the corner, and removed his hat. Long white hair fell to his shoulders as pale blue eyes regarded Tal. 'I won't be here long. Father's sent me with a message and a few questions.'

'At least sit down, Magnus.'

'I'll stand,' said the young magician. For a while Magnus had taught Tal a little about magic and logic, but of all of those who had taught Tal, Magnus was the one with whom he felt the least kinship. Tal thought it ironic, as Caleb, Magnus's younger brother, was the only man in the Conclave with whom Tal felt any sense of brotherhood. Both were hunters, both non-magic-users in a culture of magicians, both unable to understand much of what they saw around them every day. Of all those who served the Conclave, only Miranda, Magnus's mother, was more of a stranger to Tal.

Tal said, 'Forgive me, but I had a taxing day and night. I've had almost no sleep and my wits have fled.'

Magnus smiled. 'Your heroics with the bear and with the Lady Natalia, I gather?'

'You've heard?' Tal sat up, shocked. He had been back in the city less than an hour before departing the palace, which had been less than an hour ago. Which meant rumour would have had to have spread in record time. His eyes narrowed. 'You couldn't have heard. You saw!'

'Yes, I was watching.'

Tal didn't hide his displeasure. It was the second time Magnus had secretly watched Tal. 'I can almost understand you wishing to observe my fight with Raven, but why a simple hunt?'

'Because nothing involving Kaspar of Olasko is simple. Father asked me to ensure you were well on your way to ingratiating yourself with Kaspar and between the rescue from the bear and your conquest of his sister, it appears things are well in hand. Besides, it will be the last time I spy on you.'

'Why?'

Magnus held his broad-brimmed hat in both hands. 'First the questions. Are you ready to take service with Kaspar?'

'Almost, but not quite.'

'Soon, then?'

'Yes, soon.'

'Has either the Duke or his sister mentioned the man Leso Varen to you?'

'No. I would have taken note.'

'Father's last question: do you have any idea why Kaspar seeks to put troops on the border of the Kingdom of the Isles, hundreds of miles from any significant objective?'

'Not even a hint.'

'Now, a question from me: why did you save Kaspar from that bear?'

Tal shook his head and sipped his wine. 'To tell you the truth, I had no idea at the time. I just reacted. But after dwelling on it, I decided it must be the gods telling me something.'

'What?'

'It's not enough to see Kaspar die. At the very least he must know why he is dying, but even more . . .'

'What?'

'I want to see him humbled. I want to watch as he realizes that everything he's done, every murderous order given, every treacherous decision, has come to naught.'

Magnus was quiet for a moment, then said, 'Killing him will be far easier than reducing him to such a state.'

'Still, that is my goal.'

'Your goal,' said Magnus, 'if I may remind you, is to first discover why he desires a war with the Kingdom. Every shred of intelligence we have tells us you are correct in your surmise: Kaspar has some mad design on forging an alliance among the Eastern Kingdoms so he may launch a strike against the Isles.

'And I emphasize the word "mad" for none of what he has accomplished so far reveals a hint of sanity.'

Tal nodded. 'Yet I would wager my life that Kaspar is anything but mad. Devious, murderous, charming, even amusing; but he is as sane as any man. His choices may appear pointless, but there is always a design behind them.' He leaned forward and put his wine cup on the table. 'Now, Pasko and Amafi will return soon, so we must be done with this quickly.'

'Then to the message. This from my father. You are to be detached.'

'Exactly what does that mean?'

'It means no one will be calling on you at any time, Tal.' Magnus adjusted his hat. 'When you decide to take Kaspar up on his offer and enter his service, find an excuse to discharge Pasko. I leave it up to you as to what you do with this Amafi fellow. But you are oath-bound to never mention your connection to the Conclave to him, or even hint of the Conclave's existence.

'From now on, we will have no further contact with you until you seek us out. If you are in the north, find a way to send a message to Kendrick's or go there yourself. In Rillanon, seek out an inn called the Golden Sunrise, and you've already been to the Cask and Vine in Salador. Should you find yourself in Krondor, you already know the Admiral Trask. Here, see the night barman at Molkonski's Inn. We don't have any agents in Opardum, more's the pity, but if you can get a message up to the Anvil and Tong, in the town of Karesh'kaar in Bardac's Holdfast, it'll get to us.'

Tal laughed. 'Are all your agents ensconced in inns and taverns?'

Magnus smiled. 'No, but we find inns and taverns to be useful places to collect information. Devise a way to get a message to any of those locations, addressed to the Squire of Forest Deep, and it will reach us. Use the code phrase if you can. There are other inns in other cities, and Pasko can see you have a full list before you part company.'

'Why am I to do without him?'

'Two . . . no, three reasons. First, with each additional agent of the Conclave who gets near Leso Varen, the risk to us is multiplied. Mother has Lady Rowena as close to Kaspar as a woman can get – I assume in the vain hope Kaspar might let something slip among the pillow-talk – and with you there, our vulnerability increases; Pasko adds nothing of use to us, but increases the hazard.

'Second, we have other tasks for Pasko.

'And lastly, he works for the Conclave, not Squire Hawkins of Ylith, no matter what you have come to believe.'

'Point taken.'

'Now, I must make this clear: no matter what opportunity you have to revenge yourself on Kaspar, he is only part of the problem; find out what you may of Leso Varen. He is the true danger in this. Finally, if you are found out, we will see you dead before risking the security of the Conclave. Is that clear?'

'Abundantly.'

'Good. So, don't get killed, or at least try to do something useful before you do. If you get into trouble, we can't and won't fetch you out.'

Suddenly he was gone. There was a slight intake of air where Magnus had stood and the room went silent.

Tal reached out and took his wine cup and muttered, 'I hate that he always has to have the last word.'

*   *   *

Tal awoke feeling a little disoriented. He had only had one cup of wine the night before during his conversation with Magnus. The day had been uneventful, a somewhat leisurely ride down the mountain and through the city to the palace. But he hadn't slept well, and wondered if his restless night was due to the choice that now confronted him.

Kaspar was in his debt; so how was Tal to take service with him and not look overly anxious? His idea of killing Prince Matthew and having Kaspar intercede to protect him now seemed eminently plausible; Magnus was correct: Tal's status as Champion of the Masters' Court gained him many privileges, but what were the obligations? Tal pondered that for a moment.

He knew he could manipulate any number of social situations where Prince Matthew would be forced to call him out for a duel. Someone would insist it be to first blood and Tal could 'accidentally' kill him; unfortunate, but these things happen. *Ironically*, Tal considered, *they happen to me a lot, actually*. No, that wouldn't do, for a duel would be about honour and while the King might never again allow him in the palace . . .

A brawl perhaps? Matthew had an appetite for some of the seedier bordellos and gaming halls in the city. He went 'in disguise', despite the fact everyone knew him and he used his position to great advantage.

Tal discarded the idea; not public enough.

There was no easy way to kill him in such a way as to land in that magic place between being forgiven and being beheaded. And even if he did land in that magical place, and Kaspar interceded on his behalf, that would settle Kaspar's debt. Tal liked having that debt.

No, he decided as he arose, he wouldn't kill Prince Matthew.

Another idea came to him. He sat back and thought about it, and decided he had not considered his own role closely enough. There might just be a way to make himself *persona non grata* in Roldem. He could keep himself off the headsman's block yet seemingly have no social future left in Roldem. At which point it would seem as if he had no choice to but take service with the Duke.

'Pasko,' he called and a moment later Amafi entered the room. 'Magnificence, may I serve?' he asked in the language of the Isles.

'Where's Pasko?' he asked, motioning for his trousers.

The former assassin handed them to Tal. 'He went to the morning market, Magnificence, shopping for food. What may I do for you?'

Tal considered this, and then said, 'I guess now is as good a time as any for you to learn to be a valet.'

'Valet? Magnificence, I do not know the word.'

Tal had forgotten he was speaking Roldemish, a language in which Amafi could barely keep up. '*Il cameriere personale*,' said Tal in the Quegan language.

'Ah, a manservant,' said Amafi in the King's Tongue, as the language of the Isles was known. 'I have spent some time among men of breeding, Magnificence, so it will be of little matter to learn your needs. But what of Pasko?'

'Pasko will be leaving us soon, I'm afraid.' Tal sat and pulled on his boots. 'It's a family matter, and he must return to his father's side up north in Latagore.'

Amafi didn't ask for any details. He just said, 'Then I shall endeavour to match him in caring for your comfort.'

'We still need to work on your Roldemish,' said Tal, falling back into that language. 'I'm for the Masters' Court. Wait here for Pasko, then tell him to begin to acquaint you with my routines. He will explain as he goes. Become like his shadow for a while and observe. Ask questions if they do not disturb me or any in my company, otherwise keep them until the two of you are alone.

'Tell him to meet me at Remarga's at midday and bring fresh clothing. Then I will dine at ... Baldwin's, outside along the Grand Canal, then some afternoon cards at Depanov's. I'll return here to change into something more appropriate for supper.'

'Yes, Magnificence.'

Tal put on the same shirt he had worn the day before, and threw a casual jacket across one shoulder as he grabbed his sword. 'Now, find something to do until Pasko gets back and I'll see the two of you at noon.'

'Yes, Magnificence,' Amafi repeated.

Tal left the apartment and hurried down the stairs. He fastened his sword around his waist and kept the jacket over his shoulder. It was a warm day and he had elected to forgo a hat. As he worked his way along the streets to the Masters' Court, he pondered just how much damage he could do to a royal without getting himself into too much trouble.

The morning sun, a warm breeze off the ocean, the memory of the Lady Natalia's enthusiastic lovemaking – all combined to put Tal into a wonderful frame of mind. By the time he reached the Masters' Court he had a plan as to how to humiliate a royal without getting hung, and had convinced himself it might even turn out to be fun.

A week later, the gallery was full as Tal walked onto the floor of the Masters' Court. With the return of the Greatest Swordsman in the World, observing practices and bouts had become the favoured pastime of a large number of young women in the capital. Many noble daughters and a significant number of young wives found reason to take pause during their day's shopping to indulge their new-found interest in the sword.

He had been practising every day for a week since returning from the hunt, and waiting for his opportunity to confront Prince Matthew. He had finally realized the Prince was waiting until he departed to appear at Masters' Court every second day. Tal judged that the vain prince didn't wish to share the attention of those at the Masters' Court with the Champion. So this day, Tal began his practice sessions in the late afternoon, rather than the morning, as was his habit.

Tal was saluted by every member on the floor, including the instructors, in recognition of his achievement. Today Vassily Turkov was acting as Master of the Floor, head instructor, and arbiter of any dispute. Other instructors worked with students in all corners of the massive hall, but the Master of the Floor supervised the bouts at the centre.

The floor of the court was of inlaid wood, arranged in a complex pattern that after a brief study revealed itself to be a clever series of boundaries between various practice areas. The floor was surrounded by massive columns of hand-polished wood supporting the ornate high ceiling. Tal glanced up and saw that the ceiling had been repainted, white with gold leaf over embossed garlands and wreaths which surrounded large skylights. Galleries ran along one wall between the columns, while the other wall boasted floor-to-ceiling windows, keeping the entire hall brilliantly lit.

Vassily came and took Tal's hand. 'When you didn't appear this morning, I thought perhaps you'd given yourself a day of rest, Squire.' He glanced at the crowded gallery and said, 'If this continues, we may have to put up those temporary seats again.' During the Masters' Champion Tournament, temporary seating had been erected in front of the windows, to accommodate as many onlookers as possible.

Tal smiled. 'I just came to practise, Master.'

The older man smiled and nodded. 'Then I shall find you an opponent.' He saw several young men lingering nearby, eager to cross swords with the Champion of the Masters' Court. He beckoned one of them: 'Anatoli, you are first!'

Tal had no idea who the young man was, but the youth approached without hesitation. He bowed to the Master, then bowed to Tal. Master Vassily cried out, 'Rapiers! Three points to the victor!'

Both men wore heavily-padded jackets that covered them from neck to groin, over leggings and leather-soled slippers. Each donned a basket mesh helmet that allowed air and vision, but protected the entire head from injury. They advanced and faced one another.

The Master came to stand between them, holding out his sword. Each combatant raised his own weapon, touched it to the Master's and held it in place. Then the Master pulled his weapon away and the contest began.

Tal had been duelling during his nearly year-long stay in Salador. The Court of Blades was no match for the Masters' Court in terms of the number of quality opponents, but there were enough good swordsmen there to keep Tal sharp.

He had needed the time, for on Sorcerer's Isle there was only

Caleb to spar with, and he had been absent a great deal of the time, out on one mission or another for his parents. And while he was the best hunter and archer Tal knew, Caleb's blade-work left room for improvement.

Before then, Tal had been with mercenaries, and most of the niceties of the duelling floor were lost on them. They were not looking to perfect swordcraft as an art, but rather as a means of survival, and Tal was fairly certain the Masters of the Court would look dimly upon his using kicks to the groin, eye gouging, and ear biting as part of his sparring regime. Tal realized that many of the young men who would spend years of their lives here in the Masters' Court would never have to use their blades in anger. Such was the life of a young noble in the civilized bosom of Roldem.

Young Anatoli was quickly dispatched, for he was sound at basic swordsmanship but lacked any particular gift. Three other young men were also quickly disposed of, and Tal elected to leave the floor.

Rather than heading straight for the changing room, he went to a table at the end of the hall which was laden with refreshments. A crystal bowl stood in the centre, filled with water and floating slices of lemons. Tal had come to appreciate the drink after getting used to its tartness. Fresh fruit, cheeses, breads, pastries and smoked meats rested on trays. Bottles of ale and wine were also there for those who had finished with the day's practices. Tal took a cup of lemon-water from a servant, then picked up a slice of apple to nibble on while he surveyed the room.

One of the court's many servants stood next to Tal, busily restocking each dish so that the presentation always looked fresh.

He calculated the expense and considered how costly it must be to operate the Masters' Court. Any nobleman was free to use the court for the furtherance of the art of the blade. Commoners with gold could use it for a not-inconsiderable fee, and many chose to do so, for political reasons. Otherwise, the entire cost of operating this palatial undertaking was borne by the Crown.

For an idle moment, Tal wondered just how much wealth King Carol commanded. He called up from memory a book he had read on the life of the Krondorian trader Rupert Avery, and reconsidered how exaggerated the various sums mentioned by the self-aggrandizing fellow really were. Sitting alone in his little hut on Sorcerer's Isle, Talon of the Silver Hawk had thought those figures must have been inflated to bolster the author's claim of importance in the history of the Kingdom. But now that he considered how vast the palace of Roldem was, and just the cost of operating this court alone, not to mention the funding of Roldem's navy, Tal realized just how naïve Talon had been. From somewhere in his memory came the phrase, 'It's good to be king', and despite not being able to remember which of his teachers had uttered it, Talon was inclined to agree.

For a brief instant he thought he was on the edge of understanding Duke Kaspar's greed for power.

Then he saw another large party enter the floor and without needing a second glance, he knew Prince Matthew had arrived. Tal reconsidered his plan again, as he had countless times since he had dreamed it up the week before. Fresh from his heroics in saving the Duke and with the King's approval he now stood the best chance of making it work without ending up on the headsman's block, or being discreetly dumped into the harbour.

Sipping on his drink, he ambled to where the Prince stood

surrounded by his entourage. Prince Matthew was a vain man, despite the fact that by the age of thirty he had accumulated an ample girth around an otherwise slender figure. It gave the comic effect of a large reptile trying to digest an even larger ball. Still, the Prince heroically attempted to mask the result of his excesses by employing a jacket that was cinched tight around the middle and padded across the shoulders. He wore his hair short, heavily oiled, and combed forward to disguise his rapidly-retreating hairline, and affected a thin moustache that must take hours to trim each day, thought Talon. He also carried an ornate little viewing-glass, a thing of light purple quartz imported from Queg through which he would peer at things as if the glass somehow gave him a better level of detail.

Tal waited a short distance away until he was noticed, then bowed.

The Prince said, 'Ah, Squire. Good to see you back. Sorry I missed you at the gala, but I was indisposed.'

The rumour in the palace had been that the Prince had consumed so much wine the night before Kaspar's welcoming gala he dared not step more than a dozen paces from the garderobe in his quarters lest his irritated bowels rebel unexpectedly. 'My loss, Highness. It's good to see you recovered.'

'Have you duelled?' asked the Prince.

'I just finished, Highness.'

'Ah, a pity. I had hoped for some decent competition today.'

The Prince was an indifferent fencer, but for reasons political, he rarely lost a bout. Tal had no doubt he had waited in the nearby changing rooms, under the soothing hands of a masseuse, waiting for word of Tal's sessions being over. 'That's no trouble, Highness. I haven't left the floor yet, so I would be happy to accommodate you should you wish a bit of a challenge.'

Several of the Prince's party exchanged glances. On his best day the Prince would be no match for Tal on his worst, and few thought the Champion of the Masters' Court likely to allow a victory to the Prince, given that Tal had never lost a bout and if he continued to win until the next Masters' Court Tournament he would be the undisputed master of all time.

Prince Matthew forced a smile. 'Again, a pity. I've already booked my opponents.'

Three young fencers stood nearby, one of them being the youth, Anatoli. He beamed as he stepped forward and said, 'Highness, I would gladly surrender my place to allow the Champion to accommodate you.'

If looks could kill, Anatoli would have been instantly reduced to smoking debris. Instead, the Prince said, 'How kind, young sir. I shall be sure to remember.'

Tal tried to suppress a grin. 'Why don't you begin with the other two, Highness, while I finish my lemon-water? When you're finished with them, I'll be delighted to be your last opponent.'

The Prince smiled, for at least Tal offered him a way to save face. He would win his first two bouts, after which being defeated by the Champion would be no shame. And, who knows, perhaps the Champion might seek to curry favour by allowing a draw – certainly he had done so before.

Tal wandered back to the buffet and helped himself to another piece of apple. The Prince quickly disposed of both his opponents who contrived to lose in an almost convincing fashion.

Tal put down his cup of water and returned to the floor. 'Congratulations, Highness. You barely broke a sweat.' In fact the Prince was puffing like an old horse that had been run uphill all day.

'Kind of you . . . to say that . . . Squire.'

'Let's say to seven? That will give us both a good workout.'

Master Vassily glanced at Tal with narrowed eyes. To seven meant best of seven touches. The usual match was to three touches. Tal would win without difficulty, but would have to score on the Prince four touches instead of the usual two out of three. The Prince was caught exactly where Tal wanted him, unwilling to decline. He said, 'Of course.'

Then Tal said, 'And if you would be so gracious, we've already both matched with rapiers. I could use some practice with a heavier weapon. Sabres? Or longswords, perhaps?'

Everyone within hearing range fell silent. Prince Matthew was indifferent with the rapier, but it was his best weapon. The heavy cavalry blade required quick, powerful attacks, and the infantry sword required stamina. The Prince elected the lesser of two evils. 'Sabres, then, Squire.'

Tal motioned for one of the floor staff to hand him his helmet and sword, while another attendant brought the Prince a practice sabre. Master Vassily approached and whispered, 'What do you think you're doing, Squire?'

'I just thought it about time someone took some of the wind out of that pompous fool's sails, Master Vassily.'

The Master of the Floor stood dumbfounded. His entire experience with Squire Hawkins had led him to believe him a young man of exceptional social adroitness. He could charm nearly every woman he met and most men wanted to be his friend. Yet here he stood ready to humiliate a royal prince. 'He's the King's cousin, Squire!' hissed Vassily.

'The fact of which the swine makes sure we never forget,' said Tal, trying to sound venomous. 'Let's get on with it.'

From the moment they took their places, Tal knew he could have his way with the Prince, injure him, or even kill him if he wanted. Despite the padding and the helmet, a sabre – even a practice sabre with a blunted edge – could wreak great harm in the hands of a master, and no man was more of a master than Tal.

Reluctantly, Vassily took his place and raised his weapon. 'Places!'

Both men approached and touched blades, and when Vassily ordered, 'Begin!' the Prince attempted a quick but feeble over-hand strike.

Tal knocked it aside effortlessly. The Prince was already over-balanced and Tal should have without hesitation riposted with a strike to the shoulder or exposed side of the body for the point. Instead he retreated a step. 'Why don't you try that again, Highness?' he said in a voice that merely hinted at mockery. It was almost as if he was turning a practice duel into a lesson.

Tal took his position, sabre down at his side, waiting, while the Prince retreated and approached with his sword at the ready. The Prince tried the same move, even more clumsily than before, and Tal easily blocked to the side. Prince Matthew overbalanced and was open to any number of light taps that would win Tal the match, but at the last instant, Tal slashed hard with a punishing blow to the ribs, hard enough to bring an audible grunt of pain from the Prince.

'Score, Squire Hawkins!' announced Vassily, as he looked at Tal with an expression halfway between a question and outrage.

With a gasp, Prince Matthew pulled himself upright, his left hand across his stomach, clutching his ribs. Affecting concern, Tal asked, 'I trust I didn't hurt you, Highness?'

For an instant Tal wondered if the Prince was going to be sick, for his voice sounded as if he were swallowing between words. 'No . . . I'm . . . fine . . . Squire.'

Brightly, Tal suggested, 'Let's try another.'

For a moment it appeared as if the Prince might decline, but instead he returned to his position and Tal said, 'Be careful not to over-extend, Highness.'

With barely-concealed anger, Master Vassily approached. There was nothing he could do, really. As Master of the Floor he could halt any match for any reason, and over the years he had stopped several matches in which an advanced student was bullying a novice. But this was a royal prince of the House of Roldem and to halt this bout because Tal was punishing him would only humiliate the Crown.

Tal scored two more brutal touches, and by the time the Prince approached the line, Master Vassily whispered, 'Squire, this is more than enough!'

'If His Highness wishes to retire, I will not object,' Tal said with as much contempt as he could manage in his tone. He let his voice carry just enough that all those nearby could overhear.

Prince Matthew was a proud man, even if that pride was founded in vanity rather than achievement. He seemed to be choking back tears when he said, 'I'm not going to quit.'

Brightly, Tal said, 'Well said, Highness. Let's give the gallery something to remember, shall we?'

When Vassily instructed them to start, Prince Matthew held his ground, waiting for Tal to make the first move. Tal feinted and the Prince reacted. In quick order, Tal knocked the Prince's sabre from his hand, then slipped the point of his sabre under his helmet, flipping it off his head. Then he stepped past the Prince and administered as hard a blow across the buttocks as he could. The crowd's reaction was instantaneous. Gasps of astonishment were mixed with catcalls and jeers. The blow was so hard that Prince Matthew fell forward to his knees, hand stretched out before him. His face was flushed, and his eyes swollen from the tears of pain he had shed from the previous blows. But the last strike had reduced him to crying, and despite his best efforts, he could not help himself.

Courtiers rushed forward and helped the humiliated prince to his feet. Tal turned his back and walked away, another breach of decorum. In the gallery, several young women who had come to the Masters' Court in the hope of catching Tal's eye rose up and departed, contempt in their eyes as they regarded him.

Master Vassily hurried over and said, 'Are you totally bereft of reason?'

Smiling at the Prince, Tal answered, 'Quite the opposite, really, Master Vassily.'

In low, warning tones, Vassily said, 'If I were you, Squire, I'd consider a voyage somewhere very soon. Champion of the Masters' Court or not, you've just made a very dangerous enemy. The Prince may be many things, but forgiving is not one of them.'

Tal locked eyes across the room with Prince Matthew and saw that through the tears of anger and humiliation, barely-checked rage was directed at him. 'Yes, I believe you're right,' said Tal. He let the mockery in his voice sound as he allowed his words to carry to those nearby. 'But judging from this after-noon's bout, he's really not all that dangerous.'

Unable to think of another thing to say, the Master of the Floor turned and left him. Tal walked to a distant corner where Pasko and Amafi waited. Pasko understood what had taken place, but Amafi said, 'Magnificence, are you inclined to suicide?'

'No, not really. Why?'

'For the Prince now wants you dead.' With a bright smile, he added, 'And he does have enough gold that I would at least consider betraying you.'

Tal laughed, again loudly enough for those nearby to think that he was enjoying the moment. 'Then don't betray me, and I'll consider increasing your pay.'

'Yes, Magnificence.'

As they headed to the changing room, Pasko whispered, 'Be careful. Even before the bout was over, Matthew's agents were leaving the building with word of his humbling. You've made a powerful enemy.'

Tal let out his breath slowly, as if releasing the tension he had felt inside. 'Then, I think it's time to seek out a powerful friend.'

• CHAPTER FIVE •

Service

KASPAR SMILED.

'So, young Hawkins, I see you've managed to create a decidedly uncomfortable position for yourself.' Duke Kaspar sat back in a large chair, motioning for his servant to fill a pair of wine cups on a round table in a room that was part of a large apartment given to him by the King to use on his visit.

Amafi stood just outside the door in his role of manservant, while Pasko was back at the apartment making ready for his departure. The story of a sick father was acceptable to him and he had already purchased passage on a ship bound for Prandur's Gate, where he would find another ship to Coastal Watch, then by wagon to Kendrick's. He would be gone within the week.

Tal had sent the Duke a message the day before requesting an audience, and the next morning a palace page had delivered the reply. Tal was invited for a late-afternoon meeting, but advised to use one of the palace's servants' entrances rather than the main gate, for obvious reasons.

Kaspar lounged in a brocade-trimmed tunic that buttoned up to the neck, a fashion Tal had not seen; it must be something worn in Olasko, he thought. 'I judged you to be a young man of uncommon sense and calm judgment. What caused you to do such an uncharacteristic thing?'

Tal picked up his cup, and sniffed the wine out of habit. He sipped, then said, 'Ah, this must be the new vintage from Krushwin in Ravenswood!'

Kaspar's eyebrows raised and he said, 'You know your wine, Talwin. Yes, it arrived last month, and the King was kind enough to have a few bottles waiting here when I arrived. Now, answer the question.'

The last was as pointed a command as Kaspar had ever directed at Tal.

Tal tried to look sheepish. 'Prince Matthew is a boor.'

'True, but that hardly makes him unique among nobles here in Roldem. Why humiliate him in public?'

'Because I couldn't kill him and avoid the headsman, I suppose,' said Tal, taking a sip of wine to give him pause. 'Had he not been a royal I would have called him out on a matter of honour.'

'Oh?' said the Duke, his brows rising again. 'Whose honour? Certainly not yours? You seem to be a pragmatic sort, not one given to overblown principles.'

Realizing he hadn't thought this through as thoroughly as he should, Tal said, 'A lady's honour, sir.'

'You're in dispute with Prince Matthew over a lady?'

Tal knew this wouldn't undergo close scrutiny if he strayed too far from a plausible story, so he improvised. 'Not in dispute, but rather in defence. The lady in question is a widow and the Prince has been . . . too enthusiastic over pressing his attentions on her.'

'Ah, then it would be Lady Gavorkin,' said Kaspar with a chuckle. 'I have sources for gossip here as well as in my own court.'

Tal shrugged. 'The lady and I have been close. While I have no interest in marriage, she is looking for a new husband should circumstances permit, for already the Crown is considering taking away some of her estates and she fears the loss of revenue.'

Kaspar waved away further comment. 'I know her situation. Had Matthew been seen in public with her, other interested noble sons would avoid her. I understand.'

Tal wasn't certain if Kaspar believed the story or not. All Tal had go on was one remark Lady Gavorkin had made when he had come to call upon her one afternoon: that she found the Prince repellent.

'Still,' asked Kaspar with another chuckle, 'did you have to make him cry like a child in public?'

'Better than killing him,' offered Tal.

'Perhaps not,' Kaspar said, 'You have made a very bad enemy, because Matthew has no shred of forgiveness in his nature. He is the only member of the King's close family who would use his power to avenge a personal slight. Even now there may be a bounty on your head. I'd watch your back for assassins, young Hawkins.'

'That's why I've come to you.'

'With the King I might have some influence, and I am in

81

your debt. But with Matthew . . .' He spread his hands and shrugged.

'Matthew wouldn't dare attack me directly if I were in your service, Your Grace. I have decided to take you up on your offer of employment.'

Kaspar sat back. 'I understand the cause, but it seems a sudden reversal, to be blunt.'

'I weighed your offer before, Your Grace, and seriously considered it. I had hoped, however, to be able to find a position with a trading concern out of Salador, Ran and Bas-Tyra. Perhaps you've met their local agent, Quincy de Castle?'

A tiny flicker in Kaspar's eyes revealed the lie as he said, 'Don't know the man. But why trading?'

Tal paused, as if gathering his thoughts. 'I'm a noble only by the thinnest thread, Your Grace. The head of my family barely knows I exist, for I am a third cousin, once removed.' He lowered his voice. 'I only hold the title "Squire" by a deft manipulation of a local magistrate on my father's part, truth to tell. And the lands that come with that title provide no income.' Returning to a normal tone, he said, 'To advance, I need two things: wealth and fame. I could either join the army – and truth to tell, I tried that for a little while, and thrashing goblins in the cold north is no route to either – or I could marry well. But to marry well, I need wealth and fame. A circle, don't you see?'

'I do.'

'So I came east. Here is where politics and trade give a man opportunity, not out in the west. There it's all duty and service, but here a man can find prospects. So, becoming Champion of the Masters' Court gave me fame. And if I could rise financially with de Castle and his partners, then would I have wealth.'

'I appreciate the general design, Squire, but aren't there more direct routes?'

'None that I can see. My best opportunity was Lady Gavorkin, but the Crown would never approve her marrying a poor country squire from the Isles.'

'Especially now,' said Kaspar with a chuckle.

'Yes,' agreed Tal with a pained smile. 'But even had I restrained myself regarding the Prince, I think my future lies somewhere else. And now that it appears my prospects in Roldem have diminished . . .' He shrugged.

'You thought you would ride my coat-tails to greatness,' finished Kaspar.

'Yes, Your Grace.'

'Not an unwise choice,' said Kaspar. 'I have a use for clever men – assuming you resist the temptation to humiliate princes in public in the future. There's a captaincy for you in Opardum.'

'Captaincy?' Tal smiled. 'As I said, I've tried the military life, Your Grace, and found it less than ideal for my talents.'

'It's a title. If you like, you may continue to call yourself "squire", for no one will salute you and no one will have you marching around a parade ground. I have many captains in many capacities, and none of them wear a uniform.'

'Ah,' said Tal, as if he now understood. 'You seek an agent.'

'Agent is a good word. Factor is another. Or representative, depending on the need. Whatever the title, the function will be the same: to serve me with unswerving loyalty and vigour. The rewards will be quite in keeping with the effort.'

Tal finished his wine. 'Should I pack?'

'Soon,' said Kaspar. 'I linger here another week, then it's off to Rillanon and a visit with the King of the Isles, then back to

Opardum. You are not officially in my service until we reach Opardum. The reasons for this will be made clear to you then.

'Until then, however, you will be under my protection. I will send a quiet word to Prince Matthew that I would take it as a personal affront should any ill befall you, and then reassure him that I'm getting you as far away from Roldem as possible.

'Perhaps in three years' time you might return to defend your championship. It will be awkward, but at least by then Matthew will have had a chance to reflect.' He paused, then added brightly, 'Or maybe by then someone else will have killed the posturing fool.'

Kaspar rose, signalling that the interview was over. 'Return to your quarters and try to stay out of trouble, Squire.'

'Yes, Your Grace,' said Tal.

The Duke left through one door, and Tal departed through the other, finding Amafi waiting outside. He gestured for his new valet to fall in and they left the palace together, this time exiting through the main gate.

When they were safely outside the palace, Amafi asked, 'Magnificence, what transpired?'

'We are now in the service of Duke Kaspar of Olasko, Amafi.'

The former assassin grinned, for a moment looking positively lupine. Then he said, 'So, now our rise to greatness begins!'

'Yes,' said Tal, though inside he felt as if it was a descent into darkness that lay before them.

The ship beat against the rolling combers as a stiff breeze hurried it towards the most magnificent city Tal had ever seen. No, he thought, more magnificent than he could have imagined.

Rillanon stood outlined against the hills, a stunning creation of coloured stone and graceful arches. The late-afternoon sun etched its form with brilliant highlights set against deep shadows. Tal had been told of its history, that the Mad King, Rodric the Fourth, had ordered the city rebuilt with every drab façade replaced by cut stone of brilliant hue. Kings Lyam, Patrick and now Ryan had continued with the project, and now nearly every building in the capital of the Kingdom of the Isles was a study in splendour. A thing of marble and granite, Rillanon glimmered white and pink, yellow and amber, with hints of purple, green, red and blue scattered across the scene. As they approached, details resolved and both Tal and Amafi stood in mute astonishment in the bow of Duke Kaspar's ship, *The Dolphin*.

A voice from behind them said, 'Is this your first visit, Squire?'

Tal turned to see the Duke and bowed before he answered. 'Yes, Your Grace.'

Amafi stepped away discreetly, giving his master and the Duke the opportunity to speak in private.

'I am second to no man in my pride in my homeland, Squire,' said the Duke. 'Opardum is a magnificent city in its own way, but I'll concede that upon first viewing, no city matches Rillanon in beauty.'

'I must agree, Your Grace. I have read histories . . .' Tal forced himself to remember his place. 'When a student, my father insisted I master the history of the Kingdom.' He turned, and waved his hand. 'But this . . . it's beyond description.'

'Yes, isn't it?' Duke Kaspar chuckled. 'If one were to wage war upon the Kingdom of the Isles, it would be a tragedy to have to sack such a wonder. It would be far better to force them to surrender before having to storm those towers, don't you agree?'

Tal nodded. 'Though I would think *not* going to war with the Isles the wiser choice.'

'There are other means of winning a struggle besides armed conflict,' said the Duke. He spoke, as much to himself as to Tal. 'There are those who will avow that war is the result of failed diplomacy, while others will tell you that war is but another tool of diplomacy; I'm not enough of a scholar to decide if there's really any difference between those two positions.' He turned and smiled at Tal. 'Now, get to your cabin and change into your finery. We shall be dining in the King's palace tonight.' He glanced at the sails. 'I judge us to be less than an hour out of the harbour, and we shall have clear sailing to the royal docks.'

Tal went below and did as instructed, and by the time he was ready for presentation in court, he heard a knock upon his door. Amafi opened it to find a cabin boy standing before the portal.

'Yes?'

'Duke's compliments, Squire. You're to join him on deck.'

'I'll be along straight away,' said Tal.

Tal quickly adjusted his new tunic and grabbed his hat, an outfit tailored for him in Roldem prior to leaving. He had spent the week lying low as Kaspar had suggested, avoiding public places for the most part. It hardly mattered anyway, for the invitations from Roldem's elite had stopped immediately after his humiliation of Prince Matthew. Tal assumed Kaspar had sent out word that Tal was now under his protection for there had been no attempt at reprisal, at least none that Tal and Amafi could see.

Tal hurried up on deck as the ship approached the breakwater outside the harbour. If Roldem had been breath-taking the first time Tal had seen it from a ship, Rillanon was astonishing. The closer they got the more stunning the vista became. For not only was the city constructed of polished marble and granite, it was trimmed in all manner of ways: there were flower trellises, hillside gardens, colourful pennants and banners, and windows of quartz and glass. The late-afternoon sun set the stones ablaze with reflected gold, amber, rose and white highlights.

'Amazing,' said Amafi.

'Yes,' said the Duke. I always try to arrive before sunset, just to see this.'

A royal cutter flying the banner of the Kingdom of the Isles was on an outward tack, and dipped its pennant in salute to the Duke of Olasko. Sailors on both ships waved greetings, and Tal was rendered almost mute by the grandeur around him. Ships from every nation on the Sea of Kingdoms were at anchor or sailing in or out of the harbour. He saw Keshian traders, ships from the Eastern Kingdoms, and cargo-haulers from every point in the known world.

Sails were reefed and *The Dolphin* slowed as the captain allowed a smaller boat to come alongside. A rope ladder was dropped and up it scampered the Harbour Pilot, who quickly made his way to the quarterdeck. He took control of the ship: from this point on, it was his job to sail the ship into the Royal Dock.

Tal tried to drink in every sight before him. He remembered his first view of Latagore, and then Krondor, Salador, then Roldem. Each had offered new impressions and new sensations, but Rillanon eclipsed them all.

The ship's last sails were reefed, and the ship drifted comfortably into the designated slip, where dockmen waited with long poles to hold off the ship while fenders were dropped alongside the quay. Then the fore and aft lines were thrown ashore and before Tal knew it, the ship was secured.

Lady Natalia came up from her quarters, her servants behind her, and flashed a brilliant smile at Tal. 'We're here, I take it.'

'Yes, m'lady,' said Tal with a grin. 'We most assuredly are.'

Natalia's smile remained in place, but her eyes darted around, as if wary. Then she focused on Tal. 'We must be sure to be on our best behaviour, Squire.'

Tal nodded. It was an unnecessary warning. He knew he was being evaluated every minute between Roldem and their eventual destination of Opardum. This humiliation of Matthew was so untypical of him that suspicion was directed at him even by the Duke's sister. Their night of passion seemed entirely forgotten and Tal thought better of mentioning anything to her that might be perceived as an overture. In this situation, he decided, it was better to let the lady take any lead.

Duke Kaspar was the first to depart, followed by his sister then the other members of his entourage. Tal followed, since his status as a member of Kaspar's court had not yet been formalized. Then came Amafi and the other servants.

Carriages awaited, each bearing the royal crest of the Kingdom of the Isles, a golden lion rampant on a field of crimson holding a sword aloft, a crown hovering over its head. Liveried coachmen waited. Kaspar and his sister entered the first, most ornate, carriage, and the rest of the Duke's retinue followed. The coach Tal entered with Amafi behind him was serviceable and clean, but far from luxurious.

Tal half hung out of the window as the carriage wended its way through the streets of the city, taking him past shops and houses, through large squares with majestic fountains, and up the hill towards the palace. The city rested upon a series of hills, so that at times they saw the ground fall away as they crossed soaring bridges. Several times Tal looked down to see small rivers running towards the sea. 'This city is wonderful,' he said to Amafi in the King's Tongue.

'Assuredly, Magnificence,' said his valet. 'It is said that when the first King of the Isles built his fortress, he picked the highest peak here, and a series of wooden bridges protected his band of men – who were little more than pirates it is said. Over the years the city has grown up from the docks and down from the palace, so that now you have this maze of streets and bridges.'

As they crossed the second to last bridge on their way to the palace, Tal looked down and saw houses built into the very hillsides, it seemed, with clever cantilevered supports below and narrow flights of stairs leading up to the streets above them. Below them the River Rillanon raced towards the sea over a series of small cataracts, hemmed in on both sides by mighty granite walls.

As they neared the palace, Tal said, 'I wonder if those who live here get used to this beauty.'

'Undoubtedly, Magnificence. It is the nature of man to become oblivious to that which is around him daily,' Amafi commented. 'It is something a good assassin understands. The trick to not being discovered until it is too late is to become part of the expected surroundings. Stealth is more the art of blending in with the background than sneaking through dark shadows.'

'You're probably right,' said Tal.

'Of course I'm right, Magnificence, for were I not right, I would by now be long dead.'

They were speaking the King's Tongue, which seemed appropriate to their setting, but Tal realized he could be overheard.

Switching to the Quegan tongue, he said, 'There are some things you must do.'

'I live to obey, Magnificence.'

'When I do not need you at my side, I wish you to hang back, to keep a short distance away. I want you to be my second set of eyes, my second pair of ears. Watch who watches me, listen for any words about my lord Kaspar or myself.' He waved his hand to indicate everyone else around them. 'As far as anyone else is concerned, you do not speak the King's Tongue. We will converse only in Quegan.'

'As you instruct, Magnificence.'

The carriages rolled across the last bridge to the palace, and by the time the door opened, Tal could see the Duke's carriage and several of those that had followed immediately behind were already gone, having been returned to the royal carriage house. Tal stood mute.

If the palace appeared splendid from the docks, up close it was almost unbelievable. An ancient stone keep had risen upon this hilltop centuries ago, but since then wings and new buildings had been added, until it had become a sprawling creation of corridors and galleries, gardens and fountains. The courtyard itself was three times larger than the palace at Roldem. But what set this palace apart was its façade. Every inch had been covered with matching stone, a white granite flecked with gold and silver. In the rosy glow of the setting sun it was a thing of glittering pinks and dazzling orange punctuated by indigo shadows. Every window was of arched, clear glass, and high in the towers brilliant pennants flew. Flowers grew everywhere on trellises or in window boxes.

A servant approached. 'Squire Hawkins?'

'Yes?' Tal replied.

The servant motioned and a royal page appeared, a boy of no more than thirteen years of age. 'Show the Squire and his man to their quarters,' the servant instructed.

Tal knew his luggage would be brought later. He set off, his eyes upon the back of the boy who led them up the broad steps to the palace entrance. Two guards stood to the side of each step, so that a dozen men were standing to attention on the right and left. All wore polished metal helms with flared edges, and red tabards emblazoned with the golden royal lion, over black tunics and trousers. Their boots were polished to a glassy sheen and each man held a halberd.

Upon entering the palace, Tal could see directly ahead through a huge pair of open doors revealing a garden and a stone path to another open pair of doors into a gallery. Tal and Amafi followed the boy to the right and down a series of long halls, until they reached the guest apartments. The page stood before Tal's door and said, 'Sir, Duke Kaspar is at the other end of that hallway.' He pointed to the far end of the hall. 'It is a bit of a walk, sir.' He opened the door and Tal entered first.

Tal was impressed. As a minor member of Kaspar's party, he expected modest quarters, and if these were such, then Kaspar's room must rival the King's in Roldem.

There was a large bed which had a canopy with heavy curtains which were drawn back. The bed was bedecked with a heavy comforter and several bolsters and pillows. A huge fireplace stood in the opposite wall, currently cold. This time of the year there was no need, though Tal judged it probable that there was a fire going all through the winter.

Large tapestries hung on every wall, cutting the cold of the stones, for this was an older part of the palace, Tal suspected, even if not part of the original keep. The page pointed to the door on the left of the fireplace and said, 'Your man has a bed in there, sir.'

Tal opened the door and stuck his head in. It was a closet, but a closet that was bigger than his apartment in Roldem. Enough clothing to wear different outfits every night for a year could fit in here, along with the bed, table, nightstand, and chair that were in place for a servant's comfort.

Tal turned and said, 'That is sufficient.'

The page said, 'Sir, through the other door is your water closet.'

'Thank you,' Tal replied, and the boy made to depart.

As he reached the door, the page said, 'Should you need any-thing, pull this cord, sir. The reception for the Duke is in two hours, so you should have time to refresh yourself, sir.'

He opened the door and Tal saw that there was a group of palace servants outside. As the page slipped past them, his lug-gage was brought into the room. Another servant entered with a tray of delicacies, small cakes, fruit pastries, and bunches of fresh grapes. Yet another servant brought in a tray laden with goblets of chilled wine diluted with fruit juices, and a pewter pitcher of ale, with half a dozen cups.

As soon as they left, a parade of young men carrying buckets of steaming water entered, making straight for the bathing room. Tal waited until they had finished their work and gone, then went to inspect what they had done.

The bathing room turned out to be a private bath, a stone tub lined with tiles. Tal stuck his hand in and said, 'It'll cool to the perfect temperature by the time I get undressed. Amafi, lay out my best clothes for tonight, the russet-and-black tunic, with the grey leggings and my black ankle-boots with the golden buckles. I'll wear the silver-handled rapier and the black felt hat with the hawk's feather.'

'Yes, Magnificence,' Amafi said and set to unpacking the luggage and putting away the clothing, while Tal stripped off his travel clothing.

As Tal settled into the tub he noticed an odd mechanism hanging over it. It consisted of a brass pipe with a flared head dotted with small holes. Next to it hung a chain with a handle. He sat up and pulled on the handle. Instantly he was showered with cold water. He yelped in surprise and pulled the handle again, causing the water to stop.

Hearing the cry, Amafi was in the room almost instantly, a dagger in his hand. Seeing nothing except Tal sputtering and his hair now drenched, he said, 'Magnificence, what is the matter?'

Laughing, Tal said, 'Nothing. I was just not prepared for a dowsing. It is to rinse you off. But the water is rather cold.' Tal found a large bar of scented soap on the side of the bath and began to wash. 'When I've finished, feel free to use the tub, Amafi. The water will still be fairly clean.'

'You are generous,' said the Quegan.

'And bring me some wine, please,' he asked, and moments later, the servant returned with a chilled cup of wine.

Tal finished his bathing and settled back with the wine for a moment to relax. Thinking of how much more lavish the King's apartments must be, he smiled and muttered, 'It *must* be good to be king.'

*   *   *

If Tal had been impressed by the royal court at Roldem, he was rendered nearly senseless by the throne room of the King of the Isles.

As one of Kaspar's retinue, he was permitted entrance after the Duke, but no formal presentation was made. He stood to one side of the hall while the King welcomed Kaspar and his sister.

King Ryan was a young man, no more than twenty-three years of age. His father, King Patrick, had died unexpectedly a few years before, ending what had been a troubled reign. Patrick had been a man of temper and questionable judgment, who had followed two kings, Lyam and Borric, who had been quite the opposite. Patrick had ruled in Krondor during the troubled rebuilding of the Western Realm after the horror that was called the Serpentwar. Myth and history collided, and depending on which sources one was inclined to believe, Pantathian Serpent Priests, creatures of dark legend, had engineered a monstrous invasion of the Kingdom at Krondor, sailing a fleet of a thousand or more ships around the world. Whatever the truth of the story, the fact of the aftermath was simple: Krondor had been reduced almost to rubble. Patrick had to contest with Kesh on two occasions during his rule in Krondor. When his father, King Borric, had died, Patrick had already been a tired and worn-out man. His rule had not been a happy one.

Ryan was considered an unknown quantity, and Kaspar's visit was intended in part to assess the young monarch's abilities. One of Kaspar's captains, Janos Prohaska, stood next to Tal. He whispered, 'The King must be concerned about our master.'

As the formal introduction droned on, Tal whispered back, 'Captain, why do you say that?'

'Do you not know your own nation's nobility?' he asked softly.

'Not by sight,' admitted Tal.

Half a dozen men stood on either side of the King, who being unmarried sat alone on a single throne on the dais. Kaspar was thanking the King for his welcome while those six men studied him.

Prohaska said, 'Next to the King stands Lord Vallen, Duke of Rillanon, but next to him stands Lord James, Duke of Krondor. The King has his two most powerful dukes at his side. They rule the Eastern and Western Realms on his behalf. With no prince in Krondor, James is also Regent of the West.'

Tal studied both men. They were similar in stature, elderly, but still tall and powerful with keen eyes and the calm confidence of men who had wielded power for decades. Beside the Duke of Krondor stood another man, somewhat younger, who was talking quietly to the Duke. Prohaska said, 'That man talking to Lord James is Lord Williamson Howell, the King's Chancellor of Finance and the Exchequer. He's a court duke, but as powerful in his way as the other two. He is considered to be as shrewd with gold as any man living. Behind him, the two old soldiers?'

Tal nodded. 'Yes, I see them.' A man of middle years, with the upright military bearing of a career soldier, wore a royal red tabard, but the other wore a tabard matching that of Duke James, a blue tabard bearing a circle of light blue, upon which an eagle could be seen flying above a mountain peak. He looked to be a man in his late seventies, and Tal could see he had once been very large and powerful. His muscle had softened with age, but Tal would still count him a dangerous opponent.

'That's Sir Lawrence Malcolm, Knight-Marshal of the Armies of the East, and next to him is Erik von Darkmoor, Knight-

Marshal of Krondor. Behind him stands the Admiral of the King's Eastern Fleet, Daniel Marks, and his adjutant.

'If this wasn't a reception, I'd say it was a war council.'

Tal studied the men, and was forced to agree. They didn't possess any of the festive demeanour of those attending a gala. The light, celebratory mood that was always there in Roldem was absent in this court tonight.

The Master of Ceremonies stepped forward as the Duke backed away from the throne, and struck his iron-shod staff of office on the stone floor. 'My lords, ladies and gentlemen, His Majesty bids you come forth and dine in the Great Hall.'

Tal followed the others and found his place with the help of a page. Here too, the mood was far more subdued than what he had experienced in Roldem. People chatted and he was engaged in light conversation by several local minor nobles in turn, but while Roldem's court was alive with music and performers, here a small ensemble of musicians played softly in the background.

The food was superb, as was the wine, but Tal couldn't help but feel a sense of foreboding. As Tal was about to finish his meal, a palace page appeared at his elbow. 'Sir, the King commands your presence.'

Tal stood, uncertain why he was being singled out, but he followed the page along the side table until they reached the gap between it and the head table. He was escorted to a place directly before the King and found himself under the scrutiny of the entire assembly.

The King sat in his high-backed chair, with Duke Kaspar on his right as the honoured guest. To his left sat the Lady Natalia, and from what Tal could see, she had charmed the King. The other nobles of the Isles were arrayed along the table.

The page said, 'Majesty, Squire Talwin Hawkins.'

Tal bowed as effortlessly as he could manage, but found that he was nervous. He hid it well, but he felt it. He had no trouble passing himself off as a minor Kingdom noble in other nations, but here he stood before the monarch of the nation in which he was supposed to have been born, and worse, just four chairs away sat the duke to whom his so-called cousin owed fealty; he forced himself to breathe deeply.

The King was a fair-skinned man with sandy-coloured hair. His dark brown eyes studied Tal. He looked intelligent, thought Tal, and even if he wasn't a king, most women would find him attractive. Then he smiled and said, 'Welcome, Squire. You do us honour.'

Tal said, 'Your Majesty is too gracious.'

'Nonsense,' said the King. 'You bring honour to the Isles as Champion of the Masters' Court. We have several times enquired as to your whereabouts.'

Duke James studied Tal closely. 'Your kinsman Baron Seljan Hawkins had no idea how to find you.' There was something in his tone that led Tal to believe the Duke was suspicious.

Tal nodded. 'Your Majesty, Your Grace, I am forced to admit that by the most generous accounting I am a shirt-tail cousin to the Baron. I believe him to have been ignorant of my birth until news of my victory reached him. His grandfather and mine were brothers, and all we have in common is the family name. My claim to the rank of squire is only through my father's adroit influences with the Office of Heraldry, as I understand it.'

The Duke grinned. 'In other words, your father bribed someone.'

Tal returned the smile and shrugged. 'He never said, and I never asked. I only know that the estates my father claimed

97

consisted mostly of swampland outside Ylith and I've never seen a copper from them in rents.'

This brought a round of laughter from everyone at the table. Tal's self-deprecating humour had eased the mood.

'Well, even if your father was skirting the edge of the law in this matter, I hereby do affirm your rank and titles, even if the land you own is worthless,' said the King. 'For to have one of our own as Champion of the Masters' Court warrants reward.'

He signalled and a page brought forth a purple cushion upon which rested a sword of stunning beauty. It had a silver filigreed basket-hilt, and the blade was of the finest steel Tal had ever encountered. 'This is from our foundry at Rodez,' said the King. 'It is agreed that the finest blades in the world are made there, and this is a suitable blade for a champion, we think.'

Tal took the blade and the ornate scabbard that was handed to him by another page and said, 'Majesty, you overwhelm me.'

'We understand that you have taken service with our friend Duke Kaspar.'

'Yes, Majesty, I have.'

The King sat back and his smile faded. 'Serve him well, but should time and fate bring you back to your homeland, Squire, know there will be a place for you here.' Glancing sidewise at Kaspar, the King said, 'We can always use another swordsman in our service, especially one so talented.'

Tal nodded and with a wave was dismissed by the King. He followed the page back to his place at the table, but the King's last words had again dampened the mood in the room.

As he sat down, Tal considered Prohaska's words and was forced to agree: this was no festive gala. This was a council of war.

• CHAPTER SIX •

Rillanon

*T*AL WATCHED.

He stood upon a balcony near the royal apartments. He had been requested to wait there for Duke Kaspar, who was closeted with the King. Below, the city stretched out and Tal was struck again by its beauty. He wished time permitted him to explore: for had he not taken service with Kaspar that is what he would have been doing this very moment. However, as Kaspar's retainer, he awaited his master's pleasure.

'Quite a sight, isn't it?' came a familiar voice at his shoulder.

He turned to find Lady Natalia approaching, so he bowed. 'That it is, m'lady.'

'My brother will be out shortly and will have something for you to do, I have no doubt.'

Tal rarely felt disquiet in the presence of any woman, but

since the night after the hunt, he had wondered what he should expect from Natalia, or more to the point, what she might expect from him.

As if reading his thoughts, she smiled and came close. Touching him lightly on the cheek, she said, 'Don't worry, Tal, our time together was fun, nothing more. I am an instrument of the state, my brother's tool, much as you are. He has plans for me, so you're safe from the need to make any declarations to me.'

Tal grinned. 'It wasn't a declaration that worried me, m'lady. Only if I was to be cast aside or . . . if my attentions were required again.'

She paused, then regarded him. 'Why do I suspect that either choice is of little importance to you?'

Tal took her hand. 'That's not true, m'lady. You are without peer among women.' He came close to the truth with that statement, for few women in his experience were as ardent as Natalia had been.

'Liar. You use women as I use men. We are too alike, Tal. Have you ever loved?'

Tal hesitated, then he said, 'I thought so once. I was mistaken.'

'Ah,' said Natalia. 'So, you're armoured against love because of a broken heart?'

Tal made light. 'If it pleases you to think so, then so be it.'

'I think sometimes having no heart is a better condition. My brother's Lady Rowena is like that. She lacks something.'

Tal could only silently agree. He knew her well, for she had been the woman who had broken his heart, the harshest lesson taught him by the Conclave. Alysandra, as she was named there, indeed lacked *something*. She had no heart, and had wounded Tal deeply.

'I will marry for reasons of state. So I take my pleasures where I might.' She paused, then asked, 'What think you of this young king?'

'Ah,' said Tal. 'Your brother seeks to make you Queen of the Isles?'

'Perhaps,' said Natalia with a grin. 'There is no suitable match from Roldem, with the eldest princess being merely eleven years old. I suppose Ryan could wait until she was of age, but I think Lord Vallen and the others are anxious for him to wed and start breeding heirs. I am the most advantageous match among the ladies of the eastern courts, and Isles needs allies to the east.'

Feigning ignorance of regional politics, Tal said, 'I thought Isles had treaties with Farinda, Opast and Far Lorin.'

'They do, but those states are . . . inconsequential. Ryan needs Olasko as an ally.'

Tal's mind raced. All signs pointed to a coming conflict between the Isles and Olasko, otherwise Kaspar's campaigns in the region made even less sense than they did now. Trying to fish for information, Tal asked, 'But they provide a buffer. It seems to me Olasko and the Isles have little cause for contention.'

'Indeed,' said a voice from behind.

Both Tal and Natalia turned to see Duke Kaspar there. Tal bowed and said, 'Your Grace,' while Natalia approached and kissed her brother on the cheek.

Kaspar came to stand next to Tal. 'The city is quite breathtaking, isn't it, Squire?'

'Yes, Your Grace.'

Kaspar was dressed in a white tunic buttoned up the right side, with yellow piping. He wore red leggings and slippers and his only decoration was the ornate silver buckle on his black leather belt. 'Natalia,' he said. 'We dine with the King tonight. A page will come and fetch you at the seventh hour. Squire, I have no need for you this afternoon. Why don't you keep my sister amused until supper, then feel free to take your man and visit the city. Rillanon is quite an interesting place; you should avail yourself of the opportunity to learn about it.' He studied Tal's face and softly added, 'Learn it well.'

'Yes, Your Grace,' Tal said with a slight bow.

'Now, I must go to another meeting. Run off and find something to do, you two, and I'll see you this evening, my dear.'

Natalia kissed her brother again and he departed. When he was gone, she turned brightly to Tal and said, 'My brother commands us.'

Tal laughed. 'Yes, and what is my lady's pleasure?'

She slipped up close to him and kissed him deeply. 'Pleasure is my pleasure. And I know exactly what will amuse me, Squire.'

Tal glanced around to make sure they weren't being observed. It would not do for a potential Queen of the Isles to be seen embracing a lowly squire on the balcony of the castle. 'This is hardly the place,' he whispered.

She smiled even more broadly, and said, 'Then let's go and find the right place.'

Turning, she didn't wait to see if he followed her, but walked imperiously into the hallway, turning away from her apartments, and without asking, led him back to his own room.

She opened the door to find Amafi busy polishing a pair of Tal's boots. The Quegan rose and bowed.

'Leave us,' commanded Natalia as Tal entered the room. Amafi threw Tal a look as if asking confirmation, and Natalia's voice rose. 'I said *leave us*!'

Tal nodded. 'Leave us for an hour,' he said in Quegan.

As Amafi moved to the door, Natalia spoke in Quegan as well 'Make that two hours.'

Amafi found himself standing outside the door, a pair of Tal's boots in one hand, and a rag in the other. For a moment, he stood uncertain of what to do, then he decided the King's boots must need cleaning, so he'd go and find a page and ask directions to where such matters were addressed. Remembering he was to speak only Quegan outside the rooms, he hoped he could find one who might understand him.

Tal put down his cards and said, 'Not this time.'

The man sitting directly across from him also folded his hand. The man to Tal's right laughed as he raked in the coins. 'Not your night, eh, Squire?'

Tal smiled. 'Can't win every night. Where would be the fun in that, Burgess?'

Tal was playing cards at a modest tavern called the Black Bull, located by the northern gate of the city. It was inhabited mostly by locals and the occasional farmer or miller from up the island staying there.

Tal had followed Kaspar's instructions. He had spent the last three nights and two days, learning everything about Rillanon he could. As he had suspected he might, after his first foray into the city Kaspar had peppered him with questions. They ranged from the location of critical intersections, where he had seen soldiers of the Crown, to what sort of people were on the streets after dark.

Each day more exploration and each day more questions. Tal's skills in hunting and tracking, and his sense of place and direction served him well. At this point he could probably draw a map of the city and get most of it right.

Kaspar informed him he was to continue his explorations until the end of the week, when the Duke's party would be leaving for home. Tal had been to some of the seedier waterfront inns and several of the most luxurious brothels, gambling halls both low and high, and nearly every tavern worth mentioning. His only regret was that Rillanon lacked the dining establishments that were now all the rage in Roldem, so most of the food he encountered outside the palace was unremarkable.

'Your deal,' said the merchant.

Tal picked up the cards and began his shuffle. He had met Lyman Burgess the night before in a gambling hall down near the central market square, and the affable trader in luxury goods had suggested they meet at this inn. As promised, it was a convivial little establishment with decent food, better drink, and a friendly game of poker.

Everyone tossed in a coin and Tal began the deal. Burgess had expressed interest in making Tal's acquaintance the night before when he had discovered his identity. While a few others had recognized his name as Champion of the Masters' Court, Burgess had been more interested in his relationship to Duke Kaspar.

Burgess dealt in rare trade items, gems, fine jewellery, ornate statuary and other items of value. His clientele were the very wealthy and the nobility of the city, including according to him, the palace, where several of his more extravagant items were on display. He made no effort to hide his interest in making the Duke's acquaintance.

Tal looked at his cards and saw no hope in bettering his hand. When it came to his turn to bet, he again folded. He caught indifferent cards as the deck made its way around the table and it was his deal once more. While dealing out his cards, he glanced around the room. Besides the five of them playing cards, there were half a dozen other men in the room. Amafi was one of them, sitting a discreet distance away, watching everything.

After the hand, Tal tossed in a coin, and waited for the next hand. As if making conversation, he asked Lyman, 'Do you ever trade down in Roldem?'

Burgess picked up his cards. 'No, not really. I've sold some items here to Roldemish traders, but have never been there myself.'

'You ought to go,' said Tal, looking at his own cards. He at last had a hand worth betting, so he waited, then called the bet before him. As he tossed in two cards and picked up the replacements, he said, 'Quite a market for luxury goods, I'd say.'

Burgess looked at his cards. 'So I hear. But it's a hard place to get a foothold. Very old firms with a stranglehold on commerce down there.' He shook his head. 'This will never do,' he said, and threw in his hand.

'I have a friend in Roldem,' said Tal. 'He's a Kingdom man. He might be able to help.'

'Really?'

Tal showed his cards, the winning hand, and gathered in the coins with a chuckle. 'The cards have turned.' As the deck was passed, he added, 'Yes, he's a trader of some influence in the city, by the name of Quincy de Castle. Perhaps you've heard of him.'

Tal studied Burgess's face. There was a tiny flicker, but Burgess said, 'Can't say as I have.'

Tal knew he was lying.

The game went on for another hour, Tal neither winning nor losing. By night's end, the two travelling traders had done well, a local merchant had broken even, while Burgess had lost big. Tal had lost only a little. 'Let me buy a drink before we say good night,' he said to Burgess as the others departed.

'Fine,' said the merchant.

Tal motioned for the serving girl and said, 'Wine, the best you have.'

The girl appeared with a bottle and two goblets, and removed the cork. She poured out a tangy young red, loaded with the flavours of fruit, spices, and oak. Burgess sipped it and said, 'This is good.'

'A blend of several grapes, from somewhere near Salador, I guess.'

'You know your wines,' said Burgess.

'I lived in Salador for a while. It's a familiar blend. If I hadn't been drinking ale earlier, I might even presume to guess which vintner made it.'

Burgess laughed. 'I've never been much of one for wine. I prefer stout ale.' Seeing Tal was about to call to the girl, he said quickly, 'But this is good. I'm content to drink it. Especially as you're paying for it.'

Tal took a long sip then said, 'I could learn to love living here, I think.'

'It's a wonderful city,' said Burgess. 'Though I've never been to Opardum.'

'Neither have I,' admitted Tal.

'Oh, I thought you were in service to the Duke.'

'I am,' said Tal, taking another sip of wine. 'But only recently.

We met in Roldem, after the Tournament at the Masters' Court.'

'That's quite an achievement, Tal.'

Tal shrugged. 'Every man has a skill or two. Some of us are more gifted in one thing than another. I'm a good hunter and swordsman. You?'

'I'm a successful trader,' admitted Burgess, 'even if I'm a dreadful card player.'

'Married?'

'Yes,' said Burgess. 'My wife is visiting her family in Dolth. That's why I'm out and about the city these nights. The house gets lonely.'

'Children?'

'A boy. He's in the army, serving in the King's Own.'

'That's quite a position.'

Burgess pushed himself back from the table. 'I've been selling items of art to the palace for twenty years, Tal. I've made some deals that have cost me profit to keep people like Lord Howell happy. My son's commission didn't come cheap, but he always wanted to be a soldier and I didn't want to see him manning some battlement with the Border Barons up in the frozen north.

'Besides, if he rises through the ranks, there's a chance for a good marriage, perhaps even the daughter of a noble.'

Tal nodded. 'Ambitious for your son.'

'What father isn't?'

Tal remembered his own father. His people had been so different in their outlook on life. For a moment he felt a distressing stab of nostalgia, then forced it down. Dwelling on the past only brought pain. His father was ambitious in the way of the Orosini; he wanted Talon to be a good father, husband and man of the village.

Finally Tal said, 'I think you're right. My father wished me to succeed.'

'And you have,' said Burgess. 'You're Champion of the Masters' Court and in service to Duke Kaspar of Olasko. You have a bright future ahead of you.' Seeing no one nearby, Burgess leaned closer. 'And I can help make it bright for you, Tal.'

Lowering his voice, Tal said, 'I'm listening.'

'Without knowing what you're privy to, let's say there are those here in Rillanon who would welcome a friend in Kaspar's court.'

Tal sat back as if digesting the statement. 'You want me to spy?'

Burgess shook his head and said, 'Nothing of the sort, Tal. I have a desire to be presented to the Duke should I come to Olasko, and if you hear of this or that, something that might gain me and my associates a trading advantage, well, let's say the rewards might prove generous.'

Tal again paused, then said, 'How generous?'

'That depends,' said Burgess. 'If you can get my trading consortium an audience with Duke Kaspar, you'll be well rewarded. If we can arrange for trade concessions, you'll be wealthy.'

Tal remained silent, as if pondering the offer. 'As long as I don't find myself violating my oath to the Duke.'

Burgess spread his hands. 'We would never consider asking you to do something like that.'

'Well, I might be willing to see what I can do.'

'Wonderful. My offices are well known; they are down by the dockside, not too far from the Royal Docks. Anyone there can direct you to me. Should you decide to cooperate, either come visit or send word. If I am back home with my wife when she returns, one of my associates will be there.' He stood up. 'Now, Squire, I best be to bed. This has been a pleasant, if costly night.' They shook hands and Burgess departed.

Tal waited a few moments, then rose and crossed the room to where Amafi sat. 'Wait, then follow. See if anyone comes behind me,' he said as he walked past.

Amafi nodded slightly as Tal departed.

Tal stepped out into the night air, aware that the city had fallen quiet. There were still plenty of signs of life, but none of the din that accompanied the business of the day. He walked along the cobbled road, heading towards the palace. He was going to be walking alone for at least half an hour, so he set his mind to thinking about what he needed to do next.

Either Burgess was an agent of the Isles Crown, or he was as he said, an ambitious trader, but either way his first concern wasn't serving the Duke or Tal's enrichment. He would have to be carefully dealt with.

Halfway to the palace, Tal realized he was being followed. He kept alert for attack, but none came by the time he reached the palace gates. He identified himself to the guard on duty and informed him that his manservant would be along shortly, and that he didn't speak a word of the King's Tongue. The guard captain said they would send him along, and Tal reached his quarters without incident.

Less than a quarter of an hour later, Amafi entered the rooms. 'Magnificence, it was as you thought. You were followed.'

'An agent of the King of the Isles, no doubt,' said Tal as he removed his boots.

'No, Magnificence. I recognized the man who followed.'

'Who was it?'

'Captain Prohaska. The Duke had you followed.'

'Ah,' said Tal. 'That changes things.'

'What will you do, Magnificence?'

Tal motioned for Amafi to take away his dirty clothing. 'Why, that's obvious. Tomorrow, I will go to the Duke and confess everything. Now, blow out the candle and go to sleep.'

Tal waited as the Duke considered a parchment message that had been delivered by messenger from Opardum. When he put it down, he said, 'You wished to see me, Squire?'

Tal said, 'Your Grace, last night I was approached by someone I believe to be an agent of the King of the Isles.'

'Oh, really? Tell me about it, Tal.'

Tal outlined his encounter with Burgess two nights before, and his conversation the previous night. When he finished, Kaspar nodded and didn't speak for a moment. Then he said, 'You're probably correct. This man Burgess may be part of Lord Vallen's very capable spy network. Lord James's grandfather established it back during the reign of King Lyam, first in Krondor, then here in Rillanon. It's endured, grown, been refined, and is now the match of the Keshians'.' He looked out of the window towards the city and added, almost to himself, 'Lacking their resources, I must rely on other solutions.' Kaspar turned back to Tal, studied him, then went on, 'You acted correctly, informing me of this contact. I would like you to seek out this man Burgess and tell him you are willing to act as interlocutor upon behalf of his trading concern.'

Tal showed his surprise in his expression, but said only, 'Yes, Your Grace.'

'It may be this Burgess is exactly who he appears to be, and perhaps some good will come of this; he might actually have some goods that I'll purchase, or perhaps a more beneficial trade arrangement can be made with the Isles than we've had heretofore – they tend to need little of what we have to offer, and many things we need, so trade with them is usually disadvantageous.

'But it also may be that Burgess is attempting to recruit you as a spy.'

'I would never violate an oath, Your Grace!' said Tal.

'I know, but while you seem a capable young man, Tal, you have no idea how devious these people can be. This man would probably let you think for some time to come that he was who he claimed, and allow you to provide some information that seemed harmless enough, but eventually, you would find yourself confronted by Burgess who would then produce some sort of "evidence" that if put before me would make you look guilty of betraying Olasko. And from that point forward, you would be Burgess's creature.

'No, let us play this out for a while and see what happens. Eventually it will be clear which of the two men Burgess is, the spy or the trader.' Tapping his chin with his forefinger, Kaspar added, 'It also might prove useful if he is a spy, for then we can tell him what we want the Isles to know.'

'Whatever Your Grace wishes,' said Tal.

Kaspar said, 'We have two more days here, then we are off for Opardum. Keep studying the city and find this man Burgess and do as I said. You may go now.'

'Yes, Your Grace,' said Tal.

Tal left the Duke's quarters and hurried to his own. It was

barely an hour past dawn, and the city would be bustling. Already he felt sorry to be leaving this fabled city behind, but he had a duty. Reaching his own quarters, he found Amafi waiting for his instructions.

'Lay out a change of clothing. I'm going to spar with the officers of the Royal Guard, then I'll want a bath. Wait an hour, and order up hot water. Then lunch in the city and more sightseeing.'

'Yes, Magnificence,' said Amafi.

Tal closed the door and headed for the Royal Armoury.

The armoury had none of the grandeur of the Masters' Court, or even the elegance of the Court of Blades in Salador. It was a drab building near the southern gate of the palace complex, fashioned from stone, with high windows that let in just enough light to keep the hall in a state of near gloom. Five large wheels set with candles were hung from the ceiling and provided additional light.

The room was filled almost to capacity, as word spread through the palace that the Champion of the Masters' Court would be sparring with the best the Kingdom of the Isles had to offer.

They cheered when Tal disposed of his third opponent, a gifted young knight-lieutenant who pushed him quite hard. Laughing, Tal shook his hand and said, 'Bravo, my friend. Had you been in the last tournament, I wager you might have been in the round of eight! Well done!'

The King's Swordmaster, in charge of training the soldiers of the Royal Household Guard, said, 'Squire, I have seen forty years of service under three kings, and while I may have seen swords to match yours, there haven't been many. Thank you for the entertaining and instructive display.'

The assembled officers cheered and for an odd moment, Tal felt a kinship with them. He was not from the Isles, yet so long had he worn the false colours of a noble of this nation he felt almost as if he were one of them. He lifted his sword in salute, then bowed his head. 'You honour me, Swordmaster.'

The officers began to disperse and Amafi handed Tal a towel. 'Your bath is ready,' he said in Quegan.

Another voice from behind, also speaking Quegan, said, 'Isn't the plumbing here in Rillanon wonderful?'

Tal turned to see Lord James approaching. He bowed. 'Your Grace.'

In the King's Tongue, James said, 'I have a lot of dealings with Queg. It helps to speak the language.' He glanced at Amafi. 'How did you come to have a Quegan manservant?'

'It's a long story, Your Grace,' said Tal.

'Some other time, then,' said James. 'You're quite remarkable with that sword, young sir.'

'Thank you. It's a gift, and I really take no more pride in it than a bird does in singing. It's something I can do.'

'Modest?' The Duke raised his eyebrows. 'Surprising. Most young men would be howling to the moon over their achievements. But then, you're not like most young men, are you, Squire?'

'I don't take your meaning, sir.'

In Quegan, James said to Amafi, 'Go ahead and prepare your master's bath. I shall see he comes to no harm.' The servant glanced at Tal who nodded once; Amafi bowed and left them. By now the rest of the officers had departed, and they were alone in the armoury. 'Let's have a talk, shall we?'

'I am at Your Grace's service.'

'Not really, since you serve Duke Kaspar. Come, I'll walk with you a way.' They left the building and as they crossed the yard, James asked, 'How is it you have a Quegan assassin as a bodyguard, Tal?'

Tal tried not to look surprised. 'Assassin?'

'Petro Amafi is not unknown to us. In fact there's a warrant out for him in Salador. Did you know that?'

'No,' said Tal honestly. Now Amafi's desire to take service with Tal made a great deal more sense.

'I would have him arrested, but as part of Duke Kaspar's company, he benefits from a certain diplomatic immunity. I trust you're taking him with you when you depart?'

'Yes, of course.'

'Good. He's not the only one who isn't what he seems to be,' said the Duke as they walked across the empty parade ground.

'Your Grace?'

'Whoever you are, my young friend, your papers don't bear scrutiny. I've seen your patent of nobility and it's perhaps the best forgery ever, but it's still a forgery.'

Tal attempted to look shamefaced, without looking guilty. 'As I said to His Majesty, Your Grace, how my father got the patent accepted I don't know. I have never traded upon the rank and I've never attempted to collect rents from anyone on those estates.'

James laughed. 'A good thing, as your "tenants" consist of frogs, mosquitoes, black flies, swamp pigs, some poisonous snakes and a few smugglers. It is as you said, worthless swampland near Ylith.

'I don't know who put those patents in the hall, your father or someone else. Either way, I now face something of a dilemma.'

'What would that be, Your Grace?'

James stopped as they reached the steps leading into the heart of the palace. 'The King acknowledged your rank in front of witnesses; whatever the origin of those patents, they are now as valid as if his father had bestowed them upon your father.

'Moreover, you are something of a hero here in the Isles. You are the first non Islesman to be Champion of the Masters' Court.

'Lastly, if you were staying in Rillanon, I would ask Lord Vallen to keep a close watch on you, but you're not. You're leaving in two days for a very distant city.

'But I can't help thinking you may be a very dangerous man, Tal. My grandfather taught me to appreciate what he called his "bump of trouble", that itch on the back of his neck that told him something was wrong. And you, sir, make my neck itch.

'So, should you ever return to the Isles, expect to be watched very closely. And should you ever return to the Western Realm, expect that I'll be watching you closely, Talwin Hawkins, Squire of Morgan River and Bellcastle, Baronet of Silverlake.

'Because there is one fact I can't seem to get my mind around.'

'What would that be, Your Grace?'

'You're reputed to have been a Bannerette Knight-Lieutenant for the Duke of Yabon. But my old friend the Duke can't find one man who remembers serving with you. Odd, isn't it?'

Seeing no easy way out, Tal said, 'Well, Your Grace, while the patent was my father's invention, truth to tell, the claim of service was my . . . embellishment, if you will.'

The Duke said nothing for a long moment, merely looking at Tal. Then he said, 'Good day, Squire.'

'Good day, Your Grace,' said Tal as Lord James walked away.

Tal exhaled slowly. He couldn't help but feel that he had come very close to a disastrous encounter. But he didn't find any comfort in having avoided it, for he now was under the scrutiny of Lord James of Krondor, and everything Tal had seen of the old noble convinced him the Duke was a *very* dangerous man.

• CHAPTER SEVEN •

Oath

*T*HE SHIP BEAT AGAINST the waves.

The Dolphin raced north by northwest, heeling over on a close haul against a southbound autumn squall. The rain bit through the oil-soaked canvas cloak and Tal found his tunic clinging to his skin, but he could not take another minute in the close quarters assigned to him and Amafi. Sailors huddled miserably in the lee of whatever shelter they could manage, waiting for the call to trim sails as the ship was about to swing to a westerly tack.

The call came and Tal watched in fascination as barefoot seamen scrambled aloft or hauled on sheets to move booms and yards. The ship came around with a shudder and a groan of wood, then settled into another rhythm as the sails took what they could from the wind and the rolling waves struck the hull from another angle.

The sky was a canvas of roiling clouds, all black and grey, and Tal wished he could fix the image in his mind, for to paint the subtle differences would be an achievement. All his life he would have said that during a storm the sky was a uniform grey, but now he realized that at sea the rules were different.

Then he saw the light.

To the west, a shaft of light broke the gloom as a single ray of sunlight cut through, and at that moment, he felt the rain lessen. Within minutes the sky began to clear, with patches of blue appearing in the west. A sailor nearby said, 'We're through the squall, Squire,' and started to gather up rope off the deck.

'That was something,' said Tal.

'Not really. You ought to try tacking through a big blow, say a week or more in the teeth of a gale. Or a day and night running from a hurricane. Now, *that's* something to remember.'

With a grin, Tal said, 'I think I'll find another way to amuse myself.'

Scrambling up the ratlines, the sailor said, 'Suit yourself, Squire.'

As the storm abated, the breeze turned warmer, or at least with the absence of rain it felt that way to Tal. The ship seemed to ram through the water, a low rolling motion that reminded Tal of a cantering horse, up and down. The rhythm gave him the illusion of riding into sight of Opardum's towers.

The lookout aloft shouted, 'Land ho!' and Tal caught a glimpse of Opardum as the weather broke.

While Rillanon was the most spectacular city he had ever seen from the deck of a ship, Opardum was impressive.

The ship heeled over and they were suddenly on a southwestern tack, racing straight for the city with a following wind. Directly ahead Tal saw a brilliant sun-drenched morning revealed as the clouds above blew away, like so many curtains being pulled aside.

Tal knew the geography of this region from the maps he had studied, but those lines of ink on parchment did little to prepare him for the sight which lay ahead. He knew that the south-eastern corner of Olasko was a network of islands and waterways, with only one habitation of any size, the port city of Inaska. Hundreds of villages dotted the thousand or more islands, which rested in what was in reality the mouth of the Anatak River. The rest of the islands were lush plantations of fruits, cotton and flax, intercut by glades full of exotic trees and animals, and a few hills high enough to encourage dry-land faming. But on the north shore of the river, above a small but thriving harbour, rested Opardum.

The city seemed to be carved out of the face of the mountain, which was an illusion, Tal knew, as they raced towards the harbour. But from the sea, it looked as if a jumble of spirals and towers had sprouted out of the rock-face of a mountain thousands of feet in the air.

Tal knew from his reading that the mountains were really a massive cliff, and at the top a relatively flat grassland ran downhill for a dozen miles to the west. There a series of fault lines cut canyons and crevasses across the entire region, making use of that land impossible to anything that couldn't fly to reach it. Beyond that jumbled landscape lay vast grasslands and woodlands, still wild for the most part, until the city of Olasko Gateway was reached.

The ship's captain called out orders and sailors scrambled aloft to reef sails. Amafi came up on deck. 'Magnificence, I brought you a dry coat.'

Tal slipped off the soaked oil-treated canvas covering he wore, and thankfully took the dry coat. Amafi asked, 'This, then, is our new home?'

'Yes,' said Tal, 'and you must learn to speak the local tongue.'

The language of the region was similar to Roldemish, as settlers from that island had founded the various nations that comprised the Eastern Kingdom. The exception being the Duchy of Maladon and Semrick, which had been settled by men from the Kingdom city of Ran. They spoke both the King's Tongue and a local dialect of Roldemish.

Tal said, 'It's Roldemish to all intents and purposes, but it has local idioms and some different words. You'll learn quickly, understood?'

'Yes, Magnificence,' said Amafi.

As they began the final tack into the harbour, the ship slowed as the captain turned into the wind. Drawing closer to the city, details began to emerge in the bright light of day.

'The calm after the storm, as they say,' said Lady Natalia from behind them.

Tal turned and grinned. 'I believe the expression is the calm *before* the storm, m'lady.'

'Whatever the case may be,' she said. 'Home.'

Tal conceded that it might be home to her, but to him it was just another alien place. The harbour beckoned and inbound ships gave way to *The Dolphin*, for she flew the ducal banner. Compared to Rillanon, Roldem, Salador or even Krondor, it was a small harbour. Behind it the city was relatively flat, then suddenly rose up on an incline, an almost evenly sloped face of soil and rock that had been terraced over the years and connected by ramps and streets. Then suddenly the citadel rose up behind, hard against the cliff-face, and from what Tal had been told by members of the Duke's retinue, dug back deep into the rock.

It struck him as incongruous that the original builders had chosen to use a white, or very light grey, stone to fashion the place, for it stood out dramatically against the darker colours of the cliff.

The citadel was massive, rising ten storeys above the foundations, as far as Tal could judge, and surrounded by a wall of less than half that size. At the corners, towers rose up another twenty or so feet, so that overlapping archer fire could stop anyone coming up through the city to the citadel.

Tal turned his attention away from the city itself, looked towards the south. He could make out little of the southern islands at this distance, save what looked to be brown smudges on the horizon.

Natalia put her hand on his shoulder and said, 'We shall have fun, Talwin.'

He patted her hand, somewhat distracted by the events of the last two days in Rillanon. He had followed Kaspar's instructions and located Burgess, for whom he had promised to intercede with the Duke. The trader would arrive in Opardum in a month or so with samples of trade goods, seeking concessions and licences.

But something didn't feel right. No matter what he said, Burgess just didn't ring true as a merchant trader, the way Quincy de Castle did. De Castle might be an agent for the Crown of the Isles, but he was truly a trader. Tal had played cards with too many merchants, as well as gained some insights into their nature by reading the biography of Rupert Avery, but Burgess was something else. Under that apparently soft exterior, Tal was certain he was dangerous.

The ship rolled into the harbour, and unlike the Kingdom cities or Roldem, no pilot came aboard. The captain simply directed the ship to the Duke's personal slip, at the far end of the quayside, closest to the most direct road to the citadel.

With years of practice, the captain saw his ship safely into its berth, and by the time the lines had been tied, the ship made secure, and the gangplank run out, the Duke was on deck, ready to depart. He hurried down to his waiting carriage, followed by his sister and his senior captains.

Tal followed in the third carriage, along with a Lieutenant Gazan, whom he knew only slightly, and a junior clerk who had come to the dock to give the Duke messages his staff felt needed his immediate attention. Amafi rode above, on a small bench behind the carriage, next to the coachman.

By the time they departed for the citadel, Tal was genuinely curious about Opardum. He considered his expectations about the place might have been coloured in part by his attitude towards Kaspar. While affable enough on the surface, the Duke was a man without scruple capable of wholesale murder. For that reason, perhaps, Tal had expected the city to be a sombre, even dour place. In the midday sunshine, it looked anything but.

Broad-bottomed skiffs plied the harbour, running small loads of cargo to and from ships. Smaller trading vessels up from the southern islands deposited their wares on the quay. As the carriage rolled through the city, Tal saw that most of the buildings were whitewashed, made brilliant by the sun, and the roofs were mainly of colourful clay tiles of red or orange. Many small temples dotted the squares, which were centred around graceful fountains. Traders hawked their wares in the markets, and many shops were thronged with customers. By all appearances Opardum was a prosperous, thriving and busy city.

They passed over a canal and Tal saw more signs of commerce, as riverboats just off the Anatak River were slowly manoeuvred through a series of locks by polemen labouring on the decks, heading for the harbour quays for loading and unloading. Olasko had two cultivated regions, the islands to the south, and the great rolling meadowlands and hills between Olasko Gateway and the border with the Principality of Aranor. Most of the land between Opardum and Olasko Gateway was forest and wild prairie, very dangerous to cross, so most commerce between the two cities was by the river.

They reached the citadel and entered the main gate, but had turned at once to the right, moving around the side of the old bailey past what looked to be a parade ground to what was obviously the stabling area. A huge carriage house and stables large enough for perhaps fifty or more horses were snug against the outer wall.

Grooms ran out to take the horses, while the coachman opened the door. A page sought them out, asking, 'Are you Squire Talwin?'

'Yes.' Tal glanced around, realizing that Kaspar and Natalia were already up the stairs and into the citadel.

The boy smiled and said, 'I am Rudolph, Squire. I am to guide you to your quarters.'

To Amafi, Tal said, 'See to the luggage,' and turned to follow the boy.

Rudolph was a lad of about eleven or twelve years of age, from what Tal could judge, handsome in his palace togs of red leggings and a black tunic. The crest of Olasko, a charging boar of silver on a field of black, was sewn above his heart.

The boy moved quickly and Tal had to hurry to keep up. 'You'll like your quarters, Squire,' said the lad. Moving purposefully on, he barely gave Tal time to take note of his surroundings.

They entered a side entrance to the citadel, one that Tal assumed the Duke preferred, which meant it was probably close to his personal quarters. Tal took note of landmarks, which door they entered, the corridors they used, what stairs they climbed, and while he had a rough sense of where he was by the time they reached his quarters, he was certain he had a good chance of getting lost for a while if he ventured out on his own.

The suite was comprised of a full five rooms. A sitting room with large windows greeted Tal as he entered. It was decorated with tapestries to minimize the cold from the stone walls, a fine carpet, and several tables and chairs. He could entertain up to six people here in comfort, he judged. A big fireplace rested between two other doors.

To the right, Rudolph showed him a large bathing room, with a drain in the centre of a tiled floor. A brass tub sat nearby and there was a pair of seats, as well as a particularly well-fashioned mirror. 'A barber will call upon you every morning, sir, if you wish.'

'I prefer to let my manservant shave me,' said Tal.

'I'll mention that to the housecarl, sir.'

He then showed Tal the bedroom, which had a low but huge bed, with multiple comforters, many cushions and pillows, and a smaller fireplace, which Tal judged must share the chimney with the one in the sitting room. A door to the right led to a small room, which also had a door onto the sitting room. It was a servant's room, and would be given over to Amafi.

On the left was one more door, which led to another, smaller bedroom, which Tal assumed meant that once a family with children had occupied these apartments. He said to Rudolph, 'Thank you. I think I shall be fine now. Make sure my servant arrives with my luggage.'

'Yes, Squire.' The lad moved to the door to the hall and asked, 'Is there anything you require before supper, sir?'

Tal judged supper to be several hours away. 'I wouldn't mind a bit of a tour of the citadel.'

'I can arrange that, Squire. I've been detailed to be your page until you're at home. I'll run to the housecarl and tell him about the shaving, sir – I mean about you preferring to have your manservant shave you – and then I'll be straight back.'

'Not too straight,' said Tal. 'Say an hour after my luggage arrives. I need to bathe and change out of these travel clothes.'

'Very well, sir. I'll have hot water sent up straight away.'

'Good,' said Tal, taking a liking to the affable boy.

'The Duke will expect you at supper, Squire, so we must be back in time for you to change again.'

Tal raised an eyebrow in question, but said nothing.

Reading the gesture, the boy said, 'His Grace always has a gala when he returns home, so something festive is in order.'

'Very good. Come back when I've finished cleaning myself up.'

The boy stepped into the hall. 'Here comes your man with the luggage now, sir,' he said. 'I'll be back in an hour.'

Amafi showed the porters where to put the two large bags, then dismissed them. Then he glanced around the rooms. 'Very nice, Magnificence.'

Tal said, 'Get used to it. It's home for a while.'

But inside he knew it would never be home, and he knew that he had to blend in and become one of Kaspar's creatures, or his long-term plans for the Duke's destruction would never succeed. But he couldn't help but feel that he had walked straight into a trap, like a wild bull charging into a net with a band of hunters just out of sight.

Tal followed Rudolph as the boy scampered up yet another flight of stairs. Tal was working diligently at memorizing every hallway, flight of stairs and significant room in the citadel. He was drawing a map in his mind.

They reached a landing where stairs headed down in two directions, to the right and left, and Tal said, 'That way leads back to my quarters.' He was pointing to the right.

'Yes, Squire. Very good,' said the boy with a grin.

'Where does that lead?' He pointed to the left.

The boy said, 'I'll show you,' and they were off.

For almost two hours they had been exploring the vast edifice that was Opardum's citadel. Tal believed the boy when he said that between the extra rooms, outer buildings inside the wall and some of the older tunnels into the rock, the entire population of the city might take shelter there if the need arose. The place was massive. For some reason the Dukes of Olasko had over the years felt the need to keep adding to the citadel.

Half an hour later, they reached a hallway and Rudolph stopped. They had just passed the large hall that led to the Duke's great hall and his private quarters, a vast apartment comprising more than a dozen rooms. Rudolph said, 'Down this hall is a stairway, Squire. No one is allowed to go there.'

'Really?'

'Yes. The Duke is most emphatic on that subject.'

'What's up there?'

'Leso Varen,' whispered the boy, looking as if even speaking the name frightened him.

Tal pretended ignorance. 'Who or what is a Leso Varen?'

The boy took Tal's hand as if to pull him along. 'We need to keep moving. He's an advisor to the Duke. He's supposed to be a wizard, everyone says. He looks like everyone else, but . . .'

'But what?'

'I don't like him,' said the boy, again in a whisper. 'He scares me.'

'Why?' said Tal with a laugh, as if trying to make light of it.

'I don't know, Squire. He just does.'

Tal feigned indifference, but he marked the entrance to Varen's quarters clearly in his mind. Then a faint aroma came to him and his eyes widened. He recognized the scent, the particular perfume and the hint of the skin that it had touched. Alysandra! Or, Lady Rowena as she was known here. The other agent of the Conclave of Shadows, a woman of cold calculation and remarkable beauty. What had she been doing near the magician's lair?

'We should start back now, Squire,' said Rudolph, bringing Tal out of his reverie with a solid yank on his hand. 'We need to make sure you're ready for the Duke's gala.'

Tal nodded as Rudolph released his grip on his hand, and fell in behind the boy. From what he'd learned of the citadel thus far, Tal knew the lad was taking a circuitous route back to his quarters to avoid passing by the hall leading to the wizard's quarters. As he followed, his mind returned to the question of what Rowena had been doing in the company of Leso Varen.

Tal had been astonished to discover new clothing waiting for him. Amafi had laid everything out. The jacket was sewn with seed pearls and what appeared to be garnets, on a fabric of lavender hue. The leggings were white, and a pair of ankle boots with silver buckles stood by the bed. A new belt for his sword from the King of the Isles completed the ensemble. There was no hat, so Tal went bareheaded.

The Duke's hall was huge, almost as large as the King of Roldem's. Tal recognized that once this had been the central keep of the citadel, a huge single room in which an ancient noble and all his retinue once lived. A massive fireplace housed a huge fire behind the Duke's chair, far enough away that Kaspar and those at his table were comfortable. The Duke's table sat on a raised platform; two lower tables running perpendicular to the head table, forming a 'U'. From his elevated vantage point, Kaspar could see every guest at his table. Sitting at Kaspar's right hand was Natalia, and at his left was the Lady Rowena. Tal caught Natalia's eye and smiled slightly, but purposely ignored Rowena, though he marked her. He found himself once again amazed at her ability to be whoever she wished to be, and yet at the same time the beautiful girl who had beguiled him on Sorcerer's Isle, overwhelming him to the point of his thinking he was in love with her, only to discover she was completely without compassion or affection. Now, effortlessly, she was a lady of Kaspar's court, a lovely trophy for the lord's arm, and one who enthusiastically shared his bed. Tal wondered if it was possible that Kaspar suspected the woman he bedded was one capable of plunging a dagger into his throat without feeling an echo of remorse. *Probably not*, Tal concluded. For if he had, Rowena would be dead already.

Tal was escorted to the left flanking table near the Duke. He sat next to a man of middle years who introduced himself as Sergey Latimov, the Duke's Assessor, or collector of taxes.

The dinner went on quietly, without the entertainers in other courts. As the last dishes were being removed, Duke Kaspar stood up. 'My friends,' he said, loudly. 'There is an addition to our company I would now like to introduce. He is a clever young man of many talents who will be an asset to Olasko. Squire Hawkins, please stand.'

Tal stood, and Kaspar said, 'It is my pleasure to introduce you all to Squire Talwin Hawkins, late of the Kingdom of the Isles and Champion of the Masters' Court in Roldem. Tonight he enters our service.'

There was a polite round of applause. Lady Rowena displayed just the right amount of interest, then returned her attention to the Duke. Tal noticed one significant member of the Duke's table was not applauding. Captain Quint Havrevulen, most senior of Kaspar's officers, sat silently, observing the young stranger. As Tal resumed his seat, he wondered if the Captain's lack of enthusiasm stemmed from a general dislike of Islemen or because at the Masters' Court Tournament he had killed one Lieutenant Campaneal, Havrevulen's aide-de-camp.

As the meal ended, Kaspar stood up and said, 'Squire, please attend me.' He walked away from the table, leaving the Lady Rowena unattended.

Tal nodded to Amafi – who had stood behind his chair

throughout the meal – to return to their quarters, then hurried to the Duke's side. Kaspar put a large hand on Tal's shoulder and said, 'Now is as good a time as any to get the matter of your oath taken care of. Come with me: there's someone I want you to meet.' Over Kaspar's shoulder, Tal could see Natalia's expression was drawn as if she were concerned.

To Tal's surprise, no servants or guards accompanied them as Kaspar led Tal through a series of hallways. Then Tal saw they were at the flight of stairs that Rudolph had said was forbidden. Kaspar said, 'This area of the citadel is not to be entered, unless you are summoned by myself, Squire. Is that understood?'

'Yes, Your Grace.'

They climbed the stairs and went down a hall, to a large wooden door. Without knocking, Kaspar opened the door and motioned for Tal to enter.

The room was large, but sparsely furnished, containing just one table and a chair. Tapestries covered the walls against the cold, but otherwise the room was without comfort. A fire burned in a large hearth, and three men were waiting.

Two were guards, who quickly came to stand on either side of Tal and grip his arms. 'Tie him in the chair,' said Kaspar.

Tal realized the futility of resisting and let himself be lashed to the chair as the third man came to examine him. He was slender, of middle height, with long dark hair that reached past his shoulders. His face was almost pinched, with a prominent nose that would have dominated his face had it not been for his eyes. The eyes were black, and something in them made Tal fearful. The man came to stand before Tal and said, 'Hello, young man. Duke Kaspar says you are a talented lad with great potential. I certainly hope so.' He looked past Tal at Kaspar for a moment, then back at Tal. 'Because if you are not, you will not leave this room alive.'

He turned his back on Tal and went to the table. He picked something up and returned to stand before Tal. 'Shall we begin?' he asked the Duke.

Tal sat motionless. Behind him Duke Kaspar said, 'Begin.'

Suddenly there was a faint buzzing sound in Tal's ears, just at the edge of being recognizable. It sounded like the distant murmuring of voices. He found his eyelids growing heavy and he felt his body become heavy, as if he were on the verge of sleep.

Then a voice said, 'Your mind is mine, and you may not hide any falsehood.'

Tal felt an oddly familiar tingling along the base of his scalp, just above his neck, and recognized the use of magic. He had known such a sensation many times at Sorcerer's Isle as he had been subjected to many different types of magic spells. He could only trust that whatever Pug, Miranda, and Magnus had done to him over the time he was there would see him through this ordeal.

Duke Kaspar came to stand within Tal's field of vision. 'Do you, Talwin Hawkins, swear an oath upon your life, to serve me and my line, until such time as you are released by me? Do you serve freely, without reservation, emendation, or subterfuge? Do you offer your life if false?'

'I do,' said Tal, and his voice felt thick in his own throat. He thought of his father, before a fire late one night, and the words that he could still recall. 'Never offer an oath lightly. For you pledge not only your life and sacred honour, but your people's honour as well. To break an oath is to be without honour, to be without a spirit, and to be apart from the people.'

'I do,' he repeated.

After a moment, the strange sensations vanished and the odd-looking man said, 'He offers his oath truly.'

'Good,' said the Duke. 'Untie him.'

Tal sat rubbing his wrists for a moment as the Duke said, 'I have many enemies, Tal, and my enemies have many agents. You wouldn't be the first of those to seek my service.' He smiled. 'I had no doubt you would be found to be a man of your word.' Turning, he said, 'This is my most trusted advisor, Leso Varen.'

The man inclined his head politely, but his eyes were fast upon Tal. 'You are an unusual young man, Squire,' he said.

Tal stood up. 'Thank you, sir.'

The Duke waved the guards away and took Tal by the arm. Steering him towards the door he said, 'Go now and rest for the night. I have business here with Leso. Tomorrow we have some tasks to set you on.'

'I thank Your Grace for the opportunity to serve.'

With a laugh, Kaspar opened the door and said, 'Don't be so quick to thank me, young Hawkins. You haven't heard the tasks yet. You may not be so grateful when you see what plans I have for you.'

With that, he ushered Tal through the door and closed it behind him. Tal set off down the stairway, thinking that whatever might have been said, Leso Varen had reservations which were expressed in his eyes, if not his words. He would have to tread carefully around the magician, Tal knew.

Still, he had endured the first trial and was still breathing, and as it was said, so far, so good.

CHAPTER EIGHT

Task

*T*AL SLOGGED THROUGH THE swamp.

A company of Olasko soldiers wearing knee-high boots and heavily-padded jackets were trudging through calf-deep water. Kaspar had given Tal his first task the month before: *By fast ship go to Inaska and dispose of a band of smugglers who are causing problems for the local merchants.* They were also pirates, Tal discovered after two days in Olasko's southernmost city. He had spent hours in seedy taverns and seedier brothels, but after two weeks of spreading gold around he had got the information he had needed.

He had presented himself to the garrison commander at Inaska, shown his warrants from the Duke, and hand-picked the twenty men who now were working their way towards the smugglers' camp. Leading the locals was a sergeant who seemed to be the toughest of them, a snake-eater named Vadeski. He had a forehead like an anvil and a jaw that jutted like the ram on a Quegan war-galley, and his shoulders were as wide as the Duke's, though he was a full head shorter. Tal had seen his type in many a tavern: a brawler, bully, and, probably, a murderer, but he was exactly the type of man Tal needed for a thankless job like this.

The other men all were either trappers or hunters at one time, for Tal knew he would need men familiar with the local area. For the first time in his life, Tal found himself feeling lost. He had hunted in the mountains, and lowland forests, and across grasslands, but never in the swamps.

They had taken a boat from Inaska to a village called Imrisk, where they had secured provisions and commandeered a pair of large shallow-draught boats. Those had been paddled to the windward side of the island, opposite where the pirates had their camp.

Two small coast-sailers were reputedly anchored on the lee side, along with a dozen or more of the shallow-draught boats identical to the ones Tal's men used. Tal expected no more than thirty smugglers to be in camp. A quick attack, take some prisoners for questioning, fire the boats and base – these were his plans.

He motioned for Vadeski to hold the men in place, telling him, 'I'm going to scout ahead.'

'Yes, Captain,' answered the sergeant.

Tal moved through alien-looking trees with their underwater roots, having no idea what they were called. He kept his eyes busy, looking for danger, human or otherwise. The swamp held many predators, alligators, lizards, and especially a ferocious big cat; most of those would give the soldiers a wide berth, but there was also a particularly deadly water snake that had no fear of men.

When he saw dry land ahead, he climbed out of the water, moving as silently as possible, to a rise before him. He smelled the faint tang of smoke. Glancing over the rise, he saw a long depression running for nearly a quarter of a mile to another ridge. From the other side he saw the smoke from campfires, a faint haze against the sky, being blown away by the wind.

He returned and motioned for his men to follow, and led them down the shallow gully. At the far end, they halted, and Tal signalled for them to wait. He peered over the rocks and saw the pirates' camp. Then he sat down and swore silently. He beckoned for the sergeant to join him and when the old veteran was at his side, they both took a look.

Tal counted close to ninety or a hundred men, three large sailing boats riding at anchor off the beach, and more than a dozen of the shallow smugglers' boats.

'See those?' said Vadeski, whispering in his ear, pointing to the boats. 'They come rippin' out of the islands and swarm ya. If'n they can, they'll offload all the goods, then fire the traders' boat to the waterline. Those three big 'uns are to haul plunder.'

'How often do they move to new camps?'

'All the time,' said Vadeski.

Tal sat down quickly. Then he led the men back to the other end of the gully. When they were safely away from the camp, Tal said, 'Who is that lying bastard who told us there would be about thirty or so smugglers here, Sergeant?'

'Jacos of Saldoma; he's a trader o' sorts, Captain,' answered the Sergeant.

'Remind me to have him flogged when we get back, assuming

we get back. There's close to a hundred men in that camp.' He turned and did a quick inventory. He had twenty men, and only four crossbows.

'Five to one ain't all that bad, is it?' said the Sergeant with a grin.

'Only if we have an advantage,' said Tal. 'Let's head back to the water's edge in case one of those lads decides to come over that rise to take a piss, and we can ponder this.'

Tal knew that to return for more men would be a waste of time. The smugglers moved their camp on a regular basis, so he assumed they'd scout around every once in a while. There was no way any experienced scout would miss the signs of twenty-one men down in that gully and on this beach. He glanced down as they reached the water's edge.

'What's this?' Tal asked, kneeling. The shore was covered in a crushed white substance that didn't look like sand or rock.

One of the others said, 'Looks like broken shells, Captain.'

'Shells?'

'Swamp oysters,' said another. 'They're common enough around here. Not much for eating unless you're starvin', but some do.' He pointed. 'Look over there.'

Tal looked where the man indicated and saw a large mound of shells. Something started nagging at him. He remembered something about oyster shells but couldn't recall what.

They walked over to the pile and he said, 'Someone put these here.'

'Probably lookin' for pearls,' said the first man who spoke. He picked one up. 'Got a pearl ain't worth much, not like those that come from the sea, but some'll buy 'em. All kind of blokes range through these swamps, set up camp, abide a while, then move on.'

Tal was motionless as he held the shell. Then he said, 'What happens when you burn these?'

'You get a white ash,' said another man. 'Did it all the time in my village. I grew up in these islands, Captain.'

'White ash?' asked Tal, thinking. 'What do you use the ash for?'

'Well, me mum made soap by mixing it with tallow. Nasty stuff'll take the skin right off you if you leave it on too long, but it'll get your face and hands clean enough. Good for clothes, too, if you get it all out. Otherwise it'll eat a hole in a shirt.'

Tal grinned. '*Now* I remember. Something I read a while ago!' He motioned to the Sergeant. 'Set two pickets at the near end of the ravine. If they see anything, tell them to come running.' Vadeski detailed two men to do as ordered. Tal then said, 'Start a fire, there.' He pointed to a spot just above the water. 'Start gathering shells,' he instructed the other men. 'As many as you can find. Then empty out your kits.'

The men did as ordered, dumping the contents of their backpacks on the ground. They gathered shells and then once the fire was going, Tal started dumping shells into the flames.

They let the fire burn throughout the afternoon, and Tal watched as a huge pile of ash formed. As the sun lowered in the west, Tal said, 'We attack at sundown. The evening breeze should be at our backs, right, Sergeant?'

Vadeski said, 'Right, Captain. Wind's pretty constant across these islands. Still as the grave at sunrise, nice little zephyr every sundown.'

Tal said, 'We've got dirty work ahead, Sergeant.'

With a grin that was positively evil, Vadeski said, 'That's the kind I like, Captain!'

* * *

Twenty-one men crouched below the top of the rise. Tal peered over and saw that the pirates were gathered around a large cook-fire, or lounging nearby. He signalled to his men, and they spread out along the low ridge, two crossbowmen in the centre, one each at either end of the line.

He had given clear instructions to his men; now he had to wait for the wind to freshen. As the sun touched the horizon, he felt the breeze pick up. He nodded and spoke in a quiet tone. 'Now.'

His men stood. They waited until one of the smugglers saw them, and shouted. The smugglers all grabbed up weapons and made ready for an attack. Tal had ordered his men to hold their ground.

The two groups stood motionless, facing each other, until Vadeski shouted, 'Well, what are you waiting for, you ugly buggers?'

The pirates shouted and charged. The distance from the beach to the rise where Tal waited was less than a hundred yards, and most of it was slightly uphill. Tal waited until the first smuggler was only twenty yards away and then he shouted, 'Now!'

The men picked up their backpacks and started throwing handfuls of the white ash into the air. It was picked up by the wind and blew into the eyes of the attackers. Suddenly men were dropping their weapons and screaming in pain.

The four crossbowmen fired, and four of the pirates went down. A few of them kept their eyes covered, and managed to get to the line, where they were quickly cut down by Tal's men. Of the ninety or more charging pirates attacking, only a dozen reached Tal's line, all dying quickly.

'Now!' shouted Tal and the soldiers dropped their packs and

charged. There wasn't much fight left in the pirates, as many of them were blind. Tal shouted, 'Get me some prisoners!'

Tal leapt among the smugglers, many of them flailing about wildly with their swords, doing more damage to their companions than to any of Tal's men.

In less than ten minutes, the slaughter ended. Tal had only two wounded men, both with superficial cuts, and four prisoners who were sitting down by the boats trying to wash out their eyes with wet rags.

Sergeant Vadeski approached. 'Captain, there's somethin' you should see.'

Tal followed him to where his men were digging graves for the dead. 'What is it?'

'Look at the feet,' said the Sergeant.

Tal did so and noticed that a full dozen of the corpses were wearing boots. 'Those aren't sailors.'

'No, sir,' said the Sergeant. He bent over the closest man with boots on and pulled open his shirt. 'Look at this, sir.'

Under the dead man's shirt was a pendant. 'Bet you'll find the same as this on the others, sir.'

'What is it?'

Vadeski pulled it off the man and handed it to Tal. He looked closely and saw that the medallion was embossed with the head of a roaring lion. 'It's worn by the Black Lions, sir.'

Tal shook his head. 'I don't understand.'

'The Black Lions are a special group, sir. Soldiers workin' for the Prince of Salmater. These ain't pirates, sir, but soldiers come across the border to do mischief.'

Tal looked at the four prisoners and saw that one of them was wearing boots. He went to stand over the man and nudged him with his foot. The man looked up and blinked. 'I think I'm blind.'

'Most likely,' said Tal. 'Or at least for a while.'

'What is this?' asked the man, pointing to his swollen eyes.

'Lye,' answered Tal. 'Ash containing lye. Now, *I'll* ask the questions. Who was your officer?'

'I don't know what you mean,' said the prisoner.

Tal nodded at Vadeski, who kicked the man as hard as he could in the side. The prisoner couldn't see the kick coming and he doubled over, crying out in pain. He lay on the sand, unable to catch his breath for almost a full minute, finally inhaling with a great rasping noise.

'You're not bloody pirates,' said Tal. 'You're soldiers of Salmater. You're across the border in Olasko territory. If I take you back to Opardum, it'll mean war.'

'I'm a smuggler,' the man said weakly.

Tal looked around. 'Right.' He motioned to Vadeski. 'We'll stay the night, and tomorrow we'll burn all the boats but one.' He pointed to the three large boats anchored off the shore. 'Send four lads to see if there are any more of these cut-throats hiding aboard, and if not, what cargo they hold. If you can, move all the cargo to one of the boats, and we'll sail it back to Inaska. Detail four men to fetch our boats on the other side of the island. I want to get this news back to the Duke as quickly as I can.'

'What about him?' said the Sergeant.

Tal looked at the man huddling in the sand, blind and hunched up in such a way that Tal suspected Vadeski had broken some of his ribs. Without pity, Tal said, 'Make him talk.'

'Gladly, sir,' said the Sergeant.

The old soldier started shouting orders while Tal went over to the cook-fire. A large iron pot bubbled over the flames. He lifted a wooden spoon out of it and tasted the contents of the pot; it was a simple but acceptable fish stew. He beckoned over one of the soldiers and said, 'Pass the word; hot supper tonight. After burial, I want pickets posted, then the men can start eating.'

'Yes, Captain.'

Tal knelt and took a quick inventory. There was enough hard bread and dried fruit to last his men four or five days. More than enough to compensate for the provisions they had dumped to accommodate the ash in their packs. Tal sighed. This was the first of many bloody tasks Kaspar would set for him, he was certain.

If he was to realize his ambition, to utterly destroy the Duke of Olasko, he must be a good and faithful servant until such time as the Duke revealed his true nature and betrayed Tal. Then he would be free of his oath and could bring Kaspar down.

But that day was a long way off, for there was still much to know. And Tal was patient in many ways.

He got a wooden bowl from a nearby pile and used a ladle to pour out some hot stew. Then he tore off a chunk of bread and sat down, noticing some bottles of wine nearby. He decided to leave those for the men. As he put the bread into the stew and took a bite, he could hear the prisoner starting to scream.

Tal stood quietly as Kaspar read the report. 'You did well, Tal,' he said as he put down the parchment. 'Your report is detailed. The goods recovered will pay for the cost of the trouble we went to, but what do we do about the Prince of Salmater?'

'Send him a message, sir?'

'Yes, my thoughts exactly.' He picked up one medallion from the pile Tal had deposited on the table before him. 'I think returning these to him might get the point across.'

'Will it, Your Grace?'

Kaspar leaned back and regarded Tal. 'You have something on your mind, Squire?'

'The smuggling was no more than a nuisance, Your Grace. It harmed some merchants and perhaps diverted some duty money from your treasury, but it was only a small-scale problem. Why detail crack troops to such an undertaking?'

'You have something for me?'

'Only a thought, Your Grace. The soldier we captured knew nothing, but his officer had orders not shared with the men. We got that from the soldier before he died. The other three prisoners were common riff-raff, nothing more than thugs and dock rats working for the promise of easy booty.

'But we did find this.' He motioned to a servant who deposited a bundle before the Duke. Inside was a case, which Kaspar opened, revealing fine writing instruments. The parchments that were folded below the box lid revealed pages covered in cryptic notes, and other pages with line drawings.

Finally the Duke asked, 'A mapping expedition?'

'Yes, Your Grace.'

'To what end?'

'A straight route from Micel's Station to Olasko Gateway. I studied the maps of the area in your collection before leaving. Having just returned from the region, I know they are incomplete and inaccurate. What looks to be a large waterway turns out to be shallow and filled with debris, and there are islands marked where none exist, sandbars that build up and shift, all manner of hazards to any deep-draught vessels.' He pointed to one of the line maps. 'If I have understood their codes and these drawings, they were returning from a successful expedition – and not the first.' His finger pointed to another page. 'They were almost finished. I know from more reliable sources that there is only one viable route from the point where they stopped to the river itself. They would have found it on their next trip, I am certain.'

He rubbed his chin absently for a moment, then added, 'If war were to come to the north, having a direct route that would allow seizing the Gateway without having to confront your forces at Inaska and here in Opardum would give an enemy a strategic advantage: he would hold a fortress city on your western flank and cut off any supplies from the heartlands of Olasko. Another attack on Inaska from inside the island group coupled with a sea assault could take the city in less than a week, in my estimation.'

'Really?' said the Duke, smiling. He turned to Captain Havrevulen and said, 'What do you think, Captain?'

In neutral tones the Captain said, 'I think we should fortify Inaska and send a strong message to Salmater.'

'So do I,' said Kaspar. He looked at Tal. 'You've done well, young Hawkins.' To the Captain he said, 'Draw up plans to fortify Inaska and get them to me by tomorrow.' The Captain bowed and departed.

To Tal, Kaspar said, 'I want you to start tomorrow in incorporating this information on our maps. Bring them up to date.' He leaned back in his chair and said, 'Clean up and rest before dinner. That will be all.'

Tal bowed and departed. He returned to his quarters and found a hot bath, and Amafi, waiting.

'Magnificence, next time you must take me with you; you need eyes watching your back.' Amafi lowered his voice. 'The servants hear things. This is not a happy place. Many political rivals and much plotting.'

'Your command of the language is improving, I see,' said Tal as he slipped into the hot tub.

'You command, I obey, Magnificence.' Amafi started soaping a large cloth, and motioned for Tal to lean forward so he could scrub his back. 'It is to my advantage that most here don't realize I'm learning fast, and think me ignorant of their tongue. So, they gossip, and let slip things.'

'So, what have you found out?'

'The entire household is afraid of that man, Leso Varen. Those who serve him are in and out, do not linger. The only people who visit with him are Duke Kaspar and sometimes, the Lady Rowena.'

'Hmmm,' Tal said, wondering what Rowena might be up to. He observed the instructions of the Conclave, and made no attempt to speak to her outside the normal social contact that resulted from them both serving in Kaspar's court. When a dinner or some other function brought them together, both observed their roles impeccably and neither hinted at their prior relationship. Still, Tal had to admit to devoting a lot of time to considering what her mission might be. That she was spending time with Varen piqued his curiosity.

Amafi went on, 'No one has said Varen has done bad things, but it is a feeling of those here that he is a wizard and a bad man.'

'I'll concede that point,' said Tal. He took the cloth from Amafi and continued washing. 'What else?'

'Most of those who have been here a long time remember Duke Kaspar as a different man; the older servants who talk about him as a boy. Most blame Varen for Kaspar's changed nature.'

'A man makes choices,' Tal said.

'True, but what choices a man makes depends on what choices he is offered.'

'You're occasionally profound, Amafi.'

'Thank you, Magnificence. Duke Kaspar is devoted to his sister. The Lady Natalia is refused nothing. She likes men, horses, fine clothing and galas. There are many entertainments here in the citadel, at least one a week. Many seek her hand in marriage, but Kaspar is keeping her for a special alliance.'

'He wants her to be Queen of the Isles, I think,' said Tal.

'I am no expert on politics, Magnificence, but I think that will not happen.'

'I agree,' said Tal, standing.

Amafi wrapped him in a towel, then asked, 'What is your pleasure until supper, Magnificence?'

'A bite. You go fetch some bread, cheese and wine, while I dress myself. Then find that page, Rudolph, and tell him to come here. I think it's time to see more of the citadel.'

'More?' Amafi shrugged. 'I thought you had seen it all.'

Tal smiled. 'Hardly. There are things here that I have only imagined, Amafi.'

'Very well, Magnificence. I shall do as you command.'

Amafi bowed and left the room, and Tal finished drying off.

There was so much to learn, if only he could manage to stay alive long enough to learn it.

Tal followed Rudolph. The boy took him through a hallway that was clean, but rarely used. 'These quarters are empty, Squire,' said the boy. He reached the farthest door and rattled the handle. 'All locked up proper, sir.' He turned around. 'Well, that's it, then. You've seen it all, from one end of the citadel to the other.'

Tal smiled. 'Not all, I warrant.'

'Well, all the stores back inside the caves . . .'

'Caves?'

'There are caves used as storehouses behind the citadel, Squire. Big nasty, draughty dark places, and some of them I hear go back for miles. No reason to go there, but if you must . . .' He started to walk.

Tal put his hand on the boy's shoulder, restraining him. 'No, some other time perhaps. How do I find these caves?'

'There are several entrances, Squire. One lies behind the armoury, but that door is always locked and only Captain Havrevulen and the Duke himself have keys to that door. There's another one behind the kitchen, through a door that's behind where you go to dump the kitchen waste to the midden, and there's another one down off that old room I showed you that had all the different furniture in it that we keep around for Lady Natalia when the mood strikes her to change things. Then there's the dungeon, but you don't want to go there.'

'No,' agreed Tal.

'There's one other door that comes up somewhere else, but I don't recall exactly where.' He looked at Tal and said, 'I've shown you everywhere I know about, sir. All that's left then is the wizard's apartments, Squire, but you don't want to go there either.'

'I've been there,' said Tal to the boy's open-mouthed amazement. 'No, I was thinking of the servants' passages.'

'The serving ways? But none of the gentry want to know about those. Even I don't know all of them, sir.'

'Why don't you show me what you do know?'

Rudolph shrugged and walked past Tal. 'This way, then, sir, but if you ask me, it's a bit odd.'

Tal laughed. 'Then why don't we keep this between ourselves?'

'Mum's the word, Squire,' said Rudolph as he led Tal towards the kitchen.

An hour later they walked through a narrow hall, barely wide enough for Tal to move without his shoulders brushing a wall. Rudolph held a candle up. 'This leads to the Duke's quarters, Squire. Can't go too close, unless we're summoned.'

As Tal had anticipated, there were passages out of sight of the residents and guests of the citadel that were used by the servants to fetch and carry all sorts of things. Laundry and food, soil-buckets and water were lugged through these narrow hallways, so as not to inconvenience the residents and, as Tal knew, they were often used as shortcuts from one part of the building to the next.

He suspected that more than one noble had skulked through these passages on his way to the bedroom of a visiting noble's wife or daughter, and more than one pretty maid had made her way towards a nobleman's quarters that way as well.

They passed a ladder and Tal asked, 'Rudolph, where does this lead?'

'Next floor up, Squire,' the boy answered, now very bored with exploring.

'I know that, boy. *Where* on the next floor?'

'Can't say as I rightly know, sir. Most of us don't use the ladders. Some of 'em are so rotten with age and you can fall and break your neck. When you're carrying a tray or a bundle, you can't climb up or down. So most people don't use them.'

Tal closed his eyes for a moment, calling up what he remembered of the passages above, and had a fair idea of where that ladder exited. As he suspected, while entrances below in the citadel – primarily in the kitchen and laundry areas – were regular doors, almost all the exits above were disguised as wall panels or behind closets or through doors behind tapestries. He wondered if even the Duke knew all these passages, though he found it hard to believe that a man as thorough as Kaspar would remain ignorant of what could turn out to be a vulnerability; but on the other hand, even the smartest people took too many things for granted, and if Kaspar's parents had been ignorant of all these byways in the citadel, then Kaspar might be as well.

They moved on through the dark tunnel and Tal decided he would return to these tunnels and explore on his own some time soon. Just as he would visit the dungeon and the caves as well.

The only places he would give a wide berth were Kaspar's apartment and the rooms occupied by Leso Varen.

Tal said, 'I think that's enough. Show me the fastest way back to my room.'

'Thank you, Squire,' said the boy, not hiding his relief. 'The housecarl's going to beat me if I don't get back soon.'

'Don't worry. I'll tell him I required your services.'

'That's all right, Squire. It won't do me any good. My master reckons I've got to learn to be in two places at once sooner or later.'

Tal laughed and followed the boy.

Tal stood silently, feeling something akin to triumph. He was in the mouth of a cave, looking across a deep ravine still shrouded in darkness as the early morning light began to illuminate a cliff-face less than half a mile away. Looking down he felt almost giddy with delight.

A few days after returning from his mission down to the Southern Islands, Tal was called into Kaspar's presence and informed they would be hunting for a week starting the next day. Tal had instructed Amafi to prepare his travel bags, had secured new strings for his bow from the Duke's armoury and chosen two dozen arrows. Then just before dinner, his stomach had rebelled and Tal had come down with a murderous stomach flux, either from something he had picked up on the way back from the southern islands or something he had eaten that morning. Tal had spent the day in bed or in the garderobe. He couldn't even keep water down without having it come right back up.

The Duke's healer had come to see him, giving him a foul-tasting concoction to drink, but Tal vomited that back up a minute later. Shaking his head, the chirurgeon had prescribed bed-rest and waiting it out. He had informed the Duke that Tal would be bedridden for at least three days. Kaspar then sent a note wishing Tal well and inviting him to join the party in a day or two should he quickly recover.

The afternoon after Kaspar's departure, Tal had endured a fever for half a day. He had awoken thirsty and the water had stayed down. He had rested for that night and the next morning informed Amafi he would not be joining the Duke immediately. And then he decided to use the time he had to further explore the caverns behind the citadel.

Dressed in black, carrying a lantern, he had slipped out that night into the lower basement of the citadel, quickly negotiating the servants' passages and making his way to the pantry. Since the Duke and much of his household were out hunting, kitchen activity had been at a minimum, so he easily avoided the few cooks' helpers working late at night, located the ancient caves Rudolph had told him about, and explored them. As the boy had promised, some went on for miles. His first night had been difficult, for while the fever and flux had left him, he was still feeling weak.

On the second night he had found a long tunnel unmarked by any sign of human passage for a very long time and had followed it to a huge gallery with three passages leading eastward. One of them contained a barely noticeable draught of air and he had followed it.

It had taken him three nights of exploration, but at last he had discovered the exit where he now stood. He put down the lantern and studied the crevasse that the maps in the Duke's library clearly marked as the biggest barrier across the escarpment. High above he could see the brightening sky between the two opposing faces of the deep cut in the earth. And directly across from him Tal saw something totally unexpected, a pathway down from the opposite side of the crevasse. He moved to the edge of the entrance and looked down and beheld another stone pathway leading down. Tracing the route with his eyes in the early-morning light, he saw what he had never dreamed might exist: the means of traversing the chasm that had safely guarded the rear of the citadel for ages. These paths were not natural. Some ancient war chief or early Duke of Olasko had cut those narrow paths into the face of the cliffs. They were little wider than goat trails, but two or even three men could walk abreast down one side and up the other. They were not marked on any documents in Kaspar's library. Tal judged that some past ruler had wanted to make sure there was a fast way out of Opardum that few, if any, besides himself knew about.

Tal made his way carefully down the path to the bottom of the cliff. It was not a difficult journey, although the descent was steep, for the path was wide and free of obstacles. At the bottom he found a pair of stone pillars. A matching pair mirrored them on the other side of a broken, rocky gully. Once in the past water must have flowed through this part of the gorge, Tal decided, but at some later stage the water source had been diverted or dried up. He negotiated his way across the broken gully to the other side and looked up. It would be an annoying climb to the path above, but he could manage it if he wished. But he knew he wouldn't bother: because when he came here next, it would be from the other side with a company of engineers who would have a bridge across the gully in a matter of hours.

Tal started back. It would be dark before he reached his room, and Amafi would keep servants away from his 'sleeping' master, fighting off what was going to turn out to be the last of his fever. Tomorrow Tal would awaken sufficiently recovered to join Kaspar on his hunt, and no one would know that he had discovered the citadel's glaring weakness. For a moment he considered telling Amafi then decided against it; he could not confess what he didn't know. Besides, no matter how loyal the former assassin had been since coming into Tal's service, Tal wasn't certain he would always remain so. Remembering the story Nakor had told him, of the scorpion who had killed the frog crossing the river, thereby dooming himself as well because it was his nature, Tal decided that Kaspar might not be the only scorpion he had to contend with.

Since killing Raven in the Land of the Orodon, Tal had dreamed of how he might defeat Kaspar. He had imagined finding him alone and killing him with a sword in hand, telling him who he really was at the last. He had imagined sneaking into his quarters in the dead of night, using the hallways and servants' passages to win his way past his guards. Now it seemed he might have another choice. He felt positively buoyant as he made his way back through the caves.

Tal sat in mute amazement as the servants brought in the bear. It had been given to a taxidermist in Roldem who had prepared the trophy for display, and had been delivered the day before Kaspar and his companions returned from their most recent hunting trip. The bear rose up on his hind legs, his muzzle set in a snarl. The assembled nobles and privileged commoners of Opardum gawked at the creature.

'My lords, ladies, and gentlemen,' declared the Duke, 'my view of this animal the last time he rose up like that was lying at his feet, as he was preparing to devour me. I would not be here this evening if it hadn't been for the quick and heroic action of your newest member of the court. My friends, I present to you Talwin Hawkins, my emissary at large.'

He motioned for Tal to stand. Tal did so to a round of polite applause. He sat down again as quickly as he could. Kaspar went on to add, 'This bear will stand on display with the other prizes in the Trophy Hall, with a plaque detailing Squire Hawkins's noble achievement. Now, please continue with the festivities.'

A low buzz of conversation returned to the room. The officer next to Tal, a Lieutenant Adras, said, 'Good luck, Squire. None rise so fast as those with luck.'

Tal nodded. Natalia glanced over at him while pretending to be listening to a story one of the Duke's senior advisors was telling. She threw him a quick smile, then returned her attention to the courtier.

The Lieutenant said, 'Slowly, Squire. Our lady is known to . . . let's leave it that she rarely takes prisoners,' he finished with a chuckle.

Tal looked at him. 'Really?'

'Not that I have first-hand experience, you understand, Squire. I'm merely a lowly lieutenant of cavalry, not even a member of the Household Guard. A few of us are allowed to dine here from time to time, but I expect my next turn will be a year or more coming around.' He pointed to the far end of the table, where Captain Havrevulen dined, and said, 'Our esteemed Captain Quint is the only soldier in the duchy who would think of so lofty a prize. The rest of us may merely gaze on in adoration.' He sat back, appraising Tal. 'You, Squire, have noble lineage, are Champion of the Masters' Court, and – judging by the size of that bear – no mean hunter. Since our lord and master is not given to overblown praise, he is also in your debt. So, you have a chance, slim as it might be, to court our lady.'

'The lady is the Duke's most important treasure,' observed Tal. 'She will be wed to whichever ruling prince most advantages Olasko, I'll wager.'

With a laugh, the Lieutenant said, 'You're no country boy, Hawkins, that's for certain.'

The banquet continued for another half an hour and Tal put the conversation with Lieutenant Adras behind him. He knew that if he continued his affair with Natalia he was putting himself in harm's way, but to spurn her advances might make him a powerful enemy who was close to the Duke.

He glanced at a lovely blonde woman sitting to the left of the Duke who was engaged in conversation with another of the many courtiers present. The Lady Rowena had entered tonight on Kaspar's arm, and it was Tal's first opportunity to see her since he had come back to Opardum from the Southern Islands.

She had been absent when he first came to the city, ostensibly away visiting her family. Tal knew she had no family, as she had been raised on Sorcerer's Isle, so he wondered what she had been up to. He knew that it would be impossible to find out. Both he and his former lover were deep in their roles, so neither would acknowledge the existence of Talon of the Silver Hawk or Alysandra.

Seeing her always made him consider the emotional punishment he had gone through at her hands. He felt only a hint of pity, for he knew she was a broken thing, devoid of true feelings for any person, content to take instruction from Miranda, mistress of Sorcerer's Isle, and the only person who could effectively control the young woman.

As the banquet ended, a page appeared and said, 'Squire, the Duke requests your presence in his private apartment.'

Tal followed the page and soon entered a luxurious room with a low round table and half a dozen chairs spread around it. Sideboards, candlestands of gold, mirrors and tapestries decorated the place. On the table rested a crystal decanter and several crystal goblets.

Kaspar sat alone. He motioned for Tal to take another seat. A servant poured wine for them then departed.

'I've decided to send you to Salmater, Talwin. You will take my message to His Highness, the Prince of Salmater.'

'Sir?'

'It will be short, albeit very flowery, very diplomatic, but the heart of it will be this: he will acknowledge me as his liege lord and submit, or else I will reduce his city to rubble around his ears.' With a grin, he asked, 'How do you think he'll react?'

Tal sipped his wine, to gain a moment in which to consider this. Then he said, 'Not knowing the man, that might be hard to anticipate, but I can't imagine he'll be pleased.'

Kaspar laughed. 'No, he most certainly won't be. But he is a fool and someone is using him.'

'Who, Your Grace?'

'Almost certainly Paul of Miskalon. It might be someone else, but I doubt it. Prince Janosh of Salmater is wed to Duke Paul's sister, and she rules the Prince. She might meet with an untimely accident . . .'

'Your Grace?'

'Not yet, but that is a possibility.' Kaspar reached down behind his chair, drew out a map and placed it on the table. 'Here are the disputed lands, Tal. Olasko, Salmater, Miskalon, Roskalon,

Maladon and Semrick, Far Lorin, and Aranor all have claims to part or all of those lands.' He sat back. 'Some of us have better claims and others of us have bigger armies.'

Kaspar watched as Tal studied the map.

Then the Duke said, 'Olasko has four frontiers to be concerned with. You've already uncovered a problem on one of them, among the islands that comprise our southern province.

'To the north we have the thugs up in Bardac's Holdfast. As long as they stay thugs, I don't worry. I keep enough troops in the City of the Guardian to make them think twice about raiding south, and they have their own problems to the north with County Conar – that merry band of murderers would make anyone nervous.'

Tal said nothing, but he remembered stories about the men from Conar; they were close enough to the land of the Orosini that there had been conflicts before.

'To the west,' continued Kaspar, 'is my cousin in Aranor, about whom I have no concerns.

'That leaves the east.'

'Which is the sea,' said Tal.

'Which is the sea,' agreed Kaspar. 'The sea can be a great barrier, but it also can be a highway. If you study the histories of the late war in the Kingdom some thirty years ago, you'll find that an army came from halfway around the world by ship, and they laid waste to nearly half the Western Realm before being destroyed.'

Tal said, 'So you seek to secure borders?'

'Yes,' said Kaspar. 'And more. Some of which I'll tell you later, but for now consider this: while Kesh and the Isles have been raising up mighty nations, under one rule of law, under one common administration in each nation, the Eastern Kingdoms have been squabbling like poor relatives at a feast over kitchen scraps.

'Only Olasko's unique relationship with Roldem keeps the Kingdom of the Isles at bay. Roldem's navy is vast, for she is an island nation, and just the presence of that fleet makes our eastern frontier secure.' With a chuckle, he said, 'As long as we stay on good terms with Roldem.

'No, it's to the south I must look right now, and eventually in other directions, but before I have finished, I mean to bring all these squabbling, petty little rulers to heel and then what is now a collection of independent little kingdoms, principalities and duchies will be fused into one nation, with one ruler.'

Tal said nothing, but he realized now that what he had suspected before was true: that Kaspar craved power. He just hadn't anticipated the particular vision that served Kaspar as the vehicle for his ambition.

'So, go and rest. Tomorrow you leave for Salmater. I will have all the necessary papers for your office drawn up, as well as my message for Prince Janosh.'

Tal rose and bowed, departing quickly. He hurried to his quarters, thinking that now he was becoming fully Kaspar's creature.

• CHAPTER NINE •

Emissary

*T*AL STOOD SILENTLY.

Before him rose the throne of Prince Janosh of Salmater, a slender man with a distracted expression who blinked constantly and appeared to have difficulty sitting still. Next to him sat Princess Svetlana, who eyed Tal coolly as the Prince's First Minister read the missive from Duke Kaspar.

When at last the reading of the demand for submission was over, the Prince said, 'Well, I never.' He looked at his wife and said, 'Madam, have you ever?'

Ignoring her husband, the Princess addressed Tal. 'So, Kaspar is seeking war?'

Tal inclined his head. 'No, Majesty. My Duke is seeking resolution for a problem that has plagued this region for generations. I am instructed to make this as clear as I can.' He turned and motioned to Amafi, who today was dressed as finely as Tal. The manservant stepped forward and handed a pouch of black velvet to his master, who opened it and turned it upside down, allowing a dozen medallions to fall to the marble floor with a clatter. 'These twelve medallions were taken from the corpses of a dozen "pirates" who were on a mapping expedition of sovereign Olasko territory. Had these men been simple merchants, my lord Kaspar would have been more than obliging in seeing they had up-to-date charts of the acknowledged trading routes. We can only assume they were up to mischief.'

'Medallions?' said the Prince. 'What have medallions to do with maps?'

The First Minister, a whip-thin man named Odeski, looked at Tal with a narrowed gaze, his blue eyes trying to ascertain the quality of the man before him. Tal looked from him to the Princess, ignoring the Prince for a pointed moment, then speaking to the monarch. 'Majesty, those medallions belong to your Black Lions.'

'My Black Lions?' The Prince positively fluttered with confusion. 'What have my guards to do with this?'

Odeski said, 'Majesty, I think it best if we adjourn from the court and retire to less public quarters, where we may discuss this matter at leisure.'

'Yes, that sounds capital,' said the Prince, rising.

The Princess followed her husband, and as she passed, she studied Tal minutely. When they had departed, Odeski said, 'We shall be in chambers for the afternoon. I suggest you return to your allotted quarters and stay in them. Diplomatic status protects you only in the palace. Our more common thugs do not care if Duke Kaspar gets upset over your demise.'

'Your point is made,' said Tal.

A court page escorted Tal and Amafi back to the quarters they had been given upon arrival the day before. Tal glanced around, as if expecting to be ambushed at any minute, but they reached the apartment without incident.

Tal motioned to Amafi to check to ensure they were alone, and when the assassin-turned-manservant did so, he nodded. At the table, Tal took out a writing pack. He unfolded it and said aloud, 'I wonder what the Prince's answer to the Duke might be.'

'Who can say, Magnificence?' Amafi replied.

Tal took out a charcoal and wrote on a parchment, 'Can you do it?' Then he showed this message to Amafi.

Amafi smiled. 'I should find my way to the kitchen, Magnificence, and see to having some fruit and wine sent here. Our hosts have been remiss in providing for the comfort of an envoy from a neighbouring nation.'

He bowed and left the room, while Tal crossed over to the fireplace and threw the parchment in. They could be certain they weren't being watched, but they had no certainty someone wasn't listening close by.

Tal threw himself down on the bed and stared at the ceiling. His mind returned to the first night at sea on the fast ship which had sped them south from Opardum. The Duke had given him a portfolio which contained his documents, instructions, the medals from the dead soldiers, and a note with the ducal seal on it which said, 'Open when you are alone at sea.'

He had waited until after dark to open the note, and within found only one instruction: *Kill Princess Svetlana*. Then he had gone up on deck and threw the message overboard.

He now understood Kaspar's instruction. Without his iron-willed princess, Prince Janosh was a fool who could be easily controlled.

A short time later, Amafi returned to find Tal half-dozing on the bed. 'Magnificence,' he said softly.

Tal sat up. 'I am awake. I was just thinking.' He got up and went over to the table and wrote, 'What did you find?'

Aloud, Amafi said, 'I got lost, master, and a servant was kind enough to direct me to the kitchen. The major domo of the palace is beside himself that no one saw to your comfort and food will be arriving shortly.' Then he wrote on the parchment, 'I have found a way.'

Tal said, 'Well, that will be welcome. I'm feeling peckish.'

He threw the parchment into the fire just as a knock came at the door. Amafi opened it and three servants entered with trays. One bore cheeses, breads, and fruit, the next pastries and sweet candy, and the last wine and glasses.

Tal waited until they were gone, then sampled the wine. 'Good,' he said, and meant it.

'Shall I leave you to rest?' Amafi asked.

'Yes,' said Tal. 'While we wait for a response from the Prince, hurry into the city and see if you can find a gift suitable for the Lady Natalia. And while you're at it, find an apothecary and see if they have something for sea sickness. That last trip was damned uncomfortable.'

'At your command, Magnificence.' Amafi hurried out. He would go to the Captain of the Palace Guard, requesting an escort, and would be detailed a pair of bored palace guards, who would follow him as he ambled from shop to shop. Along the way, besides some pretty trinkets for the Duke's sister, Amafi would secure some items of a less felicitous nature.

The atmosphere at the state dinner that evening proved as warm as the mountain streams of his youth in winter, thought Tal. The Prince and Princess ignored Tal absolutely as much as possible without breaching political decorum. He had been politely greeted once, moved to a table occupied by military officers who spoke in monosyllables and otherwise ignored him, and at one point during the meal, the Prince politely asked him if he was enjoying his food and wine, to which Tal had graciously replied in the affirmative.

Tal had been back in his quarters for less than half an hour, inspecting the gifts Amafi had found, when a knock came at the door.

In Quegan, Tal said, 'It can't be a reply to the Duke at this late hour, can it?'

Amafi smiled and shrugged. 'Anything is possible, Magnificence.'

Tal opened the door to find a young woman standing there. She said, 'Sir, the Princess requests your presence in her apartment.'

Tal looked over his shoulder at Amafi and said, 'Anything is possible.'

He followed the young woman through a corridor, then past a pair of guards at their post. She led him along another long hallway that led past the throne room, and down a side corridor. At a large ornate doorway, the girl paused and knocked. 'Enter,' came a voice from the other side.

The girl opened the door and let Tal enter first. He stepped through and found himself in a large drawing room, lit by only a few candles. The girl said, 'The envoy, Highness.'

Princess Svetlana sat on a long divan, her legs drawn up under her in a very casual pose. She said, 'Leave us.'

The girl bowed and departed, leaving Tal alone with the Princess. He took a quick look around the room and kept a straight face, for he had an impulse to smile. He bowed and said, 'Ma'am?'

The Princess wore a lounging robe of a nearly-diaphanous silk, with a sleeveless over-jacket of the same material. It was of a pale blue which accented her vivid eyes. She was still a striking woman, thought Tal as he heard her demand, 'Approach, Squire.'

Tal moved to stand before her and she patted the divan, saying, 'Sit.'

He did as instructed. Despite being in her forties, she showed only a slight dusting of grey in her otherwise dark hair. She had a thin face, but her eyes were wide and expressive, and her neck and shoulders – shown to good advantage by the clothing she had chosen – were elegant. Tal took it all in with a glance, the full bosom and long legs and, despite the fact that she had given birth to two children at an early age, her small waist.

Kaspar had given Tal all the information on the Princess that he possessed, which was extensive: she was the sister of the Duke of Miskalon, at one time had been all but thrown at Kaspar as a possible duchess, had married a man she basically despised, and was all that kept Salmater from being overrun or controlled by one of its neighbours. Her son, Serge, was as big a fool as his father, and her daughter Anastasia was a simpering, spoiled brat. Svetlana's passions included politics, hunting and men. Tal had noticed all the palace guards in the Princess's retinue were uniformly young, handsome and tall.

'I trust you don't mind the informality, Squire.'

Tal smiled, a polite and unrevealing expression. 'Not at all, Highness. I am at your service.'

The Princess laughed. 'Hardly. Kaspar would never send a fool with a message that is one rude word shy of a declaration of war. What does he *really* want?'

Tal realized the seductive setting was designed to throw him off balance and distract him. He had no doubt he stood a fair chance of the Princess dragging him off to bed in the next room. He could read a woman's moods as well as the next man, indeed better than most, and he knew she found him attractive. She was also the true ruler of this nation and used to indulging her every whim – women who rule through weak husbands, Tal had discovered reading his history, had decided advantages in their personal choices. As she was an attractive enough woman by any measure, he would be more than willing to indulge her in any fashion she desired before he killed her. Given the curves of her slender body, he would certainly enjoy it.

'I make no presumptions about my master's desires, Princess,' Tal answered. 'He stated his brief clearly in his message to you and the Prince.'

'Well, then, Squire,' said the Princess, leaning forward to pour two goblets of wine, and opening up the top of her gown enough to give Tal a clear view of her very attractive body, 'let's play a game, shall we?'

'Ma'am?'

'Let's pretend we're both seers, and we are able to read Duke Kaspar's mind.' She handed him a goblet. 'Now, you go first.'

Tal laughed. 'Highness, I would be doing my master a disservice if I attributed to him motives or desires beyond the message he sent.'

'I've known Kaspar since before I came to this throne, Tal – I may call you Tal, may I?' He nodded. 'I've known him since we were children, though I am only a few years older.' She sipped her wine. 'I know him for the double-dealing, lying, murderous bastard he is, and love him anyway.' She smiled and Tal found her even more attractive. 'He's one of my favourite enemies and lovers – that was before I married Janosh, of course. Besides, we're playing a game, aren't we?'

Tal considered. He quickly arrived at something that would not compromise his position, yet might help him resolve this little impasse. The sight of the Princess by candle light was beginning to captivate him. He smiled, 'Yes, it's just a game, Princess.'

'Call me Svetlana when we're alone, Tal.'

She leaned forward. 'Now, what does Kaspar really want?'

'I can only guess, but I think he means to ensure you don't end up aiding other enemies. The mapping expedition was clearly designed to find a clear route through to Olasko Gateway, and that's of great concern to the Duke.'

'Understandable,' said the Princess, dipping her finger in Tal's wine, then playfully outlining his lips with the finger.

Tal felt himself growing warm, and would have merely attributed it to the wine and the Princess's seductive play, except that his training at Sorcerer's Isle told him that something else was going on. He sipped his wine, applying his tutored palate to the task, and after a long sip identified a strange and ever-so-slightly bitter quality in the finish of the wine that was not supposed to be there.

He wasn't certain what had been added to the wine, but he suspected a particular powder made from a certain tree bark. It was sold throughout both the Kingdom of the Isles and in Roldem as a curative for older men whose ardour was flagging. At his age it was unnecessary, but it certainly did seem to be working.

He put the goblet aside. 'I think what my lord Duke really wants is to find one of his borders secure, so he can turn his mind to other things. He has ambitions –'

'As well we know,' said Svetlana, moving even closer as she started tracing Tal's jawline with her finger.

'– ambitions that require he not fear for the safety of Olasko on multiple fronts.

'He sees your husband as a tool of Miskalon or Roskalon, or perhaps even the Isles, and would like to find an absolute way to end that threat.'

She kissed him, then moved back slightly and whispered, 'We must find another way to reassure our beloved Kaspar, but we will never swear fealty. Perhaps you could attend a meeting with my husband's Cabinet tomorrow and we shall ponder things a little while longer.'

Tal whispered back, 'I am at your service.'

Smiling, she pulled him forward as she lay back on the divan and said, 'Yes, you are.'

As morning drew near, the Princess said, 'Time to go.'

Tal dressed. As he pulled his boots on, he said, 'I thank Her Highness for her hospitality.'

Svetlana laughed, a genuinely amused, warm sound. 'I thank the Squire for his enthusiasm.'

'That was easy enough, m'lady.' He leaned over and kissed her. 'The drug in the wine was unnecessary.'

She feigned a pout. 'At my age one worries.'

'With your beauty, you needn't.'

She rose up, ignoring her nakedness. Embracing him, she said, 'You have no idea how difficult it has been. Since our two children were conceived, our last over a decade ago, my husband . . . let's say he prefers the company of others.'

Tal shrugged. 'His loss.'

'And it's so difficult sometimes to convince a young man of the court that . . . well, they fear the Prince's wrath.' Her voice turning bitter, she added, 'When they should expect his thanks and relief.'

'I might fear him, save I expect to be departing tomorrow, perhaps with a declaration of war following me.'

She escorted him to the door of her apartment. Kissing him deeply, she said, 'All is not lost. You're a wonderful boy and I admire you, but I shall not bend my stance for your protection. However, I will tell you that war is a last resort and I see no joy in it. I will expect you to make a persuasive brief to the Cabinet this afternoon, Tal. Give me something to work with and we can prevent it.' Lowering her eyes, she said, 'Either way, I expect we shall talk about this alone, later tonight?'

'My pleasure, Highness,' said Tal before kissing her once more, then leaving the apartment.

If the palace guards were surprised to see a visiting envoy leaving the Princess's private apartments at dawn, they did a masterful job of disguising the fact. They held their positions with eyes forward as Tal returned to his own quarters.

He entered the room and found Amafi asleep in a chair, feet

out before him, next to a table covered in vials and jars. As the door closed with a faint click of the latch, Amafi came awake.

'Magnificence,' said Amafi. He stood and pointed to the table. 'It is done.'

Tal looked at Amafi in surprise. 'After you left,' Amafi said, 'I took the liberty of completely inspecting these premises. Salmater observes the formalities of diplomacy. There are no secret listening posts or peep-holes, of that I'm certain.'

Tal nodded, then looked at the clutter and said, 'Which one?'

Amafi picked up a tiny blue vial and said, 'This is the one.'

'No one is suspicious?'

'I paused at three apothecaries, buying different ingredients at each, telling the guards I could not find that which I needed for your health. They were bored and distracted by the time I had wasted the entire morning in several shops seeking more gifts for Lady Natalia.' He pointed to another table in the corner, where several objets d'art, items of personal jewellery and bottles of rare perfume rested.

'Natalia will be most amused,' said Tal.

'How was your night, Magnificence?'

'Pleasant enough,' said Tal. 'It's a shame, in a way. She thinks me a young fool and will try to play me to her advantage while I am sent back to Kaspar with a clever little request from her husband. It's a ploy to buy time.

'It's a shame we can't find out who she sends messages to, and identify the true architect of this plot against Olasko.'

'You might if you could find a source of information inside the palace. Minister Odeski seems a man of ambition.'

Tal grinned. 'My assessment as well. But all this cannot play out in one night. We must get back to Olasko before the unfortunate events that are to take place transpire.' He motioned to all the apothecary items on the table. 'Make sure everything is destroyed.'

'Of course, Magnificence. I will drop a vial into different garderobes throughout the palace. No one will be sifting through the middens, I am certain.'

The waste from the palace would be hauled away by wagons and perhaps dumped outside the city or spread out in the midden fields to dry and later be used for fertilizer on local farms. Either way, should a farmer find a tiny blue glass bottle in his fertilizer, he would have no idea where it came from.

'Very well, that should do it.'

'What then, today, Magnificence?'

'Today I rest until called before the Prince's Privy Council, at which time I can sit and watch the Princess run the nation. It should be entertaining, if predictable.' He moved to the door to his bedroom. 'Wake me at an hour after noon, and have some food ready. I expect to be in with the council all afternoon. Then another banquet.'

'Then the Princess?' asked Amafi.

'Then the Princess, assuming a handsome young palace guard doesn't take her fancy during supper.'

'Not to worry, Magnificence.'

'The Princess seems a woman of fickle appetites, and you seem sure of yourself.'

'I know women, Magnificence, or at least as well as any man might. You are a novelty, and from what I heard before taking your service, well regarded by the ladies. And even if he's a very handsome young guard, he will be here next week, and you will not.'

Tal smiled. 'You are probably right.' He took the blue vial and put it in his belt pouch, then entered his bedroom and closed the door. As he fell into bed, he could hear Amafi clearing up the accumulated items and was sound asleep by the time Amafi left to get rid of the evidence.

The meeting was proceeding exactly as Tal had anticipated. The Cabinet appeared unconvinced of Duke Kaspar's resolve and Tal had on several occasions to inform them that he had been given no latitude to negotiate.

First Minister Odeski tried more than once to beg more time of Tal, and each time Tal gave the same answer: any reply to Kaspar that wasn't full acquiescence would be seen as defiance. Salmater would come to heel or be crushed. Tal managed to convey this choice in as diplomatic a fashion as possible, but he gave no hint of leeway.

As the meeting dragged on, Tal realized the truth of Kaspar's observation. Princess Svetlana let Prince Janosh prattle on at length, but whenever it became time to move to the next item of discussion it was the Princess who made that decision.

Tal used his training to stay calm and appear unconcerned, for he had his own orders and no matter what the outcome – including a complete capitulation – his one task was clear: Princess Svetlana must die.

Finally, the Prince said, 'We shall prepare a response to Duke Kaspar's demand, and I must tell you, young sir, it will not be to his liking. Not in any way! Then we shall see you off on the morning tide. I bid you good evening!' He rose, and all those in the chamber rose as well. The Prince left and as she followed her husband, Princess Svetlana smiled at Tal in such a way that he knew she would send him an invitation after supper.

When the Prince and his wife had departed, First Minister Odeski said, 'Squire, a moment of your time, please?'

Tal bowed. 'I'm at your service, Minister.'

'Walk with me a way,' said the older man. When they were out of earshot of the other ministers, Odeski said, 'We have something of a mess here, don't we?'

'If by we, you mean Salmater, sir, then yes, you do.'

'War profits no one, and Kaspar's demands seem to me to be a rather extreme response to a relatively minor offence.'

'Mapping expeditions disguised as smugglers, in Olasko's sovereign territory, in anticipation of military action is hardly "minor", Minister.'

'You're from the Kingdom, Squire, so perhaps you're ignorant of our history here in the East, but we spar, feign, threaten and generally play rough with one another as a matter of course. I've been in the Prince's court and his father's before him for thirty years, and I've seen half a dozen border clashes with Olasko, an equal number with Miskalon, two naval conflicts with Roskalon, one with Roldem, another with the Isles, and the disputed lands are a constant battleground any time one of the local rulers gets ambitious.

'But never in that time has one ruler demanded of another an oath of fealty.'

Lowering his voice, Tal said, 'My master seeks stability. He sees a time when this region will come under the scrutiny of either the Isles or Kesh. Roldem's navy can protect the region from Kesh to a point, should they honour their treaties with Aranor and Olasko, but who can protect Roskalon, Miskalon, and Salmater from the Isles if they decide to march? Roldem might challenge a Keshian war fleet in the Sea of Kingdoms, but they will not land troops on the mainland to lend support against the Isles.'

'The Isles have never sought eastern expansion. Her eyes have ever been turned to the west.'

'But who can say that has not changed?' Tal lowered his voice even more. 'I do not say this lightly, but it is in all our interests that Salmater and Olasko remain good neighbours.' He glanced around. 'I would hate to see this lovely palace reduced to rubble.' As Pasko would say, Tal had just shown the mule the stick, now it was time to show him the carrot. 'My lord is very generous with his friends. He would appreciate any good work done by any member of the Privy Council in avoiding this war.'

Odeski looked as if he might say something, but he closed his mouth and remained silent for a moment. Then he said, 'I will caution reason to Their Highnesses.'

'I shall keep in mind your good works when I report to my master.'

'Good day, Squire,' said the First Minister, leaving.

Tal realized Amafi's reading of the older noble was correct. Odeski wouldn't blatantly betray his prince, but he would be willing to work on behalf of any peaceful settlement that kept him in his place of privilege.

And once the Princess was dead, the royal household would be in turmoil and the Prince would be as unable to govern as a chicken in a thunderstorm. Odeski would almost certainly take charge of the council and from that point on, Kaspar would have his way in Salmater.

*   *   *

Tal stood alone on the deck of the ship. He was four days out from Opardum and by his calculations, Princess Svetlana should be dead by now. The concocted poison Amafi had blended for him was one he claimed would not take the Princess's life for a full week after being administered, and would make it appear she had succumbed to heart problems. The beauty of the poison, said the former assassin, was that symptoms were misleading, looking like a fever, which would cause chirurgeons and healing priests to attempt cures that would avail them nothing. Death came swiftly, so unless a healing priest of great power intervened quickly, there was little chance of the Princess surviving.

It had proven easy enough to administer, as Amafi had said it would. While she slept, Tal took out a slender silken cord and a tiny vial of the poison. He had slowly dripped the poison, one drop at a time, down the cord onto the Princess's lips. As Amafi had predicted, she had licked them in her sleep and when she stirred, Tal paused. The poison had a sticky, sweet taste, and by the next morning what residue was left on her lips had been made harmless by being left to dry. Tal kissed her awake without fear. They had made love before dawn, Tal knowing that she was already dead by his hand.

Tal felt a stirring of remorse, and he pushed it down inside. Despite her charm, he knew Svetlana was as ruthless in her own way as Kaspar and that sex was but one of her many weapons, that her passion and the sweet things she whispered into his ear were meaningless, only part of the experience, and not to be taken seriously.

His mission was black and he had already given up his soul to pursue it. Like the scorpion, Kaspar's nature was betrayal, and eventually Tal would be betrayed, and then free from his

oath and able to strike at the man responsible for the obliteration of his people. Even if he should die while taking Kaspar's
life, he would have done his duty to his ancestors.

But before Kaspar, one other had to die: Captain Quint
Havrevulen, the man who personally oversaw the murder of Tal's
family. Yes, he would have to watch for an opportunity to destroy
the Captain before Kaspar. If he survived, if he killed Quint and
destroyed Kaspar, only then would Tal mourn the loss of his
own soul.

If he survived.

CHAPTER TEN

Discovery

*T*AL WAITED.

Kaspar sat back reading a message and at last put it down and smiled. 'Word just in from our agents in Micel's Station. Princess Svetlana was unexpectedly taken by a sudden fever that caused her heart to stop beating. Prince Janosh is beside himself with grief, and the Privy Council has declared him unfit to rule. Prince Serge has been named ruler, but as he is only a boy, Minister Odeski will rule as regent in his name until such time as he reaches his majority.' He put down the parchment. 'Brilliant, Tal. How did you achieve such a perfect resolution?'

Tal spoke calmly. 'My manservant, Amafi, knew of a particular poison that could be concocted from seemingly harmless ingredients – a few of them difficult to find – and visited several apothecaries in the city. He prepared the poison, and I found means of administering it the night before my departure. The Princess should have died in a week's time.'

'There is no clear connection between your visit and her death.' Kaspar positively beamed. 'My boy, I am very happy with your work. I expect we'll hear from the First Minister within days asking for some "clarification" or another on my last message so that he can try to negotiate his way out of my demand.'

Tal said, 'Will I return to Micel's Station?'

'No,' said Kaspar. 'My insistence on fealty will go away. I wanted Svetlana dead, though I will miss the old harridan.' He held up his hand, finger and thumb separated by only the tiniest margin. 'You know I came that close to being wed to her? My father thought it a good match, but I persuaded him otherwise. One of us would have killed the other.' Suddenly, Kaspar laughed and said, 'Well, one of us did!' He stood up. 'I reward excellence, Tal, and for this you are now a baron of my court. I'll have the patent drawn up and will find a useless piece of land to give you to go with the useless land you own in the Isles.

'But you will find other benefits awaiting you if you continue to serve me this well.'

'Thank you, Your Grace. I will always do my best.'

'Come, let us have some lunch and see what other mischief we can dream up for you.'

Tal followed Kaspar out to a balcony overlooking the harbour. The day was cold, as autumn was fully upon them, and both men wore heavy coats. Yet Tal found the chilly air invigorating as servants put food and wine on the table between them.

Kaspar motioned for the servants to withdraw, and when they were a discreet distance away, he said to Tal, 'I must say I was prepared to hear you had been arrested and executed, which would have given me an excuse to march down there and avenge you. Not that I needed an excuse, but you take my meaning.'

'Yes, Your Grace.'

'Now I can probably wring concessions out of Minister Odeski and save myself the bother of a war.'

Tal said, 'I was under the impression you wanted total subservience, Your Grace.'

'From Svetlana and her idiot husband, yes. If you failed in your mission. Remember, never rely on one plan, Tal. Always have two or more in place when you undertake something perilous. If the first one fails, go to the second plan. If the second plan fails, go to the third.'

'If the third plan fails, Your Grace?'

Kaspar laughed. 'Then run like hell if you're still alive.'

Tal laughed, though his heart wasn't in it.

Kaspar said, 'If I had gone to Svetlana with a reasonable demand, insisting Salmater stop working on behalf of my enemies, she would have insisted we talk and by the time I left, I would have a concession from her that Salmater would stop working for my enemies every other week.

'By demanding fealty and a complete surrender to my rule, I knew they'd be so busy wondering what madness had taken possession of me, they wouldn't give much thought to the possibility I had a different ambition.'

'To rid yourself of Princess Svetlana.'

Kaspar nodded. 'Yes, as much as I regret it. She's never had the resources to challenge me directly, Tal. She's always had to depend upon others to bolster her position. At various times she's acted in concert with Roldem, the Isles, and this time it was Miskalon. She really never forgave me for refusing to marry her.'

Tal sat back, his expression betraying his thoughts.

Kaspar said, 'Yes, a lot of what passed between Svetlana and me was over my refusal to take her as my wife. Not that she was in love with me, you understand.' He chuckled. 'We were two of a kind, in many ways: ambitious, remorseless, unrelenting. Had she been a man, I'd have taken her for my first general without hesitation, then watched my back. But as a wife . . .' He shrugged. 'She needed a puppet like Janosh to control. But her most recent intransigencies were beyond forgiveness. Working with Miskalon to take Olasko Gateway . . . that was too much. It was the first time she'd attempted to abet a direct attack on Olasko soil, and that I could not tolerate.' He slapped the table with a grin. 'But it is of no matter. She is gone, and soon I will have a new treaty with Salmater, and it might as well be Olasko's southern province by the time I'm done with them.' He sat back. 'Now I can turn my attention to other matters.'

Tal said nothing, merely sipping his wine and taking a small bite of food.

Kaspar did likewise, then after swallowing said, 'Do you discern any plan here, Tal? Any pattern that leads you to believe you understand what I'm trying to do?'

'In truth, Your Grace, I do not. I think there are some obvious things, such as securing your borders and making sure you're protected from potential enemies, but beyond that, nothing obvious.'

'Good, because you are a very astute young man, and if you see nothing obvious, then there is nothing obvious to see.

'Now, about your next undertaking. I want you to rest and enjoy your new rank for a week or so. Then, when I tell you, I wish you to voyage to Salador. I have a variety of errands and tasks for you in that city. But I want you established by the Midwinter Festival as a resident of that city.'

'That will be no difficulty, Your Grace. I have resided there before and can easily revive old friendships and establish myself again.'

'Good. Because Duke Varian Rodoski will be attending a festival hosted by the Duke of Salador. Do you know him?'

Tal said, 'I have seen him, and was briefly introduced to him once, but I do not claim to know him.'

'Do you know his importance to the throne of Roldem?'

'He is the King's cousin, and in line for the crown after . . . Prince Matthew?'

'And Prince Michael, Constantine, and the Princess. In short, he stands sixth in line of succession. So, he is among Roldem's most important dukes, if not among the more powerful.'

'So, Your Grace. I am in Salador and so is Duke Rodoski. What is your pleasure?'

'My pleasure, young Hawkins, is to see you leave Salador after the festival, while Duke Rodoski doesn't.'

'You wish him not to return to Roldem?'

'Yes, exactly.'

'And how long do you wish the Duke to remain in Salador, Your Grace?'

'For the rest of his life, my friend,' said Kaspar. 'As short as it may be.'

Tal said nothing for a moment, then said, 'I will see what I can do, Your Grace.'

'I know you will not displease me, Baron Talwin,' said the Duke with a cruel, thin smile.

Tal sat back and watched the distant harbour. The cold air caused his breath to steam as he exhaled: but for the first time since sitting down he felt the chill.

Tal sat at the table three seats away from Lady Natalia. With his elevation to the rank of court baron came his ascension to the Duke's head table at supper. To his immediate left sat another young baron, Evegeny Koldas, and between him and Natalia sat Captain Quint. Everyone had congratulated Tal on his new rank, though Tal could see Quint was only being polite. There was a distance between the two men that had existed from the moment they had met, and Tal did not know if it was caused by some sort of personal aversion, a rivalry for Natalia's attention, or a sense of Tal's ultimate hostility, however well masked it might be.

If fate permitted, Tal would see Quint and Kaspar dead, and then . . .

Tal had no idea what he would do after that, if he survived. He realized he was dwelling on that overly long when Evegeny Koldas said, 'Baron?'

'Sorry,' said Tal. 'I'm just a little overcome by His Grace's generosity, and my mind wandered. You were saying?'

'I was saying that should you have the time, I would enjoy taking you up the river, to the wilderness beyond the Broken Lands. Your reputation as a hunter makes me desire to see what I can learn from you.'

Tal judged Koldas a sincere sort, not given to empty flattery, so he smiled at the compliment. 'If time permits, I think I would enjoy that.'

The supper went on in typical fashion; Tal had grown used to the tempo of the court in the months he had been in residence. The Duke was an unusual ruler in so far as he didn't require his courtiers to be in constant attendance. A fair amount of Kaspar's time was spent in the company of Leso Varen, who almost never left his quarters, but on those rare occasions he did it was always in the Duke's company.

Tal watched closely on those occasions, and attempted to learn as much about the man as he could on behalf of the Conclave. He decided that his best choice at first was to be entirely passive in the matter. He never brought up Leso's name or asked about him. He merely listened if anyone else spoke of him.

After months in Opardum, Tal now began to think of Leso Varen as The Man Who Wasn't There. His name never came up in any context, save one: when the Duke was not around, occasionally someone would remark, 'He's up in Varen's suite.'

Tal was not in any hurry, but he was curious. He decided the day would come when he asked questions, but that day wasn't here yet.

Amafi had also been instructed to do likewise with the other servants in the citadel. To listen, but not to question. All he could discover was that twice a day a meal was left outside Varen's apartment door, and every week a pile of clothing to be laundered was left outside. No servant was permitted inside except on rare occasions, always at his request, and always involving a particularly repugnant task. One servant had been overheard to complain that if Leso Varen wanted another corpse dragged out of his quarters in the dead of night, he could bloody well do it himself, and another once remarked that whatever the black stains were on the walls of one of the rooms up there, they were nearly impossible to scrub off.

Tal instructed Amafi in his role of manservant and found him to be Pasko's rival in the common matters of the day. Tal's clothing was always clean, laid out impeccably, and his messages were delivered in a timely fashion. The man could blend into the background, despite his somewhat colourful choice of clothing upon occasions, and he remembered everything he saw and heard.

After supper, Natalia motioned to Tal to join her and whispered, 'Have you some time for me later?'

Tal nodded and replied in low tones, 'As much as you require, m'lady.'

With a smile, she accepted her brother's invitation to depart with him and over her shoulder said, 'I'll send word.'

Tal nodded. Captain Quint Havrevulen turned to Tal and said, 'Getting ambitious, Baron?'

Tal pretended not to take the Captain's meaning. 'Sir?'

'Just watch yourself, Baron. Our lady has many suitors and some of them do not abide competition well.'

'I am merely our lady's servant, sir,' Tal said, then with a smile and nod he turned and walked away.

Amafi fell into step beside his master and said, 'Our dear captain wants you dead, Magnificence.'

'Well, then, the feeling is reciprocated.'

They reached Tal's apartment and Amafi said, 'What is your pleasure, Magnificence?'

'Our master has no need for me, it seems, tonight.'

'Shall we go into the city?'

'No, tonight I wish to explore for a short while,' said Tal. 'Kaspar has no need for me later, but I suspect Natalia will, probably after the eleventh hour. So, I need to be back here should the call arrive.'

Amafi said, 'Magnificence, that's less than two hours away.'

'Should it come before I return, send word I am . . . bathing . . . have some hot water drawn, and I will be along shortly.' Tal quickly stripped off his ornate tunic and donned a plain one of dark grey. He went to the door and glanced out, looking quickly each way. 'I'll be back shortly,' he said.

When Amafi looked out a moment later, he saw that the corridor was now empty. 'Very good, Magnificence,' he said softly and then shut the door.

Tal moved quietly through the dim hallway. Every chance he had since the first day young Rudolph had guided him into the servants' network, he had explored on his own.

He had already discovered two cave networks, apparently unknown to the servants, that ran back into the cliff for miles. One ran downward, and Tal had ceased exploring due to time constraints. The other ran slightly upward, and ended at a loose fall of earth and stone, and Tal was convinced that with a little digging he might have found a way to the surface of the plateau above the citadel.

Now he was seeking a hidden entrance into Leso Varen's private apartments. He had unsuccessfully tried several hallways that ran parallel to the halls leading to that part of the citadel, and now he was exploring an old hallway above that. He had almost taken a punishing fall trying one of the other ladders to the upper levels, for as Rudolph had warned, the wood was old and rotten.

But he had found three sound ladders that took him to a series of halls higher than any other he had seen. They started in the distant wing of the citadel that was sealed off, and worked across the highest level of rooms. He had mentally mapped every room in the citadel he could see, and had a firm grasp on his location every step of the way.

He also knew he was running out of time and would have to be back to his quarters quickly. He came to a door.

Tal paused. If he judged direction and distance correctly, on the other side of this door would be a hallway, one that should lead within a hundred feet to some sort of servants' entrance to the hallway outside Leso Varen's private apartments. He inspected the door and as soon as he touched it, the hair on his neck and arms stood up.

There was a ward on the door. Even in this forgotten passage, the wizard had ensured his privacy. Tal quickly pulled away. He hoped that merely touching it hadn't alerted the spell-caster. He thought it improbable, since enough rats travelled these halls to make it likely he'd be up here checking to see if someone breached his privacy two or three times a week.

Tal decided to call it a night and return to his quarters. He took the shortest route back and after climbing down half a dozen ladders and travelling nearly half a mile of hallways, he cracked open the servants' door across from his own rooms. He peered out, saw the hall was empty, and quickly crossed the hall.

Letting himself into the apartment, he saw Amafi waiting. 'The Lady Natalia sent word.'

'How long ago?' asked Tal, stripping off his very dusty tunic.

'Ten minutes, perhaps. I said as you instructed that you were bathing and would be along shortly.'

Tal tore off his remaining clothes and climbed swiftly into the tub. 'I can't very well show up covered in dust.'

He washed rapidly and was drying himself with a large towel a minute later. Amafi tried to comb as much water as possible out of Tal's shoulder-length hair.

Still feeling slightly damp, Tal said, 'This will have to do,' and left the room.

He hurried along as best he could without drawing attention to himself. He reached the door to Lady Natalia's suite and knocked. The two guards on either side of the room ignored him, so he knew he was expected.

A servant girl opened the door and admitted him. As Tal stepped into the apartment, the girl exited through the same door, leaving him alone. He found his way to the door to Natalia's bedchamber and opened it.

'You bastard,' she said, sweetly. 'You kept me waiting.' She sat propped up by a mountain of pillows, covered to her shoulders by a snowy-white sheet. Her bare shoulders and neck were bathed by the light of a single candle, as she had chosen to pin up her long black hair.

'I was in my bath,' said Tal. He crossed the room and sat next to her.

She let the sheet drop as she reached out and pulled him towards her. 'Most men are not so fastidious.'

'Any complaints?' he asked just before she kissed him.

After a lingering, deep kiss, she said, 'No, though I will admit I like your smell – in moderation – better than the soap you use. I shall have to send some I found in Rodez that I like.'

'I'll be happy to use it.'

'Now, shut up and take off those clothes.'

'Yes, m'lady,' said Tal with a grin.

As morning came, with the sun lingering just below the eastern horizon, Natalia stirred as Tal tried to disentangle himself from her. She woke and clutched at him. 'Don't go.'

'I must. If your brother summons me, it would be better for everyone if the page found me in my quarters.'

'Oh, bother,' she said, pouting. At times Tal thought she really was a little girl.

As he dressed she lay on her back, staring at the canopy above the bed. 'I wish sometimes you were a prince or at least a powerful duke somewhere, Tal.'

'Why?'

'Because then my brother might consent to us marrying.'

Tal felt an unexpected stab in his stomach at those words. He turned and said, 'Natalia . . .'

She laughed. 'Don't look so panicstricken, Tal.' She rolled over and sat up, hugging a pillow in front of her. 'I'm not in love with you.' She narrowed her eyes. 'I don't know if I could be in love with anyone. I think it's been bred out of me. And I know you're not in love with me. I don't think either of us is that sort.

'But you are great fun. If I must be married to a man I don't love, it might as well be to one whom I enjoy. You know so many things and have done so much for a man of your few years. And I think you might be . . . I don't know, something special.'

'You flatter me, Natalia.'

'Yes, I do, but you deserve it. You are the youngest man ever to be named Champion of the Masters' Court – I had a clerk research it. The way you saved Kaspar from that bear. You speak many languages, know food and wine, and what else do you do? Play music?'

'Poorly,' Tal admitted as he pulled on his boots.

'What else?'

'I paint a little.'

'You *must* do my portrait!' she said with glee. 'See, you are so many things most of the men in my life are not. You are not dull. I am never bored when you are around. Oh, do something truly great, Talwin Hawkins, so my brother will have to consent to our marriage. Go conquer a country or overthrow a dynasty for Kaspar.'

Tal laughed. The girl's uncharacteristic romantic impulse amused him. 'Your brother might consent if I could lay a nation at his feet, but short of that, I suspect we must plan on going our separate ways in the future.'

As he made ready to stand up, she lunged forward and threw her arms around his shoulders. 'Not for a long time, Tal. I may not be able to love, but if I could, it is you I would love, deeply and with all my heart.'

For a brief, uncomfortable moment, Tal didn't know what to say. He had bedded many women in his time, but he didn't claim to understand them beyond that point. This was something he had never encountered: Natalia was unlike any woman he had known, and he wasn't sure if she was indulging herself in a fanciful moment, or if she were revealing a hint of something that lay buried deep within. He sought a facile way out of this uncomfortable moment and kissed her, then said, 'If a woman like you could love a man like me, deeply and with all her heart, that would be a truly remarkable thing. Even the gods would notice.'

She looked at him and grinned. 'Well said. Now, before you flee, tell me, did you sleep with Princess Svetlana before you killed her?'

Suddenly Tal knew that here was the other side of Natalia, the cold, calculating, vicious side. 'M'lady?'

Natalia laughed. 'Not to worry, Tal. Kaspar has told me little, but I know enough to see clues and draw conclusions. You may leave me now.'

Tal bowed and hurried out. The morning staff were busy in the citadel, hurrying about their business, less than an hour before the Duke's retinue would be up and asking for their morning meals.

He slipped into his own quarters and found Amafi already awake, with a change of clothing waiting should Tal require it. Tal motioned towards the tub. It was steaming, so Tal knew it had just been refilled. He smelled of Natalia and her perfume, and knew that would bring raised eyebrows should he get too close to the other members of the court today.

As he slipped into the water, he said to Amafi, 'Should I ever forget, please feel free to remind me that Natalia is every bit as dangerous in her own way as her brother.'

Amafi motioned for Tal to lean forward so he could scrub his master's back. 'No, Magnificence, she is *more* dangerous.'

Tal couldn't think of any reason to argue.

Tal looked up as Amafi came into the room. He was covered in what appeared to be blood. 'Gods, what happened?'

'Something extraordinary, Magnificence. Put on simple clothing, quickly.'

It was almost midnight and Tal had just returned from a late supper with Kaspar and some other members of the court. The meal had turned into an after-dinner bout of drinking and story-telling with no one but Natalia leaving the table for hours. She had excused herself, claiming fatigue, and with one quick glance had communicated her frustration to Tal. With an equally quick shrug and tilt of his head, he had responded that that there was nothing that could be done, and he would have to visit her some other time.

Tal changed into a tunic and leggins he wore for exercising in the marshalling yard.

'The boots will not do,' said Amafi.

'I have nothing plainer.'

'Then come barefoot.'

As Tal stood, Amafi came over with a handful of ashes from the fireplace. These he rubbed across Tal's face and into his hair. 'Magnificence, try to look like a lowly peasant, and perhaps we will both live through this night.' Then he rubbed some blood off his tunic and onto Tal's tunic and face.

Tal followed as the former assassin led him straight to the wing of the citadel used by Leso Varen. As he neared the wizard's quarters, what he saw would have caused him to falter, had he not had a strong stomach.

Servants, all of them ashen-faced and many trying not to be sick, were carrying bodies out of the wizard's apartment. Mixed among the servants were faces Tal did not recognize, perhaps workers from the city. Someone shouted, 'You two!' pointing at them. 'Fetch that tub in here and be quick about it.'

Tal and Amafi grabbed up a large wooden tub filled with water mixed with something caustic. Even breathing the fumes made Tal's eyes water. Turning his head to one side, he helped his manservant haul the tub into the wizard's apartment.

Leso Varen stood off to one side, studying a pile of parchments on a table before him. He would glance up every so often to watch the work, but his attention was focused on the writings.

The room they first entered was the very room in which Tal had been sworn to oath, and it was flanked by large doorways on either side. The doors on the left were open, and Tal and Amafi were directed to lug their burden into the adjoining room.

Tal set the tub down. For a moment he couldn't believe his eyes. He did not have the words to describe what he saw before him. The room was stone, without a tapestry or any other item of comfort to be seen. Shelves lined one wall, filled with books and scrolls. The wall opposite the door was adorned with a series of shackles hanging from chains, and from the abundance of blood splattered there and on the floor below them, it must be where the bodies had come from, Tal decided. The third wall revealed a solitary window. In front of that sat a small desk upon which a solitary inkwell and quill rested. To the immediate right of the door stood a large table covered with vials, jars, and boxes. The floor had a large drain in the middle, and blood was trickling towards it.

Tal didn't need to feel the hair on his arms and neck stand up to tell him that foul magic permeated this room. He remembered enough of his training from Sorcerer's Isle to have some idea of what was going on here. Dark spells of binding and powerful incantations designed to confound enemies, as well as many other arcane practices, all were made more puissant by human death and blood. This Leso Varen was a necromancer, a master of the magic of death, and he had undertaken some great spell recently. From the distracted expression he wore as he consulted his notes, Tal deduced things hadn't gone well for him.

Tal took up a brush and began scrubbing the floor, while Amafi worked on the walls. Tal used his task to memorize every detail he could about the place. He worked his way over towards the bookshelves, attempting to read titles if possible. Many of the volumes bore no lettering on the spines, while others revealed glyphs and markings he could not understand. But a dozen or more were readable, in the language of Kesh, Roldemish, the Isles, and a few other tongues he knew. He memorized them all, determined to make a copy of those titles against the day he reported back to the Conclave.

So intent was Tal on this that he almost didn't sense someone coming up behind him. As he lowered his head, he felt a hand upon his shoulder. He turned, keeping his eyes low in case it was someone who might recognize him, and saw a pair of bare feet below a long dress with a filthy hem. He glanced up and saw a young woman holding a fresh bucket of water. In heavily-accented Roldemish, she said, 'To clean.'

He nodded, stepped away and put his hand on the wall as his head swam. She didn't pay him a second glance as she threw the water on the floor, washing away the bloody mess and leaving a clean area behind.

He stood motionless as the girl walked away, taking the bucket to a larger tub of clean water. Amafi saw Tal standing and yanked hard on his sleeve. Whispering, he said, 'You're staring, Magnificence. Keep your head down!'

Tal returned to scrubbing, all thoughts of recording titles of books driven from his mind. The work went on for another hour and then he was ordered to carry the tub out of the room. Outside, he found a stairway leading down, and he and Amafi ducked down it. Halfway down a long corridor, he opened a hidden entrance to the servants' passages, and led Amafi back to their quarters. The tub from that day was still full, and Tal said, 'We'll both have to use it, then you will have to empty it by the bucket. We can't have anyone seeing all this blood.'

Amafi said, 'Magnificence, what happened back there? You looked as if you had seen a ghost.'

Tal looked up. 'Almost, Amafi. Almost.' He pulled off his blood-soaked tunic and tossed it to his servant. 'Burn these,' he instructed, taking off his filthy trousers. He sat in the tub and closed his eyes. But the face of the young woman hung in his mind's eye like a portrait burned into his memory. Every hair on her head, the smudges on her cheek, and the marks on her face – bruises, some old, some new.

But he remembered her in a time when her face was dusted with freckles by the sun, and her honey-coloured eyes narrowed as she regarded him in a way that made him want to die. He ducked his head under the water and washed his hair. As he came up spluttering, he covered his face with his hands, for he *had* seen a ghost. He knew that tall, slender body. He had seen her run with the other girls at Village Kulaam, back when Talwin Hawkins had been named *Kielianapuna* – Little Red Squirrel – and she had been called Eye of the Blue-Winged Teal.

Amafi came and said, 'What is it, Magnificence?'

Tal felt the urge to shout, *I am not the last of my kind*, but knew to do so would mean telling Amafi more than he wished to share with the former assassin. Finally he said, 'That girl, in Leso Varen's room, with the blonde hair.'

'Yes, Magnificence?'

'She . . . put me in mind of someone I have not seen for years.'

'Ah,' said Amafi, as he began peeling off his blood-stained clothing. 'A startling resemblance.'

'Very startling.'

They exchanged places and Tal dried off with a towel. As he got ready for bed – knowing that sleep would probably not come – he said, 'Tomorrow, while the Duke gives me my final instructions before we leave for Salador, I want you to find out what you can about who those people were who came to clear away the bodies. It must be someone the housecarl trusts to keep silent. Find out what you can.'

'About the girl?'

Tal considered. 'Not yet. For the time being, just find out where she is, and who her master is.'

'Yes, Magnificence.'

Tal sat in front of the fireplace, trying to get warm, and discovered it took far longer than it should have done.

• CHAPTER ELEVEN •

Salador

*T*HE CARRIAGE ROLLED DOWN the street.

Tal and Amafi were heading to a house that had been rented through one of Kaspar's agents in Salador. He was not acting in any official capacity for the Duke on this journey. There were no envoys, no diplomatic tasks, no representing Olasko in the palace of the Duke of Salador. No one was to know he was Kaspar's agent, or of his installation as a court baron of Olasko. To everyone in Salador, he would continue to be Squire Tal Hawkins, returning to a city he had resided in years ago.

He had a plan, and he knew what was expected of him, and what his fate would be if caught, or if he failed. Still, he forced himself to re-examine the plan again, for he always felt as if somehow he was missing something. For the first time since taking Kaspar's service, he felt uncertainty. Tal knew every detail of his plan, yet he was constantly distracted.

And he had been since the night he had seen Eye of the Blue-Winged Teal in the citadel.

Amafi had discovered only a little, that a trader named Bowart was the man called upon to occasionally haul away the dead from the citadel. He disposed of the bodies and no one knew where. Amafi also discovered that he ran a gang of knackers, men who carried away dead animals, horses and cattle for the most part, that had died in traces or in the field. It was rumoured he also had connections to the slave trade down in Kesh, and smugglers down in the southern islands.

If Eye of the Blue-Winged Teal had been sold to him by the raiders in Raven's party, then there might be others who had also survived. Tal understood why Eye of the Blue-Winged Teal might have been spared; she was a striking girl of rare beauty. He also understood why she might be reduced to the most menial service, for while she might survive rape, she would fight with every bit of strength she possessed, as would any woman of the Orosini, and she would never submit to working in a brothel. A slaver who had purchased her from Raven's gang for that reason would be sadly disappointed.

The frustration of knowing she, and possibly others, had survived turned Tal's world on its ear. Since the day of the raid he had assumed he was the last of his people, for no word of any other Orosini had reached Kendrick's or any other place he had visited in the region. That would make sense if whoever survived had been immediately marched back to Olasko after the raids. But Tal had no way of knowing that, and he had based his entire existence since then on the notion that no one else among his people had lived past that day. No one to care about. No one to live for.

His course was clear, but for the first time since taking the road of vengeance he now had a reason to live. Until the moment he saw Eye of the Blue-Winged Teal, he didn't care if he survived as long as he avenged his people. Now he *must* survive. He must destroy Captain Havrevulen and Duke Kaspar, and survive so he could find Eye of the Blue-Winged Teal and find any others who might have survived, and perhaps, some day, return to the mountains of home and rekindle the spark of the Orosini, no matter how faintly.

Amafi sensed a change in Tal, and on several occasions had asked his master if something was amiss. Tal had deflected the questions with vague answers that he was concerned with Kaspar's orders.

Tal constantly reminded himself that no matter what had changed, one thing remained constant; to survive, he must do Kaspar's bidding until such time as Kaspar could be destroyed, and until then, Tal must be his loyal servant.

The carriage reached the house Tal was renting and a footman opened its door. Tal exited with Amafi behind him, and Tal walked up to the house and knocked on the door.

A girl opened it and said, 'Yes, sir?'

'I am Squire Hawkins.'

She stepped aside. 'Welcome to your home, Squire. I am Magary.'

As he entered, Tal said, 'My manservant is Amafi. He will be major domo. Who else is here?'

'The cook, sir. Well, he's not here, but he's on the staff. He is at the market; we just got word of your arrival yesterday from the owners of the house. I can make tea, if you care for some.'

'That will be fine. Anyone else?'

'No one else, sir. When the house is not occupied, I keep it clean and Lucien cooks for the two of us. We never know quite what is needed until the tenant arrives.'

Tal could see a drawing room in front and a hall which no doubt led to the kitchen. Another room's door could be seen on the right side of the hall, behind the drawing room. Tal asked, 'What's in there?'

'The pantry, sir.'

'No dining room?'

'Upstairs, sir. It's a bit of an odd house, but it's a nice enough place, once you're used to it.'

Tal nodded. 'I'll be upstairs. Have Amafi bring up our luggage, then bring the tea.'

Tal went exploring. Within the space of a few minutes he found the girl's description apt. The small house had a lovely view of the central square of the city, directly across from the road that led up to the Duke of Salador's castle. At the front of the upper floor, his dining room had two floor-to-ceiling windows which commanded that view. There were two bedrooms on the floor above, one slightly larger than the other. As he examined what would be his room, Tal realized why this house had been picked by Kaspar's agent in Salador. It had one unique quality: a small, inconspicuous door that led out to a tiny sitting area on the roof, a little deck surrounded by a low iron fence. It overlooked the city in the opposite direction from the Duke's castle, affording a clear view of the city rolling down to the harbour. There was a single tiny table and a pair of chairs. While in the shadow in late afternoon, during the summer it would be a lovely place to take a glass of wine at sunset.

It also would be a lovely way to slip in and out of the house without being seen. Tal went to the edge of the tiny deck and looked down. The wrought iron fence was primarily there to keep someone from inadvertently stepping off. On the bottom of the fence, a series of very sharp spikes pointed downward, probably to keep curious thieves from climbing up and entering through the door. Tal had no doubt that a determined thief could easily circumnavigate the hazard, but he would be more likely to find an easier target than bother, especially if the local thieves knew the house was rented, which meant it contained nothing worth stealing most of the time.

But what intrigued Tal was how easy it would be to get across the narrow alley below to the house opposite, one which appeared conveniently abandoned, if the broken windows were any indication. A stout board of sufficient length and no fear of heights were all that was needed.

Tal would have Amafi look around for such a board, or secure one from a supplier of lumber.

He went back inside to find Amafi unpacking. 'Is the house sufficient to your needs, Magnificence?'

'Yes.'

'It has no tub, and the jakes are downstairs to the rear. But they've left a very nice pot for night soils.'

Tal shrugged. He had got used to having a copious bathing tub in the room at Kaspar's citadel, but his home in Roldem had had only a tiny tub. That one was so small he had to sit with knees up to his chin in order to bathe and it didn't hold enough water to stay hot for more than a few minutes.

'Find out where the nearest acceptable bathhouse is. I know a few closer to the harbour, from when I lived here before.' For a moment he remembered his time in Salador, with Caleb and Pasko, perhaps the happiest time in his life after the destruction of his village. Perhaps some time in the next week he might revisit a few of their old haunts.

There was one gambling house he particularly liked, down by the fish market, which was a little rough compared to the others, but a friendly, honestly-run place where he and Caleb had spent quite a few nights.

He wondered what Caleb was doing. And the others, Robert de Lyses, Pasko, Magnus, Pug and Miranda ... everyone who had taken a near-dead boy from the Orosini mountains and turned him into what he was today, Baron of the Court Talwin Hawkins, anointed greatest swordsman in the world, culinary and wine aficionado, musician, painter, linguist, dancer, and dandy. Bitterly he thought, *and add to that list liar, spy and assassin. And servant of his most hated enemy.*

Then he reflected, did he truly hate Kaspar? He hated Kaspar and Captain Havrevulen for what they had done. The Captain he felt no affinity for; given the type of man he was, he did little to earn affection. And his obvious jealousy over Lady Natalia's preference for Tal's company kept things cold between the two men. But Kaspar, Kaspar was a different matter.

Kaspar had qualities Tal found attractive; he was brilliant, with perhaps the most complex mind Tal had ever encountered. He had an unusual sense of humour and often took delight in the most mundane and trivial details of life. He was ruthless and without scruple, yet he was caring and generous to those who served him.

Tal would destroy Kaspar without hesitation, revenging the wrong done his people, but he now wondered how Kaspar had come to be this dangerous, ambitious man. Not for the first time, Tal wondered where Kaspar's crimes ended and Leso Varen's influence began.

Tal decided it was time to send a message to the Conclave. He found his writing instruments, in a leather carrying-pouch, set out by Amafi on the table in his bedroom. He unrolled a piece of silken paper, very expensive, but durable and nearly impervious to water once the indelible ink had dried. He recorded on it what he had seen at the citadel, with as much detail as possible. He recounted every recognizable item on Varen's table, drew what he could remember of symbols he had seen, and listed the titles he recalled of the volumes on the bookshelves. He spent a short paragraph speculating on what influence Varen had over Kaspar. He kept the names of Varen and Kaspar out of the message, referring to them only as 'the magician' and 'the nobleman', and at the end, he signed it simply 'Talon'.

He folded the paper, sealed it with wax, but did not impress it with his ring. Then he addressed it to *The Squire of Forest Deep*. When Amafi returned, he informed Tal of a nearby bathhouse of sufficient quality to warrant Tal's patronage. Tal gave him the message, asking if he knew his way to the Cask and Vine. Amafi knew of the place, and Tal instructed him to go there and deliver the message to the owner without comment or waiting for a response, then to meet him at the bathhouse with a full change of clothing.

Amafi ran off and Tal went downstairs to interview Magary and the cook, who had returned from the market. Tal said, 'You must be Lucien.'

The cook was a young man, just a few years older than the

girl by the look of him, and was trying to look confident. 'Yes, sir.'

'Well, you're going to have an easy time of things, I think. I don't dine at home much, and I rarely entertain. So, mostly you'll be cooking in the mornings, and perhaps making up a meal at midday.'

'Very good, Squire.'

Tal detected an accent. 'Where are you from?'

'Bas-Tyra, originally, sir. A small town called Genoui, not too far from the city.'

'Ah,' said Tal with delight. 'The food of Bas-Tyra is famous. What are your specialities?'

Lucien launched into a list of dishes he favoured, and Tal interrupted to ask him how he prepared one in particular. As Lucien started to describe the preparation, Tal asked questions, often offering alternative spices or herbs, and quickly the cook seemed to light up. 'You know your food, sir.'

'I worked in a kitchen, once,' said Tal noncommittally. 'I am not what you would call a rich squire,' he said when Lucien and Magary looked at him in surprise. Tal laughed. 'Poor squires have to eat, too.'

He saw the way glances passed between them, so then he asked, 'Are you married?'

Magary was a pale girl with light brown hair, but her colour changed to a deep red as she blushed. 'No, sir . . . not yet, but we would like to some day.'

'I'll tell you what,' said Tal. 'I was planning on dining out tonight, and for social reasons I must, but tomorrow why don't you prepare some of your specialities? I don't care if you make too much for me to eat – you two and Amafi can finish off what

I don't try, but I would like to see if you cook as well as you talk about cooking.'

'You won't be disappointed, sir.'

Tal said, 'Well, I'm off for a bath and massage. I'll expect to eat an hour after first light . . . wait, make that two hours. It may be a late night. By the way, where are your sleeping quarters?'

'In the basement, sir. We have a tiny room we share, and there's a bed for your manservant there, as well.'

'That won't be necessary. He's also my bodyguard and will sleep in the small room upstairs next to mine. You can keep your privacy.'

Magary looked relieved and Lucien positively beamed. 'Yes, Squire!'

Tal left the house and started his walk to the bathhouse. Looking around the city, he realized that he had missed Salador. *What is becoming of me?* he wondered. *I am not sentimental by nature, yet now I feel as if I've come back to a place that's dear to me.*

Then he realized the place wasn't dear to him, it was the memory of the time he had spent here that was dear. He and Caleb had studied together, got drunk together, and even whored together. He had learned about wine, food, and the arts in Salador. He had learned to play music and to dance, to paint, and had learned how to be charming and seduce women of quality. It had been the only time he had felt free of the dark urgency that was revenge, and he had not thought about his future, living only in the moment.

Now he found he missed Caleb, and he longed to save Eye of the Blue-Winged Teal. And most surprising of all, he found he missed Natalia.

*   *   *

The meal was stupendous. He looked up at Lucien and said, 'I've had better meals.' The cook's face started to sag a little, but then Tal said, 'But not many. You do honour to your craft.'

'Thank you, Squire.'

Tal considered. He knew his tenure in Salador would be brief, despite the fact they were making it appear as if he was settling in. The weather was turning cold and soon people would begin preparing for the Midwinter's Festival. Duke Rodoski would be in the city in slightly more than a month. But he would like to do something to help this young couple.

'What are your long-term plans, Lucien?'

The young man shrugged. 'Plans, sir? I don't know. I am rather fortunate to have this employment. There are more cooks than jobs in Salador these days. It would be nice to have steady work with someone who took advantage of my ability, sir, such as yourself,' he finished up in a rush.

Tal laughed. 'Have you thought of perhaps finding someone to back you in establishing your own place?'

'A tavern?'

'In Roldem, private dining clubs are all the rage.' Tal described Dawson's, the Metropol, and a few others. 'The very best cooks, or what you in Bas-Tyra would call *gran chefs*, are men of stature, and very rich.'

Magary, who had been looking on, said, 'Oh, sir, that would be a wonderful thing.'

'I'll be doing some entertaining. Let me see if I might find you a backer.'

'Sir, that would be . . . beyond imagining,' said Lucien.

'Well, just keep cooking like this and we'll both be happy.' Tal pushed himself away from the table. 'But I will say the pudding could have used a touch more ginger.'

Lucien seemed ready to argue, but he caught himself in time. 'Perhaps you're right, Squire.'

Tal laughed. 'The pudding was just fine. I was seeing if you could keep your mouth shut. Arguing with chefs is like trying to hold back the tide.'

Lucien and Magary both laughed and looked embarrassed.

Tal said, 'That will be all for tonight.' To Amafi, who had stood at his shoulder throughout the meal, he said, 'Grab a bite for yourself. It's quite good. Then meet me down at the club called Ruthia's Palace. It's time for Salador to remember me.'

He had dined at a small tavern the night before, and gambled at an establishment close to the city square, but in neither place had he seen one person he knew from his previous tenure in Salador. He had introduced himself to the owners of both establishments, ensuring word of his return would eventually spread, but he decided he needed a more dramatic return. Ruthia's Palace was the most popular gaming hall in the city, and he was well known there.

'Yes, Magnificence. I will follow as soon as I have eaten.'

Tal headed out into the night, and the entire way to the gambling hall he wrestled with his emotions. Since that night in the citadel, everything had changed. Now, he felt as if he had somehow been trapped within a box, made of thoughts, feelings, and not of wood, but confining nevertheless.

He felt constantly on the verge of anger, so strong was his desire to walk away from what had become his reason for existence, the desire to revenge his people. Now he suddenly felt ensnared, caught by forces pulling him this way, then that. He ached for a moment at the thought of Eye of the Blue-Winged Teal suffering one more day of hardship, and he longed for the simple joy a man like Lucien had at being told his work was good.

He stopped, leaning against the wall by a miller's shop, shuttered for the night, and felt as if he couldn't take another step. The pit of his stomach seemed to drop away, and his chest constricted. Suddenly, without warning, he wept. Pain he thought long forgotten came welling up from somewhere deep within; then anger at what the gods had visited upon him, then sadness, for all he had lost. For nearly half an hour he stayed at this quiet place, ignoring the occasional passer-by who cast him a glance, thinking him intoxicated, or perhaps mad.

Then he recognized the trap his own mind was setting for him. This way lay only destruction, he reminded himself. He could not leave Kaspar's service, nor recant his oath. He could only endure until such time as he was free, or he could die. But to survive while in Kaspar's service he must be as immovable as a mountain, as cold as ice, as hard as steel. Emotions could destroy him faster than the most dangerous swordsman.

He looked up, seeing a few stars peering from behind clouds as they swept along the coastline. He felt the breeze off the harbour and its cold bite reminded him: he was only as weak as he let himself become. His feelings of sadness, anger and remorse were all honestly earned, paid for with the blood of others, and he need not apologize to anyone, least of all himself for them. But they could not be embraced. They must be acknowledged, then let go, for to cling to them, to keep them alive in his heart, would be to doom himself and make meaningless everything he had done so far.

If he survived, and if he destroyed Kaspar, then he could wonder at what fate the gods would have for him for his dark deeds. If he survived, perhaps then he could find Eye of the Blue-Winged Teal and free her from her captivity. If he survived, perhaps he could find a true home in one of these cities he had known. If he survived, perhaps he could finance an eating establishment, with a young chef like Lucien. Perhaps he could find love again. Perhaps some day he could be a husband and father. If he survived.

He took a deep breath and drew himself upright. He must never let his feelings overwhelm him again in such a way. It was only through the kindness of fate it happened in so benign a spot. In the citadel or in any number of other places, it would have meant his death.

Step by step, he resolved to grow stronger, to use every mental discipline he had learned to protect himself, from himself. Remorse, anger, fear and hate would only undo him, and he must remember that always.

By the time he reached Ruthia's Palace, he was back within himself, strong and ready, and had vowed that never again would he betray himself.

Ruthia, the Goddess of Luck, favoured Tal again. He put down his cards with a smile and said, 'All cups, gentlemen.'

Five cards of the same suit was the best hand at the table, and Tal gathered in the gold coins on the table, while the other five players threw down their cards. Squire John Mowbry of the Duke of Salador's court was a young man, perhaps no more than seventeen or eighteen years of age. He shook his head and said,

'You must be an honourable man, Squire Hawkins, for with luck like yours, who needs to cheat?'

Suddenly those at the table went silent. Realizing he had come close to deadly insult, the young squire said, 'Apologies, sir. I was merely making a jest. Apparently a bad one.'

Tal glanced at the boy and smiled. 'Not that bad, really,' he said, then he laughed. 'Actually, now that I think of it, quite good.'

He passed the cards to the young man. 'But you win the deal.'

The young squire, obviously relieved that no insult had been taken, shuffled the cards.

'How long are you with us, Squire Hawkins?' asked a trader named Ruben of Ravensburgh.

Tal shrugged. 'Indefinitely. I have travelled and find I like Salador very much. I studied here some years ago and enjoyed my stay. I am at liberty presently and decided to return here to see what the future holds.'

Another man, an officer in the Duke's guard named Dumont, laughed and said, 'And getting out of Roldem must have been good for your health.' He had been one of Tal's regular gambling opponents when he had lived in Salador; he was, if not a friend, then an amiable acquaintance.

Tal feigned a wince at the remark, but then smiled and said, 'There is that.'

Squire John's expression as he dealt the cards indicated that he didn't understand, and Dumont said, 'Our friend here managed to publicly humiliate Prince Matthew of Roldem in such a way that it was unlikely he'd ever be invited back to the palace for a gala.'

'Really?' said another man at the table, a shipper named Vestla. 'Tell us about it.'

Tal picked up his cards, looked at them, then threw down his hand. 'Nothing to draw to.' He sat back and said, 'I'd rather not.'

Dumont said, 'What I heard was that our friend reduced the Prince to tears in public on the floor of the Masters' Court. Literally spanked him with the flat of his sword, he did.'

The men at the table laughed and Dumont added, 'I've met the Prince, once, and I'll wager not a few of those watching were silently saying "bravo" to you, Squire, for humbling that lout.'

Tal shrugged. 'I've been travelling. What's the news?'

The others laughed as they made their bets. Dumont said, 'Well, enough. We'll drop the story of your bout with the Prince. As for news, not much. Old Duke Duncan rules wisely. His son Laurie is a chap who is well regarded by all, and will be a good ruler in his own right some day. We are at peace with Great Kesh, and last time I heard, the Western Realm was quiet, so it is a time for soldiers like myself to grow lazy and fat.' He put down his cards and said, 'Three nines.'

No one could beat the hand, so Dumont pulled in the coins. 'Oh, and Duke Rodoski of Roldem will be visiting for the Midwinter's Festival.'

Tal feigned surprise. 'Varian's coming to visit the Duke?'

'An old friend?' asked Ruben.

'An acquaintance, from the Masters' Court.'

'Given your contretemps in Roldem with the Prince,' said Dumont, 'don't expect to be invited to the Duke's gala.'

'I wouldn't, normally,' said Tal as the cards were dealt again.

'Don't underestimate yourself, Tal,' said Dumont. 'When last we met you were merely a minor squire from the west. *Very* minor,' he added, and the others laughed. 'But now you are

Champion of the Masters' Court, and that is no mean thing.'

Tal picked up his cards and organized them. The bet was made and he replaced two of them. 'Well, perhaps some other time I'll earn the pleasure of an introduction to His Grace, Duke Duncan, but for the moment, I'm content to spend Midwinter's Day crawling from one tavern to the next in search of a convivial wench or two.'

The others laughed. 'Well said.' Tal won the hand, and Dumont declared, 'I must get back to the castle. I have duty in the morning.' He glanced at Squire John.

The boy rose, saying, 'I as well. Good night, gentlemen.'

Tal turned to the other three men. 'Shall we continue?'

Ruben stood up. 'I've lost enough for one night, Tal. It was good to meet you.'

The other players also left, and Tal rose. There was another game in the corner, with an open chair, but he felt he had played enough cards for the night. There were other games as well, dice and the wheel, but he felt he couldn't raise the enthusiasm for them. The goal of his visit had been achieved; while Dumont might mention him to only a few at the Duke's castle, young Squire John was almost certain to tell everyone he had gambled with the Champion of the Masters' Court.

Tal had drunk little that night, sipping at his drink and watching other players succumb to drunkenness. But he felt the need for one more before leaving. He glanced to the far corner of the room where Amafi stood silently, holding the same flagon of ale he had nursed throughout the night. Tal had insisted that when he was gambling, the bodyguard should keep his distance. Tal needed to know who watched him, and Amafi was his second set of eyes.

Tal ordered a brandy and sipped it. The pungent, bittersweet liquor warmed as it went down. As he stood silently, he felt the dark emotions that had overwhelmed him earlier that night rise up again, and he used every mental trick taught him at Sorcerer's Isle to fend them off. Then he pushed away his unfinished brandy and went to the door.

Outside, he glanced around and judged that it was six hours or less to dawn. He walked slowly, waiting for Amafi to catch up with him.

He heard footsteps approaching rapidly from behind and turned. But instead of his manservant, he saw a figure in black clothing leaping at him, dagger drawn.

Tal's almost unnatural reflexes were all that saved him. He stepped aside just enough for the blade to miss, and he was borne down to the ground, grappling with his assailant.

Tal gripped the man's right hand with his left, while he reached down to his own belt. The man's body kept Tal from reaching his dagger, so Tal reached up and clawed at the man's eyes.

The man pulled his head back, grunting in pain, then suddenly he stiffened and his eyes rolled up into his head and he went limp.

Tal saw Amafi standing above the now-dead assassin. Amafi used the man's cloak to wipe his blade clean and asked, 'Magnificence, are you all right?'

'Fine, but feeling like a fool. I heard him behind me and assumed it was you.'

'I saw him leave an unfinished drink at the gambling hall, Magnificence, as soon as you did, so I knew he was up to no good.'

Tal knelt by the man and examined him. He was slender, with

unremarkable features, wearing a black tunic, grey trousers and cloak. He carried nothing to identify him; no purse and no jewellery, just a sword and dagger.

'Who was he?' wondered Amafi.

Tal motioned for his manservant to accompany him. 'Let us away before someone else comes by. I do not want to spend the night talking to the Sheriff of Salador.'

As they turned a corner and hurried away, Tal said, 'The important question isn't who he was, but rather, who sent him.'

Amafi said, 'You have enemies, Magnificence.'

Tal nodded. 'I do.'

They hurried back to the house, and every step of the way Tal realized he was feeling something new. He was feeling what it was like to be hunted.

• CHAPTER TWELVE •

Betrayal

*T*AL LUNGED.

He struck his opponent easily, and the crowd in the gallery applauded. He saluted his opponent and then the Master of the Floor.

The House of Blades was a modest establishment compared to the Masters' Court in Roldem. Instead of dominating an entire city block, it was a single building of some size, but it lacked the complex of rooms, had no bath, and offered few of the amenities seen in Roldem. It was not subsidized by the King of the Isles or the Duke of Salador, but rather had come about as a private club for noblemen seeking to hone their skills. While frontier nobles and garrison soldiers had ample opportunity to train under the watchful eye of a swordmaster, those nobles of the court in cities such as Salador were often left to their own devices when it came to the art of the blade. Membership was not inexpensive, but Tal, as Champion of the Masters' Court, had been invited as a guest, and granted full privileges as long as he resided in Salador. It was a canny move, Tal conceded to Amafi when he got the invitation, for his attendance sparked a renewed interest in membership among the younger nobles and sons of wealthy commoners.

And as had been the case in Roldem, many daughters of wealthy families and young girls of noble birth now found watching duelling practice to be a fascinating pastime. His first visit to Salador, while mastering the role of squire, Tal had been merely a young noble of promise. Now he was famous, or infamous if the story of his affront to Prince Matthew was known, and the dashing young squire from the west was considered among the more eligible of the young courtiers in the city.

He had made his one obligatory journey to the Duke's castle, a relic of ancient days, large and draughty, despite many attempts to refurbish and modernize the place. The present Duke, Duncan, a distant cousin to the King, was a bright-eyed man in his late sixties, who welcomed the young squire to the city and offered him any help he might need, all the while communicating that it would be in poor taste for Tal to ask for anything.

The Duke's son, Laurie, stood next to his father, quietly amused by the entire affair. Tal had caught a glimpse of the young man on a couple of occasions. Unlike some noble sons, he didn't appear to waste his time and energy on too much drinking, women, or gambling. On one occasion, Laurie had been escorting a young woman of unusual beauty – later, Tal had discovered she was the daughter of a nobleman in service to the Duke of Krondor – and the other time, he had been quietly gambling for modest stakes at one of the better establishments in the city, again with the same young woman at his side. The young lady was rumoured to become the next Duchess of Salador. Tal had never seen Laurie touch a drink besides water. City gossip labelled the next Duke of Salador a modest young man of quick wit, ample skills, and a steady nature. The only remarkable quality he possessed was an unusual gift for music, as he played several instruments and sang with a strong, pleasant voice, talents inherited from his great-grandfather, according to city lore.

Tal wished that circumstances permitted him a better chance for acquainting himself with the young man, but it seemed unlikely. Laurie appeared the sort who would steer clear of notorious acquaintanceships.

Tal crossed to where Amafi waited with a towel and clean tunic, and said, 'Well done, Magnificence.'

'Thank you, Amafi.'

It had been almost a month since the attack outside Ruthia's Palace, and so far there had been no repeat of the attempt. Amafi had some contacts in the city and had tried to discover the name of the assailant which might lead to discovering who paid him. So far, he had discovered nothing.

Tal's life since then had been a constant cycle of working out at the House of Blades, dining at the better establishments in the city – though he ate at home often, given Lucien's talent – accepting invitations to various social gatherings and festivities, gambling, and spending time with a variety of charming ladies of rank.

As he paused to consider what to do next, leave for the day or try one more bout, a stir in the crowd heralded the arrival of someone else of note. Tal watched with interest as half a dozen ducal guards entered, followed by a retinue of courtiers, then Duke Varian Rodoski. For a brief instant, Tal felt self-conscious. He had considered the possibility that the Duke and he would encounter one another, but had not anticipated it might be in such a similar location to the scene of where Tal had humiliated the Duke's cousin, Prince Matthew.

The Duke was a young man, no more than thirty-five years of age, and darkly handsome; he had reputedly been quite the rogue with the ladies until his marriage to a noble woman of Kesh seven years ago. An unfortunate riding accident had widowed the Duke two years previously and he genuinely mourned the loss of his wife. Now, according to gossip, his only vice was an occasional gambling binge, wagering on horses or watching Guild League Football. Otherwise he was a devoted father to his two children, a daughter of six and a son of four years. He was dressed for swordwork, wearing the traditional heavily-padded jacket, tight leggings and slippers, and he was carrying a rapier. At his side a servant held his duelling helm, a metal basket protected the face and neck from accidental cuts.

The Duke caught sight of Tal and nodded, then as if thinking of something, he walked towards him. When he was a short distance away, he stuck out his hand in greeting. 'Squire. It's been a while.'

Tal was taken off guard, but after a moment's hesitation, he took the Duke's hand, bowing slightly. 'Your Grace. Yes, it has.'

The Duke had a face that looked untouched by guile or pretence. He leaned over to whisper, 'You know, not everyone in the family was angered by how you humbled Matthew. The only thing I wonder was why someone didn't do it sooner. He can be an unbearable prig one minute, and an excruciating bore the next. He's as annoying as a fly in the pudding. Did him good to have his bottom thumped. His mother should have done so years ago.' Then he paused, and smiled at Tal. 'Sir, would you care to engage me in a bout?'

Tal smiled back. 'You're serious, Your Grace?'

'As serious as a kick in the rump, Squire.'

Tal nodded, grinning. 'It will be my honour, Your Grace.'

The Duke said, 'Just don't thump me the way you did Matthew, and we'll get on famously.'

'My word, Your Grace,' said Tal.

They took to the floor and the crowd immediately started a low buzz of conversation. The two men squared off and the Master of the Floor said, 'Gentlemen, first to three touches.'

The match was almost predictable, given that Tal was a vastly superior swordsman to the Duke. But he refused to take several openings, and allowed the Duke to work on his technique. At last, the match was over and the Duke said, 'Well done, Squire. Your generosity is most appreciated.'

As they walked to where servants waited to help them off with their padded jackets and provide towels, Tal answered, 'My pleasure, Your Grace. Besides the fact that I regret my intemperate outburst with your cousin, you are an experienced swordsman. Should your duties in office not have put such excessive demands on your time, I suspect you might have been one of the better opponents I would have faced at the Masters' Court.'

'You're too kind, sir. I entered once, when I was young, and was ceded the thirty-second place,' said the Duke, as he towelled himself off. 'That was due to rank, I'm afraid, and they did me no service. I was humbled quickly by the first opponent

I faced. I think it would have been better to let me struggle in the earlier, open competition.'

'It is a better way to learn than being quickly ousted,' agreed Tal as he handed his towel back to Amafi.

'If you are not hurrying off, perhaps you'd join me for a cup of wine across the street, Squire. There's something I wish to discuss with you.'

Tal looked at Amafi and said, 'Fetch my clothing.' To the Duke he said, 'My honour, Your Grace.'

'Say half an hour?'

'I will be there.'

Tal changed and found his way across the street to an inn called the Cutting Edge. It was a favourite of many of those who were members of the House of Blades. He found a private room in the rear had been secured for the Duke's use, and had been there only a few minutes when Duke Varian arrived.

The Duke made small-talk while the wine was served, then sent his servants outside. He inclined his head towards Amafi, and Tal nodded to Amafi that he was to wait outside, as well.

When they were alone, Duke Rodoski said, 'So, did Kaspar send you here to kill me, Squire?'

Tal kept his face immobile, then feigned shock. 'Your Grace, is this some sort of dark jest?'

'Hardly,' said Rodoski. He sipped his wine. 'Don't be so confoundedly proud of yourself, Talwin. Your master is not the only one with agents crawling over every port and city of significance in the region. Roldem has arrangements with several other nations to share information when it's mutually beneficial. Your visit with Prince Janosh was just a little too timely relative to the demise of Princess Svetlana. I'm not sure how you did it, but . . .' He shrugged. 'While I had no enmity with her, I also don't particularly miss her.'

'Why in the world would you presume I had a hand in it?'

'Because it is exactly Kaspar's style, Squire. And because I know what Kaspar is really up to, and I suspect you do not.'

Tal sat back, interested. He had studied Kaspar's ambition and most of what he did made little sense in terms of a larger picture. The assassination of Princess Svetlana did make sense from a tactical point of view, since it secured a stable border for Kaspar as he turned his attentions elsewhere, but why Kaspar wanted Rodoski dead still made no sense to Tal.

'Let me draw you a map,' said the Duke, sticking his finger in the wine. On the table he drew a rough outline of the Sea of Kingdoms, then a line from Roldem to Aranor. Then from Aranor to Opardum. 'It is only six short steps from Olasko to Roldem. Now do you understand?'

For a moment, Tal didn't. What did the Duke mean by six short steps? Then it dawned on him. Softly he said, 'Kaspar means to be King of Roldem.'

'You're a bit brighter than most,' said Rodoski. 'Kaspar is a more than competent general, an extremely talented administrator, and a charismatic leader who can get idiots to die for him. He'd make a wonderful King of Roldem, except for the fact that I'm rather fond of my family – even that idiot Matthew – and along with seeing them stay alive, I also would like to see a ripe old age. Hence, I must frustrate Kaspar's plans.'

Tal wanted to deflect attention from himself for a moment longer while he scrambled to devise a story to keep himself out of harm's way, if possible. 'If what you say is true, why all the military activity in the north? Kaspar wiped out the Orosini, brought Latagore to heel, and is moving against Farinda.'

'Kaspar wants to put his army on the border of the Kingdom in a place where King Ryan has no choice but to respond by marching an army from Ran and Rodez up there to meet him. To protect Ran and Rodez, he will need to dispatch troops from Dolth; to protect Dolth, soldiers from Euper, and so on until the garrison from Salador is on the move.

'Kaspar won't need an army to seize control of Roldem. He'll have wrung concessions out of his cousin, Prince Phillip of Aranor, and he'll have disposed of the other six claimants to the throne before him. In short, he will arrive in Roldem with little opposition and a great deal of support, not only from agents within the King's court already loyal to him, but from others anxious for an orderly transition in government.

'King Ryan will quickly recognize the finality of things and acknowledge Kaspar's legitimate claim to the throne. He might even consent to marry the lovely Natalia as part of the bargain, and the Isles' recognition of Kaspar's reign will keep Kesh at bay.

'It's really quite a wonderful plan, except for the fact it will not be allowed to happen.'

Tal sat back. Something didn't make sense to him. 'It sounds marvellous, very complex and subtle and the like, but it seems to me that if you were certain of this plot, you wouldn't be sitting here drinking wine with me, Your Grace. I'd be dead already.'

The Duke knocked loudly on the table. The door flew open and a pair of crossbowmen entered with their weapons levelled at Tal. 'Don't try to draw your sword, Squire. You might just reach me, but I doubt it.'

Over the shoulders of the two guards, Tal could see Amafi being held tightly by two men, one with his hand clamped over the manservant's mouth, while another held a dagger at his throat. Tal sat back, slowly raising his hands above the table.

'You're right, Squire. If I wanted you dead, you'd be dead.' He paused. 'You are a goat.'

'Sir?'

'To capture a tiger, you stake out a goat and wait. Don't you consider it odd that Kaspar would send you to this city, for this festival, so soon after your debacle with my cousin, and so soon after your visit to the court of Salmater? Could it be any more obvious?'

'You still have no proof,' said Tal.

The Duke laughed. 'I need none. If I wish, you'll be found floating in the harbour at dawn, and the strongest reaction that will come from Duke Duncan will possibly be a note of condolence to your cousin the Baron.

'But I will not kill you. I will send you back to Kaspar in chains, and let him decide what to do with you. For you failed him utterly, Squire.

'You see, you were not supposed to kill me. I was supposed to kill you, while the real assassin found me after I was convinced I was safe.'

'Real assassin?'

The Duke snapped his fingers and from outside a man was carried in. He had obviously been beaten to the point of insensibility and was hanging limply between two more guards. 'Do you recognize this man?'

Tal struggled to put a name to the man, but couldn't. But he did look familiar.

'He's an officer in Kaspar's garrison.'

'Prohaska!' Tal whispered.

'So, you do know him.'

Tal sat back. 'Not well, but I recognize him.'

'Like yourself, he is a man of many guises. While in Salador, he was calling himself Coshenski, a trader from Olasko Gateway. Very influential friends got him an invitation to the Duke's gala on Midwinter's Day.'

Tal said, 'You obviously have good agents in Olasko if you knew he was coming.'

'Yes,' agreed the Duke. 'But you were a gift.'

'What do you mean?' asked Tal.

Duke Varian said, 'We were supposed to find and kill you, Talwin. You were given up to us, so that I would be caught off-guard when your compatriot Prohaska killed me at the gala.'

'I was given up? By whom?'

Rodoski laughed. 'You still don't see? You were given up by Kaspar. He uses people just like you use towels after a bath. Kaspar let our agents know you were coming to kill me. Kaspar wants you out of the way. The Lady Natalia is a little too fond of you, and you've already made enemies in his court by your rapid rise. Kaspar may even see you as a threat, for without heirs, if something happens to him and you wed his sister, who else is there to rule in Opardum? You were the goat. Do you see?'

It all made sense to Tal. He sat back. 'If you know all this, why not move directly against Kaspar?'

Varian said, 'I need no proof to dump you in the harbour. And I need no proof to have someone slit Kaspar's throat in the dead of night. But we can't get anyone that close, for reasons you know all too well.'

'Leso Varen.'

'Yes. That evil wizard is too dangerous, so we're content to let Kaspar play his games, as long as they don't become too deadly. And we block him where we can. But one day he'll go too far – and this attempt on me is as close to the limit as King Carol is willing to permit – when that day comes, we will sail our fleet to Opardum and unload soldiers from Kesh and let them destroy Kaspar.'

Tal sat back. 'So why let me live?'

'Because I need to send a message to Kaspar he can't ignore, or pretend to misunderstand. I will have the body of Prohaska delivered to him and yourself bound up in chains, and the conclusion he comes to should be clear.' The Duke stood up. 'And I'll leave you to Kaspar's tender mercies. The day may come when you wish I killed you. Oh, if you do survive, understand that you will be killed on sight if you set foot on Roldem again.' To the guards, he said, 'Take him.'

Tal was grabbed by two soldiers who quickly disarmed him and bound his arms behind him. One stepped behind him and suddenly pain exploded behind his eyes and he slipped into unconsciousness.

Tal awoke in the dark, and quickly realized he was chained inside the hold of a ship. The rocking motion told him they were already out of the harbour and out at sea. Amafi groaned next to him, and Tal said, 'Are you awake?'

After a moment came a choked groan, then Amafi said, 'I am here, Magnificence.'

'We have been betrayed,' said Tal.

'So it seems.'

Tal tried to make himself as comfortable as he could, for he knew it would be a long, cold, wet journey. After some hours a sailor came down the companionway, bearing two bowls of food, a mix of boiled grain, dried fruit, and a piece of salted pork, mostly fat. 'Eat,' he said, handing each man a bowl. 'It's all you get until tomorrow.'

Tal took the food and began to eat. It tasted salty and bland, but it filled him and he knew he would need as much strength as he could muster.

The voyage passed slowly, a seemingly endless succession of days spent in rocking darkness, interrupted only by a daily visit by a sailor who brought the same meal. On the forty-first or -second day, Tal noticed they no longer got the salt pork.

Some ten days later, the ship shuddered, and Tal realized they were making the final reach for Opardum. Before another day was out, they'd be hauled up before Kaspar.

A thought ran through Tal's mind over and over again. He had been betrayed. The king of foxes had shown he was really a scorpion, and being true to his nature, he had stung.

Tal was freed of his obligation. He could now kill Kaspar without betraying his oath.

If he survived.

They had been taken straight away to the castle. Tal had hoped perhaps he might be unchained and allowed to clean up before being dragged before Kaspar, but that hope proved to be in vain.

He was brought before Kaspar, who sat alone in his great hall, with only soldiers around him: no Lady Natalia, no courtiers. 'So, Baron Talwin,' said Kaspar without preamble, 'you've failed.'

Tal decided there was no benefit to feigning ignorance of events. 'As I was apparently destined to, Your Grace.'

Kaspar laughed. 'Well, you obviously didn't get yourself killed, so I assume Duke Rodoski had other plans, such as rubbing my nose in my failure.'

'Something like that. He did say you have now come as close to the line as King Carol will permit. One more infraction and a Roldemish fleet will be delivering companies of Keshian Dog Soldiers to Opardum.'

'Oh, he said that, did he?' Kaspar chuckled. 'Games within games, Baron. There is another level of play underway that even one so highly placed as Duke Varian is unaware of.

'Still,' he added with a wave of his hand, 'that is a matter which no longer concerns you. You've failed me, Baron. You not only didn't kill Rodoski, as I ordered, you didn't have the good grace to get yourself killed in the attempt. So, in a sense, you've failed me twice, which is one more failure than I usually permit. Still, you've been an earnest young fellow and have given me some amusement. For that sake, I will have your death be quick and painless.' To the guards he said, 'Take him away.'

As the guards seized Tal's arms, Tal shouted, 'You owe me your life!'

Kaspar sat back and motioned for the guards to stop. 'Damn me, but you're right,' said Kaspar. He shook his head. 'Very well, I will not be bound in life by a debt not paid. I will give you your life, Squire – I'm rescinding your office of baron – but you will wish before I'm done I hadn't.' He then looked at Amafi, and said, 'What am I to do with you?'

Amafi said, 'You could start by removing the chains, Your Grace.'

The Duke motioned and guards freed him. After Amafi was out of his chains, he bowed and said, 'I hope the Squire's failure does not taint my service, Your Grace.'

'No, not in the least, Amafi. You are the perfect tool. You do exactly what I bid you to do, no more, no less.'

Tal looked at his manservant and said, 'You?'

'Someone had to carry word to the Duke's agents in Salador that you were sent to kill him, Squire,' said Kaspar. 'I certainly couldn't depend on Roldemish agents here to get word back to the Duke in time. Bribing your man to betray you was a far more elegant solution. I told him how to contact one of my agents in Salador, who in turn put him in touch with a member of Duke Duncan's staff, and from there it was but one step to Duke Rodoski.'

Amafi bowed towards Tal. 'As you yourself observed the first night we met, Magnificence, "Until such time as you can successfully betray me without risk." This was such a time.'

'You will be rewarded, Amafi,' said Kaspar. 'Now, go and get cleaned up.'

The former assassin said, 'Yes, Your Grace, but may I caution you in one thing?'

'What?'

'I have served Talwin Hawkins long enough to know that despite his youth, he is an extremely dangerous man. You would do well to put aside your debt and have him killed.'

'No,' said Kaspar. 'I understand your caution, but I have my sense of honour, peculiar as it may be. He saved my life, so I can't ignore that debt.' He paused, then said, 'But I will take your warning to heart. Now, leave us.'

Amafi bowed to the Duke and departed. To Tal, Kaspar said,

'I give you your life, but it will be spent in a place no man should endure, and few have for long. You are to live the rest of your life in the Fortress of Despair. If the gods are kind, you will die quickly there. But in my experience, the gods are rarely kind.'

To the captain of the guards, he said, 'When he arrives, inform the commander of the Fortress that this man is to be fed well and not tortured. Well, not tortured after he cuts off the prisoner's right hand.'

Tal stood numbly for moment upon hearing his fate, then suddenly without further word, he was dragged off by the soldiers. His last image of Kaspar was of the Duke sitting on his throne, an expression of satisfaction mixed with regret playing across his face.

PART TWO

Soldier

'*Revenge should have no bounds*'
William Shakespeare, *Hamlet*, Act IV, Scene viii

• CHAPTER THIRTEEN •

Prison

*T*AL STOOD ON THE deck.

He had been dragged to Opardum harbour. He had been off the ship from Salador less than half a day before he was chained in the hold of yet another ship.

Rather than forty or more days, this journey took only a week. Thoughts of escape had run through his mind and more than once he had tested his chains where they passed through a large iron ring fastened to a beam. After the first day, he had fallen into a mood of dejected misery. After a week, Tal had been roughly hauled up to the deck, where the ship's captain waited.

'There's your new home, Squire,' he said in an oddly convivial tone, pointing to an island.

Tal looked where the captain indicated and felt even more hopeless. The Fortress of Despair was an old keep, six storeys tall, which overlooked the narrow passage between this island and the mainland, merely three miles away. It stood bleak against a grey winter sky, as the wind cut icily through Tal's clothing.

'One of the Duke's ancestors built it,' said the captain. 'Then it was called Fortress Sentinel. When the City of the Guardian was built up, this place sort of fell into disuse, until one of the old dukes decided to make a prison out of it.'

A longboat was lowered and Tal was forced to climb down a ladder to be yanked into the longboat by a couple of rough-handed seamen. As the boat was rowed towards the dock, the captain waved and cheerfully said, 'Enjoy your stay, Squire!'

Tal sat in the boat, the winter sky as foreboding and dark as his mood. The salt spray that struck him in the face was frigid as it whipped off the spindrift. The boat rocked as the four rowers pulled to reach the dock as quickly as possible. The sooner they were done the sooner they could be back on board the ship, back to a slightly warmer and drier berth.

Three men stood waiting on the dock, wearing heavy cloaks; the boat drew up and the sailors steadied it. They didn't even bother to tie off: two of them stood up and gripped the pilings, while another motioned for Tal to climb a short ladder. He did so, with one sailor following him, and when they both stood on the dock, the sailor said, 'Here's the writ, Governor.'

Without thanks, the man took the paper, and without another word, the sailor was back down the ladder and the boat pushed off. The man who had been handed the paper looked at Tal and said, 'Come.'

The other two men were armed guards, both looking little more than street thugs. Neither wore a uniform, and they carried large cudgels rather than swords. Tal had no doubt either man could and would quickly break his arm or leg with the clubs if he tried to escape. As he walked towards the Fortress, he looked around, and thought, *Where would I escape to?*

As if reading his thoughts, the Governor said, 'You can try to run; you look like a fast lad, so you might outrun Kyle and Anatoli here, but with them chains on, maybe not. If you did, you'd maybe find your way down to the beach up there on the north side of the island, but then where'd you go? Looks close, don't it? The mainland, I mean. Three miles, a bit more or less. But there's a current there wants to take you north, and there's sharks and other things. That's if the chains don't pull you down and you drown. But maybe you're a strong swimmer. If you made it to the beach, you're miles from food.'

They reached an old drawbridge that looked to have been down for years. As they crossed over it, Tal looked down and saw a twenty-five-foot ravine filled with broken rocks at the bottom. 'So, maybe you're a hunter,' said the Governor. 'Maybe you get by, even though it's winter. You build a fire and somehow don't freeze to death.

'Guess what?' he said and turned, and for the first time Tal got a look at his face. The governor of the prison had no left eye, just a closed lid, and a notch in the bridge of his nose, as if someone had cut him across it with a blade. His own teeth had been knocked out and he wore some sort of contraption made of wood and teeth – perhaps human or animal – that would serve him for eating. He grinned and said, 'The only civilization for hundreds of miles is the City of the Guardian, and it's a border city, so the guards look close at everyone coming in.'

They reached the entrance to the old fortress and the Governor stopped. 'Take a look around, lad. Look up.'

Tal did so.

'It's the last time you'll be seeing the open sky, I'm thinking.' He motioned and the two guards escorted Tal up the steps into the old fortress.

What had been the entrance hall was now bare, a huge room with a set of doors in each wall. They marched across the stone floor, worn featureless and smooth by centuries of feet trudging across it, and passed through another door. 'This used to be the great hall,' said the Governor. 'Now we only use it for banquets.'

The two guards laughed. 'Come along,' said the Governor.

They led Tal to what must once have been the private apartment of the commander of the Fortress. Now it was an office, containing a large table littered with food and empty wine cups as well as papers. A rat scurried off the table as the Governor waved his hand at it.

Taking off his heavy cloak, the Governor tossed it across a chair. 'Let's see, now, what we have here,' he said, unrolling the writ.

'Squire Talwin Hawkins, is it?'

Tal said nothing.

'I'm Governor Zirga. Used to be a sergeant in the Duke's father's household guards. Got this,' he said, pointing to his face, 'at the Battle of Karesh'kaar, when I was not much older than you. So as a reward, they give me this job. I get a week off a year to go to City of the Guardian and spend gold on whores and getting drunk. The rest of the time I care for you prisoners.

'So we understands one another. You don't cause trouble, and we'll get along fine. You've come here to die, more or less, and it's up to you how you fare between now and when we toss your ashes off the cliffs.' He waved the papers at Tal and said, 'Says here you're to be treated well, which means a little more food and we'll put you up in the keep, instead of the dungeon below. Them down there dies right fast. Most go in less than two years. Up above, well, you've got a bit of sunlight and some better air – though it do get bitter cold in the winter – but in the summer you'll be glad for the breezes. But I've got a couple o' lads up there been with us fifteen, twenty years.

'So, we'll get you upstairs straight away . . . as soon as we cut off your right arm.'

The Governor motioned for the two guards, who seized Tal by either arm, lifting him slightly off his feet so he couldn't get purchase on the stones. They frog-marched him out of the door and across to another door, then down a long flight of stairs, half-carrying, half-dragging him along a narrow corridor.

'We don't have a proper chirurgery here, so we have to make do with the dungeon when it comes to cutting and the like,' said the Governor. 'Occasionally one of the lads gets a cut or scrape that turns putrid and I've got to do some cutting.'

They passed a third guard who was sitting on a stool next to a table, and the Governor said, 'Fetch some brandy.'

The two guards who held Tal pulled him into a chamber that had obviously been used for torture in the past. 'From time to time the Duke sends us someone he wants *really* punished, so we bring them down here. Used to be we could do a lot with what was left over from the old days, but as you can see –' he pointed to a pile of rusty implements left on the filthy straw strewn on the floor '– we've fallen on harder times. Don't have that many good tools any more. Just some pincers and knives and the like.' He pointed to an iron ring in the ceiling. 'Used to have a dandy hook hanging there. I could hang a man on it just right and he'd be screaming for a couple of days. Last time I used it, damn thing broke off. I sent a request in for another one, but no one's bothered to do anything about it back in Opardum.'

The guard with the brandy appeared and the Governor said, 'Start a fire.'

There was a large brazier which at one time must have been used for heating torture devices, and the guard quickly got a fire started with some dry straw and kindling. He fed wood into it until it started blazing brightly. 'Heat an iron,' said the Governor. 'Can't have you bleeding to death, now, can we?' he said to Tal.

Tal was motionless. He felt as if he wanted to lash out and fight, to run, but he knew the situation was hopeless. He knew that if he was to have any chance at all for survival, he must not fight. He must just endure.

The Governor took off his jacket, revealing a dirty white shirt underneath. He went to the wall and found what looked to be a large cleaver. He put it in the fire. 'We used to have coal. I could get the sword so hot I could ruin the temper of the steel if I wasn't careful. Just the thing. The trick is to sear the wound. Used to be, when I had coal, I could slice right though your arm and the metal would be so hot your stump would hardly bleed. Now, I make do with wood. If the hot blade doesn't do it, then we'll poke at where it's bleedin' with the iron.'

The blade grew red after a few minutes in the flame, and the Governor nodded to the guard who wasn't holding Tal. He picked up a pair of bellows, like those a smith would use, and began pumping it, causing the wood to flare up and send a fountain of sparks spiralling upward.

Tal's mind was in turmoil. He was thinking up to this moment that somehow he could devise a way to escape. As the Governor said, he could outrun these two and make it to the north beach, swim to the coast . . .

Suddenly his chain was yanked hard, tugging him off balance, and he felt powerful arms wrapped around his waist. One guard held him while the other used the manacle to pull his arm straight, across a wooden table. With a swift motion, the Governor grabbed the sword out of the fire and in a single sweeping blow, severed Tal's right arm between the elbow and wrist.

Tal cried out in shock, and his head swam. The Governor looked at the wound, then took up the iron and seared a bleeding artery. Then he tossed the iron back into the fire. He picked up the bottle of brandy and took a long drink. 'This sort of work upsets me, Squire.'

Tal could barely stand and the pain that shot up his arm was excruciating. He felt faint and the Governor said, 'I'd offer you a drink, but we can't give strong drink to the prisoners. Rules are rules.' Then he poured some of the brandy over the charred stump of Tal's arm and said, 'But I did happen to discover, purely by accident one time, that if you pour a little brandy over the cut, it's less likely to fester.' He nodded to the two guards. 'Take him away. North room, third floor.'

Tal was dragged away by the two guards and fainted before they reached the first flight of stairs.

Tal lay in agony. The stump of his right arm throbbed constantly, and he was racked with fever. His mind lapsed in and out of consciousness, and at times he was lost in dreams and visions.

He occasionally got lost in memory, thinking he was once again feverish in the wagon on its way to Kendrick's, after being found by Robert and Pasko. Other times he dreamed he was in his bed in Roldem or Salador, trying to wake up from a nightmare, knowing that once he was awake, he would be fine.

On other occasions he came wide awake with a sudden start, his heart pounding, and then he would look around the cold room with the grey light and cold wind coming in through a high window. Then he would relapse into unconsciousness.

After some period of time, he awoke, drenched in perspiration, but clear headed. His right arm throbbed, and for a moment he could feel the fingers on his right hand. He tried to stretch and move them, then saw there was only a bloody stump, encased in rags and some sort of unguent.

He looked around, trying to make sense of his surroundings. He had seen the room before, many times, but now it was as if he was seeing it for the first time.

The cell was fashioned from stone, containing no furnishings. His only items of comfort were a mattress filled with old straw and two heavy blankets. His bedding was sour with the smell of sweat and urine. He saw a single door, wooden, with a small viewing-hole, locked from the other side. Opposite the door, at slightly more than his own height, a single window with two iron bars admitted daylight. In the far corner a hole in the floor, its edges crusted with filth, showed where he was to relieve himself.

Tal stood up and his knees threatened to buckle. Reflexively he put out his right hand, and was betrayed by the memory of a hand no longer there. He stumbled and fell, his stump hitting the wall, and he cried out, then fell back to the mattress, his head swimming.

He lay gasping for breath, tears running down his face as his entire body echoed the agony he felt in his arm. Shock ran up his arm to his shoulder and up his neck. The entire right side of his body felt as if it was afire.

He forced himself to breathe slowly and attempted a meditation taught him at Sorcerer's Isle, one that would help him master pain. Slowly, the pain moved farther away and became smaller, until it felt as if he had somehow put it in a box that he could hold away from himself.

He opened his eyes and stood up, this time carefully using his left hand to steady himself. His knees wobbled but at last he got his balance. He looked around. There was nothing to see.

He staggered to the window, and reached up. He tested the bars and found them deeply set in the rock. The one on the left he could twist a little in the socket drilled into the rock. He gripped it hard with his left hand and tried to pull himself up so that he could see, but the effort caused his entire body to hurt, so he decided that investigating the view could wait.

An hour after he had awoken, the door to his cell opened. A very dirty man with unkempt shoulder-length hair and a ragged beard entered, holding a bucket in front of him. He saw Tal and smiled. 'You're alive,' he said. 'That's a bit of all right, in'it? Thems who's been cut don't usually survive, you know?'

Tal said nothing, just looking at the man. He could hardly see any of his features, under the dirt and hair.

'I know how it is,' he said, holding out his left arm, which also ended in a stump. 'Old Zirga cut it off when I got here, 'cause it was festerin'.'

'Who are you?'

'Name's Will. Thief by trade until I got caught.' He set the bucket down.

'They let you come and go?'

'Oh, they do with some of us which has been here a while. I'm here ten years next spring. They're a lazy lot, so they let us do some of the work if they think they can trust us not to cut their throats when they're drunk, and besides, there's not much to do around here, so fetchin' and carryin' a bit here and there is all right. Besides, I get a little extra food and if they're not paying close attention, I can nick a bottle of wine or brandy every year or two.

'And you get to haul out the dead, which is a bit of all right.'

'Hauling out the dead?' said Tal, not believing his ears.

'It's a good time. You're outside for the afternoon, first burning the body, then digging up some ashes, then you carry it down to the cliffs over there above the north beach, and scatter them to the wind with a prayer. It's a nice little break from the ordinary, in'it?'

Tal shook his head. 'What's in the bucket?'

'That's your kit.' Will reached in and pulled out a metal pan, then a wooden spoon. 'Me or one of the other lads will be by twice a day. You get porridge in the morning and a nice stew at night. Not much by way of variety, but it'll keep you alive. Zirga told me you was one of the specials, so you'll get more.'

'Specials?'

'It's a bit of a joke, actually,' said Will, smiling and letting Tal see there was a face under the dirt and hair. 'Duke Kaspar gives orders for some extra food and an extra blanket, maybe even a coat, so the prisoner's around a long time, to "enjoy the stay", as Zirga says.

'Most of us are in the middle. We're just ordinary blokes, and if we don't make trouble, they feed us and don't beat us too often. We used to have this one guard, name of Jasper, he'd get crazy mean drunk and just beat someone to be doing it. Got drunk one night and fell off the cliff; broke his neck. No one misses him.

'Then the ones the Duke really hates are down in the dungeon. They don't last long down there, maybe a year, maybe two.

'You, you get some bread with your meals, and on special days, maybe something else. You never know. Depends on Zirga's moods.'

'Does anyone ever leave?'

'You mean like is anyone pardoned or serve out their sentence?'

'Yes.'

'No,' said Will, shaking his head. 'We all come here to die.' He sat down on his haunches and added, 'Well, strictly speakin', if I can last another twenty years, then I should be freed. Of course, by then, I'll have to remind them my sentence was for thirty, and then I've got to hope someone here cares enough to send a message to Opardum, and that someone there can find a record of my trial. Then someone else has to review the trial record, and get a judge to sign an order to release me, and bother sending it back to Zirga or whoever's the Governor here in twenty years. So, you can see, I don't put much faith in it. Mostly because no one's lived thirty years in the Fortress of Despair.'

'You seem uncommonly cheerful for a man condemned to live his life on this rock.'

'Well, the ways I look at it, you got two choices: you can curl up and be miserable, or you can try to make the best of things. Me, I count it lucky they didn't hang me. They called me an incorrigible thief. I'd been caught three times. First time, I got sent to the work-gang for a year, 'cause I was only a lad. Second time, I got thirty lashes and five years' hard labour. This time, they could have hung me, but for whatever reason, they sent me here. I think it was 'cause the last time I got caught it was breakin' into the magistrate's home, and he thought hangin' was too good for me.' He laughed. 'Besides, you never know what might happen. One day I might just wander down to the dock and find a boat there, or maybe those murderers up at Bardac's Holdfast will decide to attack and kill off all the guards, taking the prisoners with them to be pirates.'

Tal found himself laughing, despite his pain. 'You're quite the optimist, aren't you?'

'Me? Maybe, but what else can you do?' He stood up. 'They say your name is Talwin Hawkins. That right?'

'Call me Tal.'

'Tal it is.' He looked around. 'Well, I've got to head back to the kitchen and get the meal ready. You should be hungry by now.'

'I could eat. How long has it been?'

'They cut off your hand three days ago. Didn't know if you were going to make it or not. After I bring around the meal, let me take a look at your wound.' He held up his own stump. 'I'm somethin' of an expert.'

Tal nodded, and Will left. Tal leaned back against the stones and felt cold sucking the warmth right out of his body. He pulled his blanket around his shoulders, fumbling as he tried to do it with only one hand. At last he had it around him, and he settled in. He had nothing to do but wait for food.

Will looked at the wound and said, 'That's healing nicely.' He rewrapped the bandage. 'I don't know what that muck is Zirga puts on the rags, but it works. Smells like a pig died under the house a month ago, but it keeps the wound from festerin', and that's what it's about, in'it?'

Tal had eaten the stew, a watery broth with a few vegetables and a hint of flavour that suggested that meat had once touched the pot the broth was made in. He had also got half a loaf of a very coarse bread, which Will said was to last him the week. He said only the specials got bread every week.

Tal asked, 'So, how does someone become like you, someone the guards trust?'

'Well, you got to not make trouble, and do what you're told. Sometimes we get turned out to work, but not often. If a storm hits really hard, we might have to go clean up debris, repair the dock, or fix leaks in the cookhouse when it rains. If you do the work good, and the guards like you, then you get out of your cell.

'If there's something special you can do, that helps.'

'What do you mean?'

'Zirga says he wishes they'd convict a smith, so he could get some things around here repaired. We had a fellow claimed he was a smith, but he wasn't, so Zirga put him in the dungeon. Problem was, Zirga forgot he was down there and the bloke starved before anyone remembered.'

'What other things?'

'I don't know. I'll ask. But even if you can do something they need, specials never get out of their cells.'

Tal shrugged, trying to get comfortable and finding it almost impossible. 'Why didn't you say that to begin with?'

'Well, you didn't ask me if you could get out of the cell; you asked how someone could get like me.'

Tal laughed. 'You're right. I was just thinking you were wasting my time, but then that's the only thing I have any more, time.'

Will turned to walk away. 'You've got that right, Tal. Still, you never know. Zirga doesn't always do things by the rules; he likes being in charge too much, and no one ever comes out here to check on him. So, I'll mention you to him. What can you do?'

Tal thought. 'I used to play instruments.' He held out his stump. 'I guess that's pointless.' He said, 'I can cook.'

'Cookin's pretty simple around here.'

'So I've noticed,' said Tal. 'But I was thinking maybe Zirga and the guards might like something a bit more tasty.'

'Could be. I'll mention it to him. What else?'

'I paint.'

'Not much call for that, leastwise not so I'd notice. Haven't painted anything around here since I've been here, 'cept this one time we had to whitewash a fence out where they keep the pigs.'

'I mean I paint portraits and landscapes.' He looked at his severed arm. 'At least I used to before –'

'Oh, like them fancy pictures the swells have on their walls. I've seen 'em a time or two when I was boostin'.'

'Yes, like that.'

'Seems we got less call for that than whitewashin'.'

Tal said, 'I used to play music, too, but . . .' He waved the stump for emphasis.

'That's a shame, in'it?' Will smiled. 'But I'll mention the cookin' to Zirga.'

'Thanks.'

Tal lay down when Will left, trying to keep his feelings under control. He felt like a caged animal, and he had seen trapped beasts throw themselves against the bars of their cages until they bloodied themselves. He knew that he could not escape as things stood, and that his only hope for getting off this island was to first get out of this cell. He would bide his time, for that he had in abundance.

Tal pulled hard, lifting his body up to the window. He had seen the view a dozen times in the last half hour, but he wasn't interested in another look at the frigid winterscape he could see once he pulled himself up. He was trying to regain some strength and after a month of sitting in his cell, occasionally talking with Will, the boredom was threatening to take his sanity. The first time he tried to pull himself up by his left arm, he managed one quick peep out of the window before having to let himself down again.

From his window he could see the north yard of the fortress. He couldn't see the livestock pen, but he could hear the pigs, sheep and chickens. Occasionally a dog would bark. He could see what looked to be the old marshalling yard, now under a sheet of white snow, broken up with patches of grey and brown.

Over the last month he had come to prize that little view of his world, a patch of snow-covered earth, a section of wall, and a cliff beyond. In the distance, he could see the sea when the weather lifted enough. Otherwise it was a grey blanket beyond the cliffs.

He found the food monotonous and barely sufficient. He knew he had lost weight, due to the injury and simple fare, but he wasn't starving. The bread for all its coarseness was filling and had bits of nut and whole grain in it. The stew was little more than thin soup with a vegetable or two in it, but as Will said, occasionally there was a piece of meat as well. The porridge was merely filling.

He wished he could bathe, and realized how much he had come to enjoy being clean. As a child of the Orosini, he had gone most of the winter without bathing and thought nothing of it, but now he was a 'civilized' man and enjoyed hot baths, massages, unguents and oils.

He had asked Will if he would be given clean clothing, and was told that if someone in Opardum or City of the Guardian purchased clothing for him, and paid a bribe to the captain of the next ship that came bringing prisoners or supplies, then he could have them, as long as there was a bribe for Zirga included.

Realizing that was more than unlikely, Tal knew he would have to do with what he had, unless someone died. Then he might get that man's clothing, said Will, if they didn't fit someone else the guards liked better.

Tal fought every day to keep despair at bay, for he knew that he would not give up and let death take him without a struggle. He had also wounded or trapped animals which stopped struggling, which just laid back and let the hunter take their lives. He would not be such an animal.

He would survive.

• CHAPTER FOURTEEN •

Cook

*T*AL AWOKE.

Sitting in the window was a bird. He moved slowly, so as not to startle the creature. He tried to identify what variety of bird it was, but couldn't. It looked somewhat like the mountain finch of his homeland, but the bill was different, longer and narrower, and the feathers had a slight white band on the wings the mountain finches lacked. He tried to get as close as he could, but when he approached the wall, the bird flew away.

He jumped and grabbed the bar and pulled himself up. He peered through the window and saw that the last of the ice and snow was gone. The breeze was cool, but not bitter. He let himself down.

Another spring had come.

He had now been in the Fortress of Despair for more than

a year. He had come to accept that for an unknown time he would simply abide there.

He had developed a routine to keep from losing his sanity, one based upon three tenets: that despair was the first killer; that his mission in life to avenge his people would fail if he died; and that his mind must remain alert so that any opportunity for escape, even the smallest, would not go unnoticed.

To fill his hours he did mental exercises learned at Sorcerer's Isle, to remember things – books he had read, chess matches played, conversations with other students and lectures by instructors. He could remember things as if he were reliving them, so for hours at a time he would be submerged in memory, experiencing again things he had already once lived.

He avoided the trap of becoming lost in those memories, though, choosing not to remember the loving arms of women, the thrill of the hunt, the pleasure of winning at cards. Those memories were a snare, an avoidance of the suffering he endured at the Fortress, no aid in preparing himself to end his captivity.

And to further avoid the lure of pointless memories, he forced himself to endure an hour a day of bleak observation, either of the stonework of his walls and floor, or through the window of his cell.

He ignored his own filth as best he could. He had convinced Will to bring him a little extra water when he was able, and Tal used that water to try to keep clean. It was a scant comfort, but it was comfort of a kind, and anything he could do to alleviate the unrelenting bleakness of his situation he did. Nakor had once said to him that joy in life often came from the small victories, the tiny triumphs, and while seizing pleasure out of a damp cloth and cold water seemed improbable, he took it.

As best he could, he sought to stay fit. Given the meagre food and constant cold made it difficult. He knew he had lost a great deal of weight, but now that the weather was turning warmer, he felt renewed. He exercised within the confines of his cell, walking and running in place, pulling himself up by his one hand on the bars of his cell. He contrived ways to take the exercises he had learned from Nakor at Sorcerer's Isle and adapt them to his surroundings. He was not whole, and he was hardly strong, but he was as fit as he could manage under the existing conditions.

He maintained his regime and he kept his mind agile. He tried to master patience, and he waited. Eventually, he knew – in a month, a year, or perhaps ten – something would happen. Something would change. And when that change came, he would be ready.

At the end of his second winter in the Fortress, Tal had learned to use his damaged arm to the limit of its ability. He could do more than simply use it for balance when he exercised; he had contrived ways to push, pull and carry with it. He was sitting on his straw pallet one afternoon, when the door to his cell opened and Will walked in.

Will was empty-handed, and Tal asked, 'It's not time for supper and you're not carrying anything. Is this a social visit?'

'I came to tell you supper will be late.'

'Why?'

'Charles the cook is dead.'

'What happened?' asked Tal, always anxious for anything that broke the monotony of his days. He scratched at his beard, which was now long enough to reach below his breastbone.

'Don't rightly know,' said Will, sitting down on the floor. 'I carried out the porridge like usual this morning, then when I got back to the kitchen, I found old Charles lying face down on the floor. I rolled him over and his eyes were wide open, like he had been startled by something. His face was pale and his lips was blue. Very disturbing, if you don't mind me saying.'

'So, who's taking his place?'

'I don't know. But I assumed as long as it takes Zirga to figure out who's cooking, it'll be that much longer before supper is ready. Not to mention, even longer, if whoever's going to cook has to help burn Charles.'

'Thank you for telling me.'

'You're welcome.'

As Will turned to leave, Tal said, 'Will?'

'Yes,' said Will over his shoulder.

'If it comes up, remind Zirga that I know how to cook.'

Will nodded. 'If it comes up, yes,' he said, and left the cell.

Tal sat back. He wondered if this might be the opportunity he had been waiting for. Trying to keep anticipation to a minimum, he returned to his meditations, but just in case, he started recalling his cooking lessons with Leo at Kendrick's.

Supper never came.

There weren't many prisoners in the Fortress, apparently, for the next morning when the early meal didn't arrive, Tal heard only a small number of voices complaining. He waited.

Sometime in the mid-morning, Tal heard the latch to his cell move, then the door opened. Will entered, followed by Anatoli, one of the two guards who had met him at the dock, and after them came Zirga.

Tal stood up.

'You cook?' asked Zirga.

'Yes,' answered Tal.

'Come along, then,' said Zirga.

And so, Tal left his cell for the first time in more than a year. He walked down the long steps that led to the ground level of the keep, then followed Zirga and the others through the old main hall into the kitchen.

The place was a disaster. Someone had tried to boil up porridge and had burned it. Zirga turned to him and said, 'We have a problem.'

'Apparently,' said Tal. 'You have no cook.'

'Yes, and I have fourteen prisoners, three guards, and myself to feed.'

'Cooking for eighteen people is no problem,' said Tal.

'For you, perhaps, if what you say is true. But for Anatoli here, it is a problem.'

The large guard looked up, embarrassed, but said nothing.

'He claimed he remembered how his mother made porridge, and we can see the result. So, needless to say, I have no wish to see him make stew for the prisoners, or cook supper for the guards. Can you do this?'

'I can, but I'll need help,' said Tal.

'Why?'

Tal held out his stump. 'There are things in the kitchen I could manage with one hand, if I were cooking for myself alone. Cooking for eighteen? I will need help.'

Zirga thought about it a moment, then said, 'I am breaking rules by allowing you out of your cell. Specials are never let out of their cells.'

'But you need to eat,' said Tal. 'And who else is to know?'

'Yes, that is true. Very well. You may have these two to help.' He waved at Will and Anatoli. 'What can you do?'

Tal said, 'Give me a moment,' and hurried over to the pantry. He took a quick inventory and said, 'I can make a stew. Is there any meat?'

Zirga said, 'In the summer house. Will will show you.'

As the Governor turned to leave, Tal said, 'But I'll need to take a bath first.'

Zirga turned. 'A bath? Why?'

Tal held up his left hand, shoving fingernails black with filth right under Zirga's nose. 'Do you want this in your stew?'

Zirga paused and looked at Tal, really studying him for the first time. Then he looked at Will and Anatoli. 'All of you, take a bath.'

'We'll need clean clothing,' said Tal.

'There's clothing in the armoury. Anatoli will take you there.'

Less than two hours later, a fully revived Tal stood over two large pots of bubbling broth. He and the others had to endure a cold bath, as there was no time to heat the water, but Tal didn't mind. As a child he had bathed in the streams of the Orosini Mountains in the early spring, when the water consisted of ice-melt. Will had seemed less thrilled about being clean than Tal, but after a bath and fresh clothing, he looked like a different man. Will did have a face under the grime and hair. It was narrow and constantly set in a grin, with eyes that seemed always to squint.

Anatoli looked like a large round egg with a head, arms and legs. His muscle had all gone to fat and Tal knew that he could easily best him in a sword fight, even using only his left hand.

Tal suspected Kyle and Benson, the other two guards, were also limited in their fighting gifts. Big and powerful, perhaps, but not quick. And after five minutes of conversation with Anatoli, Tal was silently adding to himself, not very bright, either.

Tal had done a quick inventory of the spring-house, a cellar dug under the ground behind the keep, where meat and cheese were kept cool. It was still almost freezing down there as the soil below the surface held the winter's cold well into the summer. Later in the summer, when stores were used up, they would slaughter an animal as needed; cattle were pastured in a small meadow on the east side of the island, along with sheep, and there were pigs penned up downwind from the keep.

With Anatoli and Will to help him, Tal felt almost as if he had two hands again. He found the thief to be dextrous and they quickly adapted to each being one half of a pair of hands. Anatoli proved useful for simple tasks, such as washing vegetables and cleaning pots.

Tal found a box of jars of spices in the pantry, old but still useful. He knew that none had been used to flavour his meals since he had come to the Fortress, so even faded spices would be a welcome change.

He set water to boiling, then tossed in beef-bones for stock, and added vegetables and chunks of diced beef. He also started boiling some turnips he had found that weren't too far gone, and set out some cheese and fruit. He showed Will and Anatoli how he wanted things placed on Zirga's table, where he ate with the three guards, and started organizing meals for the fourteen prisoners.

The meal was hastily prepared, but still it was the best meal seen in the keep in years, Tal wagered. While Zirga and the three guards ate, Tal got Will started on taking stew to the prisoners. He made sure each plate had a good-sized hunk of meat in it, and a healthy helping of potatoes, onions, carrots and turnips. It took the better part of an hour to distribute the plates to the other twelve prisoners. When they were finished, Tal had seen every occupied cell in the fortress.

He now had a sense of the place's true size, how to navigate it, and where he could find the items necessary for his escape.

Zirga came into the kitchen while Tal and Will ate their supper at a small table. 'That was good,' he said to Tal. 'I think you should cook until they send me someone to replace Charles. Now, stop eating and return to your cell.'

Anatoli approached Tal as if to escort him back, but Tal said, 'I can't.'

'Why not?' said Zirga, looking at Tal suspiciously. 'You can come back down here in the morning.'

'But tonight I must bake bread. That takes most of the night.' He pointed to a place on the floor by the ovens. 'I can sleep there while the bread is rising, then put it in the ovens so that it's ready in the morning.'

Zirga thought about it, then shrugged. 'Well, it's not as if there's anywhere for you to go, is it?'

Tal nodded, keeping a straight face.

As Zirga started to leave, Tal said, 'I'll need Will to help me.'

Zirga looked over his shoulder. 'Fine. Keep him.'

'And Anatoli first thing in the morning.'

'All right, you can have him.'

If the guard had any reaction to this, he kept it to himself. Zirga and Anatoli left, and Will said, 'How did you do that?'

Tal shrugged, pointing to the pots they would have to clean

before making the bread. 'Zirga forgot what good food tastes like.'

'I did, too,' said Will. 'That stew was the best I've ever had.'

Tal smiled. 'I think you just don't remember. If I can get Zirga to order in some fresh spices and other things, I can keep us in this kitchen for as long as we need.'

'Need?' Will dropped his voice. 'What do you have in mind?'

'Many things, my friend. Many things.'

They started washing, with Will scrubbing out pots that Tal held still for him. Then he set about showing Will how to help him make dough. The kneading was the most difficult part, but after a few false starts, they got a rhythm going and got it done.

Tal started fires under the ovens, then let them burn down and banked the fires. He put away the iron poker and rolled out a ragged bed roll, big enough for the two men to share.

'Now we sleep,' said Tal, 'and let the bread rise. At dawn, we put it in the ovens, and start the porridge.' After they were both lying down, Tal said, 'Tell me about the other prisoners.'

'What do you want to know?'

'Who they are. What crimes they have committed. What skills they might have.'

Will whispered, 'You're planning an escape!'

Tal said, 'More.'

'What?'

'I'm building an army.'

Weeks went by, and when another prisoner was delivered, Zirga sent the boat back to the ship with a list of provisions Tal had drawn up, along with a request for a new cook. Tal was convinced he might get the provisions, but hoped the request for a cook would be ignored. After all, Zirga had requested that a new guard be assigned when the one Will had told him of, Jasper, had died, and yet after four years, no replacement had arrived.

Tal found the kitchen a haven. He quickly organized Will and Anatoli so that the preparation of meals became easy. He then started adding variety to the diet, startling Zirga one morning with a heap of pan-bread and honey, with slabs of ham, rather than porridge. He interspersed cuts of beef, pork or roasted chickens with the stews, which he also varied, including a fish stew after he had convinced Zirga and the guards to spend a day fishing off the dock.

Subtly, he usurped command of the Fortress, letting his natural leadership quietly assert itself, while Zirga unwittingly fell back into the role of sergeant, a man comfortable giving directions once tasks had been identified. Often the idea came in the form of a question, one couched in terms that made the answer obvious, and never let the former soldier suspect for a minute that he was following instructions. Zirga gladly took credit for every improvement in their daily lives, as if the ideas were his own, and Tal was happy to let him take the credit.

Quietly, Tal got the two prisoners in the dungeon moved to better cells. One of them was a murderer, a powerful man who could pick up Anatoli and throw him across the courtyard if he took a mind. His name was Masterson. Tal had snuck down to visit him and found him slightly deranged, a bully who was prone to violence. But when Tal promised him a better cell and food, Masterson agreed to do as Tal told him.

The other man was a political prisoner, the former Baron

Visniya, who quickly agreed to whatever Tal's terms might be, against the chance of freedom and revenge on Duke Kaspar.

Tal held little hope that these men would prove reliable in the end, but for the moment, he wanted everyone who wasn't working for Kaspar on his side when the time came to move. He had a plan, but he was keeping it to himself, not even sharing the details with Will.

The former thief had become as faithful as a puppy. Besides his undying thanks for the improvement in his lot, he was now convinced that Tal was capable of anything he truly wished. But all Tal ever did was smile and merely say, 'Just keep your mind on today's business, Will.'

Weeks passed, and then another ship arrived, this time with provisions and a new cook. Zirga came to the dock and when he saw that Tal was no longer needed in the kitchen, the Governor visibly wilted.

Tal was in the kitchen when the new cook was shown in. The cook looked around and said, 'This will do.'

Tal glanced at Will, then started to leave. Zirga said, 'Where are you going?'

'Back to my cell, Governor.'

'Wait a minute.' He turned to the cook. 'What is your name?'

'Royce.' He was a stocky man of middle years, and it looked as if he had been drinking. His face was puffy and his jowls hung loosely, and there were dark circles underneath his eyes.

'Why are you here?'

The cook blinked like an owl caught in lantern-light. 'What?'

'Why are you here? What did you do to get yourself discharged from your last position?'

Royce hesitated and said, 'Well, I . . .'

'Don't lie to me!' shouted Zirga. 'You got drunk on the job, didn't you?'

The man lowered his eyes and nodded. 'Yes, sir. I worked at an inn called the Tumbled Maiden, and fell asleep while cooking a lamb on a spit. The fat caught fire and . . . the inn burned to the ground.'

'Ha!' said Zirga. 'I thought so.' He pointed at Royce. 'I asked for a guard, four years ago! So, you are now a guard.' Then he pointed at Tal. 'You are still the cook until they send me one who won't burn the keep down.'

Royce seemed about to protest, then thought better of it. He shrugged and looked at Zirga. 'What do I do?'

'For the time being, you help out here in the kitchen. Anatoli, you come with me.'

Tal smiled, and said to Royce, 'You get to sleep over there.' He pointed to the room that had been used by Charles, the previous cook. 'Put your belongings there. Then come back and wash vegetables.'

'I can do that,' said Royce as he picked up his bag and moved to the door.

Will said, 'Well, he can't be any worse helping around here than Anatoli was.'

Tal winced. 'Don't say that. Ruthia listens.'

Will nodded, making a good-luck sign at mention of the Goddess of Luck.

The addition of Royce was a stroke of good fortune for Tal. Although he was a drunk, he was experienced in the kitchen and quickly adapted to a routine that freed up much of Tal's time.

Tal utilized this free time wandering the island. He did it by increments, letting Zirga find him outside in the old marshalling yard, inspecting the chickens or pigs, then a month later, when Zirga came upon Tal down in the tiny meadow on the lee side of the island, seeing how the cattle and sheep were doing, Zirga didn't object.

By the onset of Tal's third winter, he knew the island as well as he knew the mountains of home. He knew the fastest way to the north beach, where there was a stand of trees containing a hive of bees. He smoked the bees out and robbed their honey the way his grandfather had taught him, and Zirga was inclined to say nothing about his forays as long as the food continued to be wonderful.

None of the guards seemed to notice Tal had moved two prisoners out of the dungeon, all assuming that Zirga had ordered it, and Zirga never bothered to inspect their quarters. And as far as Tal could see, Zirga assumed everyone was doing just fine until otherwise notified.

Tal had got to know every prisoner well. He had managed at one time or another to bring food personally to each of them. Between the information Will had already provided and his own discussions with the men, Tal had a good idea of what they were capable of.

It was an interesting mix, mostly political prisoners, which gave him a core of five men who were former nobles, like Visniya, men who were familiar with Kaspar's court or the administration of Olasko. These men Tal was determined to see safely home if possible. They would give him allies once he returned to Opardum, for they all had friends and families still at liberty.

The other thirteen men were common murderers, rapists,

habitual thieves and robbers, men who had been condemned to the Fortress of Despair because of some oddity in their case, or because a judge had wished them more suffering than a quick hanging would bring. These men were expendable to Tal, but at the start he would need strong and ruthless men if any of them were to survive.

So Tal was doing his best to keep everyone alive. He organized excuses to get prisoners out of their cells – such as the honey raid – or to clean away deadwood from the cattle meadow, or to chop firewood for the coming winter. Everyone got some exercise and much-needed sunshine and fresh air. He even convinced Zirga to allow the men to gather in the courtyard for a small celebration on Midsummer's Day, Banapis. Several men wept openly at the day spent outside and the food on the table.

None of these men would be fit for combat when he mounted his escape, and some would die along the way. But he was going to ensure they would survive as long as possible.

One night, as autumn approached, Will sat at the small table in the kitchen with Tal. He said, 'I talked to Donal today.'

'How is he?'

'The coughin' has stopped. He thanks you for that tea you sent 'im.'

'It's an old family recipe,' said Tal.

'You know, these men would die for you, Tal.'

Tal nodded.

'You've given them hope.'

Tal was silent, then said, 'I pray that's not a cruelty.'

'Me, too.' Will was silent as he chewed on a piece of ham. After he swallowed, he said, 'You remember when we first met?'

Tal nodded.

'You said I was "uncommonly cheerful for a man condemned to live his life on this rock". Remember?'

Tal nodded again.

'Back then, I had nothin' to lose. Now I find I'm not so happy, if'n you take my meaning.'

'I do,' said Tal. 'Now you feel as if you have something to lose.'

'Ya,' said Will. 'I feel like I got somethin' to lose.'

'Hope.'

'Hope,' Will agreed. 'So, let me cut right to it. When we goin' to escape?'

Tal was silent a moment, then said, 'Next spring. I don't know when exactly, but it'll be the day after the next ship puts in.'

'We goin' to boost a ship?'

'No,' said Tal. 'The men here are fitter than they were when I got here, but they're no match for Zirga's four guards and a ship full of healthy sailors.

'But there's a reason I want to go the day after the next ship puts in, and I'll tell you about it when it's time.'

'And that'll be . . . ?'

Tal grinned. 'The day the first ship puts in next spring.'

Will sighed, and resigned himself to having to wait another six months. After all, he'd already waited twelve years. What was another half year?

CHAPTER FIFTEEN

Escape

*T*AL WATCHED.

The ship lay off the point and Zirga and two guards, Anatoli and Kyle as always, waited to see if a new prisoner was being delivered. Tal observed from the entrance to the keep, hanging back in the shadows. Will stood behind him, also watching.

The longboat rowed from the ship to the dock and Tal saw a prisoner sitting in the centre of the boat. As was the case when Tal arrived, the sailors were efficient in getting the prisoner off the boat and up the ladder. As was the case when Tal arrived, Zirga didn't bother reading the writ on the dock, but directed the prisoner to follow him up the hill to the keep.

Tal felt the hair on the back of his neck rise. There was something very familiar about the prisoner, about the way he moved and carried himself. Before the man's features became clear, Tal was stepping back and saying to Will, 'Follow me.'

Will hurried along as Tal returned to the kitchen. When they reached the kitchen, they found Royce asleep in a chair, head on the table, an empty brandy bottle lying next to him. One of Tal's discoveries was that the ancient wine cellar of whatever noble had built this keep was intact, and while most of the wine still down there was long past being drinkable, there was an ample supply of spirits that hadn't gone bad. Tal had also discovered that Royce was very manageable if Tal let him get drunk once or twice a week.

Tal looked around and Will softly said, 'What is it?'

'The new prisoner, I know him,' whispered Tal.

'Who is he?'

Tal looked thoughtful. 'Someone I never expected to see again, unless I was running him through with my sword. He's Quentin Havrevulen, Duke Kaspar's Special Captain.'

'You mean he *was* Kaspar's Special Captain.'

'Apparently.' Tal thought. 'Don't talk to him when you take him his first meal. Just deliver it and see how he acts. I need to know if he's really a prisoner here or if this is another of Kaspar's schemes.'

'Why would the Duke exile his senior captain here?'

'That's what I intend to find out,' said Tal, 'but only when I'm ready.'

'We still go tomorrow?'

Tal had to decide quickly. He said, 'Yes. We go tomorrow, but tell no one. I know exactly what it is I wish to do and I don't want anyone tipping our hand before it's time.'

Will nodded. 'I'll do exactly what you say, Tal.'

Tal said, 'So, let's get back to making supper.'

Will said, 'With luck, our last one on this rock.'

Royce finished his meal and yawned. 'Think I'll turn in.'

Tal said nothing, but nodded. When Royce's door closed, Tal picked up his water cup and wooden spoon, put them on his plate, and carried them over to a big sink. Will followed suit. When they were as far away from Royce's door as possible, Tal said, 'What do you think of our new prisoner?'

'If he's workin' for Kaspar, he missed his callin', Tal. He should'a been an actor. He's no agent; I'll wager my life on it. He's got that look.'

Tal knew what Will meant. It was an expression of shock and disbelief, a sense that somehow a horrible mistake had been made. Only the hardened criminals didn't have it. Seven prisoners had arrived since Tal, although four had died, despite Tal's attempts to help. Three had simply not had the will to survive, and the fourth had suffered a gash on his hip that had turned putrid before it had been treated.

Zirga thought nothing of this, but to Tal every man lost was a lessening of his chance of survival. Still, he had a net gain of three men since he had formulated his plan, and those who had died would most likely have been among the first to fall after reaching the mainland.

Now Tal wrestled with what to do with Havrevulen. He would eventually see the man dead, and nothing would please him more than to leave him here with Zirga and the guards, except the risk that somehow Quint would turn that to his advantage and find a way to gain Kaspar's forgiveness.

Even the slightest possibility that Havrevulen might somehow survive forced Tal to one of two choices: either he kill him outright before they fled the island, or take him with them. There was no alternative but to talk to the man.

Tal waited until Zirga and the guards were asleep, then woke Will. 'One man at a time, have the prisoners come to the armoury. Tell them to keep quiet until I get there.'

'Where are you going?'

'To speak with our newest guest.'

Will and Tal parted company on the first landing of the keep, as Will continued going upward, and Tal found Quint's cell. Tal carried a kitchen knife under his tunic and made sure he could quickly reach it before he lifted the latch to Quint's cell door.

Quint came awake as Tal entered. 'Who is it?'

Tal stood in the gloom, his features hidden. 'Tal Hawkins,' he said quietly.

Quint rolled over, and sat up on the straw pallet, his back against the wall. 'How'd you find me?'

'You'll find things are lax around here, and if you know how, you can wrangle a few privileges.'

'Hmm,' said Quint noncommittally.

Tal said, 'What happened?'

Quint made a sound halfway between a grunt and laugh. 'Failure is what happened. You know Kaspar when it comes to failure.'

Tal knelt, keeping his hand on the knife's handle. 'Tell me.'

'Why?'

'Because I'm curious, and because I might be able to help.'

'Help? How?'

'I run the kitchen. If nothing else, I can make sure you get enough to eat.'

Quint's expression was hard to read in the gloom, but Tal sensed he was considering this. 'What have I to lose?' he said at last. 'I'm not going anywhere. All right, I'll tell you.

'Kaspar is not given to patience. After *you* didn't kill Duke Rodoski, I was sent on a mission, and I failed. Kaspar was not interested in my excuses, and here I am.'

Tal was silent for a moment, as if thinking, then said, 'You were his senior officer, his Special Captain, Quint. You commanded his entire army. It must have been a critical mission.'

'It was. I took a company of men dressed as bandits into the Mountains of Aranor. Intelligence told us that the Prince and his family were en route to their palace at Lake Shenan, to enjoy spring in the mountains. We were supposed to fall on the camp, overpower the guards, and kill the royal family.'

'Why?' said Tal in surprise. 'Phillip has always been Kaspar's lapdog, and Kaspar keeps him on a short leash. He's no threat. So why kill him?'

Quint shrugged, the gesture almost lost in the gloom. 'I don't know. Kaspar's been doing unpredictable things as long as I've been in his service, but lately . . . they border on the insane. He spends more and more time with that wizard and . . . I don't know.

'Somehow Aranor's men knew we were coming, or they just decided at the last moment to send out a much larger company of guards, but for whatever reason, while Prince Phillip was killed, Princess Alena fled to safety, to Opast, then on to the Isles. Now she and her sons are in Rillanon and both the Isles and Roldem are threatening Kaspar.'

Tal was silent again. After he thought about it, he said, 'Kaspar must have a traitor in his service, if they knew it was his men behind the attack.'

'I think so. Your man Amafi rose quickly after betraying you. Kaspar sent him out on one errand after another. At the start, I thought him a useful tool, but he is more than that.'

'Much more than a tool. He's a practised assassin.'

'Kaspar's plan was simple at first: to put himself in line for the throne of Roldem, then engineer a tragedy which would end King Carol's life along with his entire family at once; a ship sinking while they were all aboard would have been ideal.

'But things began to go wrong, starting with your failure to kill Duke Rodoski.'

Tal laughed. 'That was Kaspar's doing, didn't you know?'

'No,' said Quint quietly. 'I had no idea.'

Tal explained how he was to have been sacrificed while Prohaska carried out the actual murder. When he had finished, Havrevulen said, 'We were told that you had been discovered and that you gave up Prohaska, and that's why Kaspar sent you here.' Softly he added, 'Prohaska was a friend; I would have happily murdered you myself when I heard you betrayed him, Tal.' He shook his head in the gloom. 'To find out it was Kaspar . . .'

'Maybe not. In all of this, there's another hand at play.'

'I see that now. In the last two years Kaspar has asked me to draw up plans for several contingencies. Each time, after reviewing them, he rejected my plans and adopted plans that can only be called . . . strange.'

Tal considered his options. He had no desire to see Quint live one moment longer than necessary, but he also recognized him as a potential ally, if only for the short term. He had just arrived, so he hadn't suffered any debilitation from his imprisonment, and Tal knew he was a skilled swordsman, an experienced officer, and as cold-blooded as anyone he had met. He would be an asset during the escape. *If* he could be trusted.

Tal decided to explore a bit more.

'I suspect this Leso Varen's hands may be on this.'

'Probably. Kaspar has been becoming increasingly dependent upon him, spending more and more time in that abattoir Varen calls home.' Quint was quiet for a moment, then he said, 'I'm a soldier, Tal. I don't claim to be a . . . deep thinker. I'm a very good soldier, which is why I rose so high, but this is all beyond anything I have ever seen . . . it's beyond what I can imagine.

'I know we've never been . . . friends. I've sensed something between us since you first appeared. I even wondered if Campaneal's death in the Tournament of Champions was an accident or if you meant for him to die. And I never liked the way Natalia took to you.

'I guess what it is I'm trying to say is that fate has put us here together, so I see no reason for us to be at odds. After all, we're both going to be here a very long time, and neither of us needs more enemies.'

Tal stood up. 'Not that long.'

'What do you mean?' asked Quint.

'Come with me,' said Tal, pushing open the door.

Quint followed him and the two men moved quietly through the keep, past the guards' room, where Kyle lay sleeping on the floor, rather than sitting at his post. Once they were in the bowels of the keep, Tal said, 'Zirga counts on the island preventing our escape.'

'You're planning an escape?'

'No, we're escaping, right now.'

Reaching the armoury, Tal found all but three of the prisoners waiting, and a moment later, Will, Masterson and a man named Jenkins appeared with a single lantern. Tal spoke in a whisper. 'I doubt anyone can hear us, but let's err on the side of caution.'

'What are we doing?' asked one man.

'Escaping. I will tell you my plan. There is no debate. If you come with me, you follow orders, without question. If you won't, you stay behind with Zirga and the guards. Is that understood?'

Every man nodded or muttered agreement.

Tal said, 'Put on as much clothing as you can comfortably wear. You will be wet and cold before we are through.' Tal turned up the wick on the lantern and the room was illuminated. He pointed to a large pile of clothing in the corner.

Most men threw off their filthy rags and put on two or three pairs of trousers, and multiple shirts. 'In those chests are boots. Try to find a pair that fits.'

In less than ten minutes, the men stood dressed and every man wore sturdy boots. Tal said, 'Weapons,' and indicated the racks behind the men.

All the political prisoners, as well as Captain Quint, picked swords. The others picked cutlasses, falchions, and shortswords. Masterson, the huge murderer, favoured a large axe, and Tal considered he could probably cut a man in half with it.

Will found a pair of shoulder belts with loops for daggers and put it on, then filled the loops with six or seven blades. Tal chose a rapier, and a baldric with scabbard he could set on his right hip. He said to Quint, 'I wish I had practised more with my left hand back at Masters' Court.'

Quint chuckled. 'We're armed and outfitted, but how do we get off this rock?'

Tal motioned for everyone to follow and they quietly moved to the pantry. He pointed to a pile of bundles and whispered, 'Each man takes one.'

They did so and he led them back into the kitchen. 'Open them,' he instructed softly.

Inside each bundle was flint, steel, twine, and other useful items, as well as a handful of jerked beef and hardtack. Tal went to a barrel of apples and quickly tossed two to each man, then said, 'Will, get the waterskins.' While Will did that, Tal quickly went through the stores and added another half a dozen food items to the men's bundles.

Masterson said, 'Why all the skulking around? Why don't we just kill Zirga and the others?'

'And risk injury? You want to be left behind with four corpses and a broken arm?' Nobody spoke. 'Quint's the only man here fully fit. We're going to need every man here if any of us are to have a chance.'

Baron Visniya asked, 'Shouldn't we carry more food?'

'How far are we going?' asked another.

Tal said, 'Silence!' When they all stopped muttering, he said, 'Either follow orders or return to your cells. Questions are over.'

No man said another word, and Tal motioned for one of the prisoners to help Will pass out the waterskins. 'Fill them outside at the well.'

They followed him outside, and once the waterskins were filled, Tal led the group to the north beach. They went down a steep path and when they reached sand, Tal motioned for them to keep close, lest anyone get lost in the darkness. All three moons were down and Tal could barely find the small cave he had discovered two years ago.

A few minutes later, he found it. 'Move those rocks,' he said.

Some of the men moved a few small boulders that were keeping a pile of driftwood in place, and when that was removed, the cave opening was revealed. It was shallow and low, and two men had to kneel to enter. A few feet back, they found long poles and shorter logs, along with bundles of ropes, a small cask of nails and a hammer.

'What next?' asked Havrevulen.

'Build a raft,' said Tal, 'and we have less than four hours in which to do it.'

He gave instructions and the men laid out the logs that Tal had painstakingly cut and hauled down to the beach. He had scraped himself, dropped logs on his feet, fallen down the trail and earned bruises, twisted muscles and splinters, but over the past two years he had managed to cut down eight trees, strip them, and drag them down the trail from the woods above. The poles had proven far easier, since he had discovered them in storage in an abandoned warehouse near the outer wall. The wood was old, but still serviceable. Those he had got to the cave in a week.

A few of the men lashed the poles on top of the logs, and when they had done that, a frame lay on the sands. Tal raised a single mast, held to the centre by four interlocking boards, nailed fast to the two centre logs. The sail was a bedsheet, folded over and sewn to form a triangle, tacked to the top of the mast. It could be pulled open at the bottom and tied to the rear pole.

'We can't all stand on this thing,' said one of the men.

'We're not,' said Tal. He said to Will, 'There's another pile of driftwood over there.' He pointed in the dark. 'Take some men and move it.'

Will did as instructed and returned with large folded bundles of oil-treated canvas. It was laid on the left side of the raft. 'Put all your bundles into the canvas, along with your weapons.' After this was done, Tal said, 'Tie it securely, then lash it to the poles.'

When the bundle was in place, Tal said, 'Here's the plan. It'll be a month-and-a-half to three months before the next ship arrives. That gives us six to twelve weeks to get off the island and head to safety before Zirga can send word to Olasko we've escaped. If the ship goes straight to Opardum, that's another two weeks we're away from here.

'There's a strong current, and we're going to let it do some of our work for us pushing us north while we head for shore. Most of you are too weak to swim more than a few hundred yards, if that, but you can hang on, and the rest of us will kick. The wind will do a little of the work for us. We'll take turns pushing this raft towards the beaches. A man gets too weak to hang on, he can rest on the logs a bit. I reckon it'll take us a few hours to get to the mainland and carry us north while we're doing it. We should land five, maybe six miles north of here.'

'Where are we going?' asked Masterson.

'Karesh'kaar to start.' Tal looked around and said, 'In Bardac's Holdfast we'll be a company of mercenaries. After we get there, I will tell you what's next. I'll tell you this much now: some of you will not make it. Some of you will die in the attempt, but you were dead men in those cells anyway, so you will die free.

'For those who reach Karesh'kaar, I promise this much: if you want to quit and strike out on your own, I won't stop you. But if you stick with me, and if the gods favour us, one day we will be standing on the battlements of the citadel of Opardum, with Kaspar's head on a pike!'

The men actually cheered, and Tal said, 'Get the paddles.' He pointed to the cave.

Four men returned with the roughly-carved pieces of wood, barely recognizable as paddles. He had found four matching pieces of wood that he'd carved with a kitchen-knife. 'They're not much,' said Tal, 'but they are all we have. Now, get this raft in the water.'

The men picked up the makeshift vessel and waded quickly into the sea. With the moons down the breakers were rolling lightly, breaking at chest-height. After getting completely soaked, Tal and Will stood at the mast, and Tal said, 'Four men will sit on each outer log, and take turns paddling. The rest of you will hang on to the rear of the raft and you must kick and push. We have less than an hour before sunrise. Zirga and the others will be up within an hour after that, and I want to make sure we are far enough away that they can't see us from the top of the keep.' He detailed the eight strongest men, including Masterson and Quint, to paddle. The others hung on the back of the raft and let it carry them along until ordered to kick.

The current moved them northward, while the paddlers and kickers made slight headway towards the mainland. Except for Quint and Masterson, most of the men had almost no stamina, so at intervals, Tal had two men change places, coming out of the water to paddle, while those who had just paddled rested on the makeshift canvas deck. He hoped by rotating the duty more men might survive to reach the shore.

The progress was torturously slow, but when at last the sun rose over the eastern horizon, the keep was a distant dot to the southeast. Tal had better eyesight than most men, and he was convinced no one left at the keep would be able to see them from the roof.

At least that was his hope.

Zirga yawned as he left his quarters and scratched his backside. He saw Kyle standing at the door of the guards' room and knew instantly something was wrong. 'What is it? Did someone die during the night?'

Kyle shook his head and said, 'No. It's the prisoners.'

'What about them?'

'They're gone.'

'What do you mean they're gone?'

'None of them are in their cells.'

'That's impossible.' Zirga hurried to look in the cells himself, as if not trusting the guard's word. After a few minutes, he said, 'Someone's playing a game. Look in all the cells.' He shouted and in a few minutes Anatoli, Benson and Royce also appeared, looking equally confused. Zirga told them to search the entire keep, and when they returned reporting no one was around, he shouted, 'Then search the island!'

They took off and Zirga headed up to the roof of the keep. He blinked at the rising sun and looked around in every direction. For a brief instant he thought he saw a speck to the northwest, just on the horizon, but after a moment, he saw only water and sky. Knowing what he would hear when his men returned, Zirga descended slowly and walked to the kitchen.

As he suspected, there were clear signs that the armoury and pantry had been raided. He sat at the small table where Tal and Will ate every night and waited. Within an hour, the men returned, all reporting the same thing: no sign of the prisoners anywhere.

Zirga said, 'Who looked at the north beach?'

Benson, a portly man with almost no chin, said, 'I did, sir.'

'What did you see?'

'A beach, sir.'

Zirga shook his head. 'You idiot! I meant did you see tracks or signs of a boat being dragged up on the sand?'

'Not so's you'd notice, but then . . . I wasn't looking.'

Zirga shook his head and his expression was one of disbelief.

'I mean, I was lookin' for the men. You want me to go back and look for tracks?'

Zirga said, 'No need. They're not on the island.'

Anatoli said, 'What'll we do?'

Zirga took a deep breath and let out a long sigh. To Royce he said, 'Cook us something to eat.' To the others he said, 'We wait.'

'Wait? For what?' asked Kyle.

'For the first ship to show up and take us away.'

'Away? Where are we going?' asked Royce as he moved towards the pantry.

'Anywhere but Opardum,' said Zirga. 'When the Duke finds out we let seventeen prisoners just walk off this island, he'll send another governor and four new guards and we five will be the first new prisoners in this place.'

'I wouldn't like that,' said Anatoli.

Zirga just shook his head and covered his eyes. 'Bring me some brandy. That's a good lad.'

Anatoli did as he was told, and Zirga sat back, looking around the kitchen. 'I've got some gold put by, so maybe I can find something to do up in County Conar. I've got a cousin down in a village near the border of Salmater. He might have a place for me. Wherever I end up, lads, it's going to be far from here.' He heaved a regretful sigh. 'But I'm going to really miss those meals.'

The other three nodded and voiced agreement as Royce started to cook.

By midday Tal judged they had gone farther north than he had anticipated, and it was more difficult moving towards the mainland. They seemed to get no closer to land no matter how hard they paddled. He could faintly see white water breaking on the shores, so he knew they were no more than two miles out, but for the last hour they didn't seem to have been closing.

He looked at the men in the water and saw that several were showing signs of succumbing to the cold water. He ordered the paddlers into the water, then motioned for Will to follow him into the sea. He then told those looking weakest to get out and try to get as dry as possible in the sun as fresh paddlers took up their positions. There was a breeze blowing, which would help them dry out, but to Tal's irritation, it was blowing to the north-east, so the primitive sail would be of no use to them.

Tal watched closely and saw that two of the men who had just come out of the water were in serious trouble. Their teeth were chattering uncontrollably and they could barely hang on as they crouched on the logs. 'Sit athwart and let your feet dangle, and keep your hands on the log, so you don't fall in,' he instructed them. He knew that once their shirts dried they'd start feeling the heat of the sun, but it would be a close thing.

He gauged the progress they were making as best he could from in the water, but after nearly ten minutes, he thought if anything they were farther away. To those in the water with him, he said, 'Kick.'

He put his one good hand around the pole before him, then started kicking as hard as he could. The others followed his example while the paddlers redoubled their effort. After a few minutes, he shouted, 'Are we getting closer?'

'Yes,' came the answer from one of the men sitting before the mast. 'I'd say we were. Keep it up.'

For nearly half an hour the men in the water kicked, but except for Captain Quint, they were tiring quickly. Tal called out, 'Who feels fit to get in the water and kick?'

Four of the men who had been in the water an hour before indicated they were willing to trade places, and Tal organized a rotation of men in and out of the water. When it came time for him to climb out and rest, he could barely hoist himself up onto the logs without help. He huffed and took several deep breaths until he caught his wind, then he moved forward, scooting along on a log, until he could stand by the mast.

He saw they were making progress towards the mainland. 'Another hour!' he yelled encouragingly. 'That's all it will take and we'll be in the breakers!'

That seemed to revive the men in the water a bit and they redoubled their efforts. Tal looked around and considered himself fortunate. He had thought he might lose as many as four or five men getting to the mainland, but at the moment it looked as if all of them would get to shore.

Then he saw the first shark fin cutting towards the raft.

• CHAPTER SIXTEEN •

Survival

*T*AL STARED.

In mute horror he watched as the shark fin turned and moved in on the man at the far edge of the raft. Before he could give cry to a warning, the man's head vanished under the water, as if he had been grabbed by a giant hand and pulled under.

A moment later he popped back to the surface, his eyes wide in surprise, not quite sure what had happened. Then he started to gasp and a low cry came from his throat, rising in pitch to a terrified scream.

'Sharks!' shouted one of the paddlers, pointing to the right of the raft where more fins were cutting through the water. Tal counted and three more were coming in from that side, as another joined the one that had struck the first swimmer.

Men started shouting. Tal shouted back, 'Don't try to climb up! We'll all be swamped.'

He glanced around and saw that the men were verging on mindless panic, so he screamed, 'Kick! Kick as hard as you can!'

Suddenly the water was foaming as men thrashed, trying to propel the raft towards the beach as quickly as possible. The man whom the shark had attacked made eye contact with Tal for moment, his mouth working, although no sound emerged. Then his eyes rolled up in his head and he went under. When his body bobbed back to the surface, he upended, and both legs were missing.

Then Tal saw the blunt nose of the shark as it rose up from the depths and struck the corpse, seizing it in its mouth, and pulling it under.

'Kick, damn you!' shouted Will.

The men who were sitting between the paddlers put their outside hand down in the water and paddled desperately, as if that little bit of effort would somehow help speed them. Tal scanned the waves in all directions, looking for another fin, and saw one coming in from the right. He shouted, 'Shark!' and pointed. Then he told the paddler nearest to the monster, 'Hit it!'

The man looked at the shark heading almost straight at him and reflexively tried to stand up. Shouting in panic, he lost his balance and fell over, right into the path of the shark.

'Get out!' Tal cried.

Another shark came in fast behind the first, and the man was abruptly yanked downward, only to come up for a moment, trying to scream but making only gurgling noises as he choked on water, the sea around him churning white water and blood.

Tal leapt into the waves and with one stroke of his arm reached the paddle. He turned and kicked to bring himself back towards the raft. Holding his breath, he kicked twice more and felt hands pulling him out of the water.

'Are you mad?' Baron Visniya cried.

'We need the paddle!' Tal said, spitting out water.

He held it out and Visniya took it, replacing the man who had fallen. 'If they come close,' shouted Tal to those on the raft, 'hit them with the paddles!' To the men frantically pushing the raft he yelled, 'If they get near you, kick them, hit them, gouge their eyes, do anything to make them leave you alone!'

Tal glanced towards the coast and saw they had moved slightly closer, but their progress was still torturously slow. Clinging helplessly to the mast, he stood up and watched the sharks circle. Two or three of them darted in where the last two had pulled the paddler over, drawn by the blood.

Suddenly a third man was pulled under, and the men on either side of him shouted and one tried to climb back on the raft. Captain Quint shoved him back in, shouting, 'Kick, damn you!' then he jumped in next to him and replaced the man who had just been killed.

Will whispered, 'Three men, Tal!'

A man sitting to the fore on the left side of the raft threw himself into the water and started swimming to the shore. Tal had seen enough good swimmers in his lifetime to recognize that this man was unpractised. His strokes were frantic and unco-ordinated, wasteful of energy, so he did not have much forward momentum and would tire rapidly. Tal said to Will, 'He should have taken his boots off.'

No shark came near the man, seeming content for the moment

to feed on the ones already taken, but halfway between the raft and the breakers the swimmer's head went under and didn't reappear.

Tal again judged their progress and saw they were now drawing closer to the breakers. The rise and fall of the raft was increasing as the combers rolled in to the shoreline. 'Kick harder!' he shouted. 'We're almost there!'

Then the raft jerked as if it had hit a rock, and two men fell over on the right side. A second hard bump came from below and Tal shouted, 'There's one underneath us!' Both men were desperately trying to get back on the raft when one disappeared under the water before Tal's eyes. The other made it to the raft and climbed aboard, his paddle lost. The first man never reappeared, but the water turned dark with blood.

Tal shouted, 'Everyone, into the water!'

He leapt in next to the men propelling the raft from behind, put his one good hand on the raft and started kicking.

With less weight on the raft and more men pushing, the raft picked up speed. In a few minutes the surge of tide picked up the raft and moved it closer towards the mainland. Tal shouted, 'Swim for shore!'

Tal had been a powerful swimmer as a boy, but he had never swum with just one arm. He struggled to keep some sort of rhythm and kicked as hard as he could.

Suddenly his right foot touched something and he reached down with his left, and miraculously felt sand. The waves were breaking shallowly along the coast, no more than two or three feet high. He started to wade in and looked around. Men were still swimming behind him or wading through the surf towards the shore.

Behind the others he saw Captain Quint and shouted, 'Grab the raft!'

The Captain turned to see the raft riding in on the low breakers and he shouted for the others to help him pull it ashore. The two nearest men ignored him, they were so frantic to be out of the water, but another turned and did as told and soon others joined in and they were pulling the raft into the dry beach.

Men fell weeping to the sand. Exhausted, weak and frightened, they were nevertheless now free.

Tal looked around and started counting.

When he had done so, he knew the horrible fact: there were only eleven of them on the beach. One man had drowned himself and he had seen the sharks take four, so one more had been taken or drowned trying to reach the shore.

Baron Visniya, Masterson the murderer, Captain Quint, Tal and seven other men sat drenched on the sand. Then it hit Tal: Will wasn't there.

He looked out at the rolling water, listened to the sounds of breakers and the panting of the exhausted men. For a brief moment he expected to see Will pop out of the water and start walking towards them, but after a minute he acknowledged the truth: Will was gone.

Tal looked at the sky. It was an hour after noon. The journey from the island had taken seven hours and cost six lives, and they still had several hundred miles of trekking ahead of them before they reached civilization. The only solace at the moment for Tal was knowing that he was free and that pursuit wouldn't commence for weeks, perhaps months. He could concentrate on moving at a steady pace, keeping the men alive, and getting to somewhere where he could begin to put his plan into effect.

After taking one more look out to sea, he turned and said, 'Let's get the weapons and provisions off the raft, then we need to find a campsite and start a fire.'

Slowly the men got to their feet and moved to carry out their leader's orders.

Jenkins lay still, his face a mask of agony as Tal cut at his leg with a knife. The snake he had just killed lay a few feet away, still writhing after Tal had cut off its head.

'Is he going to die, Tal?' asked Quint.

'No, but he's going to wish he had before the poison runs its course.'

Tal had cut above the fang marks and he now sucked out as much of the blood and poison as he could. Quint looked around. They were in a rocky lowland, ten miles inland from the sea, following a series of ravines that ran along a line of foothills which paralleled the coast. Filthy, tired men stood and watched as Tal worked on Jenkins's leg.

Quint studied the sky and then the fallen man. 'All right,' he said. 'That's it for today. Get some wood and let's get a fire started.'

Tal said nothing. Quint had let his natural habit of leadership come to the fore and had assumed the position of second-in-command, and Tal didn't voice any objection. Order was welcome in this company.

Tal glanced from face to face as the men started to make camp, something in which they were well practised. Eleven men had walked out of the surf and now three weeks later, there were eight left in the company. Rafelson had fallen to his death as they climbed over a rather innocuous hill, stumbling and striking his head on a rock. Vilnewski had simply been found dead one morning under his cloak. Jacobo had died after being gored by a boar they had hunted. No one could stop the bleeding.

The men were weak and tired, and Tal had no idea how much longer they could endure this journey. He had a rough idea of where they were and realized at their present rate it would probably take them another month to reach the river that was the boundary between Olasko and Bardac's Holdfast. He thought Quint and Masterson had a good chance of making it to the end, and Baron Visniya had proven unexpectedly tough. Jenkins might make it if he survived the night with the snake's venom, but Tal was being optimistic. A healthy man would survive the snake bite, but Jenkins was far from healthy. They had lived on forage for three weeks now, and were the worse for it. Sleeping outside didn't help, because even though it was spring, the nights this far north were not gentle.

Tal motioned for Quint to move closer to him and said quietly, 'We need shelter. We need to have a place to rest up for a week, maybe more, a place where we can hunt and bring in some stores and get the men stronger.'

Quint nodded in agreement. 'We're a month from Bardac's, at least,' he said. 'Even if Jenkins hadn't found that snake he's not likely to make it.' He pointed towards three men who were looking for wood, but moving at a very slow pace. 'Donska, Whislia, and Stolinko are dead men within a week if we don't rest up.' He glanced around. 'But where?'

'A cave, maybe,' said Tal. 'You get the men comfortable about the fire, and I'll see if I can find shelter. I'll be back before dark.'

Tal returned two hours later, having found a cave up in a

ravine. He told the men, 'We'll stay here one more night, without moving Jenkins, then we'll head up there tomorrow.'

After a meagre meal of berries found along the way and the last of the dried boar meat, the men gathered close to the camp-fire and went to sleep. Jenkins groaned and his breathing became ragged and shallow.

Tal watched the man's face, seeing the perspiration running off as he whimpered.

Quint came over and softly asked, 'He going to make it?'

'Maybe,' said Tal. 'We'll know in the morning.'

Quint took Tal by the arm and moved him a little way from the others. 'Tal, you've said nothing about what we're going to do when we get to the border.'

'I'm counting on you to get us across, Quint. You know the Olaskon military better than anyone. Sometime or another you must have read a report or heard about a place we can cross, then circle around and get north of Karesh'kaar, so we can enter the city that way.'

Quint said, 'Maybe. I heard of some bog-land south of the river, maybe forty miles inland, where no one patrols; it's too treacherous. But even if we do get across, once we're in Karesh'kaar, what then?'

'We eat, we rest, we heal, then we start recruiting.'

'I thought all that "building an army" talk was just bravado.'

'I'm serious. I plan on sacking Opardum's citadel with Kaspar in it.'

Quint laughed. 'Have you ever seen a mercenary company, let alone been in one?'

Tal smiled. 'As a matter of fact, I have. Truth to tell, I was captain of a company.'

'Really?' said Quint. 'You never mentioned it.'

'I didn't think Kaspar would appreciate hearing about it.'

'Why?'

Tal said, 'Because I'm the man who killed Raven and destroyed his company, blunting Kaspar's attack into the land of the Orodon.'

Quint said nothing for a long moment. Then he laughed. 'My first reaction was to throttle you, because Kaspar was as mad as a bull with a porcupine up his arse, but now that I think of it, good for you. I served with Raven once. He was an evil bastard if there ever was one. I am a soldier, but I've no love for war. That man enjoyed slaughter. I saw him kill babies.'

Tal said nothing for a while, then asked, 'Why didn't you try to stop him?'

'I'd have had to kill him. And I was there as a military liaison, just making sure Raven found the right targets, not a commander telling him how to do his work.

'I saw him butcher women, order archers to shoot at old men, saw him ride over children . . .' Quint looked down for a moment as if the memories were uncomfortable. 'I saw him shoot down a boy, couldn't have been more than thirteen, fourteen. Poor lad was covered in blood, carrying a sword far too large for him, wobbly-legged, and half-dead already. I just warned Raven in case the lad got close enough to maybe take a cut at him, but instead of knocking him down or riding away, the bastard shot him with a crossbow.' He was silent for a bit, then added, 'Glad to hear you're the one who killed him, Tal. Makes me think you might have some hope of seeing this mad plan of yours work. But I have one question.'

'What?'

'Armies need gold. Last time I looked we weren't lugging any along with the supplies. How do you propose to get gold?'

Tal said, 'Get us to Karesh'kaar and I'll get us some gold.'

'I'll do my best,' said Quint. 'Why don't you turn in? I'll take the first watch.'

'Wake me in two hours,' said Tal. He found his own bundle, unrolled it and lay for a while thinking of what Quint had said. He remembered the day Quint had mentioned, for he had been the boy Raven had shot with the crossbow. He could recall in detail the Captain turning to Raven, while Lieutenant Campaneal sat on the other side, and Quint's mouth moving as he warned Raven of Tal's approach. And he well remembered the casual way in which Raven had raised his crossbow and shot him.

Tal rolled over. Liaison or not, Quint had still been there when his village had been destroyed. His distaste for Raven didn't change a thing. One day Quint was going to die at Tal's hands.

But before he fell into slumber, Tal wondered if it had been Quint who had saved Eye of the Blue-Winged Teal, and if there had been others saved as well.

He slept for two hours, was awakened by Quint, and then after two hours he awoke Visniya and returned to sleep. In the morning he awoke and stretched, then looked across to the campfire. Jenkins was dead.

The cave had been their home for a week, and the men were slowly growing stronger. Tal had set snares around the area and had caught enough rabbits, squirrels and one fat turkey that they were eating relatively well. He had found wild berries and a stand of plants he recognized from his homeland; the roots were edible and nourishing if slowly heated in water for a few hours. Lacking a pot, he contrived a way to cook them; he wrapped the tubers in leaves, and put them in a pit, which he filled with heated rocks, steaming the roots by pouring water over the rocks. The process was tedious and had to be repeated many times, but the men welcomed the addition to their diets.

Tal felt stronger than he had since leaving the Fortress, and he knew that in a few more days they would need to start the next leg of their journey. Quint came over to where Tal was sitting and asked, 'Do you think Kaspar will try to find us?'

'You know him better than I do. What do you think?'

'Depends.' The old soldier had become gaunt since leaving the Fortress and now had a ragged beard and matted hair. 'He may be too busy with another of his mad plans to send soldiers after us, but he'll surely have his agents around the region keeping an eye out for us.'

'He has agents in Karesh'kaar?'

Quint smiled. 'Everywhere. Some work directly for him, like you did, and others are just men who know that Kaspar pays well for certain information. There are a fair number of Olaskons living in Bardac's, and I've seen the reports. I don't know who's writing them, but Kaspar's got eyes everywhere.'

'So what? Once we're out of Olasko, he can't arrest us.'

'But he can kill us,' said Quint. He laughed. 'My only pleasure these days is imagining him fuming when he hears we've escaped. It will annoy him no end not knowing where we are. Given his nature, he will assume we're sitting in some tavern right now, drinking, eating and whoring, laughing at him and calling him a fool. Brooding is his downfall.'

Tal didn't smile. 'I take no comfort from Kaspar getting distressed.' He held out the stump of his right arm. 'He has this and many more things to answer for. You might be content to get away from him and find service elsewhere, Quint, but I mean to see him dead at the end of my sword.' Tal's eyes became cold. 'And not until I've taken everything from him. First I destroy his power, then I take away his wealth, *then* I kill him.'

Quint said, 'Dreams are nice, Tal, but look where we are.'

Tal looked around the rocky hills, which were broken only by stands of trees and brush. The afternoon wind was blowing, hot with the promise of summer to come, and birds could be heard in all directions. He looked back at Quint. 'Well, I didn't say I was going to do it today.'

Quint laughed. 'Very well.'

Tal stood up. To the other men he said, 'I think after a couple more days of hunting we'll start moving north again. I'd like to sleep in a bed before another month goes past.'

The men nodded and Tal turned to Quint. 'I think I'll check the snares.'

Quint nodded and watched as Tal walked away, carrying a spear he had made from a sapling, a knife at his belt, his sword cast aside in his bedding for the time being. The former captain shook his head. Tal looked nothing like the Champion of the Masters' Court, nor would he even if he had had both arms. But then, Quint considered, he looked nothing like the commander of the Armies of Olasko, either. He decided to head down to the lake they had passed on their way up to the cave and try his hand at fishing.

Five ragged men waded through the bogs. Fetid pools covered in green slime were bounded by muddy flats. Trees with stunted branches dotted the landscape, small markers by which they judged their position as they moved north.

Tal, Quint, Masterson, Visniya and another former nobleman, Stolinko, all who were left from the escape from the Fortress of Despair, waded through ankle-deep water. Flies plagued them, and the day's heat beat down on them. Even after the cave's brief respite Donska and Whislia had deteriorated during the arduous journey and they also had been lost.

'You'd think with this heat this damn place would dry up,' said Masterson, his huge axe carried over his shoulder.

Quint grunted something approximating a laugh.

Tal said, 'We're downhill from a big range of mountains.' He stopped a moment, wiping his brow, then continued. 'It rains up there a lot and this part of the countryside is like a bloody big bowl that doesn't drain quite as fast as it fills up, no matter what the weather's like.' He pointed in the direction they were moving. 'But out there, somewhere, it *is* draining, and when we find a good-size stream coming out of this mess, it'll lead us to the river.'

Quint nodded. 'If what I remember from the maps of the area is right, we should be hitting the river in a day or two.'

'How are we getting across?' asked Visniya.

'There are fords,' said Quint. 'Quite a few, not well known, but reports list them. When we get to the river bank we turn downstream. We should find one in a couple of days.'

'If a patrol doesn't find us first,' said Stolinko. He was a dour man who didn't talk much. Tal wasn't quite sure what Stolinko had done to offend Kaspar, but he had turned out to be of a tough, reliable type who did his share of work without complaint.

Quint said, 'Our patrols don't come this far inland. No need.' He waved his hand around. 'See any reason to guard this?'

They were out of food, and there was nothing obviously edible in sight, so they staggered on, hoping to leave the bog soon. Around mid-afternoon, Tal said, 'I think we're heading into deeper water.'

The others noticed that the water was now up around their knees.

'The trees are thinning out,' said Masterson.

Tal said to Quint, 'You've never been up here before?'

'Not here. I've inspected the garrison at City of the Guardian, and ridden a patrol inland, but nothing this far out.'

'Wait here a minute,' Tal said.

He circled around them for the better part of twenty minutes then returned and said, 'The water is moving that way.' He pointed to the east.

'What does that mean?' asked Visniya.

'It means the river is *that* way,' said Tal. He headed off in the indicated direction.

They began hitting drier ground in an hour, and as sundown neared, they found the land rising ahead of them and to the right, and the bog draining off to the left, feeding what was now clearly a wide, but moving body of water. 'Let's camp up there for the night,' said Tal, pointing to an elevation that should prove dry. 'Then tomorrow we'll follow this water and see where it leads us.'

They made a cold camp, without even any food, so it was a tired and unhappy band that awoke the next morning and set off. As Tal had predicted, the water became a stream which ran quickly downhill. Two hours after they had started, they came over a rise and saw the river.

Tal studied the landscape. 'I see no signs of anyone else being around here.'

'We're too far east for patrols,' said Quint. 'This is no-man's country. The army doesn't patrol because even the smugglers avoid it.'

'Why?' asked Stolinko.

Quint said, 'No one knows. Rumours. Bands of inhuman monsters, or wild primitives who eat human flesh.' He saw the expressions on his companions' faces and laughed. 'Those are stories. There are some people living around here – the gods only know why they do – but mostly no one comes here because this land is worthless.' He pointed to the river. 'Across the river is Bardac's. There's a pretty little coastline over there and a thousand square miles of land even a pig farmer couldn't use. Bogs worse than the one we just left, salt flats, pine barrens, marshes, who knows what else? Everything in Bardac's worth taking is within fifty miles of the coast. The only exception is the city of Qulak, which guards the pass leading into Aranor. You've got a road from Karesh'kaar to there and also from Bishop's Point up north on the coast. One road from Karesh'kaar, to Traitor's Cove, to Bishop's Point. So, there you have it, four cities, three roads, and about a hundred jumped-up bandit chieftains calling themselves Baron this and Count that.

'Whenever someone tried to build anything this side of the river, bandits from across the river came down and took it. That's why everything worth talking about in Olasko is down south,' said Quint.

'So you think we'll have no trouble getting across the river?' asked Tal.

'Oh, getting across may be the least of our problems,' said Quint. He looked at his companions. 'A band of seventeen men might have been enough to prevent us from getting jumped, but the first band of rogues or the first "noble" we blunder into –' he shrugged '– they'll cut our throats first, then discover we have nothing worth stealing. The bastards won't even apologize afterwards.'

'Well, let's stop talking about it and get down there,' said Masterson.

Tal nodded. 'Let's go.'

They moved along the banks of the stream and discovered that the river was farther off than it looked. It was midday when they reached the banks just to the west of where the stream emptied into the river. Tal looked around. 'Look at the colour.'

'What about it?' asked Masterson.

'The stream must be dumping silt here. It's shallow. I'm going to try to cross.'

Tal waded into the water and found the river was running fast, but that it wasn't too deep. He moved out until he was nearly a third of the way across and the water was only up to mid-thigh. He stopped and looked, watching the currents, the swirls and eddies, then he waved for the others to follow.

The water deepened, and suddenly fell off to a channel on the side opposite where the stream flowed in. He started to swim. The men were underfed and weak with exhaustion and lack of food, but he reckoned that if a one-armed man carrying a sword and spear could get across, so could they.

A few minutes after he had reached the far shore, Masterson came across, followed by the others.

Quint looked around. 'My friends, welcome to Bardac's Holdfast.'

'I'm glad that's behind us,' Visniya muttered.

'Don't be so happy,' Quint said. 'It's now that things get difficult.'

'What do we do?' asked Stolinko.

Tal looked at Quint and said, 'I think we go north, find the road, then turn east for Karesh'kaar.'

'That would work if it wasn't for the fact that every bandit in the region uses that road. I think we find out where it is, then try to work our way west just in sight of it, but hopefully out of sight of anyone else. Any man not wearing the colours of a local noble is fair game for murder, robbery, slavers. There's law up here, but it's rough law, and it is usually a case of who has the most weapons.'

'Sounds like my kind of place,' declared Masterson, hefting his axe.

Dryly, Stolinko said, 'At least one of us is happy.'

'Well, the day's not getting any longer,' said Tal and he started hiking up the river bank, heading north.

'Man, I'm going to go mad smelling that,' said Masterson. The smell of cooking was carried towards them on the breeze.

'Keep your voice down,' whispered Tal.

They lay on their stomachs along a ridge as the sun set, over-looking the road leading to Karesh'kaar. Camped below was what appeared to be a slave caravan. About thirty young men and women were chained in a coffle, and were strung out along the side of the road, their chains secured at either end to a wagon. Six guards were posted, three at each wagon, along with a driver who tended the horses.

'What do you think's in those wagons?' asked Visniya.

Tal whispered, 'Supplies, I'm guessing.' He turned to Quint. 'Where are the slaves from?'

'Who knows? If they're coming down from the mountains, they may be from a border raid into Aranor. Or they could be some poor bastards taken in a raid from one "noble's" property by another "noble". The way things work up here, if you're more than a day's ride from your ruler's castle, you're fair game.' He pointed to the wagon in the front. 'See that banner? Holmalee, a count of sorts, with a pretty big army. He's local to this area. That's why there's only six guards, instead of sixty. This close to Holmalee's castle, no one is going to muck about with his caravan.'

'What are we going to do?' asked Stolinko.

Tal looked at his four companions. They were on the verge of collapse. Quint judged them to be a day or two more from the city of Karesh'kaar, but Tal doubted they could make it through another half-day without something to eat. It was three days since they had last eaten, and that had been nothing more than berries. It was five days since they had finished the last of the food they had carried with them.

Tal said, 'We wait until dark. Then we slip down and kill the guards.'

Masterson said, 'Wonderful.'

Visniya said, 'I don't know if I can fight.'

Tal said, 'Don't worry. I'll take out one sentry, and if they have a second, Quint will take him out. If we don't alarm the slaves, we should be able to finish them off before they are awake.'

He started moving down the incline, motioning for the others to follow. At the bottom of the rise, he led them into a stand of trees. 'We hide here just in case one of the guards is the fastidious type and comes over the rise to take a piss.'

They settled in and waited for night to fall.

Tal crept down the hillside. The sentry was sitting with his back against a wagon wheel, his head nodding as his chin touched his chest. The two other guards were sleeping near the fire. The slaves were all asleep on the ground, and at the other end of the coffle another guard sat by the other wagon. His two companions appeared to be fast asleep.

Quint was moving parallel to Tal, his task being to kill the sentry farthest from where they had come over the rise. The other three men would come out of the trees at the first hint of trouble.

Tal reached a point near his man, who suddenly started awake, perhaps sensing someone's approach. Tal slashed the man's throat before he could cry out and his hands went up, a fountain of blood spurting through his fingers as he struggled in vain to hold back the blood. Then his eyes went glassy and he fell over.

Tal quickly killed the two sleeping men.

Quint's guard died silently, but one of the sleeping men awoke, crying out in alarm. Suddenly the slaves were awake, yelling, crying and screaming, imagining that whatever new horror was about in the night would mean more suffering for them.

Masterson and the others came running out of the copse and quickly overpowered the guards and suddenly only Tal's men and the slaves were alive. No one hesitated. There was still food by the fire and all five men fell to ravenously.

Tal stood with a half-eaten chicken in his hand and saw several of the slaves were pulling on their chain, as if to rip it from the metal eyelet that fastened it to the wagon. 'Stop it!' shouted Tal in the Opardum dialect of Roldemish. 'If you want to live, stop it.'

The slaves stopped. Tal chewed and swallowed, convinced he had never tasted chicken this good in his life. He went over to inspect the slaves. There were close to twenty young women, none older than perhaps twenty years of age. All were very pretty. The men were all young as well, healthy and broad-shouldered: for slaves they appeared to be surprisingly well fed and fit.

Quint came over, chewing some bread dripping with butter and honey. 'Who are you?' he asked a young man standing next to Tal.

'My name is Jessie.'

'Aranor?'

'Yes. The village of Talabria.'

'You all from Aranor?'

'No,' said one young woman. 'I am from a village near Qulak. My father sold me to pay taxes.'

Quint looked at several more slaves then laughed. 'All heading for brothels, girls and boys alike.'

'How do you know?' asked Tal.

'Look at them. Clean them up, dress them, oil their hair, and rich merchants from Kesh will pay their weight in gold.' He paused, then said to the nearest girl, 'Did any of these men have their way with you?'

She lowered her eyes, and Tal was struck by how lovely she was. 'No, sir. The guards left us all alone.'

Quint said, 'That settles it. I'll bet most of these girls are virgins, and any guard touching them would get his head taken from his shoulders by their master.' He shouted, 'Do you know who owns you?'

One of the young men cried, 'No man owns me!'

Quint's grin spread. He walked over to the boy, who was no more than seventeen or eighteen, and slapped him on the shoulder. 'Bravely said, lad.' Then he ran his hand down the boy's face and across his shoulders. 'And some rich Keshian wine trader will pay dearly to see that skin left unblemished. Otherwise they'd have beaten any hint of defiance out of you.'

A girl said, 'These men worked for Count Holmalee. He is selling us to a slaver in the city named Janoski. I heard the guards talking.'

Tal ate enough to kill most of the hunger pangs in his stomach and said, 'Let's see what's in the wagons.' As he had suspected, there were supplies for the slaves, including a cage full of live chickens.

Quint inspected the other wagons. 'We got lucky,' he declared. 'How?'

'Count Holmalee and trader Janoski wanted this lot pretty for the auction block in Karesh'kaar. There's enough food here for three times the slaves. Each of these will bring four, five times as much on the block as the average house-servant or field-hand.' He rubbed his chin. 'So, what do you propose to do with them?'

Tal grinned. 'Free them. I told you, I'm starting an army.' To the others he yelled, 'Find the key on those guards, and turn this bunch loose.'

The slaves started talking excitedly among themselves. One girl shrieked and Tal saw that Masterson was trying to paw her.

'Masterson!' Tal shouted. 'Keep your hands to yourself. If she doesn't turn you into a eunuch, I will.'

'She's a slave! And a damn pleasure-slave, for that matter.'

'No she's not,' said Tal. 'She's free.'

At that, the slaves all started talking at the same time.

Tal shouted, 'All of you shut up!'

The talk quietened, and Tal said, 'I'm Tal Hawkins. I'm a mercenary captain.' He took down the banner of Count Holmalee and threw it on the fire. 'I need an army, so here's your choice. You can leave now, and take your chances on getting back home again. You know what it's like on the road, so you have an idea of the risks. Or you can stay with us. You'll be free soldiers, but you'll obey me. You'll get an equal share in any plunder and you'll get paid when we don't fight.' He looked at a particularly beautiful young girl with black eyes and raven tresses who stepped to the front. 'You women; there will be no camp-followers in my army. No whores. Anyone who's with us fights. That includes women too. If you don't know how to fight, we'll teach you. Now, you have until dawn to decide. Stay and fight, or leave on your own and take your chances.'

He turned and went back to the fire to find out what else there was worth eating. He settled down with a block of hard cheese and some bread. Visniya had found a wine skin and Tal took a deep drink before passing it on. With a mouth full of food, he said, 'After we eat, let's get rid of those bodies.'

Quint sat down next to him. 'One thing.'

'What?'

'You may not have the best fighters around, but damn me if you don't have the prettiest army I've ever seen.'

Tal laughed.

CHAPTER SEVENTEEN

Mercenaries

*T*HE GUARD STARED.

As strange a band of mercenaries as he had ever seen was approaching the gate of Karesh'kaar. Tal had taken the arms and armour from the six dead guards and passed it among the thirty slaves. Some wore only a helm, or a breastplate with just a dagger at their belt, while others carried a sword and wore no armour, but each had something that made them look like soldiers. Every morning before breaking camp, Tal had had his men instruct the former slaves as to the rudiments of fighting. Some learned slowly, but they grew in confidence by the day.

The sergeant of the guard at the gate studied them as the two wagons and thirty-five mercenaries rolled through the gate. They wore an assortment of ragged clothing: some wore boots, while others wore only sandals, and the women wore shifts instead of tunics and trousers – which hardly made them unique in the guard's experience – but what was strangest was most of them were young and looked like pleasure-slaves. Even odder was the leader, a one-armed man who looked as if he hadn't had a bath in months.

The guard questioned Tal briefly, then waved them into the city. Tal organized them in a small market square. 'Sell everything you can,' he instructed Quint. The wagons contained mostly foodstuffs, but also an assortment of cookware and a small box of trade items. 'I'll have gold for us in a day or two, but we need a place to stay for the night. Find the cheapest nearby inn where these children won't get raped, have their throats cut, or get enslaved again, then send word to me where you are.'

'Where are you going to be?' asked Quint.

'At a different inn, the Anvil and Tong.'

'Why don't we go there?'

'I have my reasons. Find somewhere nearby, then send word.' As Tal walked away, he looked over his shoulder and added, 'Oh, and have Masterson stand behind you when you dicker price for the horses and wagons. It should help.'

Quint nodded with a laugh and turned to oversee his charges.

Tal asked several times for directions and at last spotted an old, faded sign displaying a pair of tongs holding an anvil. He entered and saw that the inn was empty. For this time of the day he had expected one or two customers, but he was just as happy for the privacy. He went to the bar and waited. A moment later a young woman came out and said, 'Can I get you something?'

'I need to send a message,' said Tal.

The girl looked surprised. 'Sir? I don't take your meaning?'

'Then get someone who does,' he said quietly. 'I need to send a message to the Squire of Forest Deep.'

The girl nodded and left. In a few minutes, she returned with another woman, slightly older, behind her. The woman looked at him for a minute then said, 'Mayami said something about a message, sir?'

'I need to send a message to the Squire of Forest Deep.'

The second woman turned to the girl and said, 'I'll take care of this. Go to the kitchen and wait there.'

'Yes, mam.'

When the girl was gone, the woman said, 'Do you have the message?'

'No. Give me something to write on and I'll pen one, or you can just tell Magnus or Nakor or Robert to use their arts and get here as soon as they can, tomorrow if possible, though tonight would be even better.'

The woman studied Tal's face. 'I don't know what you're talking about, sir.'

Tal laughed. 'You know exactly what I'm talking about. I know I'm different from what you remember: I'm down to skin and bone, look like hell, smell like a week-dead cat, and I've lost an arm, but you spent too many nights in my bed not to recognize me, Lela.'

Her eyes widened and she said, 'Talon?'

With tears threatening to well up and run down his face, Tal said, 'It's good to see an old friend, my love. Please, I need you to get word to Sorcerer's Isle as quickly as you can, then if you don't mind, I would love a mug of ale.'

She stared at him, then put her hand on his. 'I'll take care of both.'

She left him alone for only a few moments, then came back with a large pewter jack of ale. He drank it half-empty in one gulp then put it down. 'Last I saw of you was waiting tables at the Admiral Trask in Krondor, when Caleb and I came through.'

'They move us around,' said the girl Tal had known as Lela. 'It doesn't do to have people become too familiar with a face. Here I'm called Maryanna, Talon.'

'And I'm known as Tal. I saw Alysandra in Opardum,' said Tal.

'It's better if I don't know about that.'

Tal sighed. 'I know. What you don't know, you can't betray.'

He finished his drink and suddenly felt the hair on his arms and neck stand up.

Magic.

He turned and from the back room a familiar figure emerged. A skinny man with a shoulder bag at his side entered the room.

Nakor looked at Tal and said, 'Got yourself in some kind of mess, I hear. What do you need?'

Tal smiled. 'Gold, lots of it.'

'Gold I can get. What else?'

'Weapons, horses, whatever else I need to build an army.'

'Sounds interesting.' He turned to Maryanna. 'Give me an ale and get him another.' He motioned for Tal to sit and they occupied a table. 'What else?'

'Clothing and supplies I can buy locally, but if you can, I'd like you to find a man up in Latagore named John Creed, and see if he can recruit for me and bring mercenaries south.'

'So, what are you going to do with this army when you have it?'

'I plan on sacking Opardum.'

Nakor grinned and took a swig of ale. 'That sounds like fun. Others have tried it, but you might get lucky.'

'I will if you and your friends will help.'

'What do you need from us, besides the gold, of course?'

'I need someone to keep Leso Varen out of the way.'

Nakor shrugged. 'I'll have to talk to the others about that.'

Tal told Nakor everything that had happened to him since his last visit from Magnus. He detailed his murder of Princess Svetlana and his failed attempt on Duke Rodoski. He told him of Amafi's betrayal and Kaspar's decision to sacrifice Tal.

Nakor shook his head. 'One thing I don't understand.'

'What?'

'Kaspar is nobody's fool, yet many of these things you've talked about are . . . mad. He's alienated every potential ally, and he's ensured that he will probably never get another opportunity to get at any member of Roldem's royal family. Even though no one can prove anything, they know. Even if he's there on a state visit and everyone's standing around with those painful smiles –' Nakor grimaced with his teeth clenched to demonstrate '– they're going to watch him every minute. No one will trust him ever again. What is he up to?'

'I have no idea,' said Tal. 'I just thought it was a matter of Kaspar's vanity.'

'Kaspar's arrogant,' said Nakor, 'but he's not vain. He's earned his reputation as dangerous.' He was silent for a minute. 'Whatever we think he's doing, we can almost be certain he's doing something else.' Nakor said, 'If you're cheating a man at cards, you draw his attention to the one place you don't mind him watching carefully, so you can do what you wish where you wish to do it.'

'That almost makes sense.'

Nakor grinned. 'Kaspar is blundering about trying to kill people because that's what he wants us to watch. So, where does he not want us to look?'

Tal shook his head. 'He's got agents running around everywhere, Nakor. He's got them trying to kill people. He looks as if he doesn't care if he starts a war. The only place I've seen where he doesn't want anyone looking around is that part of the citadel where Leso Varen resides.'

Nakor nodded. 'Then that's where we will have to look, my friend.'

'Well, you'll have to do something about the wizard. I've been in his quarters twice, and neither time left me confident that I can walk in there and engage him in polite conversation, let alone a duel. I suspect he'd reduce me to smoking ash or turn me into a toad or something else before I got within a sword's thrust of him.'

'You'd be surprised,' said Nakor. 'He's a very powerful magician, but sometimes such men are vulnerable to very simple things. I will have to see what we can do about him.'

Tal knew he would have to discuss it with Pug, Miranda and the other senior members of the Conclave. 'I understand. But I think Kaspar may be involved in some very black arts.'

'Oh, we know he is. That message you sent was extremely useful. It confirmed some things we already suspected.' Nakor sat back. 'Leso Varen is a very bad man, and he's trying some particularly evil magic these days. Pug will tell you about him if you live long enough to see him again. But they have crossed paths before and Varen opposes everything Pug and the Conclave stand for.'

'Am I working for you again?'

'In a manner of speaking, you always were. But yes, you are, especially if we start giving you gold, my friend.'

Tal nodded. 'Understood, but I mean to have Kaspar's head on a pike, Nakor.'

Nakor stood. 'I'd better get back. Anything else?'

With a wry smile, Tal held out his right arm, showing the stump. 'Can you fix this?'

Nakor shook his head. 'No.' Then he smiled. 'But I know someone who can.' He walked back to the door to the kitchen and said, 'Be here tomorrow, at the same time. I'll have your gold and some answers for you.'

He left Tal alone again with Maryanna. She came over with a pitcher of ale and refilled his jack. 'You look like you could use a bath.' Then she wrinkled her nose. 'Or a couple of them.'

'Do you have any old clothing?' Tal asked.

'Maybe,' she said. 'Wait here and I'll have Mayami heat some water and you can bathe in my room.' She moved towards the kitchen. 'You stay here and I'll send her to get you when the bath is hot. Want something to eat?'

'Whatever you have.'

She returned in a few minutes with a plate of fruit, cheese and some bread. Tal had eaten most of it by the time the girl returned to lead him to the tub.

As he settled back in the hot water, the door opened and Maryanna entered. She held out a small jar. 'Thought you might like this.' She poured a bit of the liquid on her hand and started rubbing his back. He caught the scent of lilacs.

There came a knock at the door and Mayami entered, saying, 'There's a man here, sir. He said to tell you your men are bedding down at the Green Wagon Wheel.'

Tal thanked her and she closed the door. Maryanna said, 'You're all skin and bones. What happened to you?'

'A bit more than three years in prison, where Duke Kaspar had them cut off my right arm, and a couple of months hiking overland from Olasko to here. Other than that, not much.'

She laughed. 'You still have that sense of humour, don't you?'

'What sense of humour?' He looked over his shoulder. 'I don't remember being particularly funny when we were at Kendrick's.'

'Oh, you were funny,' said the girl once known as Lela. 'You just weren't *intentionally* funny.'

He turned and grabbed her, pulling her into the small tub with him. She shrieked and laughed as he got her dress soaked. 'Talon!'

'It's Tal,' he said, then he kissed her passionately.

She returned the kiss then pushed away a little. 'Three years in prison?'

'Yes,' he said.

'Oh, you poor dear,' she cooed, as she started to unfasten her blouse.

Tal wanted to scratch his right arm in the worst way. True to his word, a few days after first meeting with Tal, Nakor had taken him to see a priest on an island somewhere. All Tal knew was that one moment he was standing with him in the Anvil and Tong, and the next they were on a beach in front of an ancient temple at the dead of night. Nakor spoke to the priest waiting there in a language Tal had never heard before and the priest had nodded, then examined Tal's wounded arm.

Tal got the gist of it even though he didn't understand a word.

This priest owed Nakor a favour, and Nakor sweetened the deal with a pouch of gold. Tal was made to lie on a table surrounded by candles in a room hung with tapestries bearing arcane designs. Tal had no idea which god or goddess this temple venerated, because there was not a single familiar icon or image anywhere.

The priest rubbed something on the stump of his arm and intoned several different prayers, then had Tal drink a noxious-tasting beverage. Then suddenly they were back at the Anvil and Tong.

Days went by with no apparent change in the arm. Tal busied himself with training his recruits and building his army. The gold secured them an abandoned farmhouse half an hour's ride out of the city that they'd use as a base. He bought horses, weapons, supplies and clothing.

Within a week it was clear which of the freed slaves would make soldiers and which were useless as soldiers. Four of the girls and two of the boys were given menial tasks around the property, while the remaining twenty-four continued to train with weapons.

Tal had cautioned Masterson about leaving the girls alone, unless they invited his attentions, and sent him to the city a couple of days a week to get drunk and spend time with the whores. Since arriving at the farm, Tal had established his chain of command. Quint was his deputy, while Baron Visniya was his intelligence officer. Within a few days, Visniya had messages on their way to contacts of his in Opardum. These were people he trusted, he told Tal, and he kept the language of the messages circumspect enough that if Kaspar's agents intercepted them, they would discover nothing useful. They would wait for replies before attempting to develop any intelligence about Opardum.

Stolinko turned out to be an adept quartermaster and a natural-born trader, so he often went to town to buy supplies.

One morning, Tal stood out on the porch of the farmhouse, watching Visniya teach the former slaves how to ride a horse. He absently started scratching at his stump, then pulled his hand away. It was tender.

He went inside and sat down at the table they used for meetings and started unwinding the bandage from around the stump. When he got it clear he looked at his severed arm and saw that a lot of the skin was flaking off. He picked at it a little and then noticed little bumps at the point of the stump. He examined it closely, wondering if Nakor's priest friend had somehow given him something that was making it fester. He got as close as he could without crossing his eyes and saw that there were five distinct protuberances coming up.

He studied it for a long minute, then gave up and washed the stump. The soothing bath seemed to help the itching, but did nothing to alleviate the return of the sensations he had experienced for a long time after his arm had been severed, the impression of having fingers and a hand, and the feeling of 'connection', that he should somehow be able to use those digits. He shrugged and returned to his work.

Within a few weeks he would start actively recruiting mercenaries. He had enquired about the difficulties he faced in building a private army and had been told that he could do pretty much anything outside the city as long as local officials were bribed. The power in the region was divided equally between the Lord Mayor of the city and his ruling council and the local

Baron, Lord Reslaz. An independent navy, funded by everyone along the coast with an interest in keeping their own ships afloat, was based out of Traitor's Cove. When it came time to secure transport for his army, Tal would have to talk to them; they had an office and a representative in Karesh'kaar.

Tal had introduced himself to the Lord Mayor, and offered him a sizeable gift. He had done the same with Lord Reslaz. By the time he had left the Baron's castle, they had consumed a great deal of wine and Reslaz had let Tal know that if he was looking for allies in some great undertaking, Tal could count on his support, for a reasonable split of any booty.

Tal was sitting at the table pondering the situation when Quint entered and said, 'You look lost.'

'I was just thinking. We've landed in a nation of pirates.'

Quint pulled up a chair and sat down. 'There are moments when Kaspar's desire to bring order to the region looks attractive.'

'It's how he wishes to bring order I object to,' said Tal. 'He regards people as disposable.'

'He wasn't always like that, you know,' said Quint. 'I'm not trying to make excuses for him. He was always a hard man, even when he was little more than a boy; he could be beaten bloody by older boys in a game of ball and want to get right back in to give as good as he got. But he was never murderous.' Quint reached over for a pear from the nearby counter and took a bite. 'I mean, if he had an enemy he could be ruthless, but that was only with enemies. Now, he just doesn't care who gets hurt.' Quint shrugged. 'I think it's Varen. I think he's the cause of Kaspar's change.'

'Whatever, he's got to be stopped.'

'You'll need more than that bunch of babies out at the pasture learning to ride.'

Tal laughed. 'I know. I'm keeping them around mostly because I don't know what else to do with them. I can't get them back home, and I won't sell them, and I would like to have at least a dozen or so men with swords walking around when I start to recruit.'

'When will that be?'

'A couple more weeks. I'm waiting for a message from up north.'

'From whom?'

'An old comrade-in-arms. Man by the name of John Creed. He helped me in that business with Raven. He's smart, tough, and knows mercenaries; he'll get us men who won't run at the first sign of trouble.'

'I don't know, Tal,' said Quint. 'You're going to need more than just a few mercenary companies. You're going to need a real army, and I mean support, food, weapons, chirurgeons, porters, boys for the luggage, commissaries, engineers. You're going to need horse, siege machines, and that doesn't even start to touch on what to do about that evil bastard Leso Varen.'

Tal said, 'You're wrong. I'm only going to need a crack company of maybe three hundred mercenaries, hand-picked and ready to ride at my command. The others, the engineers, the support, all that, will be provided by others.'

'Who?'

Tal shrugged. 'Roldem and the Isles.' He shrugged again. 'Maybe Kesh, Miskalon, Roskalon, some others might want to get involved too.' He hiked his left thumb over his shoulder, in the general direction of Lord Reslaz's castle. 'And we have no shortage of volunteers to help sack Olasko right around here.'

'Finding people to take booty is one thing; finding those who will fight before there's booty to take, that's another. Remember, I built up Kaspar's army for the past eleven years. It's the best force in the region.'

'I know, and I'm counting on you to help me take it apart.'

'That won't be easy, either in the doing, or for me: a lot of those lads are friends, and others I've trained.'

'How many of those men would die for Kaspar?'

Quint shrugged. 'I know a lot who would stand with me until the end.'

Tal nodded. 'But how many would willingly stand against you? For Kaspar? Look, if facing men you've trained and served with is too difficult, you know that at any time you're free to leave, Quint.'

The old soldier shrugged. 'Got nothing better to do for the time being, so I might as well stay.'

'Good,' said Tal, standing up. 'I'm going to head into the city and visit a friend.'

Quint grinned. 'A lady friend?'

'Just so,' said Tal as he departed. Over his shoulder he said, 'Don't bother waiting up for me.'

Weeks passed, and Tal saw the very best of the freed slaves turn into soldiers before his eyes. Twelve of them, seven women and five men, had turned into decent riders, adept with the sword and bow, and able to take orders. The only thing he didn't know was how they would react when blood started flowing. Two gave up on trying to serve and arranged passage to the west on caravans, hoping to return safely home. The others were put to work in support capacities.

Tal noticed that several of the girls were establishing alliances with particular men and hoped he didn't regret including women in his army. Jealousy could tear apart his little force before it ever became a coherent company. Still, what else could he do? Turn them over to a brothel-keeper?

His arm was starting to drive him to distraction. Two nights ago he had taken off the bandage to bathe the stump again and found it transformed. The five little bumps had lengthened and now what appeared to be a tiny hand was growing on the end of his stump. It didn't look so much like a baby's hand as it did a tiny replica of his own before it had been severed. He wondered how long it would take to grow to full size, if it ever did. Given Nakor's quirky nature, discovering the priest did a half-baked job wouldn't surprise Tal.

By the end of the second month at the farm, Tal had recruited a core of seasoned fighters. He had decided to hire only the very best, both in terms of experience and reliability. He wanted a cadre of men around him he could rely upon, and knew that if things turned sour in battle, many mercenaries would throw down their weapons rather than fight to the death. He also knew that if his core fighters were the sort of men who could be counted on to fight until the end, those around them might be more resolute in the face of adversity.

It was midsummer, a week before the festival of Banapis, when one of the young former slaves ran into the farmhouse shouting, 'Captain! Riders to the north.'

Tal stood up from the table where he had been reading

messages and went outside. He looked northwards and saw that a large company of riders was indeed approaching. By the time he could make out any details, he saw there were close to two hundred in the party. 'Get everyone ready,' said Tal.

The youngster ran off and spread the word. As they approached, Quint came to stand at Tal's side. 'Trouble?'

'If they keep riding in a file, no. If they spread out, they're going to hit us.'

The column stayed in a file and at last, the lead rider could clearly be seen. Tal put his sword away and said, 'It's all right. It's a friend.'

Tal walked forward and waved his left hand. The lead rider urged his horse forward to a trot. He was a brawny man with a drooping moustache and an oft-broken nose. When they reached one another, the rider reined in and said, 'Tal Hawkins!'

'John Creed,' Tal answered. 'You got my message.'

Creed got down from his horse. 'Indeed. Though I'll tell you it was delivered by the most irritating little man I've ever met.' They embraced and Creed asked, 'What happened to your arm?'

'Long story.'

'Well, your man said you were down here looking to build an army and could I bring some bully-boys from the north. I've got two hundred of the best I could find.' He motioned for his men to dismount and they did.

Tal turned to his own people and shouted, 'Help them get those horses cared for!'

A dozen of his young mercenaries ran forward and started directing Creed's men towards a large pasture area. Tal introduced Creed to Quint and said, 'What did you mean the messenger was irritating?'

'He was a funny little fellow, looked almost like he might have been a monk or priest, but he was a demon with a deck of cards. Took most of my gold before he left.'

'Nakor,' said Tal shaking his head. 'Well, gold is the least of my problems.'

Creed said, 'Given how well you paid last time, I had no trouble getting this lot to come along. I hope that's enough for you.'

'It's a start,' said Tal as they entered the farmhouse. 'Before I've finished, I'm going to need a thousand more, perhaps two thousand.'

'What are you thinking of?'

'I'm going to sack Opardum,' said Tal.

Creed stopped and stared at Tal, an expression of bewilderment on his face. 'You don't think small, do you?'

'As I said, it's a long story,' said Tal. 'I'll explain over a drink. Wine? Ale?'

'Whatever's close.'

They sat at the table and Tal fetched a wine bottle. He poured drinks for himself, Quint, and Creed, and said, 'Kaspar's got out of control and there are two, perhaps three, nations ready to jump him any day now. When that happens, I plan on being there for the kill.'

'Well, that's all well and good,' said Creed after taking a drink, 'but revenge doesn't pay the bills.'

'Same as last time. Pay while you're waiting and booty when the fighting's over.'

'That's enough,' said Creed. 'I can get more men if you need them.'

'Send messengers. I want them here by the end of summer.'

'I can do that.'

'How many men?' asked Quint.

'A hundred or so down in Inaska; that's where I was born and I've still got friends there. Another two or three hundred from along the borders of the disputed lands. I can have them meet up at Olasko Gateway and sail here from Opardum. As long as no one there knows what the coming fight is, they should have no trouble passing through.'

'It might be a good way to get some intelligence about what Kaspar is doing, too,' opined Quint.

'Is there one man in the area you can trust?' Tal asked Creed.

'I'll see if I can find an old comrade of mine, Daniel Toskova. He's smart and will keep his mouth shut. If I can get word to him, he'll have a thing or two to tell. Last I heard he was up in Far Reaches. Getting word to him will be the trick.'

'Leave that to me,' said Tal. 'I can get messages out there.'

Creed said, 'So what is the plan?'

'I want at least five hundred swords here before we leave, and I'd like to have made contact with two or three reliable companies we can join up with for the assault.'

'That's a full battalion,' said Quint. 'The logistics will be a nightmare if you're out in the field for more than a week or two.'

Tal said, 'I don't plan on being out in the field that long. I plan on no more than a week from the time we touch down on Olaskon soil until we're inside the citadel.'

'How so?' asked Creed.

Tal said, 'Because I know a way into the citadel that even Kaspar has no idea exists.'

Quint said, 'I've been over every inch of the citadel, and I know every door and passageway. There is no such entrance.'

Tal said, 'With respect, you're wrong. And if you were still commanding today, you'd not have a hint how we got in while my men were storming the walls from the inside in support of those who were scaling the walls.'

'You'll have to tell me about this one,' said Quint.

'In due time. First I have some errands to run.' To Creed he said, 'Give me a list of mercenary captains you trust and where I might find them, and if they can be reached we'll have word to them by the end of this week.'

'What? Are you using magic?'

'In a word, yes,' said Tal. To Quint he said, 'Make John here our third-in-command, then start getting his men into shape.'

'Where are you going to be?' asked Quint.

Tal grinned. 'After I finish sending the messages, I've got to take a short trip.'

'Why? What are you going to do?' asked Creed.

Tal said, 'Why, I've got to go and start a war.'

• CHAPTER EIGHTEEN •

Deception

*T*AL WAITED.

The tension in the court was palpable. That this was no conventional audience was made evident by the company of royal household guards lining the walls, and the dozen cross-bowmen in the galleries on either side of the hall and above the throne.

King Ryan of the Isles sat motionless, his dress casual, for this meeting had been hastily called. To Tal's right stood a man in black robes, who despite his short stature exuded power. Pug, the legendary Black Sorcerer, and distant relative to the royal family by adoption, waited.

The King motioned for the two men to approach and they did, until a line of soldiers stepped before them, halting their progress.

The King looked at the two men and said at last, 'My father warned me you might appear some day, Pug. From what he said, I take it your parting with him was less than convivial.'

Pug smiled. 'That's an understatement, Majesty.'

'As he recounted things, you renounced your allegiance to the Isles, gave up your hereditary titles, and said some fairly unflattering things to him.'

'Again, an understatement, Your Majesty.' Pug paused, then said, 'In his youth, King Patrick was not the patient and reflective man you knew in later years. He was given to hot temper and rash judgment. I acted out of altruistic motives; I didn't wish to see him plunge the Isles into a war with Great Kesh mere months after having seen half the Western Realm devastated by the armies of the Emerald Queen.'

'Yes,' said the King. 'That's something along the lines of what I heard. Nevertheless, your renunciation of your titles is considered treason by some. So, let's put this aside for the time being and get to the point. Why are you here?' Then he pointed at Tal. 'And why have you brought this assassin into my court?'

'Because Talwin Hawkins was a young man put at risk then sacrificed by Duke Kaspar of Olasko for Kaspar's own personal gains. He was duped, then betrayed, and by way of atonement, he wishes to warn Your Majesty of a grave threat to the Isles. I'm here on his behalf to vouch for him, and to reassure Your Majesty that what he will tell you is true.'

Tal bowed awkwardly, somewhat hampered by the sling holding his regenerating arm. He straightened and said, 'Majesty, I am certain your own agents have kept you apprised of Kaspar's seemingly endless plots and intrigues. As you know, he was behind the death of Princess Svetlana of Salmater, and because

317

of this has managed to convince the Prince to acknowledge Kaspar as his liege lord.'

'I had not heard of that arrangement,' said the King.

Tal motioned to a guardsman and then to Pasko, who had come along with Pug from Sorcerer's Isle. Pasko handed the guard a parchment. 'This is a sealed copy, gained at much risk from Kaspar's own archives, stipulating the conditions of the relationship under which Salmater and Olasko now exist.'

The King took the document from the guard. 'How do I know this is authentic?'

'I'll vouch for its authenticity, Majesty,' said Pug.

'And how did you come by this?'

Tal answered. 'There are those still within Kaspar's court who are sympathetic to former victims of his tyranny. If Your Majesty is familiar with Baron Visniya and Baron Stolinko of Olasko, you should know that they were imprisoned with me for a while by Kaspar's personal order. They and other nobles have been murdered or imprisoned for imagined infractions, or for the personal gain of others in Kaspar's service. Those wrongly-imprisoned men still have friends within the court, friends who will undertake to keep us abreast of any conditions that may bear upon our coming assault on Opardum.'

'You mean to attack Opardum?' said the King. 'I admire your candour, young Hawkins. And your courage. Might you enlighten me as to where you have found an army to lead into such a battle?'

'Majesty, I will have three thousand dedicated soldiers at my command by the first week of autumn.'

'A significant force, for raiding a border outpost or even sacking a minor garrison, but to take Opardum you will need . . .' he glanced at the Knight-Marshal, Sir Lawrence Malcolm, who mouthed a figure '. . . twenty thousand or more. Attacking by sea and land, if I'm right.' He glanced again at his military advisor, who nodded.

'That would be true, Majesty, in a conventional assault. But my three thousand will be attacking Opardum from the rear.'

The King laughed. 'The rear? Correct me if I'm wrong, young sir, but the citadel at Opardum is hard against a cliff-face, and if I also remember correctly, there's no way to get above it.'

'True, but there is a way in, Majesty. And that is where my army will attack.'

The King seemed to be growing impatient. 'Well, then, that's splendid. I wish you well in your endeavour. Some nearby nations are bad neighbours, but Kaspar is something of a bully and I will not shed a tear to see him gone. But what has this to do with the Isles?'

'I need a diversion.'

The King sat speechless for a full minute, then he said, 'You need a *diversion*?'

'Sire, I can show you a course from within the southern islands, avoiding Inaska entirely, and you can land an army which would threaten either Opardum or Olasko Gateway. Kaspar would be forced to leave soldiers in Olasko Gateway, rather than bring them up for support.'

'Or he could march armies from both cities and crush my forces between them!'

'He'll be too busy to risk it, Majesty.'

'Why?'

'Because the King of Roldem will have a fleet at anchor off Opardum, loaded with several thousand Keshian Dog Soldiers.'

'Kesh!' the King almost yelled. 'What has Kesh to do with Kaspar?'

'Kaspar has been found out in the murder of Prince Phillip of Aranor.'

'That's hardly news, Squire, since Princess Alena is guesting here in Rillanon. We have dispatched strong messages to Kaspar on this subject, and expect he will see to her return and assure us that a regent will rule until the Prince is of an age to take the throne.'

'With respect, Majesty, that is hardly likely to happen with Kaspar in Olasko. The King of Roldem also realizes this, and he also knows that Kaspar removed Phillip, just as he attempted to remove Duke Rodoski, to put himself closer to King Carol's throne. Kaspar means to see himself King of Roldem, Majesty.'

'So it seems, but it also hardly seems likely.'

'It will be very likely if Kaspar marches his army to Farinda, and puts ten thousand men and horses on your border, Sire. You will have no option but to march your forces up to meet him there. Meanwhile, he will be in Roldem being crowned.'

'And how will he accomplish this? By magic?'

Pug stepped forward. 'Precisely, Majesty. And that is why you must act in concert with us in this matter, for if you do not, then I will wager that Kaspar will be sitting upon the throne of Roldem before year's end and moreover, he will not be content to stay there. He will move again, first against the other Eastern Kingdoms, bringing Miskalon, Roskalon and the others into line with Salmater, forming up principalities and duchies loyal to King Kaspar of Roldem, and then he'll move against Rillanon.'

The King was quiet for a moment. Then he said, 'You paint

a bleak portrait, gentlemen. Very well, I will hear more. You will meet with my council after the midday meal and present all your evidence. But I warn you, if it is not persuasive, you will be departing this palace instantly. Neither of you is trusted here, sirs, and you must show us a great deal before trust will be forthcoming. Now, your comfort will be seen to and we will meet again this afternoon.'

Pug, Tal and Pasko bowed and departed. Outside in the corridor, Tal turned to Pug and said, 'So, that's the first step.'

Pug said, 'With many more steps to follow.'

They followed a page who had been sent to show them to guest quarters where they might eat and freshen up before the afternoon meeting with the King and his council.

Inside the room they found a large table set with refreshments and two day-couches large enough to nap upon if they so desired. A servant there waited to act upon their every request, but Pug turned to him and said, 'Leave us.'

The servant bowed and left them alone. Pug closed his eyes, waved his hands, then declared, 'We are safe from being overheard by magic.' To Pasko he said, 'Wait outside the door and see we are not overheard by more mundane means.' Pasko nodded and left the room.

Tal poured a goblet of wine and inclined his head towards Pug, asking if he wished one. 'Water will do,' Pug replied.

Tal poured water for Pug, handed it to him, then picked up the wine in his left hand. He flexed the small fingers on his right hand, under the bandages, and wondered again at the magic used. Every movement hurt, but at the same time, it felt wonderful to have true sensation back there. He knew the pain would fade; Nakor had reassured him that it would lessen in time, and that exercise would hasten the healing. He knew one thing: when he faced Kaspar it would be with his sword in his right hand.

Tal said, 'So, then, it begins.'

'Yes,' said the sorcerer. 'We will have the Isles' support before the day is out.'

Tal sat in a chair and put his feet up on another. Pug sat on one of the day-couches. Tal asked, 'Is there even a shred of truth in what we told the King?'

'Truth is a negotiable concept, I've learned over the years.'

'Do I even have an inkling of what is really at play here?'

Pug said, 'I don't know if any of us does, or if we're capable of truly understanding.' He was silent for a moment, then added, 'You've been through a lot, Tal. You're not yet thirty years of age, but you've suffered more than most men do in two life-times. When this is over, if we survive, I will tell you as much as I can.'

'*If* we survive?'

'Your plan sounds brilliant on the surface, but there are forces involved far beyond you and Kaspar, or even the Conclave and Leso Varen. The Conclave will do its part in shielding you from Varen's powers. If we are correct in our surmise as to what he is trying to accomplish, most of his energies will be directed elsewhere, and if that is the case, he will be vulnerable. Even so, he will be the most dangerous player in this game, for while I am his equal in power, he has no scruples and will think nothing of destroying everything around him rather than face defeat.'

Tal said, 'You're filling me with optimism.'

Pug laughed. 'It's all a risk. But then, all life is a risk.'

'This is true,' said Tal, sipping his wine. 'So, once we convince King Ryan, what next?'

Pug smiled. 'The hard part. Convincing King Carol and the Keshian ambassador.'

Tal shook his head. 'You'd better speak fast then, Pug, for I've the death-mark on me should I set foot on Roldemish soil again.'

Pug said, 'I'll speak very fast.'

Tal sat back, thinking. He knew the plan was bold, reckless, even mad, but it was their only hope for a decisive and sudden victory over Kaspar.

However, the prospect of finally destroying Olasko didn't fill him with keen anticipation. Instead, he felt only a dull hollowness. He sipped his wine.

A delegation of Roldem's officials, as well as a full honour guard, waited at the dockside as the King of the Isles' ship was made fast at the quay. As the gangplank was run out, the officials stepped forward, ready to receive the unannounced royal visitor, for at the top of the mainmast of the ship, the pennon of the royal house of the Isles flew, telling the world that a member of the royal family was aboard.

Instead of a richly-dressed noble, however, a short man in a dark robe walked down the gangplank, followed by a figure all too familiar to many of those in attendance, carrying a single canvas travel bag.

The Chancellor of the King's House stepped forward. 'What is the meaning of this?' He pointed to Tal and said, 'Place that man under arrest.'

Pug held up his hand. 'That man is under the protection of the King of the Isles, and is a member of this delegation.'

'And who are you, sir?'

Pug said, 'I am called Pug, known as the Black Sorcerer by some, and am representing King Ryan.'

'But the royal banner flies upon the mast!'

Pug said, 'I'm embarrassed to admit I imposed upon the King to permit this, though I am a member of the royal family by adoption, albeit a distant one. My name is recorded in the archives of the house of conDoin; I was adopted by Duke Borric, great-grandfather to King Ryan.'

The Chancellor seemed totally confused by all this. 'Your credentials, sir?'

Pug held out an ornate bundle of papers, all drawn up hastily, but with attention to detail, by the scribes in King Ryan's service. They were affixed with all the appropriate seals, and they named Duke Pug of Stardock and Squire Talwin Hawkins as ambassadors extraordinaire to the Court of King Carol and to the Court of the Emperor of Great Kesh and outlined that the two emissaries had a great degree of latitude in binding the Isles to any number of agreements.

'All this seems in order . . . Your Grace.' With a dark look at Tal, the Chancellor said, 'Please come with me, gentlemen.'

As they approached a carriage, Tal threw his bag up to a coachman and followed Pug inside. The Chancellor got in after them, saying, 'Your luggage will be brought up to the palace.'

Tal said, 'I just handed up our luggage, sir.'

'You're not staying long, then, sir?'

Tal grinned. 'If we are here more than two days I will be surprised.'

The Chancellor looked at Pug and said, 'Pardon my frankness, Your Grace,' then he looked at Tal, 'but if the Squire here leaves this island alive I will be surprised.'

Tal shrugged. 'We'll let the King decide that.'

They rode in silence the rest of the way to the palace.

Duke Rodoski could barely contain his anger. The King had listened to everything Pug had said, then like King Ryan, King Carol had insisted on a full presentation before his privy council and the Ambassador of the Empire of Great Kesh. The Duke had almost drawn his sword on entering the hall and seeing Tal sitting there.

'You will behave yourself, sir!' commanded the King. 'These men are here under the banner of the Isles, and will be treated with diplomatic courtesy.'

The Duke had shot back, 'Whatever they have to say will be lies, cousin!'

'Sit down, sir!' the King roared.

Duke Rodoski did as he was told but his suspicion was openly displayed.

Pug waited as the King called his councillors to order.

The Chancellor addressed the King and his council. 'Majesty, my lords, this ... oddly-dressed gentleman is Pug, Duke of Stardock and cousin to King Ryan. I have asked him to repeat to you what he told me earlier today. Your Grace?'

Pug stood up and said, 'First I would like to make clear that the title of Duke is a courtesy only; I renounced my allegiance to the Isles back when Ryan's father, Patrick, was Prince of Krondor. I am cousin to the King, but a very distant one.

'Second, I caution you that what I am about to say will stretch your belief to its limit. You will hear things that will leave you wondering if I am bereft of all reason, but I will tell you now, my lords, I am very sane, and what I tell you is not wild imagining.

'In your archives, I am sure, will be certain reports gathered by your agents back during the reigns of Rodric the Fourth of the Isles. The fact of the Riftwar, the invasion of our world by the Tsurani is not in question; it is historic fact, but behind that fact lies a tale far more incredible than what is known.

'The war was the result of a manipulation of incredible scale which pitted two worlds against one another, and towards only one end: the use of an ancient artefact hidden under the city of Sethanon, an artefact known as the Lifestone.' He looked at King Carol. 'I would be very surprised if any of this is recorded in your archives, Majesty. Of those who survived the battle of Sethanon, when the armies of the Brotherhood of the Dark Path marched south under the banner of the false prophet, Murmandamus, the only living beings who knew the truth were myself, Tomas – consort to the Elf Queen Aglaranna – Prince Arutha, and later King Lyam, and two Tsurani magicians, now long dead.

'Twice more the Lifestone was threatened, first by Delekhan, a moredhel chieftain, and then by the armies of the Emerald Queen.'

'What is this Lifestone?' asked Rodoski. 'Why is it so important that wars are fought over it?'

'It was an ancient thing, created by a race that lived on this world before the coming of man, the Valheru, and it was supposed to be a weapon to be used against the gods. Murmandamus, Delekhan and the Emerald Queen all wished to use it to rule the world.'

'Are you claiming that Kaspar of Olasko is going to seize this Lifestone?' asked King Carol.

'No,' said Pug. 'The stone was . . . destroyed years ago. It no longer poses a threat.' He thought better of trying to explain to them that the stone had been used by Tomas's son Calis to free trapped life-essences, helping partially to restore an ancient balance between good and evil.

The Keshian Ambassador said, 'I believe we have some mention of this in our archives, Your Grace.'

Pug smiled. 'No doubt. There was a force of Dog Soldiers under the command of Lord Hazara-Khan involved in the first battle of Sethanon. I don't imagine he neglected to report everything he saw.'

'I find it incredible to believe you were there and that you knew him,' said the Ambassador. 'That was more than a century ago.'

'I age well,' said Pug dryly. 'Now, to the point under discussion. Kaspar of Olasko has been wreaking havoc over the region for the last ten years now, including the murder of the Princess of Salmater and the Prince of Aranor, as well as a planned assassination of every member of the Royal House of Roldem.'

Rodoski could not restrain himself. His hand shot out and he pointed an accusing finger at Tal. 'And *that* man was instrumental in it. He killed Svetlana of Salmater and was going to be involved in my assassination.'

Pug shrugged. 'An attempt you easily avoided, Your Grace, which brings me to this point. Kaspar's ambitions are naked and without subtlety. He seems not to care that the world knows he wishes to sit upon the throne of Roldem. And perhaps the Isles as well, some day.

'But Kaspar is not a stupid man, so you must ask yourself, why so blatant a series of moves? Why show such disregard for disguising his ambitions and contempt for your reaction to his moves?'

Rodoski sat back. Tal could tell that even the angry duke was intrigued by the question.

'The answer,' said Pug, 'is the reason King Carol must exercise the mutual defence agreement he has with Great Kesh. The Ambassador must urge the Emperor to call north those garrisons on the eastern seaboard of the Empire, and quickly. The Roldemish navy must go to those ports and then transport those soldiers to anchor off Opardum.

'King Ryan will send an army up to threaten Olasko Gateway, and Squire Hawkins will lead a force into the citadel itself. All of this must be completed before winter comes, for Kaspar is readying himself to make his true move on Midwinter's Night. In the citadel at Opardum, in a wing of the building where few are permitted, resides a man known as Leso Varen. He is a mage of great power and black arts. He serves forces of evil and chaos that seek to obliterate all laws and covenants, traditions and social contracts, all that makes men lawful and peaceful. I can not stress strongly enough the concept you must accept, that these powers dwarf your normal notion of what good and evil entail. If you're sane men, I think it impossible for you to envision the degree of horror that awaits this world if this man Leso Varen isn't stopped.'

'So you need all the eastern garrisons of Kesh and the Roldemish navy to destroy this one man?' asked the Keshian Ambassador.

Pug said, 'In a nutshell, yes.'

The King said, 'While we waited for the council, we consulted our archives regarding you, Duke Pug. If what I read is to be believed, you yourself are a magician of great power. Your age alone gives me cause to think these reports are true.

'That being the case, why have you not sought out and destroyed this Leso Varen?'

Pug smiled and there was pain in the smile. 'I've faced this man before, Your Majesty. He has used several different names along the way, but I recognize the stink of his black arts the way you know a skunk by its smell. He is not an easy man to kill. Trust me when I tell you I have tried.' His voice lowered and his eyes became reflective for a moment as he said, 'Once . . . I thought him dead, but obviously I was wrong.'

'Very well,' said Duke Rodoski. 'You've painted a bleak picture of this man's powers, and told us a story of something dangerous that was destroyed years ago. Would you like to tie this up so that we understand it?'

Pug said, 'It is my belief that Leso Varen is in the process of creating another Lifestone. And that he means to use it on the darkest night of the year, Midwinter's Night.'

The King sat back. 'Another Lifestone? What exactly will that do?'

Pug said, 'Sire, it is something that can be utilized in any number of ways, some for good in the right hands. But I will wager my life and the lives of everyone I have ever loved that in Varen's hands it will be used for evil.

'A new Lifestone will allow him to wage war on a scale not seen since the invasion of the Isles by the Emerald Queen's army.' This was something of an avoidance, for only a handful of men ever knew the truth: that the Emerald Queen had been murdered and replaced by a demon in disguise. That detail would have only confused the members of the King's court. After a pause, Pug continued, 'With each death in its proximity, the Lifestone becomes more powerful. It doesn't matter who dies, or on which side they fight. If Varen stands near the van of Kaspar's army, he will be more powerful at the end of a battle than he was at the start. And each battle will give him more strength.

'Ultimately, he will hold in his hand a weapon that will afford him the power to rule the world, and more: the power to challenge the gods themselves.

'Then war will rage in heaven and the very ground beneath your feet will be char and ash.'

'I can scarcely believe it,' said the King.

Pug waved his hand and Pasko stepped forward, holding a pile of old documents. 'These are from the archives at Rillanon. King Ryan permitted me to remove these. Here I give you every official document on file, including one by Prince Arutha's own hand, and several by me, detailing all I have said, or at least as much as was known at the time of the Riftwar. Also, there are reports from the Serpentwar, including a report made by Erik von Darkmoor. Each is authenticated and vouched for by the royal archivist.

'Beyond what I have given you, I have told you all we know.'

'Who will bear the cost of this?' asked the Keshian Ambassador. 'Not just in gold, but in suffering and lives?'

'Your Excellency,' Pug said, 'I will make you the same offer I made to King Ryan. I will underwrite the cost of your efforts. Gold I can get. But procuring brave men willing to risk all to free the world from a coming horror no man can truly imagine, that is beyond my powers.

'My lords, Majesty, if we do not act now, by Midwinter's Night this world will begin a slide into darkness beyond comprehension. You must take this decision, if not for yourselves, then for your children, and the children they will someday bear.'

Pug looked from face to face, and Tal felt the prickly sensation that he had come to associate with the use of magic. He knew that what Pug did was subtle, for anything too overt would risk a backlash. He was using a spell to calm them, to make them feel at ease with the coming decision, and to put aside their suspicion.

The King said, 'If you gentlemen will withdraw to quarters set aside for you, we shall discuss this matter.' He looked at the pile of documents Pasko had passed along and added, 'It may take us some time to read all these. I will have supper sent to your quarters and we will resume our meeting in the morning.'

Pug, Tal and Pasko bowed, and the three men left the King's hall. A page escorted them to modest quarters, and when they were alone, Tal glanced at Pasko. 'Not as nice as the rooms given to me when I fought for the Championship of the Masters' Court.'

Pasko said, 'They liked you better then. You hadn't tried to kill anyone in the royal family then.'

Pug said, 'This is more problematic than it was in the Isles.' There came a knock at the door, and Pug waved permission for Pasko to answer. When Pasko opened the door, servants entered carrying trays of refreshments and wine. After they had left, and the door was again closed, Pasko set about preparing a light meal for Pug and Tal.

Pug said, 'I think we shall convince them, but it may take a lot more discussion.'

Tal sighed. He was anxious to be back with his mercenaries.

He trusted John Creed, and despite his desire to avenge his people, had come to trust Quint and the others. But it was still a mercenary army, and trouble could erupt at any moment. And Bardac's Holdfast was not a good place for there to be problems among his men.

Tal finally said to Pug, 'What next?'

'We wait,' said Pug. 'Which is the hardest thing of all.'

Pasko nodded. 'I will arrange for baths, gentlemen, while you enjoy this repast, and I speak to the staff to see to an early supper.'

Pug rose. 'None for me. I will dine with my wife tonight, and return before dawn.' With a wave of his hand he vanished.

Tal glanced at Pasko. 'Just like Magnus. I hate it when they do that.'

Pasko nodded.

• CHAPTER NINETEEN •

Assault

*T*HE WIND CUT LIKE a blade.

Tal sat huddled under his great cloak, squeezing a ball with his right hand. Nakor had been the one who had given him the ball, made from some strange black material. It didn't bounce well, and was heavy, but it yielded just enough to give Tal's hand serious exercise. The constant pain had dwindled now to an occasional twinge or itch, or he got a throbbing dull pain afterwards if he exercised too much.

But his arm was now fully restored, and he had been using his hand in sword practice for a month. At first he could barely hold a sword for more than a few minutes, and at times the pain brought him close to tears, but he persevered. Now he barely noticed the discomfort unless he paused to think about it. And at the moment, he was too busy thinking about what was occurring before him to think about his hand.

Up a narrow trail, riding single file, three thousand merce-naries made their way onto the plateau. For hours they had been riding, and once they reached the top, they spread out, making cold camp. Still miles behind the citadel, Tal would not risk a hundred campfires. Kaspar's full attention was directed to the fleet off his harbour and the army approaching from the east along the river, but the citadel was downwind from the plateau and smoke from that many fires would travel for miles.

The Isles' army should be fully in place by now. Tal had con-vinced King Ryan he could move his army by boats up the route mapped by the agents of Salmater Tal had captured for Kaspar, then land on the north shore of the river, placing a force of five thousand men between Olasko Gateway and Opardum.

Tal felt tremendous impatience, for he knew he was close now to his final accounting with Kaspar. He wished for a moment that the Conclave could use its arts to magic his army inside the caves, rather than wait for engineers to construct a new bridge across the bottom of the ravine. But he knew that was impos-sible. Pug had warned Tal that Leso Varen would detect any spell used within miles of the citadel. He must think until the very last instant that the attack was conventional, for forewarning would doom this attempt to failure. Even if Kaspar was taken, Varen was the true target and he must not escape. While Tal wanted Kaspar dead, he knew that his first objective had to be the magician's rooms, for there he would find the wards that pro-tected the sorcerer from Pug and the others, and there Tal would have to destroy them before Varen killed him, else all would fail. Kaspar would endure, the dark magic of Leso Varen would go unchecked, and Tal's entire life would prove futile and pointless.

Tal had sent two of his best scouts forward with the engineers. He had given them clear directions to follow. Once the bridge was up, they were to cross over, climb the long path, then wait inside the first large gallery, where he would take over and lead the soldiers through the maze of tunnels that led to the one cave big enough to hold his forces. From there it was a short march to the abandoned cellar in the citadel that would prove Kaspar's undoing.

Tal regarded his army as they filed past, making their way to campsites where they would unsaddle their mounts and leave them in the care of lackeys. They were a mix of veterans recruited by John Creed, and recruits from farms and villages near Karesh'kaar, young men and a few women who felt they had no future in Bardac's. Tal had promised everyone who fought that after the war they would be permitted to settle in Olasko . . . assuming they won, of course. Tal watched as the last of the riders crested the rise and moved off to find a place to rest. Pack animals brought up the rear, and as they came into sight, Tal rode to the most forward camp.

Quint Havrevulen, John Creed and the Barons Visniya and Stolinko waited. They had been over the plan a hundred times, but Tal said, 'Once more. Report.'

Quint said, 'Signals from our scouts to the rear show all is clear and no one suspects we are here.'

Creed said, 'Everyone knows his job, Tal.'

Tal said, 'It's in my nature to worry at this point.'

Visniya said, 'When the Keshians land, they'll find key defences have been left unattended, or orders are confused. We have friends who will ensure the outer city defence is token, at best.'

Stolinko said, 'It was never much, anyway, given the layout

of the city. By sundown tomorrow, Kaspar's forces will either be in full retreat in the city, or already behind the walls of the citadel.'

Tal nodded. It would take a full day to reach the citadel's basement by the tunnels he had mapped. 'Then at dawn in two days' time, we take the citadel.'

There was something bothering him: he knew that he would have preferred to wait until all his men were in place before assaulting the citadel from within. There simply wasn't enough room in the caves or basements for that. He had to lead two hundred men up a flight of stairs and hope that they reached the top landing before any alarm was sounded, and could hold a key corridor long enough to allow the balance of his forces to start feeding into the citadel.

If he or his men were trapped on that stairway, a squad of six men with swords and crossbows could hold them there for a week.

Tal gave his horse to a lackey then squatted down where the others sat. He pulled the glove on his right hand off and flexed it. 'If I hadn't seen that stump,' said Quint, 'I wouldn't have believed your hand had ever been cut from you.'

Looking at his fingers as he flexed them, Tal said, 'It helps to have friends who know "tricks".'

'Well,' said the dour Stolinko, 'I hope you have some more good ones for the next two days.'

John Creed said, 'From what Tal's told us, I don't think we're going to need tricks. This looks to be a straight-up fight, and whoever has the greatest will wins.'

No one said anything after that.

*   *   *

For hours they crept through the darkness. Every tenth soldier carried a torch. Tal's ability to remember details of the route after more than four years since his last visit saved them time and lives. There were treacherous falls and dead-end passages all through this region. His nocturnal explorations in his first months of service to Kaspar were now serving them all well.

The caves were dry at this time of year, and mostly of bare rock, though occasionally a vein of hard-packed earth was exposed between rock-faces. Lichen in the lower chambers gave way to dry granite walls and dusty floors as they rose to the surface. Everything smelled musty.

Tal paused in the last gallery of any size before reaching the outer limits of the citadel. He beckoned to a young woman, one of the freed slaves from earlier that year, and said, 'Pass the word back. We rest for an hour. I'm going ahead to scout.'

She turned and passed the word, and Tal took a torch, lit it from one already burning, and moved on. He turned a corner and vanished down a tunnel.

Everything was as he remembered it, and he quickly found his way to the narrow passage that led to a storage area, which had been abandoned long ago. The only footprints on the ground in the dust were his own, now grown faint after more than four years.

At the far end of this cave was a single door, and Tal inspected it closely before attempting to open it. It was stiff and moved slowly, but he took his time and when it was barely wide enough to admit him, he slipped through.

He entered a room. Now he was in the citadel proper. Three walls had been chiselled out of the rock, but the far wall was made from mortar-set stones around a door. He opened the door in that wall and looked down a deserted hallway.

Tal quickly inspected the route and reached the last door he would open, for after this room came a part of the stronghold that might be in use: a short auxiliary pantry that led to the stairs he would have to use to get into the heart of the citadel. This was the pantry farthest off the kitchen, and while it was rarely occupied, occasionally someone came down to refill salt cellars from the large barrels kept here. He took out a red rag and a heavy tack, and pinned the rag to the door.

He then started backtracking, putting rags on every door his forces would pass through.

At one junction, he put up two rags, one red, one blue, and then moved off in a different direction. An hour later a second path had been marked in blue.

By the time he returned to where the vanguard of his army waited, three routes up into the citadel would be marked. John Creed would lead a force up along the yellow path, into the marshalling yard via a postern gate entrance, opening into the bailey between the outer walls and the citadel itself. His job would be to attack the wall from inside, in support of the Keshian soldiers attacking from the city.

Quint Havrevulen would lead the second column, coming up along the blue path, directly into the armoury, attacking the main strength of the forces inside the citadel. He would most likely be the first of the three of them to face the main strength of Kaspar's forces.

Tal's task was the most dangerous, for he was to lead an assault along the red path into Leso Varen's apartments. He knew it earned him a good chance of a quick and messy death. He had argued with himself over this choice, but felt he could not order any other man to do it. Additionally, he now realized that with victory in sight, he no longer cared. All he felt was cold inside. For years he had anticipated the day when he would crush Kaspar and let him know why he was being destroyed. The thought of revenge on his enemies no longer gave him comfort. In fact, it felt just the opposite. Vengeance had started to lose its appeal after the death of Raven.

Years spent in anticipation of this moment now seemed somehow wasted. In the short time before committing himself to an all-or-nothing gamble, he wished more than anything that he could just walk away. He thought of all he had lost, all he had let go in the past without thought because of his determination to punish Kaspar.

Now he wondered what use it would be? For Kaspar's death would not bring back his father, Elk's Call At Dawn, or his mother, Whisper Of The Night Wind. His brother, Hand Of The Sun, and his little sister Miliana would remain dead. The only time he would hear the voice of his grandfather, Laughter In His Eyes, would be in his memory. Nothing would change. No farmer outside Krondor would suddenly stand up in wonder and say, 'A wrong has been righted.' No boot-maker in Roldem would look up from his bench and say, 'A people has been avenged.'

If he could just expunge Kaspar with a thought, he would gladly turn away from the slaughter to come. Hundreds, perhaps thousands, of men and women were about to die, and not one in a thousand would have an inkling of why their lives were ending. Not one of them would understand that they were dying because a boy had survived the obliteration of his people and an ambitious man had made a pact with an evil magician.

Tal sighed. Try as he might, he could not hate Kaspar or

Quint any more than he could hate a bear for acting like a bear. They were creatures of their own nature. With Kaspar that meant he was sick with ambition and devoid of scruples. With Quint it meant he followed orders blindly and did as he was told, no matter how repugnant and without morality those orders might be.

Yet now Tal was using one of those men's natures to help destroy the other. He found the irony far from amusing.

He returned to the vanguard and found his officers had all made their way to the front. Quint said, 'We're all in place and ready.'

Tal sat on the stones. 'So, now we wait.'

The cellar was empty and Tal motioned his men to follow to the far end. He pushed open the door and in the distance could hear faint noises. Nothing very distinct, but he knew it was the echoes of men and women in the citadel rushing to whatever place was appointed them during battle. Soldiers would man their posts, while servants would hurry to prepare everything required to withstand the assault: food, blankets, water, sand to fight fires, and bandages and unguents for the wounded.

Tal motioned and the first group moved up the narrow stairway. He peered through the door and saw that the corridor was empty. He pushed it open and held it aside as the first twenty men raced up the stairs, ten going to the right and ten to the left. They were ordered to hurry to the far end of the hall and to hold until a full company was in place.

After the first score of mercenaries were in place, the others came up like a steady stream, one man after another, and when a full fifty were in position Tal signalled. Both companies hurried off to their specified destinations. Each band had one mission: to find a particular place in the lower citadel and hold it. They would barricade the intersections between halls – using tables, chairs or anything else they could find – then hold those positions using longbows and crossbows until Tal had reached his objective. They would be protecting the flanks of those fighters sent into the lair of the magician.

Tal motioned for those behind him to move as silently as possible. He had hand-picked twenty-five of the toughest men in the army, led by the huge murderer, Masterson, who still carried the massive axe he had taken from the Fortress of Despair. Tal knew that if need be, he could chop through an oak door with it in moments.

Tal turned the corner, headed down a short corridor, then up a flight of stairs. At the top he was confronted by stairs leading back down again, while two other flights went up on either side. Companies following his own would head up those stairs with orders to attack any units of Kaspar's men they sighted. Tal led his twenty-five men down the central set of stairs towards Leso Varen's quarters.

He hurried down the corridor that led into the wizard's first room and as he neared the door, he felt the hair on his arms and neck stand up. He halted and without hesitation, shouted, 'Back!'

Those behind him hesitated for a moment, then the retreat began, just as a shrieking sound of unbearable volume split the air. Men covered their ears and howled in pain. Tal, who was closest to the door, suffered the worst. His legs wobbled and threatened to buckle as he staggered backwards.

When he reached the far end of the corridor, the sound stopped, and Tal shook his head to clear his vision. Without a word, he signalled to Masterson to tear down the door. Masterson nodded, rage etched upon his face, and charged the door.

If Varen had expected Tal and the others to have fled, or to be lying stunned in the hallway, he was mistaken. Masterson's massive axe struck the wood to the centre of the hasp, and shattered it, sending splinters flying. He struck it three more times and the planks fell away. With a kick of one huge foot, he smashed the wood between hinges and lock plate and the door fell open. He charged in with Tal only steps behind him.

Twenty-five men entered the room with Tal. At the far end the magician, Leso Varen, stood alone. The slender magic-user looked more annoyed than fearful and all he said was, 'This really is just too much.'

Then he waved his hand and abruptly Tal was engulfed in pain. He could barely stand and his sword fell from fingers that refused to obey him. Other men writhed on the floor, or fell to their hands and knees, vomiting.

Tal saw men falling unconscious on all sides. Only Masterson seemed able to keep his feet and the large man staggered with each step. Seeing that the huge fighter was somehow resisting his magic, Varen sighed as if he was out of patience. He picked up what looked to be a slender wand of dark wood, pointed it at the axe-wielding man and spoke a few words.

Flames surrounded Masterson's head and shoulders and he howled in agony, letting the axe fall. He went to his knees slapping uselessly at the flames, which were tinged an evil green colour, and which filled the room with an oily smoke and the stench of burning flesh.

Tal struggled to move forward, although every one of his muscles tried to contract in spasm. He could not will his fingers to close around his sword where it lay near his open hand. In a desperate act of will he drew the dagger from his belt, mustered his remaining strength and hurled it at the magician.

It flew true but Varen merely stood still and the blade halted inches from him, falling to the floor with a clatter as if hitting an invisible wall. Then he walked to stand over Tal and looked down on him.

'Talwin Hawkins, isn't it? I am surprised,' he said softly, his voice just loud enough to cut through the moans and weeping of the other men in the room. He glanced at Tal's right arm, and said, 'I thought they were going to chop that off you.' He sighed. 'That's the problem with Kaspar's people. You just can't rely upon them to attend to details. First you were supposed to die in Salador and didn't have the grace to do that, then you turn up here unexpectedly with an army . . . it's all very annoying, Talwin!' He glanced around the room. 'If Kaspar can't keep this city of his, I'm going to have to move . . . again! That is really upsetting.' He leaned over so that his face was only inches from Tal's as the young man fought to stay sitting upright, refusing to fall to the floor. 'You're quite a stubborn boy, aren't you?' asked Varen. He gently pushed Tal to the right, and Tal promptly fell over.

'I don't suppose this is all your fault; after all, you can't just whistle up a Keshian army . . . not to mention that bunch down on the river from the Isles. I'd love to know how you contrived to get Ryan and Carol to agree on anything, but time is limited, so I just can't spare a moment to chat.' Leso Varen walked away and looked out of the window. 'Now, that doesn't look good. Keshians on the wall and a troop of men I don't recognize opening the gate to the bailey. This just won't do.'

He opened the window and directed his wand out of it. Tal could feel him discharging his magic at those below. But Tal noticed that each time Varen did this the pain he was experiencing lessened slightly. His vision no longer threatened to fail him and he could move a little.

After a few moments of raining burning terror down on those below, Varen turned to Tal again. 'Well, as much fun as this has been, it's time for you to die,' he said. He put away his wand and took a dagger out of his robe. With purposeful steps he crossed the floor, heading directly for Tal.

Creed's men were on the walls before the Olaskon defenders realized they had been taken from the rear. The Keshians had come through the city like a prairie fire in summer, and those Olaskon soldiers who had been ordered to retreat in order had hit the gate in full flight.

Men on the walls with their eyes on Keshian Dog Soldiers carrying scaling ladders and siege-turtles suddenly found enemies on the wall beside them, with others hurrying up the stone stairs to the battlements. Archers who should have been raining fletched death down on the Keshians were now struggling in hand-to-hand combat with armed invaders.

Creed looked around and nodded in satisfaction as his flying company reached the gate, overpowering the squad there, and began opening it to admit the Keshians.

Just then an explosion of fire struck to the right of the gate, sending men on both sides flying through the air. A second, then third detonation of energy caused men to duck for cover or just turn and run. Creed spun to see a man in a robe look down for a moment, then turn away.

Whatever the magician thought he was doing, he created more confusion, which aided the invaders. Creed shouted orders for his company to finish opening the gate, and once he saw it thrown open he knew this part of the fight would be over in less than another half an hour. Seeing the state of the struggle up on the wall, Creed began directing soldiers still coming out of the tunnels towards a pair of doors at the base of the citadel. So fast had the attack been that they still stood open. He could send his soldiers inside to support Quint's and Tal's forces.

He glanced up at the citadel and wondered how the fighting there fared. With the Keshians inside the walls, the battle was decided; Kaspar's army would be defeated – he saluted Tal's ingenuity and hoped the lad lived long enough to see the end of it.

As Keshian soldiers hurried through the gate carrying scaling ladders, Creed waved over to the captain in command of the Keshian assault forces. 'We're inside already!' yelled Creed, pointing to the gates. 'Set your scaling ladders there, and there –' he pointed to two spots '– and we'll shred their forces from both sides.'

The captain acknowledged the suggestion and sent his men to the indicated locations. Creed took one last look around to ensure that everything was going as planned and saw with satisfaction that Olaskon soldiers were throwing down their weapons and begging quarter up on the wall.

Creed motioned for a squad held in reserve to follow him

inside the citadel. He hoped Captain Quint was having as easy a time as he had.

Captain Quint Havrevulen knelt behind a makeshift barricade – an overturned table in the soldiers' mess. He and his men had entered the armoury, only to discover that the Duke's ready company of reserves had been billeted in the mess so they could be easily dispatched to any part of the citadel.

Unfortunately for Quint, he could not get enough men through the door to mount a sustained assault. Twice he had led a dozen or so men out from the large pantry from which they accessed the mess, only to be driven back. Now they had archers on the balcony above the mess and any man of Quint's who moved was likely to be sprouting arrows.

The only thing that had kept the invaders from being over-whelmed was the breastwork of tables they had erected, for every soldier of Olasko who tried to come over it was killed. A mer-cenary next to Quint winced visibly every time a shaft struck the wood or the wall behind him. 'We going to find a way out of this, Captain?' he asked.

'Damn me if I know,' answered Quint. 'But I'm getting pretty bored just sitting here.' He glanced around. 'Here, help me push this table farther out.' He motioned to another pair of men to help him. They moved the table forward about four feet, and Quint signalled for some other men to do likewise with the tables on either side. Soon they had enough room for an additional dozen men to crawl out of the pantry and prepare for another assault.

Just as Quint was getting ready to charge, a voice shouted out, 'You dogs ready to surrender?'

Quint shouted back, 'Who died and put you in charge, Alexi?'

There was a moment of silence, then the voice said, 'Quint? Is that you?'

'None other,' shouted Quint.

'We thought you'd be dead by now.'

'Sorry to disappoint you, but I had other plans.'

'The Duke will reward me greatly if I bring him your head, my captain.'

'All you have to do is come get it,' shouted the former Special Captain of the Olaskon army. When no answer was forthcoming, he added, 'Or perhaps you'd like to talk about things first?'

'What do you have in mind?'

'Parlay.'

Again there was silence, then the officer named Alexi said, 'I can hear you just fine from here. Speak your mind.'

'A couple of thousand Keshian Dog Soldiers should be through your gates by now, Alexi. There are two other companies of mercenaries already in the citadel and more coming through from tunnels back behind you every minute. You may have us bottled up here, but I'll warrant if you send runners you'll find that other units are hard pressed on all fronts. You can't win. But if you call a halt to the fighting, you and your men can live.'

'And if I call a halt to the fighting, and you're telling tales, the Duke will have my guts for garters.'

'Send runners. Ask for intelligence. I can wait.' Quint grinned at the soldiers nearby. 'I'm not in a hurry as long as my side's winning.'

There was a very long silence then the officer named Alexi said, 'You're a lot of things, Captain Quint, but you've never been a liar. What terms are you offering?'

'We've no issue with men who are only following orders. Put down your weapons and you'll be paroled. I don't know who's going to be running things after this is over, but whoever it is, he'll need soldiers to keep the peace in Olasko. There you have it. Wait, and when the other companies start breaking down the doors at your back, we'll come over these damn tables. If you surrender now, everyone gets to live another day. We can even sit down and have an ale together when the dust settles. What'll it be?'

'I'll send runners, Quint, and I'll tell my men not to shoot as long as you stay down behind those tables. Agreed?'

'Agreed!' Quint put his sword away, indicating to his men that they could relax and lie down for a while without worry. 'This may work out well,' he whispered. He ventured a look and saw the bowmen had put their bows down and were leaning on them, while the crossbowmen had lowered their weapons. He sat back. 'Hope things are going this well elsewhere,' he said.

• CHAPTER TWENTY •

Resolution

*T*AL WATCHED.

Leso Varen approached slowly, the dagger hanging loosely in his grip. Tal felt pain in every part of his body, but it was manageable, less than he had endured after his rescue by Pasko and Robert, less than when he had been attacked by the death-dancers, less than when his arm had been cut off. He focused on that, that he had endured more pain and lived.

He drew strength from within and waited, for he knew he would get only one opportunity to strike at the magician. Tal let his head loll as if he had no strength to raise it.

Varen ignored the other soldiers nearby. When he got close, he said, 'Talwin, I am impressed. You're far more resilient than I would have thought.

'You know, I told Kaspar I thought there was something odd

about you when I examined you on the night you took oath. It wasn't that you revealed duplicity, but rather that you were . . . without any sort of doubt. I suspected you had been trained somehow, but had you been a magic-user, you would not have lived more than a minute once you were inside this room.' He gestured. 'I've placed wards everywhere.' He sighed, as if over-tasked. 'I have enemies, you know.' He waved his hand at a far wall and it shimmered, then faded away. It had been an illusion, and now Tal saw that the room was a full ten feet longer than he had thought. A figure hung from chains on the far wall, naked and bloody. Tal knew instantly who it was: Alysandra. He couldn't tell if she was alive or not, and it took all of his concentration to ready himself for one last attempt to defend himself. Varen said, 'Our lovely Lady Rowena tried to kill me.' His voice rose to a near shriek. *'She tried to kill me!'*

He turned his back on Tal and hurried to where the limp form hung. 'She thought to seduce me!' He laughed, then turned to face Tal and spoke quickly. 'Look, I enjoy a tumble as much as the next man, but there are times when such things are merely a distraction. Besides, the energies are all wrong for what I'm doing these days. It's terribly life-affirming and generative and all that, but right now, my efforts are entirely concentrated in the opposite direction, if you take my meaning. So, rather than some fun between the sheets – and a dagger in my back – I thought she could contribute to my work in a good way – or bad, from her point of view.' He laughed, and Tal knew that by any measure the man was completely mad.

Varen reached up and gripped her chin. 'A little life left in there, yet, isn't there, my dear?' He regarded her intently. 'Slow death is the best death . . . for me. Right now, I imagine it's pretty miserable being you.' He laughed and let her chin drop. Then he started walking back towards Tal. 'It wouldn't surprise me to discover you both work for an old enemy of mine. Sad to say, I haven't time to put you on the wall and find out. But even if you don't, you've been a serious nuisance, Talwin. Bringing an army, sacking the city, all that *noise*.' His eyes widened and he nodded enthusiastically. 'I do enjoy the screaming and the blood, though. That's a nice touch.' He reached Tal and knelt beside him. 'Now, it's been lovely seeing you again, but I must put an end to our time together. I fear Kaspar is about to lose his city, and that being the case, I must depart for a new home.' He smiled. 'Goodbye.' Then he reached out with his dagger, as Tal had expected, and started to slice down on Tal's exposed neck. Tal used every ounce of strength he possessed to slash upward with the dagger he had pulled from his belt, and block Leso's move. Varen was a powerful magician, but in the use of a blade he might as well have been a baby compared to Tal. Varen's blade flew from his hand and went clattering across the floor.

Tal then slashed out again, only to find his blade deflected from Varen's skin by some sort of arcane armour. But the blow caused the magician to fall backward, landing hard on his rump, and suddenly the pain racking Tal's body ceased.

Taking a deep breath, Tal rose to his feet. 'So, steel can't touch you?'

'I'm afraid not,' said Varen, his eyes narrowing. He scrambled to his feet. 'You know, this is no longer amusing. Please die *now*!'

He put out his hand and Tal could feel energies building. Only once or twice had he witnessed Pug or Magnus gathering power, and the results were usually spectacular. Tal had no doubt that if he let the mage finish his incantation, he would not enjoy the results.

In the remaining seconds he had, he knew his sword would be as useless as his dagger. He felt a lump in his tunic, and snatched out the hard ball Nakor had given him. In a desperate move to interrupt the magician's concentration, he drew his arm back and threw the ball as hard as he could.

The ball passed through whatever energy-armour Varen possessed and struck him hard in the throat. The incantation was disrupted and Tal felt the power in the room fade.

The magician's eyes went round as he grabbed his throat. He fought for air, but Tal could see he couldn't breathe. He took two steps towards the mage, and Varen fell to his knees, his face turning red and the veins on his head starting to stand out.

A voice from behind said, 'I think you crushed his windpipe.'

Tal looked and saw one of the soldiers rising to his feet. Tal pointed at a large clay object next to the door, hexagonal in shape and covered in mystic writings. 'See that,' he said. 'Break it. Look around these rooms and you'll find more. Break them all.'

Tal walked over to the quivering magician and looked down at him. 'Hell of a way to die, isn't it?' he said. Then he knelt, pulled Varen upright, moved behind him, and put his arms on either side of his head. With one quick jerk, he broke the dark mage's neck. Leso Varen's body crumpled to the floor.

Then Tal rose and went over to the unconscious figure on the wall. He unfastened the shackles and took Alysandra down gently. He looked at the face of the woman he had once thought he loved. Stunning beauty was now terribly scarred, for Varen's use of the dagger had not been kind. Tal took his cloak off and wrapped it around her. Calling to one of the soldiers nearby, he said, 'Take her to the rear and see if the chirurgeon can save her.' The soldier cradled the girl in his arms and carried her out of the door.

When the last ward was smashed, the air suddenly sizzled with energy and three men materialized in the room. Pug, Magnus and Nakor looked down at the dead mage. Nakor said, 'You did better than I thought you would.'

Pug said, 'Get everyone out of this room, Tal. There are things here that only we three are equipped to confront.' He looked down. 'Just because this body is dead doesn't mean the magic doesn't linger. There may be traps still.'

Tal turned and ordered his soldiers out of the room.

Magnus nodded. 'Nakor's right. You did well.'

Pug said, 'How goes the rest of the fight?'

Tal shrugged. 'I don't know. I've received no word from Creed or Quint, but now that this . . . man is dead, I plan on seeing this thing ended.'

As he turned to leave, Pug grabbed his arm. Looking Tal in the eyes, he said, 'Before you find Kaspar, remember this: you've been harshly used all your life, Tal, by the Conclave as well as by Kaspar. Would I have given you up to kill this enemy of mine?' He pointed to Varen's corpse. 'A hundred times over, my friend.' For a moment pain passed behind Pug's eyes. 'You would not be the first of those I cared about to die.' His hand tightened a little on Tal's arm. 'The Conclave will ask nothing more of you: from now on your life is your own to do with what you will. In any way we can we will help, with gold, land, pardons from the Isles and Roldem. Ask what you will, and if we can do it, we will.

'But one thing above all you *must* understand. You are at a crossroads and from this moment forward who you will be is in your own hands. Decide what sort of man you wish to be . . . then act.'

Tal nodded. 'Right now I have but one goal, Pug. I will find Kaspar, then after I end his life, I'll worry about the rest of mine.'

Without another word, he picked up his sword and followed his mercenaries down the hall and away from the magician's lair.

Tal shouted orders and swung his sword. His company had encountered a room full of Olaskon soldiers who appeared determined to defend that part of the citadel with their lives. The room-to-room fighting was bloody and unforgiving. Tal passed few wounded, but a great many dead on both sides.

He had been fighting for two hours, the pain he suffered at the hands of the magician now forgotten. He had cleared half a dozen rooms since leaving the magician's wing. Runners had come telling him the outer bailey and the lower rooms of the citadel were secured, and that men were being detailed to guard Olaskon prisoners. But the closer he got to Kaspar's throne room, the fiercer was the defence.

The fighting went on for the rest of the day, and twice he had to withdraw and take water and food. His arms felt as if they had iron weights tied to them, but he kept coming back to lead his men.

After hours of fighting, Tal realized they had surrounded the throne room, and he quickly sent runners to ensure that the doors were secure. He motioned for a dozen men to follow him, for he knew there were other, less obvious, ways out of that room.

He found an entrance to the servants' passages and almost died when he opened the door. Only his exceptional reflexes allowed him to block the sword-thrust that greeted his tripping the latch.

'Pikes!' he shouted and men with pole-arms raced forward. They lowered their weapons and drove the defenders back down the narrow passage, and Tal and his men followed.

There had been half a dozen men in the passage and they turned and fled after two were struck down by the pikes. Tal hurried after them but stopped running when he realized they had found the servants' entrance to the throne room.

A peep-hole had been drilled in the door and covered by a simple piece of metal on a screw. It had been put there so that servants wouldn't interrupt the Duke when he was conducting formal court.

Tal peered through and saw Kaspar standing in the middle of the room, directing his defenders. He was wearing his black armour, and bellowing commands, looking as much like a bear at bay as the one Tal had killed protecting him those years past.

Tal judged he could possibly reach Kaspar before the Duke realized he was in the room, but he couldn't be certain. Better to wait for a few minutes and see how the assault on the three entrances went. Tal knew he could spare more soldiers than Kaspar, for by what Tal could see, he had less than a full company in the room.

From outside came a voice, speaking Roldemish but in a heavy accent:, a Keshian commander. 'Will you accept quarter?'

Kaspar laughed. 'Never!'

Tal hated to see men die needlessly. The outcome was no longer in doubt. Kaspar had been totally routed in less than a day. But there was no need for more men to die. He turned and said, 'Send word back that I want as many men as possible through here. When I open the door, I will go straight in.' To the man behind him he said, 'Go right,' then to the second man behind him he added, 'and you go left. Each man, right, then left. Flood the room and draw the defenders away from the doors. Let's end this!'

Tal waited as word was passed, then he flipped the latch and charged into the room. For a moment he moved without being noticed, then something seen out of the corner of Kaspar's eye must have alerted him, for he turned just in time to raise his sword and take Tal's attack.

Those near the Duke turned to defend him, but they were quickly engaged by other mercenaries who ran from the servants' passage. Tal swung a looping overhand blow, then turned it at the last, almost taking Kaspar's arm off at the shoulder. The big man dodged aside at the last second, his eyes widening in recognition. 'Tal!' He slashed back, forcing Tal to give ground. 'And with both arms. That must be a tale to tell.' He lashed out in a furious combination, which lacked finesse but was effective.

Tal could not risk taking his eyes off Kaspar, so determined was the Duke to defeat him, but he could sense the rhythm of the fight changing. With his own men attacking from behind, those defending the doors were being overwhelmed.

Kaspar cut and parried, his face a mask of concentration, oblivious to everything else around him as he sought to kill Tal. Tal knew that he was by far the better swordsman, but he was fatigued, still in pain, and his right hand had not recovered completely. One mistake on his part was all Kaspar needed.

All around the two combatants the din of weapons diminished as swords hit the floor and men ceased fighting. After a few minutes, the only sounds in the room were the groans of the wounded and the clang of Tal's and Kaspar's blades ringing together as they clashed.

Kaspar's face was flushed and his cheeks bulged as he puffed hard, trying to keep his wind. Tal felt his own body ache with the need to end this; but Kaspar was giving him no clear-cut opening.

Then Kaspar stepped the wrong way, and for an instant his toe touched the leg of a corpse lying on the floor. He stumbled and Tal was upon him like a cat on a mouse.

Tal got inside Kaspar's guard and engaged his blade with his own, and with one twisting move had the sword out of Kaspar's hand. The next moment Kaspar was motionless, Tal's sword point at his throat.

Kaspar braced himself for the death-stroke, but Tal just kept his sword pressing that vulnerable skin. Then he said, 'Bind him!'

At this point, John Creed came into the room. 'You did it!'

'*We* did it,' said Tal. He looked around the chamber. 'And a lot of men paid for the victory with their lives.'

Creed said, 'So, why didn't you finish him?'

Tal walked up to look Kaspar in the eyes as two soldiers bound the Duke's wrists behind his back. 'That would have been too quick,' said Tal. 'I want him to fully understand what he's lost, what's been taken away from him.' He put up his sword. 'Besides, I can hang him tomorrow as easily as cut his throat today.'

Looking around the room he said, 'Make sure everyone knows the citadel is ours. Then pass the word to stop fighting.'

The Keshian commander of the forces that had been attacking the room approached. 'Captain, we will withdraw as we agreed. The citadel is yours.'

Tal said, 'Thank you and thank your Emperor. I don't suppose there's much hope of controlling the looting on the way back to the harbour?'

The Captain shrugged. 'Booty is part of war, is it not?' He bowed his head and shouted his orders and the Keshian Dog Soldiers began withdrawing.

After the Keshians were gone, Creed said, 'If there's anything of value left in the city when those boys are gone, our lads will be surprised.'

Tal smiled. 'There's enough in the citadel to make every man here feel rich. We'll get to that tomorrow. Tend to the wounded, and get the staff in the kitchen to start cooking. If everyone else is as hungry as I am, we're going to eat the entire stores in one day.'

Creed nodded and started conveying Tal's orders. Tal glanced around the room then said to the two guards who held Kaspar, 'Keep him here for the time being, but everyone else is to be taken down to the marshalling yard and put under guard.'

Tal sheathed his sword and made his way out of Kaspar's throne room and hurried to Kaspar's family apartment, ignoring the looks he got from frightened servants. When he reached Natalia's door he found a squad of guards waiting. He looked at them and said, 'It's over. Kaspar is taken. Throw down your weapons or I will come back with fifty men. No harm will come to your lady.'

The men glanced at one another then slowly put down their

swords. 'Go down to the marshalling yard and wait; you'll be given parole in the morning.'

The guards left slowly, and when they were gone, Tal opened the door to Natalia's apartment. A blur of motion caused him to duck, and a dagger bounced harmlessly off the wall. Tal called out, 'Please don't throw anything else, Natalia!'

He looked to the far corner of the room where Kaspar's sister waited, another dagger in her hand. 'Tal!' she cried, her voice revealing a mixture of relief, happiness and uncertainty. 'Kaspar said you were imprisoned.' Then she saw his right hand and added, 'And maimed.'

Tal walked slowly towards her. 'I managed to survive it all.'

'What now?' she said. 'Is Kaspar dead?'

'No, he's my prisoner,' said Tal.

'Your prisoner? I thought we were being attacked by Kesh and Roldem.'

'You were, but in support of my attack on the citadel.' He sat on the bed, and motioned for her to come closer. She approached slowly and he took her hand. 'It's a very long story and I'll tell it to you, but I have many things to do before we can discuss those details. Right now I wish to tell you that you are safe. No harm will come to you and I will ensure that your status here is respected.'

'As what?' said Natalia. 'Am I your trophy, Tal?'

He smiled. 'You would be a very special one, I'll admit.' He stood up and took her other hand in his left, and said, 'I would be lying if I said I had no feelings for you, Natalia, but I would also be lying if I told you I loved you with all my heart.

'Moreover, your future is now even less your own than it was before Kaspar was taken. For then you were but a tool for his diplomacy. Now, you are much more.'

'What do you mean?'

Tal said, 'You are heir to Olasko. Your brother's removal leaves a deadly political vacuum in the region. Kesh will ensure that the Isles don't try to claim your nation, and the Isles will keep Kesh and Roldem at bay, but others nearby may see this as an opportunity to install their own vassals on Kaspar's throne. That can't be allowed.'

Natalia nodded. 'I understand.' She looked at Tal. 'What of my brother? Is he to die?'

Tal said, 'Only a few people know this of me: I was born in the mountains of the Orosini. Kaspar's orders destroyed my race. I am perhaps the only male survivor and the day I knew I would live, I vowed to have vengeance for my people.'

Natalia said nothing, but her face grew pale and drawn. 'I would like to be alone now, if you don't mind, Tal.'

He bowed and left. When he got outside he saw that a pair of his own soldiers had replaced the Olaskons who had surrendered. 'Guard this door and protect the lady inside. I'll have someone relieve you after a while.'

They nodded and took up position on either side of the door.

Tal moved quickly along the hallway, back towards the throne room. There was much to be done yet, but the thing he felt the most need for now was a meal. Then perhaps a hot bath. For whatever decisions needed to be made, they didn't need to be made until the next morning.

The day wore on and before Tal knew it, evening was falling. The entire early part of the day had been devoted to disarming Opardum's garrison, paroling the soldiers and directing them to billets outside the citadel. Natalia would need them back soon, but some of those who had served her brother would not be invited to re-enlist.

Administration of the government was given over to Barons Visniya and Stolinko, who between them could take care of the short-term needs of the city and surrounding countryside.

And a great deal of need was now evident, for while the invasion of the city had been completed swiftly, it had been harsh. As Tal had suspected, the retreating Keshians had taken anything of value they could find, and burned many buildings out of spite when they found nothing. Still, Tal instructed the barons to establish a curfew and enlist some men into a provost guard to protect the citizens from any further looting and violence.

A message from one of the chirurgeons informed him that Alysandra would live, but it had been a close thing. Tal sent a message to the magician's room to Pug conveying the good news.

As the day wore on, Tal found himself becoming more anxious. He had won, a victory that seemed easy if one considered only the military costs. Tal knew what price he had paid over the years to achieve this victory. And his tasks were not over yet. There were still two men alive – one now an ally – who were responsible for the destruction of his nation.

The one thing that really vexed him was Amafi. The traitorous servant had somehow managed to escape during the battle. He had given a clear description of the man to many of his officers, but Amafi was not among the dead or captured. Those prisoners who knew him said that he had vanished from Kaspar's side only a few minutes before the final assault on the throne room had begun.

Tal cursed himself for a fool, for Amafi must have used the

same servants' passages to escape that Tal had used to take the citadel. Some day, he knew, if he had the chance, he would find Amafi and make him pay the price for his betrayal.

He had eaten his midday meal apart from the others, for he had to decide in his own heart what to do before he could discuss it with anyone else. He knew that Creed would follow his orders, and should he order Quint's arrest, the former captain would be in chains in minutes.

He had seen Pug only once, and Nakor twice, and both men seemed immensely disturbed by what they had found in Varen's apartments. They did not talk about it, but made it clear that, for them, some matter of great importance was still unresolved.

Tal put aside speculation, knowing they would apprise him of the problem when the time was right. Currently, he had enough problems of his own to deal with.

Visniya approached him as the afternoon session began. 'I received a message from the representative of Roldem, Tal. They have a few demands and some suggestions, which are really just politely-worded demands.'

'What?'

'They want recompense for their fleet being used by the Keshians, which is to say, they're upset Kesh got to loot the city and they didn't. We have ample gold in Kaspar's treasury. The battle went so quickly even the men who were guarding it didn't think to grab the gold and run.

'But we'll also need that gold to rebuild.'

Tal said, 'I will bow to your decision; it's your city, not mine. But my inclination is to rebuild now and pay debts later.'

Visniya nodded. 'I agree. If we pay Roldem their blood money, we'll have to tax the people when they can least afford it.'

'What news from the Isles?'

'Nothing currently, but I expect a list of their demands to be delivered at any moment,' said Visniya dryly.

Tal went to the table where the others on his ad hoc council waited. 'What next?' he said.

Stolinko said, 'Some of the men are asking, Tal. Are you to be the new Duke?'

Tal laughed. 'Wouldn't that put a bee in the ear of the King of Roldem? He'd turn that fleet around and bring those Keshian soldiers back to turn me out of here.' He shook his head. 'No, I have other plans.'

'Then who will rule?'

Tal said, 'Natalia is the logical choice.'

'But can she hold Olasko?' asked Visniya. 'There are any number of nobles, here and among our neighbours, who would be on the march the moment our mercenaries left if she's put on the throne alone.'

'I can't very well force her to wed someone just to ensure regional stability,' said Tal.

'Why not?' asked Stolinko. 'It's been done before.'

Tal thought on it, and said, 'Send for Captain Quint and the Lady Natalia.'

He waited in silence, framing what he would say, and then when they both were in his presence, he said, 'I have a pair of problems that need to be addressed.'

Quint glanced at the Lady Natalia and bowed slightly. She ignored him.

'Quint,' began Tal, 'I have a problem. First I must confess that I have lied to you in the past.'

Quint shrugged and said, 'In this court it would have been more remarkable if you hadn't.'

'Do you remember the story you told me about the boy Raven killed?'

Quint nodded.

'Well, that boy didn't die, Quint. I was that boy.'

Quint's eyebrows raised as if he had difficulty believing his ears. 'You?'

'To the best of my knowledge, I am the last Orosini male alive.'

Quint looked uncomfortable. 'You were plotting Kaspar's overthrow all along?'

Tal nodded, and saw Natalia's eyes flash, though she said nothing. Still, Tal had a fair notion of what she thought, for they had been lovers and she now must wonder how much of what he had said to her were lies, too.

Quint studied Tal's face for a long moment, then he unbuckled his sword belt and let it fall. 'Tal, you saved my life by getting me off that rock, and you kept us alive all the way from the Fortress of Despair through the wilderness to Bardac's Holdfast. If my death is the price for the freedom I've had this last year, so be it. I won't fight you.' Then he chuckled. 'Not that I could beat you, anyway, with a sword.'

Tal said, 'I have given something said to me last night a great deal of thought. I am at a crossroads, and I must decide what the rest of my life will be.

'I am going to spare your life, Quint. For you have only been a good servant, albeit to a bad master.' He looked at Natalia, and said, 'And you had no choice in who your brother was. I know you well enough to realize that you had no part in his murderous schemes.'

She said nothing.

'Here is what must be done,' said Tal. 'Natalia, you must rule in Opardum, as Duchess of Olasko. But the region must be stabilized. You must swear fealty to Aranor, from this day forward. Aranor and Olasko will be provinces of Roldem, and never again will either have any claim on Roldem's throne.'

Visniya leaned over and said softly, 'You can ignore Roldem's demands for quite a while after that gesture.'

'But you'll need a strong hand to defend this realm,' Tal continued, 'so I'm recommending you return command of your armies to Captain Quint, and name him along with my lords Visniya and Stolinko as a council of three to advise you until you decide who you should wed. Put no fool or ambitious man on the throne beside you, m'lady, and good will come of this.'

She bowed, looking somewhat relieved. She turned to Quint and said, 'Captain, I would be pleased if you would return to the service of your nation. I need you far more than my brother ever did.'

Quint bowed.

Pug, Magnus and Nakor entered the room and took up positions behind Tal and his captains. Tal looked at them and nodded. Pug leaned forward and whispered to him, 'Alysandra will live. We've taken her back to Sorcerer's Isle. We can heal her flesh wounds, but as for the other things Varen did to her?' He shrugged. Louder, he said, 'Finish this. We will talk afterwards.'

Tal glanced around the room and declared, 'Bring in the prisoner.'

A short while later, Kaspar was brought into the room. He had been stripped of his armour and wore only a black tunic and leggings. His feet were bare: Tal assumed that an enterprising soldier had discovered his feet were the same size as the Duke's.

Kaspar's wrists were in manacles and he was hobbled with leg irons, but he still appeared defiant. When he finally stopped in front of Tal, the younger man said, 'Kaspar, what have you to say?'

Kaspar laughed. 'You won and I lost. What else is there to say?'

'You've ordered the destruction of innocents, and have murdered out of naked ambition. You've caused suffering you cannot begin to imagine. If I could contrive a way to have you live your life understanding that pain every day, I would. But alive you are a danger, so I must order you to be hanged.'

'For revenge?' asked Kaspar. 'Disguised as justice, it's still revenge, Tal.'

Tal sat back. 'I'm sick of killing, Kaspar. But there is no other way.'

From behind him, Pug said, 'Perhaps there is.'

Tal looked over his shoulder and the magician stepped closer. 'If you mean what you say, if you wish for Kaspar to be in a place where he can dwell on his crimes, yet not be a threat to anyone here, would you spare his life?'

'How can I?' said Tal. 'Too many people have suffered at his hands. Why should I spare his life?'

Pug whispered, 'Because you won't be saving his life, Talon. You'll be saving your own. You haven't begun to deal with those things you've had to do, and when ghosts trouble you in the dark of the night, this one act of forgiveness may be the difference between your survival and destruction.'

Tal felt a weight lifted off his chest and tears began to well up in his eyes. Fatigue and years of suffering threatened to overwhelm him. He remembered his family, laughing and alive, and knew that they would live on in his heart if he made room for them by casting out the hatred and anger. He thought of the things he had done, the people who had suffered and died at his hands, simply to reach this moment. What made him that different from Kaspar? He had no easy answer. At last he said, 'Kaspar, I forgive you the wrongs done to me and my people. Dwell on that wherever you go. Do with him what you will, Pug.'

Pug went over to Magnus and whispered in his ear. They conferred for a long time, then Magnus nodded. He walked around the table and put his hand on Kaspar's shoulder and then they both vanished, a slight puff of air being the only sign of their departure.

Tal rose up. 'For this day, our business here is done.'

Those in the court moved away, and Tal turned to Quint, Visniya and Stolinko. 'Gentlemen, the fate of this nation is in your hands,' he said solemnly. 'Treat her gently.'

Then he walked over to where Natalia waited. 'I hope you can find some happiness in the future, m'lady.'

She smiled at him sadly. 'And I hope that some day you find peace, Squire.'

Tal kissed her lightly on the cheek and turned away. He came to stand before Nakor and Pug and said, 'What are you doing with Kaspar?'

'I'll explain later,' said Pug.

Nakor said, 'I heard from the soldiers how you killed Varen. Very clever, throwing the ball at him.' He grinned. 'Wish I had thought of that.'

'Actually, that merely broke his concentration and cut off his wind. I killed him by breaking his neck.' He looked at Pug. 'Was it worth it? Did you find whatever it was that you feared Varen was doing?'

Pug looked unhappy. 'It wasn't the story we told the two kings. But it was something almost as bad.' Lowering his voice, Pug said, 'Varen was trying to open a rift.'

'Rift?'

'A gate between two different places,' said Nakor. 'I'll explain it in detail later, if you must know. But it's the sort of magic gateway the Tsurani used to invade –'

Tal said, 'I know what a rift is, Nakor. I read the books, remember? I'm just surprised that's what he was up to.'

'As are we,' said Pug. 'I know more about rifts than any man alive, or so I thought. This thing Varen made is unlike any rift I've encountered. He used black arts and the lives of innocents to construct his device and it appears to have been recently engaged.'

'You mean there's a rift here in the citadel?'

'No, Tal,' said Nakor. Then his voice became sombre. 'But we fear there may be one forming out there somewhere.'

'But where?' asked Tal.

Pug said, 'Only Varen knew.'

Tal sighed. 'I am glad I am not a magician. My problems seem simple compared to yours.'

Pug said, 'We have resources. We'll keep people here studying Varen's work. We'll find out what he was doing.' He smiled. 'You look done in. Go get something to eat and then go to bed.'

'No,' said Tal. 'I have one task left and it can not wait any longer.' Without explaining, he turned and walked out of the throne room of Olasko.

Nakor said, 'He could have been Duke. Natalia would have married him.'

Pug shook his head. 'No, he's looking for peace, not power.'

'Do you think he'll find it?'

Pug put his hand on his old friend's shoulder. 'When he chose to let Quint and Kaspar live, I think he started on his way to it.' He smiled. 'Come. Tal may not be hungry, but I am.'

They left the hall.

The pounding on the door was insistent, and the man whose business it was stood up fearfully. The city had been filled with rampaging Keshian soldiers until dawn, then civilian looters had followed. He had held his own with a large meat cleaver and the looters left him alone, as much because he had nothing worth stealing in his shop as because of his weapon.

But the voice that came from outside sounded as if it would not be easily scared away. 'Open up or I'll kick this door down!'

The man shouted, 'I've got a weapon!'

'Then open the door, because if you make me kick the door in, I'll make you eat that weapon.'

Clearly, the intruder wasn't going to leave. At last, the knacker called Bowart opened the door. A soldier entered, his sword at his side. He took one look at the podgy man who stood holding the huge cleaver and said, 'Don't hurt yourself with that. I'm looking for a girl.'

'We ain't got no girls here,' said the proprietor. 'We're a gang of knackers. This ain't no brothel.'

Tal pushed past the man. 'Where are your slaves?'

Bowart pointed to the back door and Tal pushed it open. He

walked across a large yard that reeked of dead animal flesh and old blood. There was a shack at the back. He moved to the door and stepped inside. A dozen beds lined the walls, and a single table sat in the centre of the room.

Eyes wide from fear of marauders regarded him. A single candle burned on the table. Tal picked it up and went from bed to bed, searching the faces. At last he found the woman he sought.

In the language of his people he said, 'Eye of the Blue-Winged Teal, I am called Talon of the Silver Hawk. You knew me as the boy Kielianapuna.'

She blinked as if confronted by a vision. Softly she said, 'Kieli?'

He nodded, extending his hand. 'I have come to take you from this place if you will go with me.'

She slowly rose and took his hand. 'Anywhere but here.' She studied his face, and recognition came into her eyes. 'You *are* Kieli,' she said softly, and behind the pain in her eyes he saw hope. Gripping his hand tightly, she said softly, 'I have a son.' She inclined her head to the next bed, where a boy of perhaps four or five years slept. 'His father was a soldier, but I don't know which one, as many men had me after I was taken.'

Tal gripped her hands and looked at the boy. He was fair-haired, like his mother, and beautiful in sleep. With emotion thick in his voice Tal said, 'I will be his father.'

She squeezed his hand tightly. Softly he said, 'We can never be what we were, Teal. Our world has been taken from us, but we can be together and teach our son what we know of our ways. Our people will not be forgotten.'

She nodded, her eyes gleaming with emotion, as tears began to run down her cheeks.

He asked, 'Are there others, besides you, from our village or the other villages?'

She said, 'I don't know. There were a few taken with me, but all of us were sold.'

'We shall abide here a while, then,' he said, 'and we shall look for them. And if we find them, then we shall give them a home.'

He let go of her hand and gently picked up the sleeping boy. Cradling him, Tal said, 'I do not know what it is we will become, Teal – Orosini or something else – but we will discover that together.' Holding the boy in his right arm, he extended his left. She took his hand, and he led her into the night, and into an unknown future.

Retribution

*T*WO MEN APPEARED.

It was just after dawn, when a moment before it had been just after nightfall. Kaspar felt disoriented for a moment, but Magnus pushed him away.

Kaspar stumbled and fell, then quickly got to his feet. 'What is this?'

Magnus said, 'You are on the other side of the world, Kaspar. This is the land known as Novindus. Here not one living soul has heard of Olasko, let alone of its duke. No one here even speaks your language.

'Here you have no servants, no army, no subjects, no allies; you have neither power nor wealth. You are at the mercy of others as others have been at your mercy for most of your life. Tal Hawkins wished you to dwell on your errors, to contemplate your sins and what you have lost. Here you may do that every day of your life, however much of it you have remaining.'

Kaspar's jaw set firmly. 'This is not the end of it, magician. I will find a way back, and I will regain that which has been taken from me.'

Magnus said, 'I wish you good fortune, Kaspar of Olasko.' He waved his hand and the shackles and manacles fell away. 'I leave you with your wits, your strength and your talents, for they are all you need, if you learn humility.' He pointed off to the east, where a faint haze of dust could be seen on the horizon. 'Those are nomads, Kaspar. Men who will either kill you or enslave you, depending on their mood. I suggest you find a hiding place and consider this your first opportunity to learn.'

Then Magnus vanished, leaving the former Duke of Olasko alone on a dirt road, halfway around the world from home, with enemies advancing.

Kaspar looked around and saw a small copse of trees on a distant hill. If he started running immediately, he might be able to hide before the nomads caught sight of him.

He looked at the rising sun, and felt a fresh breeze blowing. There was no familiar hit of sea-salt, something he had grown to take for granted in Opardum, and the air was dry.

His skin prickled in anticipation, for he had been plucked from abject failure to a new beginning. His head swam with images, and he knew that somehow he had been used by forces he didn't understand. When Leso Varen had died, it was as if a nagging ache in the base of his skull had ceased. He didn't know what that meant, but he knew he felt oddly good. Despite being thrown in a cell in his own dungeon, he had slept well, and when he had been taken from there, he had expected to die.

Now he was here, wherever *here* was, free to make his own way. He glanced around. Not much of a world to conquer from what he could see, but Kaspar expected there were better places somewhere around here. Either way, he couldn't start any sooner. He picked up his chains and hefted them, swinging them as a weapon as the riders came into view.

He grinned.